Paths of Glory

Irvin S. Cobb

DODO PRESS

PATHS OF GLORY

Impressions of War Written At and Near the Front

BY IRVIN S. COBB

AUTHOR OF "BACK HOME, " "EUROPE REVISED, ' ETC., ETC.

"The paths of glory lead but to the grave. "
—Thomas Gray

To the Memory of
MAJOR ROBERT COBB
(Cobb's Kentucky Battery, C. S. A.)

NOTE

What is enclosed between these covers was written as a series of first-hand impressions during the fall and early winter of 1914 while the writer was on staff service for The Saturday Evening Post in the western theatre of the European War. I tried to write of war as I saw it at the time that I saw it, or immediately afterward, when the memory of what I had seen was fresh and vivid in my mind.

In this volume, as here presented, no attempt has been made to follow either logically or chronologically the progress of events in the campaigning operations of which I was a witness. The chapters are interrelated insofar as they purport to be a sequence of pictures describing some of my experiences and setting forth a few of my observations in Belgium, in Germany, in France and in England during the first three months of hostilities.

At the outset I had no intention of undertaking to write a book on the war. If in the kindly judgment of the reader what I have written constitutes a book I shall be gratified.

I. S. C.

January, 1915.

CONTENTS

CHAPTER

I. A Little Village Called Montignies St. Christophe.
II. To War in a Taxicab.
III. Sherman Said It.
IV. "Marsch, Marsch, Marsch, So Geh'n Wir Weiter".
V. Being a Guest of the Kaiser.
VI. With the German Wrecking Crew
VII. The Grapes of Wrath..
VIII. Three Generals and a Cook
IX. Viewing a Battle prom a Balloon
X. In the Trenches Before Rheims..
XI. War de Luxe...
XII. The Rut of Big Guns in France..
XIII. Those Yellow Pine Boxes..
XIV. The Red Glutton..
XV. Belgium—The Rag Doll of Europe.
XVI. Louvain the Forsaken.

Paths of Glory

Chapter 1

A Little Village Called Montignies St. Christophe

We passed through it late in the afternoon—this little Belgian town called Montignies St. Christophe—just twenty-four hours behind a dust-colored German column. I am going to try now to tell how it looked to us.

I am inclined to think I passed this way a year before, or a little less, though I cannot be quite certain as to that. Traveling 'cross country, the country is likely to look different from the way it looked when you viewed it from the window of a railroad carriage.

Of this much, though, I am sure: If I did not pass, through this little town of Montignies St. Christophe then, at least I passed through fifty like it—each a single line of gray houses strung, like beads on a cord, along a white, straight road, with fields behind and elms in front; each with its small, ugly church, its wine shop, its drinking trough, its priest in black, and its one lone gendarme in his preposterous housings of saber and belt and shoulder straps.

I rather imagine I tried to think up something funny to say about the shabby grandeur of the gendarme or the acid flavor of the cooking vinegar sold at the drinking place under the name of wine; for that time I was supposed to be writing humorous articles on European travel.

But now something had happened to Montignies St. Christophe to lift it out of the dun, dull sameness that made it as one with so many other unimportant villages in this upper left-hand corner of the map of Europe. The war had come this way; and, coming so, had dealt it a side-slap.

We came to it just before dusk. All day we had been hurrying along, trying to catch up with the German rear guard; but the Germans moved faster than we did, even though they fought as they went. They had gone round the southern part of Belgium like coopers round a cask, hooping it in with tight bands of steel. Belgium—or this part of it—was all barreled up now: chines, staves and bung; and the Germans were already across the line, beating down the sod of France with their pelting feet.

Paths of Glory

Besides we had stopped often, for there was so much to see and to hear. There was the hour we spent at Merbes-le-Chateau, where the English had been; and the hour we spent at La Buissière, on the river Sambre, where a fight had been fought two days earlier; but Merbes-le-Chateau is another story and so is La Buissière. Just after La Buissière we came to a tiny village named Neuville and halted while the local Jack-of-all- trades mended for us an invalided tire on a bicycle.

As we grouped in the narrow street before his shop, with a hiving swarm of curious villagers buzzing about us, an improvised ambulance, with a red cross painted on its side over the letters of a baker's sign, went up the steep hill at the head of the cobbled street. At that the women in the doorways of the small cottages twisted their gnarled red hands in their aprons, and whispered fearsomely among themselves, so that the sibilant sound of their voices ran up and down the line of houses in a long, quavering hiss.

The wagon, it seemed, was bringing in a wounded French soldier who had been found in the woods beyond the river. He was one of the last to be found alive, which was another way of saying that for two days and two nights he had been lying helpless in the thicket, his stomach empty and his wounds raw. On each of those two nights it had rained, and rained hard.

Just as we started on our way the big guns began booming somewhere ahead of us toward the southwest; so we turned in that direction.

We had heard the guns distinctly in the early forenoon, and again, less distinctly, about noontime. Thereafter, for a while, there had been a lull in the firing; but now it was constant—a steady, sustained boom- boom-boom, so far away that it fell on the eardrums as a gentle concussion; as a throb of air, rather than as a real sound. For three days now we had been following that distant voice of the cannon, trying to catch up with it as it advanced, always southward, toward the French frontier. Therefore we flogged the belly of our tired horse with the lash of a long whip, and hurried along. There were five of us, all Americans. The two who rode on bicycles pedaled ahead as outriders, and the remaining three followed on behind with the horse and the dogcart. We had bought the outfit that morning and we were to lose it that night. The horse was an aged mare, with high withers, and galls on her shoulders and fetlocks unshorn, after the fashion of Belgian horses; and the dogcart was a venerable ruin, which creaked a great protest at every turn of the warped wheels on the axle. We had been able to buy the two— the mare and the cart—only because the German soldiers had not thought them worth the taking.

In this order, then, we proceeded. Pretty soon the mare grew so weary she could hardly lift her shaggy old legs; so, footsore as we were, we who rode dismounted and trudged on, taking turns at dragging her forward by the bit. I presume we went ahead thus for an hour or more, along an interminable straight road and past miles of the checkered light and dark green fields which in harvest time make a great backgammon board of this whole country of Belgium.

The road was empty of natives—empty, too, of German wagon trains; and these seemed to us curious things, because there had until then been hardly a minute of the day when we were not passing soldiers or meeting refugees.

Almost without warning we came on this little village called Montignies St. Christophe. A six-armed signboard at a crossroads told us its name —a rather impressive name ordinarily for a place of perhaps twenty houses, all told. But now tragedy had given it distinction; had painted that straggling frontier hamlet over with such colors that the picture of it is going to live in my memory as long as I do live. At the upper end of the single street, like an outpost, stood an old chateau, the seat, no doubt, of the local gentry, with a small park of beeches and elms round it; and here, right at the park entrance, we had our first intimation that there had been a fight. The gate stood ajar between its chipped stone pillars, and just inside the blue coat of a French cavalry officer, jaunty and new and much braided with gold lace on the collar and cuffs, hung from the limb of a small tree. Beneath the tree were a sheaf of straw in the shape of a bed and the ashes of a dead camp fire; and on the grass, plain to the eye, a plump, well-picked pullet, all ready for the pot or the pan. Looking on past these things we saw much scattered dunnage: Frenchmen's knapsacks, flannel shirts, playing cards, fagots of firewood mixed together like jackstraws, canteens covered with slate-blue cloth and having queer little hornlike protuberances on their tops—which proved them to be French canteens—tumbled straw, odd shoes with their lacings undone, a toptilted service shelter of canvas; all the riffle of a camp that had been suddenly and violently disturbed.

Paths of Glory

As I think back it seems to me that not until that moment had it occurred to us to regard closely the cottages and shops beyond the clumped trees of the chateau grounds. We were desperately weary, to begin with, and our eyes, those past three days, had grown used to the signs of misery and waste and ruin, abundant and multiplying in the wake of the hard-pounding hoofs of the conqueror.

Now, all of a sudden, I became aware that this town had been literally shot to bits. From our side—that is to say, from the north and likewise from the west—the Germans had shelled it. From the south, plainly, the French had answered. The village, in between, had caught the full force and fury of the contending fires. Probably the inhabitants had warning; probably they fled when the German skirmishers surprised that outpost of Frenchmen camping in the park. One imagined them scurrying like rabbits across the fields and through the cabbage patches. But they had left their belongings behind, all their small petty gearings and garnishings, to be wrecked in the wrenching and racking apart of their homes.

A railroad track emerged from the fields and ran along the one street. Shells had fallen on it and exploded, ripping the steel rails from the cross-ties, so that they stood up all along in a jagged formation, like rows of snaggled teeth. Other shells, dropping in the road, had so wrought with the stone blocks that they were piled here in heaps, and there were depressed into caverns and crevasses four or five or six feet deep.

Every house in sight had been hit again and again and again. One house would have its whole front blown in, so that we could look right back to the rear walls and see the pans on the kitchen shelves. Another house would lack a roof to it, and the tidy tiles that had made the roof were now red and yellow rubbish, piled like broken shards outside a potter's door. The doors stood open, and the windows, with the windowpanes all gone and in some instances the sashes as well, leered emptily, like eye-sockets without eyes.

So it went. Two of the houses had caught fire and the interiors were quite burned away. A sodden smell of burned things came from the still smoking ruins; but the walls, being of thick stone, stood.

Our poor tired old nag halted and sniffed and snorted. If she had had energy enough I reckon she would have shied about and run back the way she had come, for now, just ahead, lay two dead horses—a big gray and a roan—with their stark legs sticking out across the road. The gray was shot through and through in three places. The right fore hoof of the roan had been cut smack off, as smoothly as though done with an ax; and the stiffened leg had a curiously unfinished look about it, suggesting a natural malformation. Dead only a few hours, their carcasses already had begun to swell. The skin on their bellies was as tight as a drumhead.

We forced the quivering mare past the two dead horses. Beyond them the road was a litter. Knapsacks, coats, canteens, handkerchiefs, pots, pans, household utensils, bottles, jugs and caps were everywhere. The deep ditches on either side of the road were clogged with such things. The dropped caps and the abandoned knapsacks were always French caps and French knapsacks, cast aside, no doubt, for a quick flight after the melee.

The Germans had charged after shelling the town, and then the French had fallen back—or at least so we deduced from the looks of things. In the debris was no object that bespoke German workmanship or German ownership. This rather puzzled us until we learned that the Germans, as tidy in this game of war as in the game of life, made it a hard-and-fast rule to gather up their own belongings after every engagement, great or small, leaving behind nothing that might serve to give the enemy an idea of their losses.

We went by the church. Its spire was gone; but, strange to say, a small flag—the Tricolor of France—still fluttered from a window where some one had stuck it. We went by the taverne, or wine shop, which had a sign over its door—a creature remotely resembling a blue lynx. And through the door we saw half a loaf of bread and several bottles on a table. We went by a rather pretentious house, with pear trees in front of it and a big barn alongside it; and right under the eaves of the barn I picked up the short jacket of a French trooper, so new and fresh from the workshop that the white cambric lining was hardly soiled. The figure 18 was on the collar; we decided that its wearer must have belonged to the Eighteenth Cavalry Regiment. Behind the barn we found a whole pile of new knapsacks—the flimsy play-soldier knapsacks of the French infantrymen, not half so heavy or a third so substantial as the heavy sacks of the Germans, which are all bound with straps and covered on the back side with undressed red bullock's hide.

Paths of Glory

Until now we had seen, in all the silent, ruined village, no human being. The place fairly ached with emptiness. Cats sat on the doorsteps or in the windows, and presently from a barn we heard imprisoned beasts lowing dismally. Cows were there, with agonized udders and, penned away from them, famishing calves; but there were no dogs. We already had remarked this fact—that in every desolated village cats were thick enough; but invariably the sharp-nosed, wolfish-looking Belgian dogs had disappeared along with their masters. And it was so in Montignies St. Christophe.

On a roadside barricade of stones, chinked with sods of turf—a breastwork the French probably had erected before the fight and which the Germans had kicked half down—I counted three cats, seated side by side, washing their faces sedately and soberly.

It was just after we had gone by the barricade that, in a shed behind the riddled shell of a house, which was almost the last house of the town, one of our party saw an old, a very old, woman, who peered out at us through a break in the wall. He called out to her in French, but she never answered—only continued to watch him from behind her shelter. He started toward her and she disappeared noiselessly, without having spoken a word. She was the only living person we saw in that town.

Just beyond the town, though, we met a wagon—a furniture dealer's wagon—from some larger community, which had been impressed by the Belgian authorities, military or civil, for ambulance service. A jaded team of horses drew it, and white flags with red crosses in their centers drooped over the wheels, fore and aft. One man led the near horse by the bit and two other men walked behind the wagon. All three of them had Red Cross brassards on the sleeves of their coats.

The wagon had a hood on it, but was open at both ends. Overhauling it we saw that it contained two dead soldiers—French foot-soldiers. The bodies rested side by side on the wagon bed. Their feet somehow were caught up on the wagon seat so that their stiff legs, in the baggy red pants, slanted upward, and the two dead men had the look of being about to glide backward and out of the wagon.

The blue-clad arms of one of them were twisted upward in a half-arc, encircling nothing; and as the wheels jolted over the rutted cobbles these two bent arms joggled and swayed drunkenly. The other's head was canted back so that, as we passed, we looked right into his face. It was a young face—we could tell that much, even through the mask of caked mud on the drab-white skin—and it might once have been a comely face. It was not comely now.

Peering into the wagon we saw that the dead man's face had been partly shot or shorn away—the lower jaw was gone; so that it had become an abominable thing to look on. These two had been men the day before. Now they were carrion and would be treated as such; for as we looked back we saw the wagon turn off the high road into a field where the wild red poppies, like blobs of red blood, grew thick between rows of neglected sugar beets.

We stopped and watched. The wagon bumped through the beet patch to where, at the edge of a thicket, a trench had been dug. The diggers were two peasants in blouses, who stood alongside the ridge of raw upturned earth at the edge of the hole, in the attitude of figures in a painting by Millet. Their spades were speared upright into the mound of fresh earth. Behind them a stenciling of poplars rose against the sky line.

We saw the bodies lifted out of the wagon. We saw them slide into the shallow grave, and saw the two diggers start at their task of filling in the hole.

Not until then did it occur to any one of us that we had not spoken to the men in charge of the wagon, or they to us. There was one detached house, not badly battered, alongside the road at the lower edge of the field where the burial took place. It had a shield on its front wall bearing the Belgian arms and words to denote that it was a customs house.

A glance at our map showed us that at this point the French boundary came up in a V-shaped point almost to the road. Had the gravediggers picked a spot fifty yards farther on for digging their trench, those two dead Frenchmen would have rested in the soil of their own country.

The sun was almost down by now, and its slanting rays slid lengthwise through the elm-tree aisles along our route. Just as it disappeared we met a string of refugees—men, women and children—all afoot, all bearing pitiably small bundles. They limped along silently in a straggling procession. None of them was weeping;

none of them apparently had been weeping. During the past ten days I had seen thousands of such refugees, and I had yet to hear one of them cry out or complain or protest.

These who passed us now were like that. Their heavy peasant faces expressed dumb bewilderment—nothing else. They went on up the road into the gathering dusk as we went down, and almost at once the sound of their clunking tread died out behind us. Without knowing certainly, we nevertheless imagined they were the dwellers of Montignies St. Christophe going back to the sorry shells that had been their homes.

An hour later we passed through the back lines of the German camp and entered the town of Beaumont, to find that the General Staff of a German army corps was quartered there for the night, and that the main force of the column, after sharp fighting, had already advanced well beyond the frontier. France was invaded.

Chapter 2

To War in a Taxicab

In a taxicab we went to look for this war. There were four of us, not counting the chauffeur, who did not count. It was a regular taxicab, with a meter on it, and a little red metal flag which might be turned up or turned down, depending on whether the cab was engaged or at liberty; and he was a regular chauffeur.

We, the passengers, wore straw hats and light suits, and carried no baggage. No one would ever have taken us for war correspondents out looking for war. So we went; and, just when we were least expecting it, we found that war. Perhaps it would be more exact to say it found us. We were four days getting back to Brussels, still wearing our straw hats, but without any taxicab. The fate of that taxicab is going to be one of the unsolved mysteries of the German invasion of Belgium.

From the hour when the steamer St. Paul left New York, carrying probably the most mixed assortment of passengers that traveled on a single ship since Noah sailed the Ark, we on board expected hourly to sight something that would make us spectators of actual hostilities. The papers that morning were full of rumors of an engagement between English ships and German ships somewhere off the New England coast.

Daily we searched the empty seas until our eyes hurt us; but, except that we had one ship's concert and one brisk gale, and that just before dusk on the fifth day out, the weather being then gray and misty, we saw wallowing along, hull down on the starboard bow, an English cruiser with two funnels, nothing happened at all. Even when we landed at Liverpool nothing happened to suggest that we had reached a country actively engaged in war, unless you would list the presence of a few khaki-clad soldiers on the landing stage and the painful absence of porters to handle our baggage as evidences of the same. I remember seeing Her Grace the Duchess of Marlborough sitting hour after hour on a baggage truck, waiting for her heavy luggage to come off the tardy tender and up the languid chute into the big dusty dockhouse.

I remember, also, seeing women, with their hats flopping down in their faces and their hair all streaming, dragging huge trunks across the floor; and if all of us had not been in the same distressful fix we could have appreciated the humor of the spectacle of a portly high dignitary of the United States Medical Corps shoving a truck piled high with his belongings, and shortly afterward, with the help of his own wife, loading them on the roof of an infirm and wheezy taxicab.

From Liverpool across to London we traveled through a drowsy land burdened with bumper crops of grain, and watched the big brown hares skipping among the oat stacks; and late at night we came to London. In London next day there were more troops about than common, and recruits were drilling on the gravel walks back of Somerset House; and the people generally moved with a certain sober restraint, as people do who feel the weight of a heavy and an urgent responsibility. Otherwise the London of wartime seemed the London of peacetime.

So within a day our small party, still seeking to slip into the wings of the actual theater of events rather than to stay so far back behind the scenes, was aboard a Channel ferryboat bound for Ostend, and having for fellow travelers a few Englishmen, a tall blond princess of some royal house of Northern Europe, and any number of Belgians going home to enlist. In the Straits of Dover, an hour or so out from Folkestone, we ran through a fleet of British warships guarding the narrow roadstead between France and England; and a torpedo-boat destroyer sidled up and took a look at us.

Just off Dunkirk a French scout ship talked with us by the language of the whipping signal flags; but the ordinary Channel craft came and went without hindrance or seeming fear, and again it was hard for us to make ourselves believe that we had reached a zone where the physical, tangible business of war went forward.

And Ostend and, after Ostend, the Belgian interior—those were disappointments too; for at Ostend bathers disported on the long, shining beach and children played about the sanded stretch. And, though there were soldiers in sight, one always expects soldiers in European countries. No one asked to see the passports we had brought with us, and the customs officers gave our hand baggage the most perfunctory of examinations. Hardly five minutes had elapsed after our landing before we were steaming away on our train through a landscape which, to judge by its appearance, might have known only peace, and naught but peace, for a thousand placid years.

It is true we saw during that ride few able-bodied male adults, either in the towns through which we rushed or in the country. There were priests occasionally and old, infirm men or half-grown boys; but of men in their prime the land had been drained to fill up the army of defense then on the other side of Belgium—toward Germany—striving to hold the invaders in check until the French and English might come up. The yellow-ripe grain stood in the fields, heavy-headed and drooping with seed. The russet pears and red apples bent the limbs of the fruit trees almost to earth. Every visible inch of soil was under cultivation, of the painfully intensive European sort; and there remained behind to garner the crops only the peasant women and a few crippled, aged grand- sires. It was hard for us to convince ourselves that any event out of the ordinary beset this country. No columns of troops passed along the roads; no camps of tents lifted their peaked tops above the hedges. In seventy-odd miles we encountered one small detachment of soldiers—they were at a railroad station—and one Red Cross flag.

As for Brussels—why, Brussels at first glance was more like a city making a fete than the capital of a nation making war. The flags which were displayed everywhere; the crowds in the square before the railroad station; the multitudes of boy scouts running about; the uniforms of Belgian volunteers and regulars; the Garde Civique, in their queer- looking costumes, with funny little derby hats, all braid-trimmed—gave to the place a holiday air. After nightfall, when the people of Brussels flocked to the sidewalk cafes and sat at little round tables under awnings, drinking light drinks a la Parisienne, this impression was heightened.

We dined in the open air ourselves, finding the prices for food and drink to be both moderate and modest, and able to see nothing on the surface which suggested that the life of these people had been seriously disturbed. Two significant facts, however, did obtrude themselves on us: Every minute or two, as we dined, a young girl or an old gentleman would come to us, rattling a tin receptacle with a slot in the top through which coins for the aid of the widows and orphans of dead soldiers might be dropped; and when a little later we rode past the royal palace we saw that it had been converted into a big hospital for the wounded. That night, also, the government ran away to Antwerp; but of this we knew nothing until the following morning.

Next day we heard tales: Uhlans had been seen almost in the suburbs; three German spies, disguised as nuns, had been captured, tried, convicted and were no longer with us; sentries on duty outside the residence of the American Minister had fired at a German aeroplane darting overhead; French troops were drawing in to the northward and English soldiers were hurrying up from the south; trainloads of wounded had been brought in under cover of the night and distributed among the improvised hospitals; but, conceding these things to be true, we knew of them only at second hand. By the evidence of what we ourselves saw we were able to note few shifts in the superficial aspects of the city.

The Garde Civique seemed a trifle more numerous than it had been the evening before; citizen volunteers, still in civilian garb, appeared on the streets in awkward squads, carrying their guns and side arms clumsily; and when, in Minister Brand Whitlock's car, we drove out the beautiful Avenue Louise, we found soldiers building a breast-high barricade across the head of the roadway where it entered the Bois; also, they were weaving barbed-wire entanglements among the shade trees. That was all.

And then, as though to offset these added suggestions of danger, we saw children playing about quietly behind the piled sand-bags, guarded by plump Flemish nursemaids, and smart dogcarts constantly passed and repassed us, filled with well-dressed women, and with flowers stuck in the whip-sockets.

The nearer we got to this war the farther away from us it seemed to be. We began to regard it as an elusive, silent, secretive, hide-and-go-seek war, which would evade us always. We resolved to pursue it into the country to the northward, from whence the Germans were reported to be advancing, crushing back the outnumbered Belgians as they came onward; but when we tried to secure a laissez passer at the gendarmerie, where until then an accredited correspondent might get himself a laissez passer, we bumped into obstacles.

In an inclosed courtyard behind a big gray building, among loaded wagons of supplies and munching cart horses, a kitchen table teetered unsteadily on its legs on the rough cobbles. On the table were pens and inkpots and coffee cups and beer bottles and beer

Paths of Glory

glasses; and about it sat certain unkempt men in resplendent but unbrushed costumes. Joseph himself—the Joseph of the coat of many colors, no less—might have devised the uniforms they wore. With that setting the picture they made there in the courtyard was suggestive of stage scenes in plays of the French Revolution.

They were polite enough, these piebald gentlemen, and they considered our credentials with an air of mildly courteous interest; but they would give us no passes. There had been an order. Who had issued it, or why, was not for us to know. Going away from there, all downcast and disappointed, we met a French cavalryman. He limped along in his high dragoon boots, walking with the wide-legged gait of one who had bestraddled leather for many hours and was sore from it. His horse, which he led by the bridle, stumbled with weariness. A proud boy scout was serving as his guide. He was the only soldier of any army, except the Belgian, we had seen so far, and we halted our car and watched him until he disappeared.

However, seeing one tired French dragoon was not seeing the war; and we chafed that night at the delay which kept us penned as prisoners in this handsome, outwardly quiet city. As we figured it we might be housed up here for days or weeks and miss all the operations in the field. When morning came, though, we discovered that the bars were down again, and that certificates signed by the American consul would be sufficient to carry us as far as the outlying suburbs at least.

Securing these precious papers, then, without delay we chartered a rickety red taxicab for the day; and piling in we told the driver to take us eastward as far as he could go before the outposts turned us back. He took us, therefore, at a buzzing clip through the Bois, along one flank of the magnificent Forest of Soigne, with its miles of green-trunked beech trees, and by way of the royal park of Tervueren. From the edge of the thickly settled district onward we passed barricade after barricade—some built of newly felled trees; some of street cars drawn across the road in double rows; some of street cobbles chinked with turf; and some of barbed wire—all of them, even to our inexperienced eyes, seeming but flimsy defenses to interpose against a force of any size or determination. But the Belgians appeared to set great store by these playthings.

Behind each of them was a mixed group of soldiers—Garde Civique, gendarmes and burgher volunteers. These latter mainly carried shotguns and wore floppy blue caps and long blue blouses, which buttoned down their backs with big horn buttons, like little girls' pinafores. There was, we learned, a touch of sentiment about the sudden appearance of those most unsoldierly looking vestments. In the revolution of 1830, when the men of Brussels fought the Hollanders all morning, stopped for dinner at midday and then fought again all afternoon, and by alternately fighting and eating wore out the enemy and won their national independence, they wore such caps and such back-buttoning blouses. And so all night long women in the hospitals had sat up cutting out and basting together the garments of glory for their menfolk.

No one offered to turn us back, and only once or twice did a sentry insist on looking at our passes. In the light of fuller experiences I know now that when a city is about to fall into an enemy's hands the authorities relax their vigilance and freely permit noncombatants to depart therefrom, presumably on the assumption that the fewer individuals there are in the place when the conqueror does come the fewer the problems of caring for the resident population will be. But we did not know this mighty significant fact; and, suspecting nothing, the four innocents drove blithely on until the city lay behind us and the country lay before us, brooding in the bright sunlight and all empty and peaceful, except for thin scattering detachments of gaily clad Belgian infantrymen through which we passed.

Once or twice tired, dirty stragglers, lying at the roadside, raised a cheer as they recognized the small American flag that fluttered from our taxi's door; and once we gave a lift to a Belgian bicycle courier, who had grown too leg-weary to pedal his machine another inch. He was the color of the dust through which he had ridden, and his face under its dirt mask was thin and drawn with fatigue; but his racial enthusiasm endured, and when we dropped him he insisted on shaking hands with all of us, and offering us a drink out of a very warm and very grimy bottle of something or other.

All of a sudden, rounding a bend, we came on a little valley with one of the infrequent Belgian brooks bisecting it; and this whole valley was full of soldiers. There must have been ten thousand of them — cavalry, foot, artillery, baggage trains, and all. Quite near us was ranged a battery of small rapid-fire guns; and the big rawboned dogs that had hauled them there were lying under the wicked-looking little pieces. We had heard a lot about the dog-drawn guns of the Belgians, but these were the first of them we had seen.

Lines of cavalrymen were skirting crosswise over the low hill at the other side of the valley, and against the sky line the figures of horses and men stood out clear and fine. It all seemed a splendid martial sight; but afterward, comparing this force with the army into whose front we were to blunder unwittingly, we thought of it as a little handful of toy soldiers playing at war. We never heard what became of those Belgians. Presumably at the advance of the Germans coming down on them countlessly, like an Old Testament locust plague, they fell back and, going round Brussels, went northward toward Antwerp, to join the main body of their own troops. Or they may have reached the lines of the Allies, to the south and westward, toward the French frontier. One guess would be as good as the other.

One of the puzzling things about the early mid-August stages of the war was the almost instantaneous rapidity with which the Belgian army, as an army, disintegrated and vanished. To-day it was here, giving a good account of itself against tremendous odds, spending itself in driblets to give the Allies a chance to get up. To-morrow it was utterly gone.

Still without being halted or delayed we went briskly on. We had topped the next rise commanding the next valley, and—except for a few stragglers and some skirmishers—the Belgians were quite out of sight, when our driver stopped with an abruptness which piled his four passengers in a heap and pointed off to the northwest, a queer, startled, frightened look on his broad Flemish face. There was smoke there along the horizon—much smoke, both white and dark; and, even as the throb of the motor died away to a purr, the sound of big guns came to us in a faint rumbling, borne from a long way off by the breeze.

It was the first time any one of us, except McCutcheon, had ever heard a gun fired in battle; and it was the first intimation to any of us that the Germans were so near. Barring only venturesome mounted scouts we had supposed the German columns were many kilometers away. A brush between skirmishers was the best we had counted on seeing.

Right here we parted from our taxi driver. He made it plain to us, partly by words and partly by signs, that he personally was not looking for any war. Plainly he was one who specialized in peace and the pursuits of peace. Not even the proffered bribe of a doubled or a tripled fare availed to move him one rod toward those smoke clouds. He turned his car round so that it faced toward Brussels, and there he agreed to stay, caring for our light overcoats, until we should return to him. I wonder how long he really did stay.

And I have wondered, in idle moments since, what he did with our overcoats. Maybe he fled with the automobile containing two English moving-picture operators which passed us at that moment, and from which floated back a shouted warning that the Germans were coming. Maybe he stayed too long and was gobbled up—but I doubt it. He had an instinct for safety.

As we went forward afoot the sound of the firing grew clearer and more distinct. We could now hear quite plainly the grunting belch of the big pieces and, in between, the chattering voice of rapid-fire guns. Long- extended, stammering, staccato sounds, which we took to mean rifle firing, came to our ears also. Among ourselves we decided that the white smoke came from the guns and the black from burning buildings or hay ricks. Also we agreed that the fighting was going on beyond the spires and chimneys of a village on the crest of the hill immediately ahead of us. We could make out a white church and, on past it, lines of gray stone cottages.

In these deductions we were partly right and partly wrong; we had hit on the approximate direction of the fighting, but it was not a village that lay before us. What we saw was an outlying section of the city of Louvain, a place of fifty thousand inhabitants, destined within ten days to be turned into a waste of sacked ruins.

There were fields of tall, rank winter cabbages on each side of the road, and among the big green leaves we saw bright red dots. We had to look a second time before we realized that these dots were not the blooms of the wild red poppies that are so abundant in Belgium, but the red-tipped caps of Belgian soldiers squatting in the cover of the plants. None of them looked toward us; all of them looked toward those mounting walls of smoke.

Now, too, we became aware of something else—aware of a procession that advanced toward us. It was the head of a two-mile long line of refugees, fleeing from destroyed or threatened districts on beyond. At first, in scattered, straggling groups, and then in solid columns, they passed us unendingly, we going one way, they going the other. Mainly they were afoot, though now and then a farm wagon would bulk above the weaving ranks; and it would be loaded with bedding and furniture and packed to overflowing with old women and babies. One wagon lacked horses to draw it, and six men pulled in front while two men pushed at the back to propel it. Some of the fleeing multitude looked like townspeople, but the majority plainly were peasants. And of these latter at least half wore wooden shoes so that the sound of their feet on the cobbled roadbed made a clattering chorus that at times almost drowned out the hiccuping voices of the guns behind them.

Occasionally there would be a man shoving a barrow, with a baby and possibly a muddle of bedclothing in the barrow together. Every woman carried a burden of some sort, which might be a pack tied in a cloth or a cheap valise stuffed to bursting, or a baby—though generally it was a baby; and nearly every man, in addition to his load of belongings, had an umbrella under his arm. In this rainy land the carrying of umbrellas is a habit not easily shaken off; and, besides, most of these people had slept out at least one night and would probably sleep out another, and an umbrella makes a sort of shelter if you have no better. I figure I saw a thousand umbrellas if I saw one, and the sight of them gave a strangely incongruous touch to the thing.

Yes, it gave a grotesque touch to it. The spectacle inclined one to laugh, almost making one forget for a moment that here in this spectacle one beheld the misery of war made concrete; that in the lorn state of these poor folks its effects were focused and made vivid; that, while in some way it touched every living creature on the globe, here it touched them directly.

All the children, except the sick ones and the very young ones, walked, and most of them carried small bundles too. I saw one little girl, who was perhaps six years old, with a heavy wooden clock in her arms. The legs of the children wavered under them sometimes from weakness or maybe weariness, but I did not hear a single child whimper, or see a single woman who wept, or hear a single man speak above a half whisper.

They drifted on by us, silent all, except for the sound of feet and wheels; and, as I read the looks on their faces, those faces expressed no emotion except a certain numbed, resigned, bovine bewilderment. Far back in the line we met two cripples, hobbling along side by side as though for company, and still farther back a Belgian soldier came, like a rear guard, with his gun swung over his back and his sweaty black hair hanging down in his eyes.

In an undertone he was apparently explaining something to a little bow-legged man in black, with spectacles, who trudged along in his company. He was the lone soldier we saw among the refugees—all the others were civilians.

Only one man in all the line hailed us. Speaking so low that we could scarcely catch his words, he said in broken English:

"M'sieurs, the French are in Brussels, are they not?"

"No," we told him.

"The British, then—they must be there by now?"

"No; the British aren't there, either."

He shook his head, as though puzzled, and started on.

"How far away are the Germans?" we asked him.

He shook his head again. "I cannot say," he answered; "but I think they must be close behind us. I had a brother in the army at Liege," he added, apparently apropos of nothing. And then he went on, still shaking his head and with both arms tightly clasped round a big bundle done up in cloth, which he held against his breast.

Very suddenly the procession broke off, as though it had been chopped in two; and almost immediately after that the road turned into a street and we were between solid lines of small cottages, surrounded on all sides by people who fluttered about with the distracted aimlessness of agitated barnyard fowls. They babbled among themselves, paying small heed to us. An automobile tore through the street with its horn blaring, and raced by us, going toward Brussels at forty miles an hour. A well-dressed man in the front seat yelled out something to us as he whizzed past, but the words were swallowed up in the roaring of his engine.

Paths of Glory

Of our party only one spoke French, and he spoke it indifferently. We sought, therefore, to find some one who understood English. In a minute we saw the black robe of a priest; and here, through the crowd, calm and dignified where all others were fairly befuddled with excitement, he came—a short man with a fuzzy red beard and a bright blue eye.

We hailed him, and the man who spoke a little French explained our case. At once he turned about and took us into a side street; and even in their present state the men and women who met us remembered their manners and pulled off their hats and bowed before him.

At a door let into a high stone wall he stopped and rang a bell. A brother in a brown robe came and unbarred the gate for us, and our guide led us under an arched alley and out again into the open; and behold we were in another world from the little world of panic that we had just left. There was a high-walled inclosure with a neglected tennis court in the middle, and pear and plum trees burdened with fruit; and at the far end, beneath a little arbor of vines, four priests were sitting together. At sight of us they rose and came to us, and shook hands all round. Almost before we knew it we were in a bare little room behind the ancient Church of Saint Jacques, and one of the fathers was showing us a map in order that we might better understand the lay of the land; and another was uncorking a bottle of good red wine, which he brought up from the cellar, with a halo of mold on the cork and a mantle of cobwebs on its sloping shoulders.

It seemed that the Rev. Dom. Marie-Joseph Montaigne—I give the name that was on his card—could speak a little English. He told us haltingly that the smoke we had seen came from a scene of fighting somewhere to the eastward of Louvain. He understood that the Prussians were quite near, but he had seen none himself and did not expect they would enter the town before nightfall. As for the firing, that appeared to have ceased. And, sure enough, when we listened we could no longer catch the sound of the big guns. Nor did we hear them again during that day. Over his glass the priest spoke in his faulty English, stopping often to feel for a word; and when he had finished his face worked and quivered with the emotion he felt.

"This war—it is a most terrible thing that it should come on Belgium, eh? Our little country had no quarrel with any great country. We desired only that we should be left alone.

Paths of Glory

"Our people here—they are not bad people. I tell you they are very good people. All the week they work and work, and on Sunday they go to church; and then maybe they take a little walk.

"You Americans now—you come from a very great country. Surely, if the worst should come America will not let our country perish from off the earth, eh! Is not that so?"

Fifteen minutes later we were out again facing the dusty little square of Saint Jacques; and now of a sudden peace seemed to have fallen on the place. The wagons of a little traveling circus were ranged in the middle of the square with no one about to guard them; and across the way was a small tavern.

All together we discovered we were hungry. We had had bread and cheese and coffee, and were lighting some very bad native cigars, when the landlord burst in on us, saying in a quavering voice that some one passing had told him a squad of seven German troopers had been seen in the next street but one. He made a gesture as though to invoke the mercy of Heaven on us all, and ran out again, casting a carpet slipper in his flight and leaving it behind him on the floor.

So we followed, not in the least believing that any Germans had really been sighted; but in the street we saw a group of perhaps fifty Belgian soldiers running up a narrow sideway, trailing their gun butts behind them on the stones. We figured they were hurrying forward to the other side of town to help hold back the enemy.

A minute later seven or eight more soldiers crossed the road ahead of us and darted up an alley with the air and haste of men desirous of being speedily out of sight. We had gone perhaps fifty feet beyond the mouth of this alley when two men, one on horseback and one on a bicycle, rode slowly and sedately out of another alley, parallel to the first one, and swung about with their backs to us.

I imagine we had watched the newcomers for probably fifty seconds before it dawned on any of us that they wore gray helmets and gray coats, and carried arms—and were Germans. Precisely at that moment they both turned so that they faced us; and the man on horseback lifted a carbine from a holster and half swung it in our direction.

Paths of Glory

Realization came to us that here we were, pocketed. There were armed Belgians in an alley behind us and armed Germans in the street before us; and we were nicely in between. If shooting started the enemies might miss each other, but they could not very well miss us. Two of our party found a courtyard and ran through it. The third pressed close up against a house front and I made for the half-open door of a shop.

Just as I reached it a woman on the inside slammed it in my face and locked it. I never expect to see her again; but that does not mean that I ever expect to forgive her. The next door stood open, and from within its shelter I faced about to watch for what might befall. Nothing befell except that the Germans rode slowly past me, both vigilantly keen in poise and look, both with weapons unshipped.

I got an especially good view of the cavalry. He was a tall, lean, blond young man, man with a little yellow mustache and high cheekbones like an Indian's; and he was sunburned until he was almost as red as an Indian. The sight of that limping French dragoon the day before had made me think of a picture by Meissonier or Détaille, but this German put me in mind of one of Frederic Remington's paintings. Change his costume a bit, and substitute a slouch hat for his flat-topped lancer's cap, and he might have cantered bodily out of one of Remington's canvases.

He rode past me—he and his comrade on the wheel—and in an instant they were gone into another street, and the people who had scurried to cover at their coming were out again behind them, with craned necks and startled faces.

Our group reassembled itself somehow and followed after those two Germans who could jog along so serenely through a hostile town. We did not crowd them—our health forbade that—but we now desired above all things to get back to our taxicab, two miles or more away, before our line of retreat should be cut off. But we had tarried too long at our bread and cheese.

When we came to where the street leading to the Square of Saint Jacques joined the street that led in turn to the Brussels road, all the people there were crouching in their doorways as quiet as so many mice, all looking in the direction in which we hoped to go, all pointing with their hands. No one spoke, but the scuffle of wooden-shod feet on the flags made a sliding, slithering sound, which someway carried a message of warning more forcible than any shouted word or sudden shriek.

We looked where their fingers aimed, and, as we looked, a hundred feet away through a cloud of dust a company of German foot soldiers swung across an open grassplot, where a little triangular park was, and straightened out down the road to Brussels, singing snatches of a German marching song as they went.

And behind them came trim officers on handsome, high-headed horses, and more infantry; then a bicycle squad; then cavalry, and then a light battery, bumping along over the rutted stones, with white dust blowing back from under its wheels in scrolls and pennons.

Then a troop of Uhlans came, with nodding lances, following close behind the guns; and at sight of them a few men and women, clustered at the door of a little wine shop calling itself the Belgian Lion, began to hiss and mutter, for among these people, as we knew already, the Uhlans had a hard name.

At that a noncommissioned officer—a big man with a neck on him like a bison and a red, broad, menacing face—turned in his saddle and dropped the muzzle of his black automatic on them. They sucked their hisses back down their frightened gullets so swiftly that the exertion well-nigh choked them, and shrank flat against the wall; and, for all the sound that came from them until he had holstered his hardware and trotted on, they might have been dead men and women.

Just then, from perhaps half a mile on ahead, a sharp clatter of rifle fire sounded—pop! pop! pop!—and then a rattling volley. We saw the Uhlans snatch out their carbines and gallop forward past the battery into the dust curtain. And as it swallowed them up we, who had come in a taxicab looking for the war, knew that we had found it; and knew, too, that our chances of ever seeing that taxicab again were most exceeding small.

We had one hope—that this might merely be a reconnaissance in force, and that when it turned back or turned aside we might yet slip through and make for Brussels afoot. But it was no reconnaissance— it was Germany up and moving. We stayed in Louvain three days, and for three days we watched the streaming past of the biggest army we had ever seen, and the biggest army beleaguered Belgium had ever seen, and one of the biggest, most perfect armies the world has ever seen. We watched the gray-clad columns pass until the mind grew numb at the prospect of computing their number. To think of trying to count them was like trying to count the leaves on a tree or the pebbles on a path.

They came and came, and kept on coming, and their iron-shod feet flailed the earth to powder, and there was no end to them.

Chapter 3

Sherman Said It

Undoubtedly Sherman said it. This is my text and as illustration for my text I take the case of the town of La Buissière.

The Germans took the town of La Buissière after stiff fighting on August twenty-fourth. I imagine that possibly there was a line in the dispatches telling of the fight there; but at that I doubt it, because on that same date a few miles away a real battle was raging between the English rear guard, under Sir John French, of the retreating army of the Allies, falling back into France, and the Germans. Besides, in the sum total of this war the fall of La Buissière hardly counts. You might say it represents a semicolon in the story of the campaign. Probably no future historian will give it so much as a paragraph. In our own Civil War it would have been worth a page in the records anyway. Here upward of three hundred men on both sides were killed and wounded, and as many more Frenchmen were captured; and the town, when taken, gave the winners the control of the river Sambre for many miles east and west. Here, also, was a German charge with bayonets up a steep and well-defended height; and after that a hand-to-hand melee with the French defenders on the poll of the hill.

But this war is so big a thing, as wars go, that an engagement of this size is likely to be forgotten in a day or a week. Yet, I warrant you, the people of La Buissière will not forget it. Nor shall we forget it who came that way in the early afternoon of a flawless summer day. Let me try to recreate La Buissière for you, reader. Here the Sambre, a small, orderly stream, no larger or broader or wider than a good-sized creek would be in America, flows for a mile or two almost due east and weSt. The northern bank is almost flat, with low hills rising on beyond like the rim of a saucer. The town—most of it—is on this side. On the south the land lifts in a moderately stiff bluff, perhaps seventy feet high, with wooded edges, and extending off and away in a plateau, where trees stand in well-thinned groves, and sunken roads meander between fields of hops and grain and patches of cabbages and sugar beets. As for the town, it has perhaps twenty-five hundred people— Walloons and Flemish folk—living in tall, bleak, stone houses built flush with the little crooked streets. Invariably these houses are of a whitish gray color; almost invariably they are narrow and cramped- looking, with very peaky gables, somehow suggesting flat-chested old men standing in close rows, with their hands in their pockets and their shoulders shrugged up.

A canal bisects one corner of the place, and spanning the river there are—or were—three bridges, one for the railroad and two for foot and vehicular travel. There is a mill which overhangs the river—the biggest building in the town—and an ancient gray convent, not quite so large as the mill; and, of course, a church. In most of the houses there are tiny shops on the lower floors, and upstairs are the homes of the people. On the northern side of the stream every tillable foot of soil is under cultivation. There are flower beds, and plum and pear trees in the tiny grass plots alongside the more pretentious houses, and the farm lands extend to where the town begins.

This, briefly, is La Buissière as it looked before the war began—a little, drowsy settlement of dull, frugal, hard-working, kindly Belgians, minding their own affairs, prospering in their own small way, and having no quarrel with the outside world. They lived in the only corner of Europe that I know of where serving people decline to accept tips for rendering small services; and in a simple, homely fashion are, I think, the politest, the most courteous, the most accommodating human beings on the face of the earth.

Even their misery did not make them forget their manners, as we found when we came that way, close behind the conquerors. It was only the refugees, fleeing from their homes or going back to them again, who were too far spent to lift their caps in answer to our hails, and too miserably concerned with their own ruined affairs, or else too afraid of inquisitive strangers, to answer the questions we sometimes put to them.

We were three days getting from Brussels to La Buissière—a distance, I suppose, of about forty-five English miles. There were no railroads and no trams for us. The lines were held by the Germans or had been destroyed by the Allies as they fell back. Nor were there automobiles to be had. Such automobiles as were not hidden had been confiscated by one side or the other.

Moreover, our journey was a constant succession of stops and starts. Now we would be delayed for half an hour while some German officer examined the passes we carried, he meantime eying us with his suspicious squinted eyes. Now again we would halt to listen to some native's story of battle or reprisal on ahead. And always there was the everlasting dim reverberation of the distant guns to draw us forward. And always, too, there was the difficulty of securing means of transportation.

It was on Sunday afternoon, August twenty-third, when we left Brussels, intending to ride to Waterloo. There were six of us, in two ancient open carriages designed like gravy boats and hauled by gaunt livery horses. Though the Germans had held Brussels for four days now, life in the suburbs went on exactly as it goes on in the suburbs of a Belgian city in ordinary times. There was nothing to suggest war or a captured city in the family parties sitting at small tables before the outlying cafes or strolling decorously under the trees that shaded every road. Even the Red Cross flags hanging from the windows of many of the larger houses seemed for once in keeping with the peaceful picture. Of Germans during the afternoon we saw almost none. Thick enough in the center of the town, the gray backs showed themselves hardly at all in the environs.

At the city line a small guard lounged on benches before a wine shop. They stood up as we drew near, but changed their minds and squatted down without challenging us to produce the safe-conduct papers that Herr General Major Thaddeus von Jarotzky, sitting in due state in the ancient Hotel de Ville, had bestowed on us an hour before.

Just before we reached Waterloo we saw in a field on the right, near the road, a small camp of German cavalry. The big, round-topped yellow tents, sheltering twenty men each and looking like huge tortoises, stood in a line. From the cook-wagons, modeled on the design of those carried by an American circus, came the heavy, meaty smells of stews boiling in enormous caldrons. The men were lying or sitting on straw piles, singing German marching songs as they waited for their supper. It was always so—whenever and wherever we found German troops at rest they were singing, eating or drinking—or doing all three at once. A German said to me afterwards:

"Why do we win? Three things are winning for us—good marching, good shooting and good cooking; but most of all the cooking. When our troops stop there is always plenty of hot food for them. We never have to fight on an empty stomach—we Germans."

Paths of Glory

These husky singers were the last Germans we were to see for many hours; for between the garrison force left behind in Brussels and the fast- moving columns hurrying to meet the English and the French and a few Belgians—on the morrow—a matter of many leagues now intervened.

Evidence of the passing through of the troops was plentiful enough though. We saw it in the trampled hedges; in the empty beer bottles that dotted the roadside ditches—empty bottles, as we had come to know, meant Germans on ahead; in the subdued, furtive attitude of the country folk, and, most of all, in the chalked legend, in stubby German script— "Gute Leute! "—on nearly every wine-shop shutter or cottage door. Soldiers quartered in such a house overnight had on leaving written this line—"Good people! "—to indicate the peaceful character of the dwellers therein and to commend them to the kindness of those who might follow after.

The Lion of Waterloo, standing on its lofty green pyramid, was miles behind us before realization came that fighting had started that day to the southward of us. We halted at a taverne to water the horses, and out came its Flemish proprietor, all gesticulations and exclamations, to tell us that since morning he had heard firing on ahead.

"Ah, sirs, " he said, "it was inconceivable—that sound of the guns. It went on for hours. The whole world must be at war down the road! "

The day before he had seen, flitting across the cabbage patches and dodging among the elm trees, a skirmish party, mounted, which he took to be English; and for two days, so he said, the Germans had been passing the tavern in numbers uncountable.

We hurried on then, but as we met many peasants, all coming the other way afoot and all with excited stories of a supposed battle ahead, and as we ourselves now began to catch the faint reverberations of cannon fire, our drivers manifested a strange reluctance about proceeding farther. And when, just at dusk, we clattered into the curious little convent-church town of Nivelles, and found the tiny square before the Black Eagle Inn full of refugees who had trudged in from towns beyond, the liverymen, after taking off their varnished high hats to scratch their preplexed heads, announced that Brussels was where they belonged and to Brussels they would return that night, though their spent horses dropped in the traces on the way.

We supped that night at the Black Eagle—slept there too—and it was at supper we had as guests Raymond Putzeys, aged twelve, and Alfred, his father. Except crumbs of chocolate and pieces of dry bread, neither of them had eaten for two days.

The boy, who was a round-faced, handsome, dirty, polite little chap, said not a word except "Merci! " He was too busy clearing his plate clean as fast as we loaded it with ham and eggs and plum jam; and when he had eaten enough for three and could hold no more he went to sleep, with his tousled head among the dishes.

The father between bites told us his tale—such a tale as we had heard dozens of times already and were to hear again a hundred times before that crowded week ended—he telling it with rolling eyes and lifting brows, and graphic and abundant gestures. Behind him and us, penning our table about with a living hedge, stood the leading burghers of Nivelles, now listening to him, now watching us with curious eyes. And, as he talked on, the landlord dimmed the oil lamps and made fast the door; for this town, being in German hands, was under martial law and must lock and bar itself in at eight o'clock each night. So we sat in a half light and listened.

They lived, the two Putzeys, at a hamlet named Marchienne-au-Pont, to the southward. The Germans had come into it the day before at sunup, and finding the French there had opened fire. From the houses the French had replied until driven out by heavy odds, and then they ran across the fields, leaving many dead and wounded behind them. As for the inhabitants they had, during the fighting, hidden in their cellars.

"When the French were gone the Germans drove us out, " went on the narrator; "and, of the men, they made several of us march ahead of them down the road into the next village, we holding up our hands and loudly begging those within the houses not to fire, for fear of killing us who were their friends and neighbors. When this town surrendered the Germans let us go, but first one of them gave me a cake of chocolate.

"Yet when I tried to go to aid a wounded Frenchman who lay in the fields, another German, I thought, fired at me. I heard the bullet—it buzzed like a hornet. So then I ran away and found my son here; and we came across the country, following the canals and avoiding the roads, which were filled with German troops. When we had gone a mile we looked back and there was much thick smoke behind us—our houses were burning, I suppose. So last night we slept in the woods and all day we walked, and to-night reached here, bringing with us nothing except the clothes on our backs.

"I have no wife—she has been dead for two years—but in Brussels I have two daughters at school. Do you think I shall be permitted to enter Brussels and seek for my two daughters? This morning they told me Brussels was burning; but that I do not believe."

Then, also, he told us in quick, eager sentences, lowering his voice while he spoke, that a priest, with his hands tied behind his back, had been driven through a certain village ahead of the Germans, as a human shield for them; and that, in still another village, two aged women had been violated and murdered. Had he beheld these things with his own eyes? No; he had been told of them.

Here I might add that this was our commonest experience in questioning the refugees. Every one of them had a tale to tell of German atrocities on noncombatants; but not once did we find an avowed eye-witness to such things. Always our informant had heard of the torturing or the maiming or the murdering, but never had he personally seen it. It had always happened in another town—never in his own town.

We hoped to hire fresh vehicles of some sort in Nivelles. Indeed, a half-drunken burgher who spoke fair English, and who, because he had once lived in America, insisted on taking personal charge of our affairs, was constantly bustling in to say he had arranged for carriages and horses; but when the starting hour came—at five o'clock on Monday morning—there was no sign either of our fuddled guardian or of the rigs he had promised. So we set out afoot, following the everlasting sound of the guns.

After having many small adventures on the way we came at nightfall to Binche, a town given over to dullness and lacemaking, and once a year to a masked carnival, but which now was jammed with German supply trains, and by token of this latter circumstance filled with apprehensive townspeople. But there had been no show of resistance here, and no houses had been burned; and the Germans were paying freely for what they took and treating the townspeople civilly.

Indeed, all that day we had traveled through a district as yet unharried and unmolested. Though sundry hundreds of thousands of Germans had gone that way, no burnt houses or squandered fields marked their wake; and the few peasants who had not run away at the approach of the dreaded Allemands were back at work, trying to gather their crops in barrows or on their backs, since they had no work-cattle left. For these the Germans had taken from them, to the last fit horse and the last colt.

At Binche we laid up two nights and a day for the curing of our blistered feet. Also, here we bought our two flimsy bicycles and our decrepit dogcart, and our still more decrepit mare to haul it; and, with this equipment, on Wednesday morning, bright and early, we made a fresh start, heading now toward Maubeuge, across the French boundary.

Current rumor among the soldiers at Binche—for the natives, seemingly through fear for their own skins, would tell us nothing—was that at Maubeuge the onward-pressing Germans had caught up with the withdrawing columns of the Allies and were trying to bottle the stubborn English rear guard. For once the gossip of the privates and the noncommissioned officers proved to be true. There was fighting that day near Maubeuge— hard fighting and plenty of it; but, though we got within five miles of it, and heard the guns and saw the smoke from them, we were destined not to get there.

Strung out, with the bicycles in front, we went down the straight white road that ran toward the frontier. After an hour or two of steady going we began to notice signs of the retreat that had trailed through this section forty-eight hours before. We picked up a torn shoulder strap, evidently of French workmanship, which had 13 embroidered on it in faded red tape; and we found, behind the trunk of a tree, a knapsack, new but empty, which was too light to have been part of a German soldier's equipment.

We thought it was French; but now I think it must have been Belgian, because, as we subsequently discovered, a few scattering detachments of the Belgian foot soldiers who fled from Brussels on the eve of the occupation—disappearing so completely and so magically—made their way westward and southward to the French

Paths of Glory

lines, toward Mons, and enrolled with the Allies in the last desperate effort to dam off and stem back the German torrent.

Also, in a hedge, was a pair of new shoes, with their mouths gaping open and their latchets hanging down like tongues, as though hungering for feet to go into them. But not a shred or scrap of German belongings— barring only the empty bottles—did we see.

The marvelous German system, which is made up of a million small things to form one great, complete thing, ordained that never, either when marching or after camping, or even after fighting, should any object, however worthless, be discarded, lest it give to hostile eyes some hint as to the name of the command or the extent of its size. These Germans we were trailing cleaned up behind themselves as carefully as New England housewives.

It may have been the German love of order and regularity that induced them even to avoid trampling the ripe grain in the fields wherever possible. Certainly, except when dealing out punishment, they did remarkably little damage, considering their numbers, along their line of march through this lowermost strip of Belgium.

At Merbes-Ste. -Marie, a matter of six kilometers from Binche, we came on the first proof of seeming wantonness we encountered that day. An old woman sat in a doorway of what had been a wayside wine shop, guarding the pitiable ruin of her stock and fixtures. All about her on the floor was a litter of foul straw, muddied by many feet and stained with spilled drink. The stench from a bloated dead cavalry horse across the road poisoned the air. The woman said a party of private soldiers, straying back from the main column, had despoiled her, taking what they pleased of her goods and in pure vandalism destroying what they could not use.

Her shop was ruined, she said. With a gesture of both arms, as though casting something from her, she expressed how utter and complete was her ruin. Also she was hungry—she and her children—for the Germans had eaten all the food in the house and all the food in the houses of her neighbors. We could not feed her, for we had no stock of provisions with us; but we gave her a five-franc piece and left her calling down the blessings of the saints on us in French-Flemish.

Paths of Glory

The sister village of Merbes-le-Chateau, another kilometer farther on, revealed to us all its doors and many of its windows caved in by blows of gun butts and, at the nearer end of the principal street, five houses in smoking ruins. A group of men and women were pawing about in the wreckage, seeking salvage. They had saved a half-charred washstand, a scorched mattress, a clock and a few articles of women's wear; and these they had piled in a mound on the edge of the road.

At first, not knowing who we were, they stood mute, replying to questions only with shrugged shoulders and lifted eyebrows; but when we made them realize that we were Americans they changed. All were ready enough to talk then; they crowded about us, gesticulating and interrupting one another. From the babble we gathered that the German skirmishers, coming in the strength of one company, had found an English cavalry squad in the town. The English had swapped a few volleys with them, then had fallen back toward the river in good order and without loss.

The Germans, pushing in, had burned certain outlying houses from which shots had come and burst open the rest. Also they had repeated the trick of capturing sundry luckless natives and, in their rush through the town, driving these prisoners ahead of them as living bucklers to minimize the danger of being shot at from the windows.

One youth showed us a raw wound in his ear. A piece of tile, splintered by an errant bullet, had pierced it, he said, as the Germans drove him before them. Another man told us his father—and the father must have been an old man, for the speaker himself was in his fifties—had been shot through the thigh. But had anybody been killed? That was what we wanted to know. Ah, but yes! A dozen eager fingers pointed to the house immediately behind us. There a man had been killed.

Coming back to try to save some of their belongings after the Germans had gone through, these others had found him at the head of the cellar steps in his blazing house. His throat had been cut and his blood was on the floor, and he was dead. They led us into the shell of the place, the stone walls being still staunchly erect; but the roof was gone, and in the cinders and dust on the planks of an inner room they showed us a big dull-brown smear.

Paths of Glory

This, they told us, pointing, was the place where he lay. One man in pantomime acted out the drama of the discovery of the body. He was a born actor, that Belgian villager, and an orator—with his hands. Somehow, watching him, I visualized the victim as a little man, old and stoop-shouldered and feeble in his movements.

I looked about the room. The corner toward the road was a black ruin, but the back wall was hardly touched by the marks of the fire.

On a mantel small bits of pottery stood intact, and a holy picture on the wall—a cheap print of a saint—was not even singed. At the foot of the cellar steps curdled milk stood in pans; and beside the milk, on a table, was a half-moon of cheese and a long knife.

We wanted to know why the man who lived here had been killed. They professed ignorance then—none of them knew, or, at least, none of them would say. A little later a woman told us she had heard the Germans caught him watching from a window with a pair of opera glasses, and on this evidence took him for a spy. But we could secure no direct evidence either to confirm the tale or to disprove it.

We got to the center of the town, leaving the venerable nag behind to be baited at a big gray barn by a big, shapeless, kindly woman hostler whose wooden shoes clattered on the round cobbles of her stable yard like drum taps.

In the Square, after many citizens had informed us there was nothing to eat, a little Frenchwoman took pity on our emptiness, and, leading us to a parlor behind a shop where she sold, among other things, post cards, cheeses and underwear, she made us a huge omelet and gave us also good butter and fresh milk and a pot of her homemade marmalade. Her two little daughters, who looked as though they had escaped from a Frans Hals canvas, waited on us while we wolfed the food down.

Quite casually our hostess showed us a round hole in the window behind us, a big white scar in the wooden inner shutter and a flattened chunk of lead. The night before, it seemed, some one, for purposes unknown, had fired a bullet through the window of her house. It was proof of the rapidity with which the actual presence of war works indifference to sudden shocks among a people that this woman could discuss the incident quietly. Hostile gun butts had splintered her front door; why not a stray bullet or two through her back window? So we interpreted her attitude.

It was she who advised us not to try to ford the Sambre at Merbes-le-Chateau, but to go off at an angle to La Buissière, where she had heard one bridge still stood. She said nothing of a fight at that place. It is possible that she knew nothing of it, though the two towns almost touched. Indeed, in all these Belgian towns we found the people so concerned with their own small upheavals and terrors that they seemed not to care or even to know how their neighbors a mile or two miles away had fared.

Following this advice we swung about and drove to La Buissière to find the bridge that might still be intact; and, finding it, we found also, and quite by chance, the scene of the first extended engagement on which we stumbled.

Our first intimation of it was the presence, in a cabbage field beyond the town, of three strangely subdued peasants softening the hard earth with water, so that they might dig a grave for a dead horse, which, after lying two days in the hot sun, had already become a nuisance and might become a pestilence. When we told them we meant to enter La Buissière they held up their soiled hands in protest.

"There has been much fighting there, " one said, "and many are dead, and more are dying. Also, the shooting still goes on; but what it means we do not know, because we dare not venture into the streets, which are full of Germans. Hark, m'sieurs! "

Even as he spoke we heard a rifle crack; and then, after a pause, a second report. We went forward cautiously across a bridge that spanned an arm of the canal, and past a double line of houses, with broken windows, from which no sign or sound of life came. Suddenly at a turn three German privates of a lancer regiment faced us. They were burdened with bottles of beer, and one carried his lance, which he flung playfully in our path. He had been drinking and was jovially exhilarated. As soon as he saw the small silk American flag that fluttered from the rail of our dogcart he and his friends became enthusiastic in their greetings, offering us beer and wanting to know whether the Americans meant to declare for Germany now that the Japanese had sided with England.

Paths of Glory

Leaving them cheering for the Americans we negotiated another elbow in the twisting street—and there all about us was the aftermath and wreckage of a spirited fight.

Earlier in this chapter I told—or tried to tell—how La Buissière must have looked in peaceful times. I shall try now to tell how it actually looked that afternoon we rode into it.

In the center of the town the main street opens out to form an irregular circle, and the houses fronting it make a compact ring. Through a gap one gets a glimpse of the little river which one has just crossed; and on the river bank stands the mill, or what is left of it, and that is little enough. Its roof is gone, shot clear away in a shower of shattered tiling, and its walls are breached in a hundred places. It is pretty certain that mill will never grind grist again.

On its upper floor, which is now a sieve, the Germans—so they themselves told us—found, after the fighting, the seventy-year-old miller, dead, with a gun in his hands and a hole in his head. He had elected to help the French defend the place; and it was as well for him that he fell fighting, because, had he been taken alive, the Prussians, following their grim rule for all civilians caught with weapons, would have stood him up against a wall with a firing squad before him.

The houses round about have fared better, in the main, than the mill, though none of them has come scatheless out of the fight. Hardly a windowpane is whole; hardly a wall but is pocked by bullets or rent by larger missiles. Some houses have lost roofs; some have lost side walls, so that one can gaze straight into them and see the cluttered furnishings, half buried in shattered masonry and crumbled plaster.

One small cottage has been blown clear away in a blast of artillery fire; only the chimney remains, pointing upward like a stubby finger. A fireplace, with a fire in it, is the glowing heart of a house; and a chimney completes it and reveals that it is a home fit for human creatures to live in; but we see here—and the truth of it strikes us as it never did before—that a chimney standing alone typifies desolation and ruin more fitly, more brutally, than any written words could typify it.

Everywhere there are soldiers—German soldiers—in their soiled, dusty gray service uniforms, always in heavy boots; always with their tunics buttoned to the throat. Some, off duty, are lounging at ease in the doors of the houses. More, on duty, are moving about briskly in squads, with fixed bayonets. One is learning to ride a bicycle, and when he falls off, as he does repeatedly, his comrades laugh at him and shout derisive advice at him.

There are not many of the townsfolk in sight. Experience has taught us that in any town not occupied by the enemy our appearance will be the signal for an immediate gathering of the citizens, all flocking about us, filled with a naive, respectful inquisitiveness, and wanting to know where we have come from and to what place we are going. Here in this stricken town not a single villager comes near us. A priest passes us, bows deeply to us, and in an instant is gone round a jog in the street, the skirts of his black robe flicking behind him. From upper windows faces peer out at us—faces of women and children mostly. In nearly every one of these faces a sort of cow-like bewilderment expresses itself—not grief, not even resentment, but merely a stupefied wonderment at the astounding fact that their town, rather than some other town, should be the town where the soldiers of other nations come to fight out their feud. We have come to know well that look these last few days. So far as we have seen there has been no mistreatment of civilians by the soldiers; yet we note that the villagers stay inside the shelter of their damaged homes as though they felt safer there. A young officer bustles up, spick and span in his tan boots and tan gloves, and, finding us to be Americans and correspondents, becomes instantly effusive. He has just come through his first fight, seemingly with some credit to himself; and he is proud of the part he has played and is pleased to talk about it. Of his own accord he volunteers to lead us to the heights back of the town where the French defenses were and where the hand-to-hand fighting took place.

As we trail along behind him in single file we pass a small paved court before a stable and see a squad of French prisoners. Later we are to see several thousand French prisoners; but now the sight is at once a sensation and a novelty to us. These are all French prisoners; there are no Belgians or Englishmen among them. In their long, cumbersome blue coats and baggy red pants they are huddled down against a wall in a heap of straw. They lie there silently, chewing straws and looking very forlorn. Four German soldiers with fixed bayonets are guarding them.

Paths of Glory

The young lieutenant leads us along a steeply ascending road over a ridge and then stops; and as we look about us the consciousness strikes home to us, with almost the jar of a physical blow, that we are standing where men have lately striven together and have fallen and died.

In front of us and below us is the town, with the river winding into it at the east and out of it at the west; and beyond the town, to the north, is the cup-shaped valley of fair, fat farm lands, all heavy and pregnant with un-garnered, ungathered crops. Behind us, on the front of the hill, is a hedge, and beyond the hedge—just a foot or so back of it, in fact—is a deep trench, plainly dug out by hand, and so lately done that the cut clods are still moist and fresh-looking. At the first instant of looking it seems to us that this intrenchment is full of dead men; but when we look closer we see that what we take for corpses are the scattered garments and equipments of French infantrymen—long blue coats; peaked, red-topped caps; spare shirts; rifled knapsacks; water- bottles; broken guns; side arms; bayonet belts and blanket rolls. There are perhaps twenty guns in sight. Each one has been rendered useless by being struck against the earth with sufficient force to snap the stock at the grip.

Almost at my feet is a knapsack, ripped open and revealing a card of small china buttons, a new red handkerchief, a gray-striped flannel shirt, a pencil and a sheaf of writing paper. Rummaging in the main compartment I find, folded at the back, a book recording the name and record of military service of one Gaston Michel Miseroux, whose home is at Amiens, and who is—or was—a private in the Tenth Battalion of the —— Regiment of Chasseurs a Pied. Whether this Gaston Michel Miseroux got away alive without his knapsack, or whether he was captured or was killed, there is none to say. His service record is here in the trampled dust and he is gone.

Before going farther the young lieutenant, speaking in his broken English, told us the story of the fight, which had been fought, he said, just forty-eight hours before. "The French, " he said, "must have been here for several days. They had fortified this hill, as you see; digging intrenchments in front for their riflemen and putting their artillery behind at a place I shall presently show you. Also they had placed many of their sharpshooters in the houses. It was a strong position, commanding the passage of the river, and they should have been able to hold it against twice their number.

"Our men came, as you did, along that road off yonder; and then our infantry advanced across the fields under cover of our artillery fire. We were in the open and the French were above us here and behind shelter; and so we lost many men.

"They had mined the bridge over the canal and also the last remaining bridge across the river; but we came so fast that we took both bridges before they could set off the mines.

"In twenty minutes we held the town and the last of their sharpshooters in the houses had been dislodged or killed. Then, while our guns moved over there to the left and shelled them on the flank, two companies of Germans—five hundred men—charged up the steep road over which you have just climbed and took this trench here in five minutes of close fighting.

"The enemy lost many men here before they ran. So did we lose many. On that spot there"—he pointed to a little gap in the hedge, not twenty feet away, where the grass was pressed flat—"I saw three dead men lying in a heap.

"We pushed the French back, taking a few prisoners as we went, until on the other side of this hill our artillery began to rake them, and then they gave way altogether and retreated to the south, taking their guns. Remember, they outnumbered us and they had the advantage of position; but we whipped them—we Germans—as we always do whip our enemies. "

His voice changed from boasting to pity:

"Ach, but it was shameful that they should have been sent against us wearing those long blue coats, those red trousers, those shiny black belts and bright brass buttons! At a mile, or even half a mile, the Germans in their dark-gray uniforms, with dull facings, fade into the background; but a Frenchman in his foolish monkey clothes is a target for as far as you can see him.

"And their equipment—see how flimsy it is when compared with ours! And their guns—so inferior, so old-fashioned alongside the German guns! I tell you this: Forty-four years they have been wishing to fight us for what we did in 1870; and when the time comes they are not ready and we are ready. While they have been singing their Marseillaise Hymn, we have been thinking. While they have been talking, we have been working."

Next he escorted us back along the small plateau that extended south from the face of the bluff. We made our way through a constantly growing confusion of abandoned equipment and garments—all the flotsam and jetsam of a rout. I suppose we saw as many as fifty smashed French rifles, as many as a hundred and fifty canteens and knapsacks.

Crossing a sunken road, where trenches for riflemen to kneel in and fire from had been dug in the sides of the bank—a road our guide said was full of dead men after the fight—we came very soon to the site of the French camp. Here, from the medley and mixture of an indescribable jumble of wreckage, certain objects stand out, as I write this, detached and plain in my mind; such things, for example, as a straw basket of twelve champagne bottles with two bottles full and ten empty; a box of lump sugar, broken open, with a stain of spilled red wine on some of the white cubes; a roll of new mattresses jammed into a natural receptacle at the root of an oak tree; a saber hilt of shining brass with the blade missing; a whole set of pewter knives and forks sown broadcast on the bruised and trampled grass. But there was no German relic in the lot —you may be sure of that. Farther down, where the sunken road again wound across our path, we passed an old-fashioned family carriage jammed against the bank, with one shaft snapped off short. Lying on the dusty seat-cushion was a single silver teaspoon.

Almost opposite the carriage, against the other bank, was a cavalryman's boot; it had been cut from a wounded limb. The leather had been split all the way down the leg from the top to the ankle, and the inside of the boot was full of clotted, dried blood. And just as we turned back to return to the town I saw a child's stuffed cloth doll—rag dolls I think they call them in the States—lying flat in the road; and a wagon wheel or a camion wheel had passed over the head, squashing it flat.

I am not striving for effect when I tell of this trifle. When you write of such things as a battlefield you do not need to strive for effect. The effects are all there, ready-made, waiting to be set down. Nor do I know how a child's doll came to be in that harried, uptorn place. I only know it was there, and being there it seemed to me to sum up the fate of little Belgium in this great war. If I had been seeking a visible symbol of Belgium's case I do not believe I could have found a more fitting one anywhere.

Going down the hill to the town we met, skirting across our path, a party of natives wearing Red Cross distinguishments. The lieutenant said these men had undoubtedly been beating the woods and grain fields for the scattered wounded or dead. He added, without emotion, that from time to time they found one such; in fact, the volunteer searchers had brought in two Frenchmen just before we arrived—one to be cared for at the hospital, the other to be buried.

We had thanked the young lieutenant and had bade him good-by, and were starting off again, hoping to make Maubeuge before night, when suddenly it struck me that the one thing about La Buissière I should recall most vividly was not the sight of it, all stricken and stunned and forlorn as it was, but the stench of it.

Before this my eyes had been so busy recording impressions that my nose had neglected its duty; now for the first time I sensed the vile reek that arose from all about me. The place was one big, horrid stink. It smelled of ether and iodoform and carbolic acid—there being any number of improvised hospitals, full of wounded, in sight; it smelled of sour beef bones and stale bread and moldy hay and fresh horse dung; it smelled of the sweaty bodies of the soldiers; it smelled of everything that is fetid and rancid and unsavory and unwholesome.

And yet, forty-eight hours before, this town, if it was like every other Belgian town, must have been as clean as clean could be. When the Belgian peasant housewife has cleaned the inside of her house she issues forth with bucket and scrubbing brush and washes the outside of it—and even the pavement in front and the cobbles of the road. But the war had come to La Buissière and turned it upside down.

A war wastes towns, it seems, even more visibly than it wastes nations. Already the streets were ankle-deep in filth. There were broken lamps and broken bottles and broken windowpanes everywhere, and one could not step without an accompaniment of crunching glass from underfoot.

Sacks of provender, which the French had abandoned, were split open and their contents wasted in the mire while the inhabitants went hungry. The lower floors of the houses were bedded in straw where the soldiers had slept, and the straw was thickly covered with dried mud and already gave off a sour-sickish odor. Over everything was the lime dust from the powdered walls and plastering.

We drove away, then, over the hill toward the south. From the crest of the bluff we could look down on ruined La Buissière, with its garrison of victorious invaders, its frightened townspeople, and its houses full of maimed and crippled soldiers of both sides.

Beyond we could see the fields, where the crops, already overripe, must surely waste for lack of men and teams to harvest them; and on the edge of one field we marked where the three peasants dug the grave for the rotting horse, striving to get it underground before it set up a plague.

Except for them, busy with pick and spade, no living creature in sight was at work.

Sherman said it!

Chapter 4

"Marsch, Marsch, Marsch, So Geh'n Wir Weiter!"

Have you ever seen three hundred thousand men and one hundred thousand horses moving in one compact, marvelous unit of organization, discipline and system? If you have not seen it you cannot imagine what it is like. If you have seen it you cannot tell what it is like. In one case the conceptive faculty fails you; in the other the descriptive. I, who have seen this sight, am not foolish enough to undertake to put it down with pencil on paper. I think I know something of the limitations of the written English language. What I do mean to try to do in this chapter is to record some of my impressions as I watched it.

In beginning this job I find myself casting about for comparisons to set up against the vision of a full German army of seven army corps on the march. I think of the tales I have read and the stories I have heard of other great armies: Alaric's war bands and Attila's; the First Crusade; Hannibal's cohorts, and Alexander's host, and Caesar's legions; the Goths and the Vandals; the million of Xerxes—if it was a million—and Napoleon starting for Moscow.

It is of no use. This Germanic horde, which I saw pouring down across Belgium, bound for France, does not in retrospect seem to me a man-made, man-managed thing. It seems more like a great, orderly function of Nature; as ordained and cosmic as the tides of the sea or the sweep of a mighty wind. It is hard to believe that it was ever fashioned of thousands of separate atoms, so perfectly is it welded into a whole. It is harder still to accept it as a mutable and a mortal organism, subject to the shifts of chance and mischance.

And then, on top of this, when one stops to remember that this army of three hundred thousand men and a hundred thousand horses was merely one single cog of the German military machine; that if all the German war strength were assembled together you might add this army to the greater army and hardly know it was there—why, then, the brain refuses to wrestle with a computation so gigantic. The imagination just naturally bogs down and quits.

I have already set forth in some detail how it came to pass that we went forth from Brussels in a taxicab looking for the war; and how in the outskirts of Louvain we found it, and very shortly thereafter also found that we were cut off from our return and incidentally had lost not only our chauffeur and our taxi-cab but our overcoats as well. There being nothing else to do we made ourselves comfortable along side the Belgian Lion Cafe in the southern edge of Louvain, and for hours we watched the advance guard sliding down the road through a fog of white dust.

Each time a break came in the weaving gray lines we fancied this surely was all. All? What we saw there was a puny dribbling stream compared with the torrent that was coming. The crest of that living tidal wave was still two days and many miles to the rearward. We had seen the head and a little of the neck. The swollen body of the myriad-legged gray centipede was as yet far behind.

As we sat in chairs tilted against the wall and watched, we witnessed an interesting little side play. At the first coming of the German skirmishers the people of this quarter of the town had seemed stupefied with amazement and astonishment. Most of them, it subsequently developed, had believed right up to the last minute that the forts of Liege still held out and that the Germans had not yet passed the gateways of their country, many kilometers to the eastward. When the scouts of the enemy appeared in their streets they fell for the moment into a stunned state. A little later the appearance of a troop of Uhlans had revived their resentment. We had heard that quick hiss and snarl of hatred which sprang from them as the lancers trotted into view on their superb mounts out of the mouth of a neighboring lane, and had seen how instantaneously the dull, malignant gleam of gun metal, as a sergeant pulled his pistol on them, had brought the silence of frightened respect again.

It now appeared that realization of the number of the invaders was breeding in the Belgians a placating spirit. If a soldier fell out of line at the door of a house to ask for water, all within that house strove to bring the water to him. If an officer, returning from a small sortie into other streets, checked up to ask the way to rejoin his command, a dozen eager arms waved in chorus to point out the proper direction, and a babble of solicitous voices arose from the group about his halted horse.

Young Belgian girls began smiling at soldiers swinging by and the soldiers grinned back and waved their arms. You might almost have thought the troops were Allies passing through a friendly community. This phase of the plastic Flemish temperament made us marvel. When I was told, a fortnight afterward, how these same people rose in the night to strike at these their enemies, and how, so doing, they brought about the ruination of their city and the summary executions of some hundreds of themselves, I marveled all the more.

Presently, as we sat there, we heard—above the rumbling of cannon wheels, the nimble clunking of hurrying hoofs and the heavy thudding of booted feet, falling and rising all in unison—a new note from overhead, a combination of whir and flutter and whine. We looked aloft. Directly above the troops, flying as straight for Brussels as a homing bee for the hive, went a military monoplane, serving as courier and spy for the crawling columns below it. Directly, having gone far ahead, it came speeding back, along a lower air lane and performed a series of circling and darting gyrations, which doubtlessly had a signal-code meaning for the troops. Twice or three times it swung directly above our heads, and at the height at which it now evolved we could plainly distinguish the downward curve of its wing-planes and the peculiar droop of the rudder—both things that marked it for an army model. We could also make out the black cross painted on its belly as a further distinguishing mark.

To me a monoplane always suggests a bird when it does not suggest an insect or a winged reptile; and this monoplane particularly suggested the bird type. The simile which occurred to me was that of the bird which guards the African rhinoceros; after that it was doubly easy to conceive of this army as a rhinoceros, having all the brute strength and brute force which are a part of that creature, and its well-armored sides and massive legs and deadly horned head; and finally its peculiar fancy for charging straight at its objective target, trampling down all obstacles in the way.

The Germans also fancy their monoplane as a bird; but they call it Taube—a dove. To think of calling this sinister adjunct of warfare a dove, which among modern peoples has always symbolized peace, seemed a most terrible bit of sarcasm. As an exquisite essence of irony I saw but one thing during our week-end in Louvain to match it, and that was a big van requisitioned from a Cologne florist's shop to use in a baggage train. It bore on its sides advertisements of potted plants and floral pieces—and it was loaded to its top with spare ammunition.

Paths of Glory

Yet, on second thought, I do not believe the Prussians call their war monoplane a dove by way of satire. The Prussians are a serious-minded race and never more serious than when they make war, as all the world now knows.

Three monoplanes buzzed over us, making sawmill sounds, during the next hour or two. Thereafter, whenever we saw German troops on the march through a country new to them we looked aloft for the thing with the droopy wings and the black cross on its yellow abdomen. Sooner or later it appeared, coming always out of nowhere and vanishing always into space. We were never disappointed. It is only the man who expects the German army to forget something needful or necessary who is disappointed.

It was late in the afternoon when we bade farewell to the three-hundred- pound proprietress of the Belgian Lion and sought to reach the center of the town through byways not yet blocked off by the marching regiments. When we were perhaps halfway to our destination we met a town bellman and a town crier, the latter being in the uniform of a Garde Civique. The bellringer would ply his clapper until he drew a crowd, and then the Garde Civique would halt in an open space at the junction of two or more streets and read a proclamation from the burgomaster calling on all the inhabitants to preserve their tranquillity and refrain from overt acts against the Germans, under promise of safety if they obeyed and threat of death at the hands of the Germans if they disregarded the warning.

This word-of-mouth method of spreading an order applied only to the outlying sections. In the more thickly settled districts, where presumably the populace could read and write, proclamations posted on wall and window took its place. During the three days we stayed in Louvain one proclamation succeeded another with almost the frequency of special extras of evening newspapers when a big news story breaks in an American city: The citizens were to surrender all firearms in their possession; it would be immediately fatal to him if a man were caught with a lethal weapon on his person or in his house. Tradespeople might charge this or that price for the necessities of life, and no more. All persons, except physicians and nurses in the discharge of their professional duties, and gendarmes—the latter being now disarmed and entirely subservient to the military authorities—must be off the streets and public squares at a given time—to wit, nine p. m. Cafés must close at the same hour. Any soldier who refused to pay for any private purchase should be immediately reported at headquarters for punishment. Upper front windows of all houses on certain specified streets must be closed and locked after nightfall, remaining so until daylight of the following morning; this notice being followed and overlapped very shortly by one more amplifying, which prescribed that not only must front windows be made fast, but all must have lights behind them and the street doors must be left unlocked.

The portent of this was simple enough: If any man sought to fire on the soldiers below he must first unfasten a window and expose himself in the light; and after he fired admittance would be made easy for those who came searching for him to kill him.

At first these placards were signed by the burgomaster, with the military commandant's indorsement, and sometimes by both those functionaries; but on the second day there appeared one signed by the commandant only; and this one, for special emphasis, was bounded by wide borders printed in bright red. It stated, with cruel brevity, that the burgomaster, the senator for the district and the leading magistrate had been taken into custody as hostages for the good conduct of their constituents; and that if a civilian made any attack against the Germans he would forfeit his own life and endanger the lives of the three prisoners. Thus, inch by inch, the conquerors, sensing a growing spirit of revolt among the conquered—a spirit as yet nowise visible on the surface—took typically German steps to hold the rebellious people of Louvain in hobbles. It was when we reached the Y-shaped square in the middle of things, with the splendid old Gothic town hall rising on one side of it and the famous Church of Saint Pierre at the bottom of the gore, that we first beheld at close hand the army of the War Lord. Alongside the Belgian Lion we had thought it best to keep our distance from the troops as they passed obliquely across our line of vision. Here we might press as closely as we pleased to the column. The magnificent precision with which the whole machinery moved was astounding—I started to say appalling. Three streets converging into the place were glutted with men, extending from curb to curb; and for an outlet there was but one somewhat wider street, which twisted its course under the gray walls of the church. Yet somehow the various lines melted together and went thumping off out of sight like streams running down a funnel and out at the spout.

Never, so far as we could tell, was there any congestion, any hitch, any suggestion of confusion. Frequently there would come from a sideway a group of officers on horseback, or a whole string of commandeered touring cars bearing monocled, haughty staff officers in the tonneaus, with guards riding beside the chauffeurs and small slick trunks strapped on behind. A whistle would sound shrilly then; and magically a gap would appear in the formation. Into this gap the horsemen or the imperious automobiles would slip, and away the column would go again without having been disturbed or impeded noticeably. No stage manager ever handled his supers better; and here, be it remembered, there were uncountable thousands of supers, and for a stage the twisting, medieval convolutions of a strange city. Now for a space of minutes it would be infantry that passed, at the swinging lunge of German foot soldiers on a forced march. Now it would be cavalry, with accouterments jingling and horses scrouging in the close-packed ranks; else a battery of the viperish looking little rapid-fire guns, or a battery of heavier cannon, with cloth fittings over their ugly snouts, like muzzled dogs whose bark is bad and whose bite is worse.

Then, always in due order, would succeed the field telegraph corps; the field post-office corps; the Red Cross corps; the brass band of, say, forty pieces; and all the rest of it, to the extent of a thousand and one circus parades rolled together. There were boats for making pontoon bridges, mounted side by side on wagons, with the dried mud of the River Meuse still on their flat bottoms; there were baggage trains miles in length, wherein the supply of regular army wagons was eked out with nondescript vehicles—even family carriages and delivery vans gathered up hastily, as the signs on their sides betrayed, from the tradespeople of a dozen Northern German cities and towns, and now bearing chalk marks on them to show in what division they belonged. And inevitably at the tail of each regiment came its cook wagons, with fires kindled and food cooking for supper in the big portable ranges, so that when these passed the air would be charged with that pungent reek of burning wood which makes an American think of a fire engine on its way to answer an alarm.

Once, as a cook perched on a step at the back of his wagon bent forward to stir the stew with a spoon almost big enough for a spade, I saw under his hiked-up coat-tails that at the back of his gray trousers there were four suspender buttons in a row instead of two. The purpose of this was plain: when his suspenders chafed him he might, by shifting the straps to different buttons, shift the strain on his shoulders. All German soldiers' trousers have this extra garnishment of buttons aft.

Somebody thought of that. Somebody thought of everything.

We in America are accustomed to think of the Germans as an obese race, swinging big paunches in front of them; but in that army the only fat men we saw were officers, and not so many of them. On occasion, some colonel, beefy as a brisket and with rolls of fat on the back of his close-shaved neck, would be seen bouncing by, balancing his tired stomach on his saddle pommel; but, without exception, the men in the ranks were trained down and fine drawn. They bent forward under the weight of their knapsacks and blanket rolls; and their middles were bulky with cartridge belts, and bulging pockets covered their flanks.

Inside the shapeless uniforms, however, their limbs swung with athletic freedom, and even at the fag-end of a hard day's marching, with perhaps several hours of marching yet ahead of them, they carried their heavy guns as though those guns were toys. Their fair sunburned faces were lined with sweat marks and masked under dust, and doubtless some were desperately weary; but I did not see a straggler. To date I presume I have seen upward of a million of these German soldiers on the march, and I have yet to see a straggler.

For the most part the rank and file were stamped by their faces and their limbs as being of peasant blood or of the petty artisan type; but here and there, along with the butcher and the baker and the candlestick maker, passed one of a slenderer build, usually spectacled and wearing, even in this employment, the unmistakable look of the cultured, scholarly man.

And every other man, regardless of his breed, held a cheap cigar between his front teeth; but the wagon drivers and many of the cavalrymen smoked pipes—the long-stemmed, china-bowled pipe, which the German loves. The column moved beneath a smoke-wreath of its own making.

The thing, however, which struck one most forcibly was the absolute completeness, the perfect uniformity, of the whole scheme. Any man's equipment was identically like any other man's equipment. Every drinking cup dangled behind its owner's spine-tip at precisely the same angle; every strap and every buckle matched. These

Paths of Glory

Germans had been run through a mold and they had all come out soldiers. And, barring a few general officers, they were all young men—men yet on the sunny side of thirty. Later we were to see plenty of older men—reserves and Landwehr—but this was the pick of the western line that passed through Louvain, the chosen product of the active wing of the service.

Out of the narrow streets the marchers issued; and as they reached the broader space before the town hall each company would raise a song, beating with its heavy boots on the paving stones to mark the time. Presently we detected a mutter of resentment rising from the troops; and seeking the cause of this we discerned that some of them had caught sight of a big Belgian flag which whipped in the breeze from the top of the Church of Saint Pierre. However, the flag stayed where it had been put during the three days we remained in Louvain. Seemingly the German commander did not greatly care whose flag flew on the church tower overhead so long as he held dominion of the earth below and the dwellers thereof.

Well, we watched the gray ear-wig wriggling away to the westward until we were surfeited, and then we set about finding a place where we might rest our dizzy heads. We could not get near the principal hotels. These already were filled with high officers and ringed about with sentries; but half a mile away, on the plaza fronting the main railroad station, we finally secured accommodations—such as they were—at a small fourth- rate hotel.

It called itself by a gorgeous title—it was the House of the Thousand Columns, which was as true a saying as though it had been named the House of the One Column; for it had neither one column nor a thousand, but only a small, dingy beer bar below and some ten dismal living rooms above. Established here, we set about getting in touch with the German higher-ups, since we were likely to be mistaken for Englishmen, which would be embarrassing certainly, and might even be painful. At the hotel next door—for all the buildings flanking this square were hotels of a sort—we found a group of officers.

One of them, a tall, handsome, magnetic chap, with a big, deep laugh and a most beautiful command of our own tongue, turned out to be a captain on the general staff. It seemed to him the greatest joke in the world that four American correspondents should come looking for war in a taxicab, and should find it too. He beat himself on his flanks in the excess of his joy, and called up half a dozen friends to hear the amazing tale; and they enjoyed it too.

He said he felt sure his adjutant would appreciate the joke; and, as incidentally his adjutant was the person in all the world we wanted most just then to see, we went with him to headquarters, which was a mile away in the local Palais de Justice—or, as we should say in America, the courthouse. By now it was good and dark; and as no street lamps burned we walked through a street that was like a tunnel for blackness.

The roadway was full of infantry still pressing forward to a camping place somewhere beyond the town. We could just make out the shadowy shapes of the men, but their feet made a noise like thunderclaps, and they sang a German marching song with a splendid lilt and swing to it.

"Just listen! " said the captain proudly. "They are always like that—they march all day and half the night, and never do they grow weary. They are in fine spirits—our men. And we can hardly hold them back. They will go forward—always forward!

"In this war we have no such command as Retreat! That word we have blotted out. Either we shall go forward or we shall die! We do not expect to fall back, ever. The men know this; and if our generals would but let them they would run to Paris instead of walking there. "

I think it was not altogether through vainglory he spoke. He was not a bombastic sort. I think he voiced the intent of the army to which he belonged.

At the Palais de Justice the adjutant was not to be seen; so our guide volunteered to write a note of introduction for us. Standing in a doorway of the building, where a light burned, he opened a small flat leather pack that swung from his belt, along with the excellent map of Belgium inclosed in a leather frame which every German officer carried. We marveled that the pack contained pencils, pens, inkpot, seals, officially stamped envelopes and note paper, and blank forms of various devices. Verily these Germans had remembered all things and forgotten nothing. I said that to myself mentally at the moment; nor have I had reason since to withdraw or qualify the remark.

Paths of Glory

The next morning I saw the adjutant, whose name was Renner and whose title was that of major; but first I, as spokesman, underwent a search for hidden weapons at the hands of a secret service man. Major Renner was most courteous; also he was amused to hear the details of our taxicabbing expedition into his lines. But of the desire which lay nearest our hearts—-to get back to Brussels in time haply to witness its occupation by the Germans—he would not hear.

"For your own sakes, " thus he explained it, "I dare not let you gentlemen go. Terrible things have happened. Last night a colonel of infantry was murdered while he was asleep; and I have just heard that fifteen of our soldiers had their throats cut, also as they slept. From houses our troops have been fired on, and between here and Brussels there has been much of this guerrilla warfare on us. To those who do such things and to those who protect them we show no mercy. We shoot them on the spot and burn their houses to the ground.

"I can well understand that the Belgians resent our coming into their country. We ourselves regret it; but it was a military necessity. We could do nothing else. If the Belgians put on uniforms and enroll as soldiers and fight us openly, we shall capture them if we can; we shall kill them if we must; but in all cases we shall treat them as honorable enemies, fighting under the rules of civilized warfare.

"But this shooting from ambush by civilians; this murdering of our people in the night—that we cannot endure. We have made a rule that if shots are fired by a civilian from a house then we shall burn that house; and we shall kill that man and all the other men in that house whom we suspect of harboring him or aiding him.

"We make no attempt to disguise our methods of reprisal. We are willing for the world to know it; and it is not because I wish to cover up or hide any of our actions from your eyes, and from the eyes of the American people, that I am refusing you passes for your return to Brussels to-day. But, you see, our men have been terribly excited by these crimes of the Belgian populace, and in their excitement they might make serious mistakes.

"Our troops are under splendid discipline, as you may have seen already for yourselves. And I assure you the Germans are not a bloodthirsty or a drunken or a barbarous people; but in every army there are fools and, what is worse, in every army there are brutes.

You are strangers; and if you passed along the road to-day some of our more ignorant men, seeing that you were not natives and suspecting your motives, might harm you. There might be some stupid, angry common soldier, some over- zealous under officer — you understand me, do you not, gentlemen?

"So you will please remain here quietly, having nothing to do with any of our men who may seek to talk with you. That last is important; for I may tell you that our secret-service people have already reported your presence, and they naturally are anxious to make a showing.

"At the end of one day — perhaps two — we shall be able, I think, to give you safe conduct back to Brussels. And then I hope you will be able to speak a good word to the American public for our army."

After this fashion of speaking I heard now from the lips of Major Renner what I subsequently heard fifty times from other army men, and likewise from high German civilians, of the common German attitude toward Belgium. Often these others have used almost the same words he used. Invariably they have sought to convey the same meaning.

For those three days we stayed on unwillingly in Louvain we were not once out of sight of German soldiers, nor by day or night out of sound of their threshing feet and their rumbling wheels. We never looked; this way or that but we saw their gray masses blocking up the distances. We never entered shop or house but we found Germans already there. We never sought to turn off the main-traveled streets into a byway but our path was barred by a guard seeking to know our business. And always, as we noted, for this duty those in command had chosen soldiers who knew a smattering of French, in order that the sentries might be able to speak with the citizens. If we passed along a sidewalk the chances were that it would be lined thick with soldiers lying against the walls resting, or sitting on the curbs, with their shoes off, easing their feet. If we looked into the sky our prospects for seeing a monoplane flying about were most excellent. If we entered a square it was bound to be jammed with horses and packed baggage trains and supply wagons. The atmosphere was laden with the ropy scents of the boiling stews and with the heavier smells of the soldiers' unwashed bodies and their sweating horses.

Paths of Glory

Finally, to their credit be it said, we personally did not see one German, whether officer or private, who mistreated any citizen, or was offensively rude to any citizen, or who refused to pay a fair reckoning for what he bought, or who was conspicuously drunk. The postcard venders of Louvain must have grown fat with wealth; for, next to bottled beer and butter and cheap cigars, every common soldier craved postcards above all other commodities.

We grew tired after a while of seeing Germans; it seemed to us that every vista always had been choked with unshaved, blond, blocky, short- haired men in rawhide boots and ill-fitting gray tunics; and that every vista always would be. It took a new kind of gun, or an automobile with a steel prow for charging through barbed-wire entanglements, or a group of bedraggled Belgian prisoners slouching by under convoy, to make us give the spectacle more than a passing glance.

There was something hypnotic, something tremendously wearisome to the mind in those thick lines flowing sluggishly along in streams like molten lead; in the hedges of gun barrels all slanting at the same angle; in the same types of faces repeated and repeated countlessly; in the legs which scissored by in such faultless unison and at each clip of each pair of living shears cut off just so much of the road— never any more and never any less, but always just exactly so much.

Our jaded and satiated fancies had been fed on soldiers and all the cumbersome pageantry of war until they refused to be quickened by what, half a week before, would have set every nerve tingling. Almost the only thing that stands out distinct in my memory from the confused recollections of the last morning spent in Louvain is a huge sight- seeing car—of the sort known at home as a rubberneck wagon—which lumbered by us with Red Cross men perched like roosting gray birds on all its seats. We estimated we saw two hundred thousand men in motion through the ancient town. We learned afterward we had under-figured the total by at least a third.

During these days the life of Louvain went on, so far as our alien eyes could judge, pretty much as it probably did in the peace times preceding. At night, obeying an order, the people stayed within their doors; in the daylight hours they pursued their customary business, not greatly incommoded apparently by the presence of the conqueror. If there was simmering hate in the hearts of the men and women of Louvain it did not betray itself in their sobered faces. I saw a soldier, somewhat fuddled, seize a serving maid about the waist and kiss her; he received a slap in the face and fell back in bad order, while his mates cheered the spunky girl. A minute later she emerged from the house to which she had retreated, seemingly ready to swap slaps for kisses some more.

However, from time to time sinister suggestions did obtrude themselves on us. For example, on the second morning of our enforced stay at the House of the Thousand Columns we watched a double file of soldiers going through a street toward the Palais de Justice. Two roughly clad natives walked between the lines of bared bayonets. One was an old man who walked proudly with his head erect. He was like a man going to a feast. The other was bent almost double, and his hands were tied behind his back.

A few minutes afterward a barred yellow van, under escort, came through the square fronting the railroad station and disappeared behind a mass of low buildings. From that direction we presently heard shots. Soon the van came back, unescorted this time; and behind it came Belgians with Red Cross arm badges, bearing on their shoulders two litters on which were still figures covered with blankets, so that only the stockinged feet showed.

Twice thereafter this play was repeated, with slight variations, and each time we Americans, looking on from our front windows, drew our own conclusions. Also, from the same vantage point we saw an automobile pass bearing a couple of German officers and a little, scared-looking man in a frock coat and a high hat, whose black mustache stood out like a charcoal mark against the very white background of his face. This little man, we learned, was the burgomaster, and this day he was being held a prisoner and responsible for the good conduct of some fifty-odd thousand of his fellow citizens. That night our host, a gross, silent man in carpet slippers, told us the burgomaster was ill in bed at home.

"He suffers, " explained our landlord in French, "from a crisis of the nerves. " The French language is an expressive language.

Then, coming a pace nearer, our landlord added a question in a cautious whisper.

"Messieurs, " he asked, "do you think it can be true, as my neighbors tell me, that the United States President has ordered the Germans to get out of our country? "

We shook our heads, and he went silently away in his carpet slippers; and his broad Flemish face gave no hint of what corrosive thoughts he may have had in his heart.

It was Wednesday morning when we entered Louvain. It was Saturday morning when we left it. This last undertaking was preceded by difficulties. As a preliminary to it we visited in turn all the stables in Louvain where ordinarily horses and wheeled vehicles could be had for hire.

Perhaps there were no horses left in the stalls—thanks to either Belgian foragers or to German—or, if there were horses, no driver would risk his hide on the open road among the German pack trains and rear guards. At length we did find a tall, red-haired Walloon who said he would go anywhere on earth, and provide a team for the going, if we paid the price he asked. We paid it in advance, in case anything should happen on the way, and he took us in a venerable open carriage behind two crow-bait skeletons that had once, in a happier day when hay was cheaper, been horses.

We drove slowly, taking the middle of the wide Brussels road. On our right, traveling in the same direction, crawled an unending line of German baggage wagons and pontoon trucks. On our left, going the opposite way, was another line, also unending, made up of refugee villagers, returning afoot to the towns beyond Louvain from which they had fled four days earlier. They were footsore and they limped; they were of all ages and most miserable-looking. And, one and all, they were as tongueless as so many ghosts. Thus we traveled; and at the end of the first hour came to the tiny town of Leefdael.

At Leefdael there must have been fighting, for some of the houses were gutted by shells. At least two had been burned; and a big tin sign at a railroad crossing had become a tin colander where flying lead had sieved it. In a beet patch beside one of the houses was a mound of fresh earth the length of a long man, with a cross of sticks at the head of it. A Belgian soldier's cap was perched on the upright and a scrap of paper was made fast to the cross arm; and two peasants stood there apparently reading what was written on the paper. Later such sights as these were to become almost the commonest incidents of our countryside campaignings; but now we looked with all our eyes.

Except that the roadside ditches were littered with beer bottles and scraps of paper, and the road itself rutted by cannon wheels, we saw little enough after leaving Leefdael to suggest that an army had come this way until we were in the outskirts of Brussels. In a tree-edged, grass-plotted boulevard at the edge of the Bois, toward Tervueren, cavalry had halted. The turf was scarred with hoofprints and strewed with hay; and there was a row of small trenches in which the Germans had built their fires to do their cooking. The sod, which had been removed to make these trenches, was piled in neat little terraces, ready to be put back; and care plainly had been taken by the troopers to avoid damaging the bark on the trunks of the ash and elm trees.

There it was—the German system of warfare! These Germans might carry on their war after the most scientifically deadly plan the world has ever known; they might deal out their peculiarly fatal brand of drumhead justice to all civilians who crossed their paths bearing arms; they might burn and waste for punishment; they might lay on a captured city and a whipped province a tribute of foodstuffs and an indemnity of money heavier than any civilized race has ever demanded of the cowed and conquered—might do all these things and more besides—but their common troopers saved the sods of the greensward for replanting and spared the boles of the young shade trees! Next day we again left Brussels, the submissive, and made a much longer excursion under German auspices. And, at length, after much travail, we landed in the German frontier city of Aix-la-Chapelle, where I wrote these lines. There it was, two days after our arrival, that we heard of the fate of Louvain and of that pale little man, the burgomaster, who had survived his crisis of the nerves to die of a German bullet.

We wondered what became of the proprietor of the House of the Thousand Columns; and of the young Dutch tutor in the Berlitz School of Languages, who had served us as a guide and interpreter; and of the pretty, gentle little Flemish woman who brought us our meals in her clean, small restaurant round the corner from the Hotel de Ville; and of the kindly, red-bearded priest at the Church of Saint Jacques, who gave us ripe pears and old wine.

Paths of Glory

I reckon we shall always wonder what became of them, and that we shall never know. I hoped mightily that the American wing of the big Catholic seminary had been spared. It had a stone figure of an American Indian— looking something like Sitting Bull, we thought—over its doors; and that was the only typically American thing we saw in all Louvain.

When next I saw Louvain the University was gone and the stone Indian was gone too.

Paths of Glory

Chapter 5

Being a Guest of the Kaiser

You know how four of us blundered into the German lines in a taxicab; and how, getting out of German hands after three days and back to Brussels, we undertook, in less than twenty-four hours thereafter, to trail the main forces then shoving steadily southward with no other goal before them but Paris.

First by hired hack, as we used to say when writing accounts of funerals down in Paducah, then afoot through the dust, and finally, with an equipment consisting of that butcher's superannuated dogcart, that elderly mare emeritus and those two bicycles, we made our zigzagging way downward through Belgium.

We knew that our credentials were, for German purposes, of most dubious and uncertain value. We knew that the Germans were permitting no correspondents—not even German correspondents—to accompany them. We knew that any alien caught in the German front was liable to death on the spot, without investigation of his motives. We knew all these things; and the knowledge of them gave a fellow tingling sensations in the tips of his toes when he permitted himself to think about his situation. But, after the first few hours, we took heart unto ourselves; for everywhere we met only kindness and courtesy at the hands of the Kaiser's soldiers, men and officers alike.

There was, it is true, the single small instance of the excited noncom. who poked a large, unwholesome-looking automatic pistol into my shrinking diaphragm when he wanted me to get off the running board of a military automobile into which I had climbed, half a minute before, by invitation of the private who steered it. I gathered his meaning right away, even though he uttered only guttural German and that at the top of his voice; a pointed revolver speaks with a tongue which is understood by all peoples. Besides, he had the distinct advantage in repartee; and so, with no extended argument, I got down from there and he pouched his ironmongery. I regarded the incident as being closed and was perfectly willing that it should remain closed.

That, however, though of consuming interest to me at the moment, was but a detail—an exception to prove the standing rule. One place

Paths of Glory

we dined with a Rittmeister's mess; and while we sat, eating of their midday ration of thick pea soup with sliced sausages in it, some of the younger officers stood; also they let us stretch our wearied legs on their mattresses, which were ranged seven in a row on the parlor floor of a Belgian house, where from a corner a plaster statue of Joan of Arc gazed at us with her plaster eyes.

Common soldiers offered repeatedly to share their rye-bread sandwiches and bottled beer with us. Not once, but a dozen times, officers of various rank let us look at their maps and use their field glasses; and they gave us advice for reaching the zone of actual fighting and swapped gossip with us, and frequently regretted that they had no spare mounts or spare automobiles to loan us.

We attributed a good deal of this to the inherent kindliness of the German gentleman's nature; but more of it we attributed to a newborn desire on the part of these men to have disinterested journalists see with their own eyes the scope and result of the German operations, in the hope that the truth regarding alleged German atrocities might reach the outside world and particularly might reach America.

Of the waste and wreckage of war; of desolated homes and shattered villages; of the ruthless, relentless, punitive exactness with which the Germans punished not only those civilians they accused of firing on them but those they suspected of giving harbor or aid to the offenders; of widows and orphans; of families of innocent sufferers, without a roof to shelter them or a bite to stay them; of fair lands plowed by cannon balls, and harrowed with rifle bullets, and sown with dead men's bones; of men horribly maimed and mangled by lead and steel; of long mud trenches where the killed lay thick under the fresh clods—of all this and more I saw enough to cure any man of the delusion that war is a beautiful, glorious, inspiring thing, and to make him know it for what it is—altogether hideous and unutterably awful.

As for Uhlans spearing babies on their lances, and officers sabering their own men, and soldiers murdering and mutilating and torturing at will—I saw nothing. I knew of these tales only from having read them in the dispatches sent from the Continent to England, and from there cabled to American papers.

Even so, I hold no brief for the Germans; or for the reasons that inspired them in waging this war; or for the fashion after which they have waged it. I am only trying to tell what I saw with my own eyes and heard with my own ears.

Be all that as it may, we straggled into Beaumont—five of us—on the evening of the third day out from Brussels, without baggage or equipment, barring only what we wore on our several tired and drooping backs. As in the case of our other trip, a simple sight-seeing ride had resolved itself into an expeditionary campaign; and so there we were, bearing, as proof of our good faith and professional intentions, only our American passports, our passes issued by General von Jarotzky, at Brussels, and—most potent of all for winning confidence from the casual eye—a little frayed silk American flag, with a hole burned in it by a careless cigar butt, which was knotted to the front rail of our creaking dogcart.

Immediately after passing the ruined and deserted village of Montignies St. Christophe, we came at dusk to a place where a company of German infantrymen were in camp about a big graystone farmhouse. They were cooking supper over big trench fires and, as usual, they were singing. The light shone up into the faces of the cooks, bringing out in ruddy relief their florid skins and yellow beards. A yearling bull calf was tied to a supply-wagon wheel, bellowing his indignation. I imagine he quit bellowing shortly thereafter.

An officer came to the edge of the road and, peering sharply at us over a broken hedge, made as if to stop us; then changed his mind and permitted us to go unchallenged. Entering the town, we proceeded, winding our way among pack trains and stalled motor trucks, to the town square. Our little cavalcade halted to the accompaniment of good-natured titterings from many officers in front of the town house of the Prince de Caraman-Chimay.

By a few Americans the prince is remembered as having been the cousin of one of the husbands of the much-married Clara Ward, of Detroit; but at this moment, though absent, he had particularly endeared himself to the Germans through the circumstance of his having left behind, in his wine cellars, twenty thousand bottles of rare vintages. Wine, I believe, is contraband of war. Certainly in this instance it was. As we speedily discovered, it was a very unlucky common soldier who did not have a swig of rare Burgundy or ancient claret to wash down his black bread and sausage that night at supper.

Unwittingly we had bumped into the headquarters of the whole army—not of a single corps, but of an army. In the thickening twilight on the little square gorgeous staff officers came and went, afoot, on horseback and in automobiles; and through an open window we caught a glimpse of a splendid-looking general, sitting booted and sword-belted at a table in the Prince de Caraman-Chimay's library, with hunting trophies—skin and horn and claw—looking down at him from the high-paneled oak wainscotings, and spick-and-span aides waiting to take his orders and discharge his commissions.

It dawned on us that, having accidentally slipped through a hole in the German rear guard, we had reached a point close to the front of operations. We felt uncomfortable.

It was not at all likely that a Herr Over-Commander would expedite us with the graciousness that had marked his underlings back along the line of communication. We remarked as much to one another; and it was a true prophecy. A staff officer—a colonel who spoke good English—received us at the door of the villa and examined our papers in the light which streamed over his shoulder from a fine big hallway behind him. In everything, both then and thereafter, he was most polite.

"I do not understand how you came here, you gentlemen," he said at length. "We have no correspondents with our army."

"You have now," said one of us, seeking to brighten the growing embarrassment of the situation with a small jape.

Perhaps he did not understand. Perhaps it was against the regulations for a colonel, in full caparison of sword and shoulder straps, to laugh at a joke from a dusty, wayworn, shabby stranger in a dented straw hat and a wrinkled Yankee-made coat. At any rate this colonel did not laugh.

"You did quite right to report yourselves here and explain your purposes," he continued gravely; "but it is impossible that you may proceed. To-morrow morning we shall give you escort and transportation back to Brussels. I anticipate"—here he glanced quizzically at our aged mare, drooping knee-sprung between the shafts of the lopsided dogcart—"I anticipate that you will return more speedily than you arrived.

"You will kindly report to me here in the morning at eleven. Meantime remember, gentlemen, that you are not prisoners—by no means, not. You may consider yourselves for the time being as—shall we say?—guests of the German Army, temporarily detained. You are at perfect liberty to come and go—only I should advise you not to go too far, because if you should try to leave town tonight our soldiers would certainly shoot you quite dead. It is not agreeable to be shot; and, besides, your great Government might object. So, then, I shall have the pleasure of seeing you in the morning, shall I not? Yes? Good night, gentlemen!"

He clicked his neat heels so that his spurs jangled, and bowed us out into the dark. The question of securing lodgings loomed large and imminent before us. Officers filled the few small inns and hotels; soldiers, as we could see, were quartered thickly in all the houses in sight; and already the inhabitants were locking their doors and dousing their lights in accordance with an order from a source that was not to be disobeyed. Nine out of ten houses about the square were now but black oblongs rising against the gray sky. We had nowhere to go; and yet if we did not go somewhere, and that pretty soon, the patrols would undoubtedly take unpleasant cognizance of our presence. Besides, the searching chill of a Belgian night was making us stiff.

Scouting up a narrow winding alley, one of the party who spoke German found a courtyard behind a schoolhouse called imposingly L'Ecole Moyenne de Beaumont, where he obtained permission from a German sergeant to stable our mare for the night in the aristocratic companionship of a troop of officers' horses. Through another streak of luck we preempted a room in the schoolhouse and held it against all comers by right of squatter sovereignty. There my friends and I slept on the stone floor, with a scanty amount of hay under us for a bed and our coats for coverlets. But before we slept we dined.

We dined on hard-boiled eggs and stale cheese—which we had saved from midday—in a big, bare study hall half full of lancers. They gave us rye bread and some of the Prince de Caraman-Chimay's wine to go with the provender we had brought, and they made room for us at the long benches that ran lengthwise of the room. Afterward one of them—a master musician, for all his soiled gray uniform and grimed fingers—played a piano that was in the corner, while all the rest sang.

It was a strange picture they made there. On the wall, on a row of hooks, still hung the small umbrellas and book-satchels of the pupils. Presumably at the coming of the Germans they had run home in such a panic that they left their school-traps behind. There were sums in chalk, half erased, on the blackboard; and one of the troopers took a scrap of chalk and wrote "On to Paris! " in big letters here and there. A sleepy parrot, looking like a bundle of rumpled green feathers, squatted on its perch in a cage behind the master's desk, occasionally emitting a loud squawk as though protesting against this intrusion on its privacy.

When their wine had warmed them our soldier-hosts sang and sang, unendingly. They had been on the march all day, and next day would probably march half the day and fight the other half, for the French and English were just ahead; but now they sprawled over the school benches and drummed on the boards with their fists and feet, and sang at the tops of their voices. They sang their favorite marching songs—Die Wacht am Rhein, of course; and Deutschland, Deutschland, Uber Alles! which has a fine, sonorous cathedral swing to it; and God Save the King! —with different words to the air, be it said; and Haltet Aus! Also, for variety, they sang Tannenbaum— with the same tune as Maryland, My Maryland! —and Heil dir im Sieges-kranz; and snatches from various operas.

When one of us asked for Heine's Lorelei they sang not one verse of it, or two, but twenty or more; and then, by way of compliment to the guests of the evening, they reared upon their feet and gave us The Star Spangled Banner, to German words. Suddenly two of them began dancing. In their big rawhide boots, with hobbed soles and steel-shod heels, they pounded back and forth, while the others whooped them on. One of the dancers gave out presently; but the other seemed still unimpaired in wind and limb. He darted into an adjoining room and came back in a minute dragging a half-frightened, half-pleased little Belgian scullery maid and whirled her about to waltz music until she dropped for want of breath to carry her another turn; after which he did a solo—Teutonic version—of a darky breakdown, stopping only to join in the next song.

Paths of Glory

It was eleven o'clock and they were still singing when we left them and went groping through dark hallways to where our simple hay mattress awaited us. I might add that we were indebted to a corporal of lancers for the hay, which he pilfered from the feed racks outside after somebody had stolen the two bundles of straw one of us had previously purchased. Except for his charity of heart we should have lain on the cold flagging.

The next morning was Thursday morning, and by Thursday night, at the very latest, we counted on being back in Brussels; but we were not destined to see Brussels again for nearly six weeks. We breakfasted frugally on good bread and execrable coffee at a half-wrecked little café where soldiers had slept; and at eleven o'clock, when we had bestowed Bulotte, the ancient nag, and the dogcart on an accommodating youth—giving them to him as a gracious gift, since neither he nor anyone else would buy the outfit at any price—we repaired to the villa to report ourselves and start on our return to the place whence we had come so laboriously.

The commander and his staff were just leaving, and they were in a big hurry. We knew the reason for their hurry, for since daylight the sound of heavy firing to the south and southwest, across the border in the neighborhood of Maubeuge, had been plainly audible. Officers in long gray overcoats with facings of blue, green, black, yellow and four shades of red—depending on the branches of the service to which they belonged—were piling into automobiles and scooting away.

As we sat on a wooden bench before the prince's villa, waiting for further instructions from our friend of the night before—meaning by that the colonel who could not take a joke, but could make one of his own—a tall, slender young man of about twenty-four, with a little silky mustache and a long, vulpine nose, came striding across the square with long steps. As nearly as we could tell, he wore a colonel's shoulder straps; and, aside from the fact that he seemed exceedingly youthful to be a colonel, we were astonished at the deference that was paid him by those of higher rank, who stood about waiting for their cars. Generals, and the like, even grizzled old generals with breasts full of decorations, bowed and clicked before him; and when he, smiling broadly, insisted on shaking hands with all of them, some of the group seemed overcome with gratification.

Presently a sort of family resemblance in his face to some one whose picture we had seen often somewhere began to impress itself on us, and we wondered who he was; but, being rather out of the setting ourselves, none of us cared to ask. Two weeks later, in Aix-la-Chapelle, I was passing a shop and saw his likeness in full uniform on a souvenir postcard in the window. It was Prince August Wilhelm, fourth son of the Kaiser; and we had seen him as he was about getting his first taste of being under fire by the enemy.

Pretty soon he was gone and our colonel was gone, and nearly everybody else was gone too; Companies of infantry and cavalry fell in and moved off, and a belated battery of field artillery rumbled out of sight up the twisting main street. The field postoffice staff, the field telegraph staff, the Red Cross corps and the wagon trains followed in due turn, leaving behind only a small squad to hold the town—and us.

A tall young lieutenant was in charge of the handful who remained; and, by the same token, as was to transpire, he was also in charge of us. He was built for a football player, and he had shoulders like a Cyclops, and his family name was Mittendorfer. He never spoke to his men except to roar at them like a raging lion, and he never addressed us except to coo as softly as the mourning dove. It was interesting to listen as his voice changed from a bellow to a croon, and back again a moment later to a bellow. With training he might have made an opera singer—he had such a vocal range and such perfect control over it. This Lieutenant Mittendorfer introduced himself to our attention by coming smartly up and saying there had been a delay about requisitioning an automobile for our use; but he thought the car would be along very shortly—and would the American gentlemen be so good as to wait? There being nothing else to do, we decided to do as he suggested.

We chose for our place of waiting a row of seats before a taverne, and there we sat, side by side, keeping count of the guns booming in the distance, until it began to rain. A sergeant came up then and invited us to go with him, in order that we might escape a wetting. He waved us into the doorway of a house two doors from where we had been sitting, at the same time suggesting to us that we throw away our cigars and cigarettes. When we crossed the threshold we realized the good intention behind this advice, seeing that the room we entered, which had been a shop of sorts, was now an improvised powder magazine.

Paths of Glory

From the floor to the height of a man it was piled with explosive shells for field guns, cased in straw covers like wine bottles, and stacked in neat rows, with their noses all pointing one way. Our guide led us along an aisle of these deadly things, beckoned us through another doorway at the side, where a sentry stood with a bayonet fixed on his gun, and with a wave of his hand invited us to partake of the hospitalities of the place. We looked about us, and lo! we were hard- and-fast in jail!

I have been in pleasanter indoor retreats in my time, even on rainy afternoons. The room was bedded down ankle-deep in straw; and the straw, which had probably been fresh the day before, already gave off a strong musky odor—the smell of an animal cage in a zoo.

For furnishings, the place contained a bench and a large iron pot containing a meat stew, which had now gone cold, so that a rime of gray suet coated the upper half of the pot. But of human occupants there was an ample sufficiency, considering the cubic space available for breathing purposes. Sitting in melancholy array against the walls, with their legs half buried in the straw and their backs against the baseboards, were eighteen prisoners—two Belgian cavalrymen and sixteen Frenchmen—mostly Zouaves and chasseurs-a-pied. Also, there were three Turcos from Northern Africa, almost as dark as negroes, wearing red fezzes and soiled white, baggy, skirtlike arrangements instead of trousers. They all looked very dirty, very unhappy and very sleepy.

At the far side of the room on a bench was another group of four prisoners; and of these we knew two personally—Gerbeaux, a Frenchman who lived in Brussels and served as the resident Brussels correspondent of a Chicago paper; and Stevens, an American artist, originally from Michigan, but who for several years had divided his time between Paris and Brussels. With them were a Belgian photographer, scared now into a quivering heap from which two wall-eyes peered out wildly, and a negro chauffeur, a soot-black Congo boy who had been brought away from Africa on a training ship as a child. He, apparently, was the least-concerned person in that hole.

The night before, by chance, we had heard that Gerbeaux and Stevens were under detention, but until this moment of meeting we did not know their exact whereabouts. They—the Frenchman, the American and the Belgian— had started out from Brussels in an auto driven by the African, on Monday, just a day behind us. Because their car carried a Red Cross flag without authority to do so, and because they had a camera with them, they very soon found themselves under arrest, and, what was worse, under suspicion. Except that for two days they had been marched afoot an average of twenty-five miles a day, they had fared pretty well, barring Stevens. He, being separated from the others, had fallen into the hands of an officer who treated him with such severity that the account of his experiences makes a tale worth recounting separately and at length.

We stayed in that place half an hour—one of the longest half hours I remember. There was a soldier with a fixed bayonet at the door, and another soldier with a saw-edged bayonet at the window, which was broken. Parties of soldiers kept coming to this window to peer at the exhibits within; and, as they invariably took the civilians for Englishmen who had been caught as spies, we attracted almost as much attention as the Turcos in their funny ballet skirts; in fact I may say we fairly divided the center of the stage with the Turcos.

At the end of half an hour the lieutenant bustled in, all apologies, to say there had been a mistake and that we should never have been put in with the prisoners at all. The rain being over, he invited us to come outside and get a change of air. When we got outside we found that our two bicycles, which we had left leaning against the curb, were gone. To date they are still gone.

Again we sat waiting. Finally it occurred to us to go inside the little taverne, where, perhaps, we should be less conspicuous. We went in, and presently we were followed by Lieutenant Mittendorfer, he bringing with him a tall young top-sergeant of infantry who carried his left arm in a sling and had a three weeks' growth of fuzzy red beard on his chops. It was explained that this top-sergeant, Rosenthal by name, had been especially assigned to be our companion—our playfellow, as it were; — until such time as the long-delayed automobile should appear.

Sergeant Rosenthal, who was very proud of his punctured wrist and very hopeful of getting a promotion, went out soon; but it speedily became evident that he had not forgotten us. For one soldier with his gun appeared in the front room of the place, and another materialized just outside the door, likewise with his gun. And by certain other unmistakable signs it became plain to our perceptions that as between being a prisoner of the German army and being a guest there was really no great amount of difference. It would have taken a mathematician to draw the distinction, so fine it was.

We stayed in that taverne and in the small living room behind it, and in the small high-walled courtyard behind the living room, all that afternoon and that evening and that night, being visited at intervals by either the lieutenant or the sergeant, or both of them at once. We dined lightly on soldiers' bread and some of the prince's wine—furnished by Rosenthal—and for dessert we had some shelled almonds and half a cake of chocolate—furnished by ourselves; also drinks of pale native brandy from the bar.

During the evening we received several bulletins regarding the mythical automobile. Invariably Mittendorfer was desolated to be compelled to report that there had been another slight delay. We knew he was desolated, because he said he was. During the evening, also, we met all the regular members of the household living under that much-disturbed roof. There was the husband, a big lubberly Fleming who apparently did not count for much in the economic and domestic scheme of the establishment; his wife, a large, commanding woman who ran the business and the house as well; his wife's mother, an old sickly woman in her seventies; and his wife's sister, a poor, palsied half-wit.

When the sister was a child, so we heard, she had been terribly frightened, so that to this day, still frightened, she crept about, a pale shadow, quivering all over pitiably at every sound. She would stand behind a door for minutes shaking so that you could hear her knuckles knocking against the wall. She seemed particularly to dread the sight of the German privates who came and went; and they, seeing this, were kind to her in a clumsy, awkward way. Hourly, like a ghost she drifted in and out.

For a while it looked as though we should spend the night sitting up in chairs; but about ten o'clock three soldiers, led by Rosenthal and accompanied by the landlady, went out; and when they came back they brought some thick feather mattresses which had been commandeered from neighboring houses, we judged. Also, through the goodness of his heart, Mittendorfer, who impressed us more and more as a strange compound of severity and softness, took pity on Gerbeaux and Stevens, and bringing them forth from that pestilential hole next door, he convoyed them in to stay overnight with us. They told us that by now the air in the improvised prison was absolutely suffocating, what with the closeness, the fouled straw, the stale food and the proximity of so many dirty human bodies all packed into the kennel together.

Ten of us slept on the floor of that little grogshop—the five of our party lying spoon-fashion on two mattresses, Gerbeaux and Stevens making seven, and three soldiers. The soldiers relieved each other in two-hour spells, so that while two of them snored by the door the third sat in a chair in the middle of the room, with his rifle between his knees, and a shaded lamp and a clock on a table at his elbow. Just before we turned in, Rosenthal, who had adopted a paternal tone to the three guards, each of whom was many years older than he, addressed them softly, saying:

"Now, my children, make yourselves comfortable. Drink what you please; but if any one of you gets drunk I shall take pleasure in seeing that he gets from seven to nine years in prison at hard labor. " For which they thanked him gratefully in chorus.

I am not addicted to the diary-keeping habit, but during the next day, which was Friday, I made fragmentary records of things in a journal, from which I now quote verbatim:

Seven-thirty a. m.—about. After making a brief toilet by sousing our several faces in a pail of water, we have just breakfasted— sketchily— on wine and almonds. It would seem that the German army feeds its prisoners, but makes no such provision for its guests. On the whole I think I should prefer being a prisoner.

We have offered our landlady any amount within reason for a pot of coffee and some toasted bread; but she protests, calling on Heaven to witness the truth of her words, that there is nothing to eat in the house—that the Germans have eaten up all her store of food, and that her old mother is already beginning to starve. Yet certain appetizing smells, which come down the staircase from upstairs when the door is opened, lead me to believe she is deceiving us. I do not blame her for treasuring what she has for her own flesh and blood; but I certainly could enjoy a couple of fried eggs.

Nine a. m. Mittendorfer has been in, with vague remarks concerning our automobile. Something warns me this young man is trifling with us. He appears to be a practitioner of the Japanese school of diplomacy—that is, he believes it is better to pile one gentle, transparent fiction on another until the pyramid of romance falls of its own weight, rather than to break the cruel news at a single blow.

Eleven-twenty. One of the soldiers has brought us half a dozen bottles of good wine—three bottles of red and three of white—but the larder remains empty. I do not know exactly what a larder is; but if it is as empty as I am at the present moment it must remind itself of a haunted house.

Eleven-forty. A big van full of wounded Germans has arrived. From the windows we can see it distinctly. The more seriously hurt lie on the bed of the wagon, under the hood. The man who drives has one leg in splints; and of the two who sit at the tail gate, holding rifles upright, one has a bandaged head, and the other has an arm in a sling.

Unless a German is so seriously crippled as to be entirely unfitted for service he manages to do something useful. There are no loose ends and no waste to the German military system; I can see that. The soldiers in the street cheer the wounded as they pass and the wounded answer by singing Die Wacht am Rhein feebly.

One poor chap raises his head and looks out. He appears to be almost spent, but I see his lips move as he tries to sing. You may not care for the German cause, but you are bound to admire the German spirit—the German oneness of purpose.

Noon. As the Texas darky said: "Dinnertime fur some folks; but just twelve o'clock fur me! " Again I smell something cooking upstairs. On the mantel of the shabby little interior sitting room, where we spend most of our time sitting about in a sad circle, is a little black-and- tan terrier pup, stuffed and mounted, with shiny glass eyes—a family pet, I take it, which died and was immortalized by the local taxidermist. If I only knew what that dog was stuffed with I would take a chance and eat him.

I have a fellow feeling for Arctic explorers who go north and keep on going until they run out of things to eat. I admire their heroism and sympathize with their sufferings, but I deplore their bad judgment. There are grapes growing on trellises in the little courtyard at the back, but they are too green for human consumption. I speak authoritatively on this subject, having just sampled one.

Paths of Glory

Two p. m. Tried to take a nap, but failed. Hansen found a soiled deck of cards behind a pile of books on the mantelpiece, and we all cheered up, thinking of poker; but it was a Belgian deck of thirty-two cards, all the pips below the seven-spot being eliminated. Poker with that deck would be a hazardous pursuit.

McCutcheon remarks casually that he wonders what would happen if somebody accidentally touched off those field-gun shells in the house two doors away. We suddenly remember that they are all pointed our way! The conversation seems to lull, and Mac, for the time being, loses popularity.

Two-thirty p. m. Looking out on the dreary little square of this town of Beaumont I note that the natives, who have been scarce enough all day, have now vanished almost entirely; whereas soldiers are noticeably more numerous than they were this morning.

Three-fifteen p. m. Heard a big noise in the street and ran to the window in time to see about forty English prisoners passing under guard —the first English soldiers I have seen, in this campaign, either as prisoners or otherwise. Their tan khaki uniforms and flat caps give them a soldierly look very unlike the slovenly, sloppy-appearing French prisoners in the guardhouse; but they appear to be tremendously downcast. The German soldiers crowd up to stare at them, but there is no jeering or taunting from the Germans. These prisoners are all infantrymen, judging by their uniforms. They disappear through the gateway of the prince's park.

Three-forty. I have just had some exercise; walked from the front door to the courtyard and back. There are two guards outside the door now instead of one. The German army certainly takes mighty good care of its guests.

This day has been as long as Gibbon's "Decline and Fall, " and much more tiresome. No; I'll take that back; it is not strong enough. This day has been as long as the entire Christian Era.

Four p. m. Gerbeaux, who was allowed to go out foraging, under escort of a guard, has returned with a rope of dried onions; a can of alphabet noodles; half a pound of stale, crumbly macaroons; a few fresh string beans; a pot of strained honey, and several clean collars of assorted sizes. The woman of the-house is now making soup for us out of the beans, the onions and the noodles. She has also produced a little grated Parmesan cheese from somewhere.

Four-twenty p. m. That was the best soup I ever tasted, even if it was full of typographical errors from the jumbling together of the little alphabet noodles. Still, nobody but a proofreader could have found fault with that. There was only one trouble with that soup: there was not enough of it—just one bowl apiece. I would have traded the finest case of vintage wine in the Chimay vaults for another bowl.

Just as the woman brought in the soup Mittendorfer appeared, escorting a French lieutenant who was taken prisoner this morning. The prisoner was a little, handsome, dapper chap not over twenty-two years old, wearing his trim blue-and-red uniform with an air, even though he himself looked thoroughly miserable. We were warned not to speak with him, or he with us; but Gerbeaux, after listening to him exchanging a few words with the lieutenant, said he judged from his accent that the little officer was from the south of France.

We silently offered him a bowl of the soup as he sat in a corner fenced off from the rest of us by a small table; but he barely tasted it, and after a bit he lay down in his corner, with his arm for a pillow, and almost instantly was asleep, breathing heavily, like a man on the verge of exhaustion. A few minutes later we heard, from Sergeant Rosenthal, that the prisoner's brother-in-law had been killed the day before, and that he—the little officer—had seen the brother-in-law fall.

Five p. m. We have had good news—two chunks of good news, in fact. We are to dine and we are to travel. The sergeant has acquired, from unknown sources, a brace of small, skinny, fresh-killed pullets; eight fresh eggs; a big loaf of the soggy rye bread of the field mess; and wine unlimited. Also, we are told that at nine o'clock we are to start for Brussels—not by automobile, but aboard a train carrying wounded and prisoners northward.

Everybody cheers up, especially after ma-dame promises to have the fowls and the eggs ready in less than an hour.

The Belgian photographer, who, it develops, is to go with our troop, has been brought in from the guardhouse and placed with us. With the passing hours his fright has increased. Gerbeaux says the poor

Paths of Glory

devil is one of the leading photographers of Brussels—that by royal appointment he takes pictures of the queen and her children. But the queen would have trouble in recognizing her photographer if she could see him now— with straw in his tousled hair, and his jaw lolling under the weight of his terror, and his big, wild eyes staring this way and that. Nothing that Gerbeaux can say to him will dissuade him from the belief that the Germans mean to shoot him.

I almost forgot to detail a thing that occurred a few minutes ago, just before the Belgian joined us. Mittendorfer brought a message for the little French lieutenant. The Frenchman roused up and, after they had saluted each other ceremoniously, Mittendorfer told him he had come to invite him to dine with a mess of German officers across the way, in the town hall.

On the way out he stopped to speak with Sergeant Rosenthal who, having furnished the provender for the forthcoming feast, was now waiting to share in it. Using German, the lieutenant said:

"I'm being kept pretty busy. Two citizens of this town have just been sentenced to be shot, and I've orders to go and attend to the shooting before it gets too dark for the firing squad to see to aim."

Rosenthal did not ask of what crime the condemned two had been convicted.

"You had charge of another execution this morning, didn't you? " he said.

"Yes," answered the lieutenant; "a couple—man and wife. The man was seventy-four years old and the woman was seventy-two. It was proved against them that they put poisoned sugar in the coffee for some of our soldiers. You heard about the case, didn't you? "

"I heard something about it," said Rosenthal.

That was all they said. After three weeks of war a tragedy like this has become commonplace, not only to these soldiers but to us. Already all of us, combatants and onlookers alike, have seen so many horrors that one more produces no shock in our minds. It will take a wholesale killing to excite us; these minor incidents no longer count with us. If I wrote all day I do not believe I could make the

Paths of Glory

meaning of war, in its effects on the minds of those who view it at close hand, any clearer. I shall not try.

Six-fifteen p. m. We have dined. The omelet was a very small omelet, and two skinny pullets do not go far among nine hungry men; still, we have dined.

My journal breaks off with this entry. It broke off because immediately after dinner word came that our train was ready. A few minutes before we left the taverne for the station, to start on a trip that was to last two days instead of three hours, and land us not in Brussels, but on German soil in Aix-la-Chapelle, two incidents happened which afterward, in looking back on the experience, I have found most firmly clinched in my memory: A German captain came into the place to get a drink; he recognized me as an American and hailed me, and wanted to know my business and whether I could give him any news from the outside world. I remarked on the perfection of his English.

"I suppose I come by it naturally, " he said. "I call myself a German, but I was born in Nashville, Tennessee, and partly reared in New Jersey, and educated at Princeton; and at this moment I am a member of the New York Cotton Exchange. "

Right after this three Belgian peasants, all half-grown boys, were brought in. They had run away from their homes at the coming of the Germans, and for three days had been hiding in thickets, without food, until finally hunger and cold had driven them in.

All of them were in sorry case and one was in collapse. He trembled so his whole body shook like jelly. The landlady gave him some brandy, but the burning stuff choked his throat until it closed and the brandy ran out of his quivering blue lips and spilled on his chin. Seeing this, a husky German private, who looked as though in private life he might be a piano mover, brought out of his blanket roll a bottle of white wine and, holding the scared, exhausted lad against his chest, ministered to him with all gentleness, and gave him sips of the wine. In the line of duty I suppose he would have shot that boy with the same cheerful readiness.

Just as we were filing out into the dark, Sergeant Rosenthal, who was also going along, halted us and reminded us all and severally that we were not prisoners, but still guests; and that, though we were to march with the prisoners to the station, we were to go in line with the guards; and if any prisoner sought to escape it was hoped that we would aid in recapturing the runaway. So we promised him, each on his word of honor, that we would do this; and he insisted that we should shake hands with him as a pledge and as a token of mutual confidence, which we accordingly did. Altogether it was quite an impressive little ceremonial—and rather dramatic, I imagine.

As he left us, however, he was heard, speaking in German, to say sotto voce to one of the guards:

"If one of those journalists tries to slip away don't take any chances— shoot him at once!"

It is so easy to keep one's honor intact when you have moral support in the shape of an earnest-minded German soldier, with a gun, stepping along six feet behind you. My honor was never safer.

Chapter 6

With the German Wrecking Crew

When we came out of the little taverne at Beaumont, to start—as we fondly supposed—for Brussels, it was pitch dark in the square of the forlorn little town. With us the polite and pleasant fiction that we were guests of the German authorities had already worn seedy, not to say threadbare, but Lieutenant Mittendorfer persisted in keeping the little romance alive. For, as you remember, we had been requested—requested, mind you, and not ordered—to march to the station with the armed escort that would be in charge of the prisoners of war, and it had been impressed upon us that we were to assist in guarding the convoy, although no one of us had any more deadly weapon in his possession than a fountain pen; and finally, according to our instructions, if any prisoner attempted to escape in the dark we were to lay detaining hands upon him and hold him fast.

This was all very flattering and very indicative of the esteem in which the military authorities of Beaumont seemed to hold us. But we were not puffed up with a sense of our new responsibilities. Also we were as a unit in agreeing that under no provocation would we yield to temptations to embark on any side-excursions upon the way to the railroad. Personally I know that I was particularly firm upon this point. I would defy that column to move so fast that I could not keep up with it.

In the black gloom we could make out a longish clump of men who stood four abreast, scuffling their feet upon the miry wet stones of the square. These were the prisoners—one hundred and fifty Frenchmen and Turcos, eighty Englishmen and eight Belgians. From them, as we drew near, an odor of wet, unwashed animals arose. It was as rank and raw as fumes from crude ammonia. Then, in the town house of the Prince de Caraman-Chimay just alongside, the double doors opened, and the light streaming out fell upon the naked bayonets over the shoulders of the sentries and made them look like slanting lines of rain.

There were eight of us by now in the party of guests, our original group of five having been swollen by the addition of three others—the Frenchman Gerbeaux, the American artist Stevens and the

Paths of Glory

Belgian court- photographer Hennebert, who had been under arrest for five days. We eight, obeying instructions—no, requests—found places for ourselves in the double files of guards, four going one side of the column and four the other. I slipped into a gap on the left flank, alongside four of the English soldiers. The guard immediately behind me was a man I knew. He had been on duty the afternoon previous in the place where we were being kept, and he had been obliging enough to let me exercise my few words of German upon him. He grinned now in recognition and humorously patted the stock of his rifle—this last, I take it, being his effort to convey to my understanding that he was under orders to shoot me in the event of my seeking to play truant during the next hour or so. He didn't know me—wild horses could not have dragged us apart.

A considerable wait ensued. Officers, coming back from the day's battle lines in automobiles, jumped out of their cars and pressed up, bedraggled and wet through from the rain which had been falling, to have a look at the prisoners. Common soldiers appeared also. Of these latter many, I judged, had newly arrived at the front and had never seen any captured enemies before. They were particularly interested in the Englishmen, who as nearly as I could tell endured the scrutinizing pretty well, whereas the Frenchmen grew uneasy and self-conscious under it. We who were in civilian dress—and pretty shabby civilian dress at that—came in for our share of examination too. The sentries were kept busy explaining to newcomers that we were not spies going north for trial. There was little or no jeering at the prisoners.

Lieutenant Mittendorfer appeared to feel the burden of his authority mightily. His importance expressed itself in many bellowing commands to his men. As he passed the door of headquarters, booming like a Prussian night-bittern, one of the officers there checked him with a gesture.

"Why all the noise, Herr Lieutenant? " he said pleasantly in German. "Cannot this thing be done more quietly? "

The young man took the hint, and when he climbed upon a bench outside the wine-shop door his voice was much milder as he admonished the prisoners that they would be treated with due honors of war if they obeyed their warders promptly during the coming journey, but that the least sign of rebellion among them would mean but one thing—immediate death. Since he spoke in

German, a young French lieutenant translated the warning for the benefit of the Frenchmen and the Belgians, and a British noncom. did the same for his fellow countrymen, speaking with a strong Scottish burr. He wound up with an improvisation of his own, which I thought was typically British. "Now, then, boys, " he sang out, "buck up, all of you! It might be worse, you know, and some of these German chaps don't seem a bad lot at all. "

So, with that, Lieutenant Mittendorfer blew out his big chest and barked an order into the night, and away we all swung off at a double quick, with our feet slipping and sliding upon the travel-worn granite boulders underfoot. In addition to being rounded and unevenly laid, the stones were now coated with a layer of slimy mud. It was a hard job to stay upright on them.

I don't think I shall ever forget that march. I know I shall never forget that smell, or the sound of all our feet clumping over those slick cobbles. Nor shall I forget, either, the appealing calls of Gerbeaux' black chauffeur, who was being left behind in the now empty guardhouse, and who, to judge from his tones, did not expect ever to see any of us again. As a matter of fact, I ran across him two weeks later in Liege. He had just been released and was trying to make his way back to Brussels.

The way ahead of us was inky black. The outlines of the tall Belgian houses on either side of the narrow street were barely visible, for there were no lights in the windows at all and only dim candles or oil lamps in the lower floors. No natives showed themselves. I do not recollect that in all that mile-long tramp I saw a single Belgian civilian—only soldiers, shoving forward curiously as we passed and pressing the files closer in together.

Through one street we went and into another which if anything was even narrower and blacker than the first, and presently we could tell by the feel of things under our feet that we had quit the paved road and were traversing soft earth. We entered railway sidings, stumbling over the tracks, and at the far end of the yard emerged into a sudden glare of brightness and drew up alongside a string of cars.

After the darkness the flaring brilliancy made us blink and then it made us wonder there should be any lights at all, seeing that the French troops, in retiring from Beaumont four days before, had done their hurried best to cripple the transportation facilities and had certainly put the local gas plant out of commission. Yet here was illumination in plenty and to spare. At once the phenomenon stood explained. Two days after securing this end of the line the German engineers had repaired the torn-up right-of-way and installed a complete acetylene outfit, and already they were dispatching trains of troops and munitions clear across southeastern Belgium to and from the German frontier. When we heard this we quit marveling. We had by now ceased to wonder at the lightning rapidity and unhuman efficiency of the German military system in the field.

Under the sizzling acetylene torches we had our first good look at these prospective fellow-travelers of ours who were avowedly prisoners.

Considered in the aggregate they were not an inspiring spectacle. A soldier, stripped of his arms and held by his foes, becomes of a sudden a pitiable, almost a contemptible object. You think instinctively of an adder that has lost its fangs, or of a wild cat that, being shorn of teeth to bite with and claws to tear with, is now a more helpless, more impotent thing than if it had been created without teeth and claws in the first place. These similes are poor ones, I'm afraid, but I find it difficult to put my thoughts exactly into words.

These particular soldiers were most unhappy looking, all except the half dozen Turcos among the Frenchmen. They spraddled their baggy white legs and grinned comfortably, baring fine double rows of ivory in their brown faces. The others mainly were droopy figures of misery and shame. By reason of their hair, which they wore long and which now hung down in their eyes, and by reason also of their ridiculous loose red trousers and their long-tailed awkward blue coats, the Frenchmen showed themselves especially unkempt and frowzy-looking. Almost to a man they were dark, lean, slouchy fellows; they were from the south of France, we judged. Certainly with a week's growth of black whiskers upon their jaws they were fit now to play stage brigands without further make-up.

"Wot a bloomin', stinkin', rotten country! " came, two rows back from where I stood, a Cockney voice uplifted to the leaky skies. "There ain't nothin' to eat in it, and there ain't nothin' to drink in it, too. "

A little whiny man alongside of me, whose chin was on his breast bone, spake downward along his gray flannel shirt bosom:

"Just wyte, " he said; "just wyte till England 'ears wot they done to us, 'erdin' us about like cattle. Blighters! " He spat his disgust upon the ground.

We spoke to none of them directly, nor they to us—that also being a condition imposed by Mittendorfer.

The train was composed of several small box cars and one second-class passenger coach of German manufacture with a dumpy little locomotive at either end, one to pull and one to push. In profile it would have reminded you somewhat of the wrecking trains that go to disasters in America. The prisoners were loaded aboard the box cars like so many sheep, with alert gray shepherds behind them, carrying guns in lieu of crooks; and, being entrained, they were bedded down for the night upon straw.

The civilians composing our party were bidden to climb aboard the passenger coach, where the eight of us, two of the number being of augmented super-adult size, took possession of a compartment meant to hold six. The other compartments were occupied by wounded Germans, except one compartment, which was set aside for the captive French lieutenant and two British subalterns. Top-Sergeant Rosenthal was in charge of the train with headquarters aboard our coach. With him, as aides, he had three Red Cross men.

The lighting apparatus of the car did not operate. On the ledge of our window sat a small oil lamp, sending out a rich smell and a pale, puny illumination. Just before we pulled out Rosenthal came and blew out the lamp, leaving the wick to smoke abominably. He explained that he did this for our own well-being. Belgian snipers just outside the town had been firing into the passing trains, he said, and a light in a car window was but an added temptation. He advised us that if shooting started we should drop upon the floor. We assured him in chorus that we would, and then after adding that we must not be surprised if the Belgians derailed the train during the night he went away, leaving us packed snugly in together in the dark. This incident had a tendency to discourage light conversation among us for some minutes.

Possibly it was because daylight travel would be safer travel, or it may have been for some other good and sufficient reason, that after traveling some six or eight miles joltingly we stopped in the edge of a small village and stayed there until after sun-up. That was a hard night for sleeping purposes. One of our party, who was a small man, climbed up into the baggage net above one row of seats and stretched himself stiffly in the narrow hammock-like arrangement, fearing to move lest he tumble down on the heads of his fellow-sufferers. Another laid him down in the little aisle flanking the compartment, where at least he might spraddle his limbs and where also, persons passing the length of the car stepped upon his face and figure from time to time. This interfered with his rest. The remaining six of us mortised ourselves into the seats in neck-cricking attitudes, with our legs so intertwined and mingled that when one man got up to stretch himself he had to use great care in picking out his own legs. Sometimes he could only tell that it was his leg by pinching it. This was especially so after inaction had put his extremities to sleep while the rest of him remained wide awake.

After dawn we ran slowly to Charleroi, the center of the Belgian iron industry, in a sterile land of mines and smelters and slag-heaps, and bleak, bare, ore-stained hillsides. The Germans had fought here, first with organized troops of the Allies, and later, by their own telling, with bushwhacking civilians. Whole rows of houses upon either side of the track had been ventilated by shells or burned out with fire, and their gable ends, lacking roofs, now stood up nakedly, fretting the skyline like gigantic saw teeth. As we were drawing out from between these twin rows of ruins we saw a German sergeant in a flower plot alongside a wrecked cottage bending over, apparently smelling at a clump of tall red geraniums. That he could find time in the midst of that hideous desolation to sniff at the posies struck us as a typically German bit of sentimentalism. Just then, though, he stood erect and we were better informed. He had been talking over a military telephone, the wires of which were buried underground with a concealed transmitter snuggling beneath the geraniums. The flowers even were being made to contribute their help in forwarding the mechanism of war. I think, though, that it took a composite German mind to evolve that expedient. A Prussian would bring along the telephone; a Saxon would bed it among the blossoms.

We progressed onward by a process of alternate stops and starts, through a land bearing remarkably few traces to show for its recent chastening with sword and torch, until in the middle of the blazing hot forenoon we came to Gembloux, which I think must be the place where all the flies in Belgium are spawned. Here on a siding we lay all day, grilled in the heat and pestered by swarms of the buzzing scavenger vermin, while troop trains without number passed us, hurrying along the sentry-guarded railway to the lower frontiers of Belgium. Every box-car door made a frame for a group-picture of broad German faces and bulky German bodies. Upon nearly every car the sportive passengers had lashed limbs of trees and big clumps of field flowers. Also with colored chalks they had extensively frescoed the wooden walls as high up as they could reach. The commonest legend was "On to Paris, " or for variety "To Paris Direct, " but occasionally a lighter touch showed itself. For example, one wag had inscribed on a car door: "Declarations of War Received Here, " and another had drawn a highly impressionistic likeness of his Kaiser, and under it had inscribed "Wilhelm II, Emperor of Europe. "

Presently as train after train, loaded sometimes with guns or supplies but usually with men, clanked by, it began to dawn upon us that these soldiers were of a different physical type from the soldiers we had seen heretofore. They were all Germans, to be sure, but the men along the front were younger men, hard-bitten and trained down, with the face which we had begun to call the Teutonic fighting face, whereas these men were older, and of a heavier port and fuller fashion of countenance. Also some of them wore blue coats, red-trimmed, instead of the dull gray service garb of the troops in the first invading columns. Indeed some of them even wore a nondescript mixture of uniform and civilian garb. They were Landwehr and Landsturm, troops of the third and fourth lines, going now to police the roads and garrison the captured towns, and hold the lines of communication open while the first line, who were picked troops, and the second line, who were reservists, pressed ahead into France.

They showed a childlike curiosity to see the prisoners in the box cars behind us. They grinned triumphantly at the Frenchmen and the Britishers, but the sight of a Turco in his short jacket and his dirty white skirts invariably set them off in derisive cat-calling and whooping. One beefy cavalryman in his forties, who looked the Bavarian peasant all over, boarded our car to see what might be seen. He had been drinking. He came nearer being drunk outright than any German soldier I had seen to date. Because he heard us talking English he insisted on regarding us as English spies.

"Hark! they betray themselves, " we heard him mutter thickly to one of his wounded countrymen in the next compartment. "They are damned Englishers. "

"Nein! Nein! All Americans, " we heard the other say.

"Well, if they are Americans, why don't they talk the American language then? " he demanded. Hearing this, I was sorry I had neglected in my youth to learn Choctaw.

Still dubious of us, he came now and stood in the aisle, rocking slightly on his bolster legs and eying us glassily. Eventually a thought pierced the fog of his understanding. He hauled his saber out of its scabbard and invited us to run our fingers along the edge and see how keen and sharp it was. He added, with appropriate gestures, that he had honed it with the particular intent of slicing off a few English heads. For one, and speaking for one only, I may say I was, on the whole, rather glad when he departed from among us.

When we grew tired of watching the troop trains streaming south we fought the flies, and listened for perhaps the tenth time to the story of Stevens' experience when he first fell into German hands, six days before.

Stevens was the young American who accompanied Gerbeaux, the Frenchman, and Hennebert, the Belgian, on their ill-timed expedition from Brussels in an automobile bearing without authority a Red Cross flag. Gerbeaux was out to get a story for the Chicago paper which he served as Brussels correspondent, and the Belgian hoped to take some photographs; but a pure love of excitement brought Stevens along. He had his passport to prove his citizenship and a pass from General von Jarotzky, military commandant of Brussels, authorizing him to pass through the lines. He thought he was perfectly safe.

When their machine was halted by the Germans a short distance south and west of Waterloo, Stevens, for some reason which he could never understand, was separated from his two companions and the South-African negro chauffeur. A sergeant took him in charge, and all the rest of the day he rode on the tail of a baggage wagon with a guard upon either side of him. First, though, he was searched and all his papers were taken from him.

Late in the afternoon the pack-train halted and as Stevens was stretching his legs in a field a first lieutenant, whom he described as being tall and nervous and highly excitable, ran up and, after berating the two guards for not having their rifles ready to fire, he poked a gun under Stevens' nose and went through the process of loading it, meanwhile telling him that if he moved an inch his brains would be blown out. A sergeant gently edged Stevens back out of the danger belt, and, from behind the officer's back another man, so Stevens said, tapped himself gently upon the forehead to indicate that the Herr Lieutenant was cracked in the brain.

After this Stevens was taken into an improvised barracks in a deserted Belgian gendarmerie and locked in a room. At nine o'clock the lieutenant came to him and told him in a mixture of French and German that he had by a court-martial been found guilty of being an English spy and that at six o'clock the following morning he would be shot. "When you hear a bugle sound you may know that is the signal for your execution, " the officer added.

While poor Stevens was still begging for an opportunity to be heard in his own defense the lieutenant dealt him a blow in the side which left him temporarily breathless. In a moment two soldiers had crossed his wrists behind his back and were lashing them tightly together with a rope.

Thus bound he was taken back indoors and made to sit on a bench. Eight soldiers stretched themselves upon the floor of the room and slept there; a sergeant slept with his body across the door. A guard sat on the bench beside Stevens.

"He gave me two big slugs of brandy to drink, " said Stevens, continuing his tale, "and it affected me no more than so much water. After a couple of hours I managed to work the cords loose and I got one hand free. Moving cautiously I lifted my feet, and by stretching my arms cautiously down, still holding them behind my back, I untied one shoe. I meant at the last to kick off my shoes and run for it. I was feeling for the laces on my other shoe when another guard came to re-enforce the first, and he watched me so closely that I knew that chance was gone.

"After a while, strange as it seems, all the fear and all the horror of death left me. My chief regret now was, not that I had to die, but that my people at home would never know how I died or where. I put my head down on the table and actually dozed off. But there was a clock in the room and whenever it struck I would rouse up and say to myself, almost impersonally, that I now had four hours to live, or three, or two, as the case might be. Then I would go to sleep again. Once or twice a queer sinking sensation in my stomach, such as I never felt before, would come to me, but toward daylight this ceased to occur.

"At half-past five two soldiers, one carrying a spade and the other a lantern, came in. They lit the lantern at a lamp that burned on a table in front of me and went out. Presently I could hear them digging in the yard outside the door. I believed it was my grave they were digging. I cannot recall that this made any particular impression upon me. I considered it in a most casual sort of fashion. I remember wondering whether it was a deep grave.

"At five minutes before six a bugle sounded. The eight men on the floor got up, buckled on their cartridge belts, shouldered their rifles and, leaving their knapsacks behind, tramped out. I followed with my guards upon either side of me. My one fear now was that I should tremble at the end. I felt no fear, but I was afraid my knees would shake. I remember how relieved I was when I took the first step to find my legs did not tremble under me.

"I was resolved, too, that I would not be shot down with my hands tied behind me. When I faced the squad I meant to shake off the ropes on my wrists and take the volley with my arms at my sides."

Stevens was marched to the center of the courtyard. Then, without a word of explanation to him his bonds were removed and he was put in an automobile and carried off to rejoin the other members of the unlucky sightseeing party. He never did find out whether he had been made the butt of a hideous practical joke by a half-mad brute or whether his tormentor really meant to send him to death and was deterred at the last moment by fear of the consequences. One thing he did learn—there had been no court-martial. Thereafter, during his captivity, Stevens was treated with the utmost kindness by all the officers with whom he came in contact. His was the only instance that I have knowledge of where a prisoner has been tortured, physically or mentally, by a German. It was curious that in this one case the victim should have been an American citizen whose intentions were perfectly innocent and whose papers were orthodox and unquestionable.

Paths of Glory

Glancing back over what I have here written down I find I have failed altogether to mention the food which we ate on that trip of ours with the German wrecking crew. It was hardly worth mentioning, it was so scanty.

We had to eat, during that day while we lay at Gembloux, a loaf of the sourish soldiers' black bread, with green mold upon the crust, and a pot of rancid honey which one of the party had bethought him to bring from Beaumont in his pocket. To wash this mixture down we had a few swigs of miserably bad lukewarm ration-coffee from a private's canteen, a bottle of confiscated Belgian mineral water, which a private at Charleroi gave us from his store, and a precious quart of the Prince de Caraman- Chimay's commandeered wine— also a souvenir of our captivity. Late in the afternoon a sergeant sold us for a five-mark piece a big skin-casing filled with half-raw pork sausage. I've never tasted anything better.

Even so, we fared better than the prisoners in the box cars behind and the dozen wounded men in the coach with us. They had only coffee and dry bread and, at the latter end of the long day, a few chunks of the sausage. Some of the wounded men were pretty badly hurt, too. There was one whose left forearm had been half shot away. His stiff fingers protruded beyond his soiled bandages and they were still crusted with dried blood and grained with dirt. Another had been pierced through the jaw with a bullet. That part of his face which showed through the swathings about his head was terribly swollen and purple with congested blood. The others had flesh wounds, mainly in their sides or their legs. Some of them were feverish; all of them sorely needed clean garments for their bodies and fresh dressings for their hurts and proper food for their stomachs. Yet I did not hear one of them complain or groan.

With that oxlike patience of the North-European peasant breed, which seems accentuated in these Germans in time of war, they quietly endured what was acute discomfort for any sound man to have to endure. In some dim, dumb fashion of their own they seemed, each one of them, to comprehend that in the vast organism of an army at war the individual unit does not count. To himself he may be of prime importance and first consideration, but in the general carrying out of the scheme he is a mote, a molecule, a spore, a protoplasm—an infinitesimal, utterly inconsequential thing to be sacrificed without thought. Thus we diagnosed their mental poses. Along toward five o'clock a goodish string of cars was added to our train, and into these additional cars seven hundred French soldiers, who had been collected at Gembloux, were loaded. With the Frenchmen as they marched under our window went, perhaps, twenty civilian prisoners, including two priests and three or four subdued little men who looked as though they might be civic dignitaries of some small Belgian town. In the squad was one big, broad-shouldered peasant in a blouse, whose arms were roped back at the elbows with a thick cord.

"Do you see that man? " said one of our guards excitedly, and he pointed at the pinioned man. "He is a grave robber. He has been digging up dead Germans to rob the bodies. They tell me that when they caught him he had in his pockets ten dead men's fingers which he had cut off with a knife because the flesh was so swollen he could not slip the rings off. He will be shot, that fellow. "

We looked with a deeper interest then at the man whose arms were bound, but privately we permitted ourselves to be skeptical regarding the details of his alleged ghoulishness. We had begun to discount German stories of Belgian atrocities and Belgian stories of German atrocities. I might add that I am still discounting both varieties.

To help along our train two more little engines were added, but even with four of them to draw and to shove their load was now so heavy that we were jerked along with sensations as though we were having a jaw tooth pulled every few seconds. After such a fashion we progressed very slowly. Already we knew that we were not going to Brussels, as we had been promised in Beaumont that we should go. We only hoped we were not bound for a German military fortress in some interior city.

It fell to my lot that second night to sleep in the aisle. In spite of being walked on at intervals I slept pretty well. When I waked it was three o'clock in the morning, just, and we were standing in the train shed at Liege, and hospital corps men were coming aboard with hot coffee and more raw sausages for the wounded. Among the Germans, sausages are used medicinally. I think they must keep supplies of sausages in their homes, for use in cases of accident and sickness.

I got up and looked from the window. The station was full of soldiers moving about on various errands. Overhead big arc lights sputtered spitefully, so that the place was almost as bright as day. Almost directly below me was a big table, which stood on the platform and was covered over with papers and maps. At the table sat two officers—high officers, I judged—writing busily. Their stiff white cuff-ends showed below their coat-sleeves; their slim black boots were highly polished, and altogether they had the look of having just escaped from the hands of a valet. Between them and the frowsy privates was a gulf a thousand miles wide and a thousand miles deep.

When I woke again it was broad daylight and we had crossed the border and were in Germany. At small way stations women and girls wearing long white aprons and hospital badges came under the car windows with hot drinks and bacon sandwiches for the wounded. They gave us some, too, and, I think, bestowed what was left upon the prisoners at the rear. We ran now through a land untouched by war, where prim farmhouses stood in prim gardens. It was Sunday morning and the people were going to church dressed in their Sunday best. Considering that Germany was supposed to have been drained of its able-bodied male adults for war-making purposes we saw, among the groups, an astonishingly large number of men of military age. By contrast with the harried country from which we had just emerged this seemed a small Paradise of peace. Over there in Belgium all the conditions of life had been disorganized and undone, where they had not been wrecked outright. Over here in Germany the calm was entirely unruffled.

It shamed us to come as we were into such surroundings. For our car was littered with sausage skins and bread crusts, and filth less pleasant to look at and stenches of many sorts abounded. Indeed I shall go further and say that it stank most fearsomely. As for us, we felt ourselves to be infamous offenses against the bright, clean day. We had not slept in a bed for five nights or had our clothes off for that time. For three days none of us had eaten a real meal at a regular table. For two days we had not washed our faces and hands.

The prisoners of war went on to Cologne to be put in a laager, but we were bidden to detrain at Aix-la-Chapelle. We climbed off, a dirty, wrinkled, unshaven troop of vagabonds, to find ourselves free to go where we pleased.

That is, we thought so at first. But by evening the Frenchman and the Belgians had been taken away to be held in prison until the end of the war, and for two days the highly efficient local secret-service staff kept the rest of us under its watchful care. After that, though, the American consul, Robert J. Thompson, succeeded in convincing the military authorities that we were not dangerous.

I still think that taking copious baths and getting ourselves shaved helped to clear us of suspicion.

Chapter 7

The Grapes of Wrath

There is a corner of Rhenish Prussia that shoulders up against Holland and drives a nudging elbow deep into the ribs of Belgium; and right here, at the place where the three countries meet, stands Charlemagne's ancient city of Aix-la-Chapelle, called Aachen by the Germans.

To go from the middle of Aix-la-Chapelle to the Dutch boundary takes twenty minutes on a tram-car, and to go to the Belgian line requires an even hour in a horse-drawn vehicle, and considerably less than that presuming you go by automobile. So you see the toes of the town touch two foreign frontiers; and of all German cities it is the most westerly and, therefore, closest of all to the zone of action in the west of Europe.

You would never guess it, however. When we landed in Aix-la-Chapelle, coming out of the heart of the late August hostilities in Belgium, we marveled; for, behold, here was a clean, white city that, so far as the look of it and the feel of it went, might have been a thousand miles from the sound of gunfire. On that Sabbath morning of our arrival an air of everlasting peace abode with it. That same air of peace continued to abide with it during all the days we spent here. Yet, if you took a step to the southwest—a figurative step in seven-league boots—you were where all hell broke loose. War is a most tremendous emphasizer of contrasts.

These lines were written late in September, in a hotel room at Aix-la-Chapelle. The writing of them followed close on an automobile trip to Liege, through a district blasted by war and corrugated with long trenches where those who died with their boots on still lie with their boots on.

Let me, if I can, draw two pictures—one of this German outpost town, and the other of the things that might be seen four or five miles distant over the border.

I have been told that, in the first flurry of the breaking out of the World-War, Aix was not placid. It went spy-mad, just as all Europe went spy-mad—a mania from which this Continent has not entirely recovered by any means. There was a great rounding up of suspected aliens. Every loyal citizen resolved himself or herself into a self-appointed policeman, to watch the movements of those suspected of being disloyal. Also, they tell me, when the magic mobilization began and troops poured through without ceasing for four days and four nights, and fighting broke out just the other side of the Belgian customhouse, on the main high road to Liege, there was excitement. But all that was over long before we came.

The war has gone onward, down into France; and all the people know is what the official bulletins tell them; in fact, I think they must know less about operations and results than our own people in America. I know not what the opportunity of the spectator may have been with regard to other wars, but certainly in this war it is true that the nearer you get to it the less you understand of its scope.

All about you, on every side, is a screen of secrecy. Once in a while it parts for a moment, and through the rift you catch a glimpse of the movement of armies and the swing and sweep of campaigns. Then the curtain closes and again you are shut in.

Let me put the case in another way: It is as though we who are at the front, or close to it, stand before a mighty painting, but with our noses almost touching the canvas. You who are farther away see the whole picture. We, for the moment, see only so much of it as you might cover with your two hands; but this advantage we do have—that we see the brush strokes, the color shadings, the infinite small detail, whereas you view its wider effects.

And then, having seen it, when we try to put our story into words—when we try to set down on paper the unspeakable horror of it—we realize what a futile, incomplete thing the English language is.

This present day in Aix-la-Chapelle will be, I assume, much like all the other days I have spent here. An hour ago small official bulletins, sanctioned by the Berlin War Office, were posted in the windows of the shops and on the front of the public buildings; and small groups gathered before them to read the news.

If it was good news they took it calmly. If it was not so good, still they took it calmly. If it was outright bad news I think they would still take it calmly. For, come good or evil, they are all possessed now with the belief that, in the long run, Germany must win. Their confidence is supreme.

It was characteristic of them, though, that, until word came of the first German success, there was no general flying of flags in the town. Now flags are up everywhere—the colors of the Empire and of Prussia, and often enough just a huge yellow square bearing the spraddled, black, spidery design of the Imperial eagle. But there is never any hysteria; I don't believe these Prussians know the meaning of the word. It is safe to assume that out of every three grown men in front of a bulletin one will be a soldier.

Yet, considering that Germany is supposed, at this moment, to have upward of five million men in the field or under arms, and that approximately two millions more, who were exempt from call by reason of age or other disabilities, are said to have volunteered, you would be astonished to see how many men in civilian dress are on the streets. Whether in uniform or not, though, these men are at work after some fashion or other for their country. Practically all the physicians in Aix are serving in the hospitals. The rich men—the men of affairs—are acting as military clerks at headquarters or driving Red Cross cars. The local censor of the telegraph is over eighty years old—a splendid-looking old white giant, who won the Iron Cross in the Franco-Prussian War and retired with the rank of general years and years ago. Now, in full uniform, he works twelve hard hours a day. The head waiter at this hotel told me yesterday that he expected to be summoned to the colors in a day or two. He has had his notice and is ready to go. He is more than forty years old. I know my room waiter kept watch on me until he satisfied himself I was what I claimed to be—an American—and not an English spy posing as an American.

So, at first, did the cheery little girl cashier in the Arcade barber shop downstairs. For all I know, she may still have me under suspicion and be making daily reports on me to the secret-service people. The women help, too—and the children. The wives and daughters of the wealthiest men in the town are minding the sick and the wounded. The mothers and the younger girls meet daily to make hospital supplies. Women come to you in the cafes at night, wearing Red Cross badges on their left arms, and shaking sealed tin canisters into which you are expected to drop contributions for invalided soldiers.

Paths of Glory

Since so many of their teachers are carrying rifles or wearing swords, the pupils of the grammar schools and the high schools are being organized into squads of crop-gatherers. Beginning next week, so I hear, they will go out into the fields and the orchards to assist in the harvesting of the grain and the fruit. For lack of hands to get it under cover the wheat has already begun to suffer; but the boys and girls will bring it in.

It is now half-past eleven o'clock in the forenoon. At noon, sharp, an excellent orchestra will begin to play in the big white casino maintained by the city, just opposite my hotel. It will play for an hour then, and again this afternoon, and again, weather permitting, to-night.

The townspeople will sit about at small, white tables and listen to the music while they sip their beer or drink their coffee. They will be soberer and less vivacious than I imagine they were two months ago; but then these North Germans are a sober-minded race anyhow, and they take their amusements quietly. Also, they have taken the bad tidings of the last few days from France very quietly.

During the afternoon crowds will gather on the viaduct, just above the principal railroad station, where they will stand for hours looking down over the parapet into the yards below. There will be smaller crowds on the heights of Ronheide, on the edge of the town, where the tracks enter the long tunnel under one of the hills that etch the boundary between Germany and Belgium.

Rain or shine, these two places are sure to be black with people, for here they may see the trains shuttle by, like long bobbins in a loom that never ceases from its weaving—trains going west loaded with soldiers and naval reservists bound for the front, and trains headed east bearing prisoners and wounded. The raw material passes one way— that's the new troops; the finished product passes the other— the wounded and the sick.

When wounded men go by there will be cheering, and some of the women are sure to raise the song of Die Wacht am Rhein; and within the cars the crippled soldiers will take up the chorus feebly. God knows how many able-bodied soldiers already have gone west; how many maimed and crippled ones have gone east! In the first instance the number must run up into the second million; of the latter there must have been well above two hundred thousand.

Paths of Glory

No dead come back from the front—at least, not this way. The Germans bury their fallen soldiers where they fall. Regardless of his rank, the dead man goes into a trench. If so be he died in battle he is buried, booted and dressed just as he died. And the dead of each day must be got underground before midnight of that same day—that is the hard-and- fast rule wherever the Germans are holding their ground or pressing forward. There they will lie until the Judgment Day, unless their kinsfolk be of sufficient wealth and influence to find their burial places and dig them up and bring them home privily for interment. Even so, it may be days or even weeks after a man is dead and buried before his people hear of it. It may be they will not hear of it until a letter written to him in the care of his regiment and his company comes back unopened, with one word in sinister red letters on it—Gefallen!

At this hotel, yesterday, I saw a lady dressed in heavy black. She had the saddest, bravest face I ever looked into, I think. She sat in the restaurant with two other ladies, who were also in black. The octogenarian censor of telegrams passed them on the way out. To her two companions he bowed deeply, but at her side he halted and, bending very low, he kissed her hand, and then went away without a word.

The head waiter, who knows all the gossip of the house and of half the town besides, told us about her. Her only son, a lieutenant of artillery, was killed at the taking of Liege. It was three days before she learned of his death, though she was here in Aachen, only a few miles away; for so slowly as this does even bad news travel in war times when it pertains to the individual.

Another week elapsed before her husband, who is a lieutenant-colonel, could secure leave of absence and return from the French border to seek for his son's body; and there was still another week of searching before they found it. It was at the bottom of a trench, under the bodies of a score or more of his men; and it was in such a state that the mother had not been permitted to look on her dead boy's face.

Such things as this must be common enough hereabouts, but one hears very little of them and sees even less. Aix-la-Chapelle has suffered most heavily. The Aix regiment was shot to pieces in the first day's fighting at Liege. Nearly half its members were killed or wounded; but astonishingly few women in mourning are to be seen on the street, and none of the men wear those crape arm bands that are so common in Europe ordinarily; nor, except about the railroad station, are very many wounded to be seen.

There are any number of wounded privates in the local hospitals; but there must be a rule against their appearance in public places, for it is only occasionally that I meet one abroad. Slightly wounded officers are more plentiful. I judge from this that no such restriction applies to them as applies to the common soldiers. This hotel is full of them— young officers mostly, with their heads tied up or their arms in black silk slings, or limping about on canes or crutches.

Until a few days ago the columns of the back pages of the Aix and Cologne papers were black-edged with cards inserted by relatives in memory of officers who had fallen—"For King and Fatherland! " the cards always said. I counted thirteen of these death notices in one issue of a Cologne paper. Now they have almost disappeared. I imagine that, because of the depressing effect of such a mass of these publications on the public mind, the families of killed officers have been asked to refrain from reciting their losses in print. Yet there are not wanting signs that the grim total piles up by the hour and the day.

Late this afternoon, when I walk around to the American consulate, I shall pass the office of the chief local paper; and there I am sure to find anywhere from seventy-five to a hundred men and women waiting for the appearance on a bulletin board of the latest list of dead, wounded and missing men who are credited to Aix-la-Chapelle and its vicinity. A new list goes up each afternoon, replacing the list of the day before. Sometimes it contains but a few names; sometimes a good many. Then there will be piteous scenes for a little while; but presently the mourners will go away, struggling to compose themselves as they go; for their Kaiser has asked them to make no show of their loss among their neighbors. Having made the supremest sacrifice they can make, short of offering up their own lives, they now make another and hide their grief away from sight. Surely, this war spares none at all—neither those who fight nor those who stay behind.

Toward dusk the streets will fill up with promenaders. Perhaps a regiment or so of troops, temporarily quartered here on the way to the front, will clank by, bound for their barracks in divers big music halls. The squares may be quite crowded with uniforms; or there may be only one gray coat in proportion to three or four black ones—this last is the commoner ratio. It all depends on the movements of the forces.

To-night the cafes will be open and the moving-picture places will run full blast; and the free concert will go on and there will be services in the cathedral of Charlemagne. The cafes that had English names when the war began have German ones now. Thus the Bristol has become the Crown Prince Café, and the Piccadilly is the Germania; but otherwise they are just as they were before the war started, and the business in them is quite as good, the residents say, as it ever was. Prices are no higher than they used to be—at least I have not found them high.

After the German fashion the diners will eat slowly and heavily; and afterward they will sit in clusters of three or four, drinking mugs of Munich or Pilsner, and talking deliberately. At the Crown Prince there will be dancing, and at two or three other places there will be music and maybe singing; but at the Kaiserhof, where I shall dine, there is nothing more exciting than beer and conversation. It was there, two nights ago, I met at the same time three Germans representing three dominant classes in the life of their country, and had from each of them the viewpoint of his class toward the war. They were, respectively, a business man, a scientist, and a soldier. The business man belongs to a firm of brothers which ranks almost with the Krupps in commercial importance. It has branches in many cities and agencies and plants in half a dozen countries. He said:

"We had not our daily victory to-day, eh? Well, so it goes; we must not expect to win always. We must have reverses, and heavy ones too; but in the end we must win. To lose now would mean national extinction. To win means Germany's commercial and military preeminence in this hemisphere.

"There can be but one outcome of this war—either Germany, as an empire, will cease to exist, or she will emerge the greatest Power, except the United States, on the face of the earth. And so sure are we of the result that to-day my brothers and I bought ground for doubling the size and capacity of our largest plant.

"In six weeks from now we shall have beaten France; in six months we shall have driven Russia to cover. For England it will take a year— perhaps longer. And then, as in all games, big and little, the losers will pay. France will be made to pay an indemnity from which she will never recover.

"Of Belgium I think we shall take a slice of seacoast; Germany needs ports on the English Channel. Russia will be so humbled that no longer will the Muscovite peril threaten Europe. Great Britain we shall crush utterly. She shall be shorn of her navy and she shall lose her colonies—certainly she shall lose India and Egypt. She will become a third-class Power and she will stay a third-class Power. Forget Japan— Germany will punish Japan in due season.

"Within five years from now I predict there will be an offensive and defensive alliance of all the Teutonic and all the Scandinavian races of Europe, with Bulgaria included, holding absolute dominion over this continent and stretching in an unbroken line from the North Sea to the Adriatic and the Black Sea.

"Europe is to have a new map, my friends, and Germany will be in the middle of that map. When this has been accomplished we shall talk about disarmament—not before. And first, we shall disarm our enemies who forced this war on us."

The scientist spoke next. He is a tall, spectacled, earnest Westphalian, who has invented and patented over a hundred separate devices used in electric-lighting properties, and, in between, has found time to travel round the world several times and write a book or two.

"I do not believe in war, " he said. "War has no place in the civilization of the world to-day; but this war was inevitable. Germany had to expand or be suffocated. And out of this war good will come for all the world, especially for Europe. We Germans are the most industrious, the most earnest and the best-educated race on this side of the ocean. To-day one-fourth of the population of Belgium cannot read and write. Under German influence illiteracy will disappear from among them. Russia stands for reaction; England for selfishness and perfidy; France for decadence. Germany stands for progress. Do not believe the claims of our foes that our Kaiser wishes to be another Napoleon and hold Europe under his thumb. What he wants for Germany and what he means to have is, first, breathing room for his people; and after that a fair share of the commercial opportunities of the world.

Paths of Glory

"German enlightenment and German institutions will do the reSt. And after this war—if we Germans win it—there will never be another universal war."

The soldier spoke last. He is a captain of field artillery, a member of a distinguished Prussian family, and one of the most noted big-game hunters in Europe. Three weeks ago, in front of Charleroi, a French sharpshooter put a bullet in him. It passed through his left forearm, pierced one lung and lodged in the muscles of his breast, where it lies imbedded. In a week from now he expects to rejoin his command.

To look at him you would never guess that he had so recently been wounded; his color is high and he moves with the stiff, precise alertness of the German army man. He is still wearing the coat he wore in the fight; there are two ragged little holes in the left sleeve and a puncture in the side of it; and it is spotted with stiff, dry, brown stains.

"I don't presume to know anything about the political or commercial aspects of this war," he said over his beer mug; "but I do know this: War was forced on us by these other Powers. They were jealous of us and they made the Austrian-Servian quarrel their quarrel. But when war came we were ready and they were not.

"Not until the mobilization was ordered did the people of Germany know the color of the field uniform of their soldiers; yet four millions of these service uniforms were made and finished and waiting in our military storehouses. Not until after the first shot was fired did we who are in the army know how many army corps we had, or the names of their commanders, or even the names of the officers composing the general staff.

"A week after we took the field our infantry, in heavy marching order, was covering fifty kilometers a day—thirty of your American miles—and doing it day after day without straggling and without any footsore men dropping behind.

"Do these things count in the sum total? I say they do. Our army will win because it deserves to win through being ready and being complete and being efficient. Don't discount the efficiency of our navy either. Remember, we Germans have the name of being thorough. When our fleet meets the British fleet I think you will find that we have a few Krupp surprises for them."

I may meet these confident gentlemen tonight. If not, it is highly probable I shall meet others who are equally confident, and who will express the same views, which they hold because they are the views of the German people.

At eleven o'clock, when I start back to the hotel, the streets will be almost empty. Aix will have gone to bed, and in bed it will peacefully stay unless a military Zeppelin sails over its rooftrees, making a noise like ten million locusts all buzzing at once. There were two Zeppelins aloft last night, and from my window I saw one of them quite plainly. It was hanging almost stationary in the northern sky, like a huge yellow gourd. After a while it made off toward the weSt. One day last week three of them passed, all bound presumably for Paris or Antwerp, or even London. That time the people grew a bit excited; but now they take a Zeppelin much as a matter of course, and only wonder mildly where it came from and whither it is going.

As for to-morrow, I imagine to-morrow will be another to-day; but yesterday was different. I had a streak of luck. It is forbidden to civilians, and more particularly to correspondents, to go prowling about eastern Belgium just now; but I found a friend in a naturalized German- American, formerly of Chicago, but living now in Germany, though he still retains his citizenship in the United States.

Like every one else in Aachen, he is doing something for the government, though I can only guess at the precise nature of his services. At any rate he had an automobile, a scarce thing to find in private hands in these times; and, what was more, he had a military pass authorizing him to go to Liege and to take two passengers along. He invited me to go with him for a day's ride through the country where the very first blows were swapped in the western theater of hostilities.

We started off in the middle of a fickle-minded shower, which first blew puffs of wetness in our faces, like spray on a flawy day at sea, and then broke off to let the sun shine through for a minute or two. For two or three kilometers after clearing the town we ran through a district that smiled with peace and groaned with plenty. On the verandas of funny little gray roadhouses with dripping red roofs officers sat over their breakfast coffee. A string of wagons passed us, bound inward, full of big, white, clean-looking German pigs. A road builder, repairing the ruts made by the guns and baggage trains, stood aside for us to pass and pulled off his hat to us. This was Europe as it used to be—Europe as most American tourists knew it.

We came to a tall barber pole which a careless painter had striped with black on white instead of with red on white, and we knew by that we had arrived at the frontier. Also, there stood alongside the pole a royal forest ranger in green, with a queer cockaded hat on his head, doing sentry duty. As we stopped to show him our permits, and to give him a ripe pear and a Cologne paper, half a dozen soldiers came tumbling out of the guardroom in the little customhouse, and ran up to beg from us, not pears, but papers. Clear to Liege we were to be importuned every few rods by soldiers begging for papers. Some had small wooden sign-boards bearing the word Zeitung, which they would lift and swing across the path of an approaching automobile. I began to believe after a while that if a man had enough newspapers in stock he could bribe his way through the German troops clear into France.

These fellows who gathered about us now were of the Landsturm, men in their late thirties and early forties, with long, shaggy mustaches. Their kind forms the handle of the mighty hammer whose steel nose is battering at France. Every third one of them wore spectacles, showing that the back lines of the army are extensively addicted to the favorite Teutonic sport of being nearsighted. Also, their coat sleeves invariably were too long for them, and hid their big hands almost to the knuckles. This is a characteristic I have everywhere noted among the German privates. If the French soldier's coat is over-lengthy in the skirt the German's is ultra-generous with cloth in the sleeves. I saw that their hair was beginning to get shaggy, showing that they had been in the field some weeks, since every German soldier—officer and private alike—leaves the barracks so close-cropped that his skin shows pinky through the bristles. Among them was one chap in blue sailor's garb, left behind doubtless when forty-five hundred naval reserves passed through three days before to work the big guns in front of Antwerp.

We went on. At first there was nothing to show we had entered Belgium except that the Prussian flag did not hang from a pole in front of every farmhouse, but only in front of every fourth house, say, or every fifth one. Then came stretches of drenched fields, vacant except for big black ravens and nimble piebald magpies, which bickered among themselves in the neglected and matted grain; and then we swung round a curve in the rutted roadway and were in the town of Battice.

No; we were not in the town of Battice. We were where the town of Battice had been—where it stood six weeks ago. It was famous then for its fat, rich cheeses and its green damson plums. Now, and no doubt for years to come, it will be chiefly notable as having been the town where, it is said, Belgian civilians first fired on the German troops from roofs and windows, and where the Germans first inaugurated their ruthless system of reprisal on houses and people alike.

Literally this town no longer existed. It was a scrap-heap, if you like, but not a town. Here had been a great trampling out of the grapes of wrath, and most sorrowful was the vintage that remained.

It was a hard thing to level these Belgian houses absolutely, for they were mainly built of stone or of thick brick coated over with a hard cement. So, generally, the walls stood, even in Battice; but always the roofs were gone, and the window openings were smudged cavities, through which you looked and saw square patches of the sky if your eyes inclined upward, or else blackened masses of ruination if you gazed straight in at the interiors. Once in a while one had been thrown flat. Probably big guns operated here. In such a case there was an avalanche of broken masonry cascading out into the roadway.

Midway of the mile-long avenue of utter waste which we now traversed we came on a sort of small square. Here was the yellow village church. It lacked a spire and a cross, and the front door was gone, so we could see the wrecked altar and the splintered pews within. Flanking the church there had been a communal hall, which was now shapeless, irredeemable wreckage. A public well had stood in the open space between church and hall, with a design of stone pillars about it. The open mouth of the well we could see was choked with foul debris; but a shell had struck squarely among the pillars and they fell inward like wigwam poles, forming a crazy apex. I remember distinctly two other things: a picture of an elderly man with whiskers—one of those smudged atrocities that are called in the States crayon portraits—hanging undamaged on the naked wall of what had been an upper bedroom; and a wayside shrine of the sort so common in the Catholic countries of Europe. A shell had hit it a glancing blow, so that the little china figure of the Blessed Virgin lay in bits behind the small barred opening of the shrine.

Of living creatures there was none. Heretofore, in all the blasted towns I had visited, there was some human life stirring. One could count on seeing one of the old women who are so numerous in these Belgian hamlets—more numerous, I think, than anywhere else on earth. In my mind I had learned to associate such a sight with at least one old woman—an incredibly old woman, with a back bent like a measuring worm's, and a cap on her scanty hair, and a face crosshatched with a million wrinkles—who would be pottering about at the back of some half- ruined house or maybe squatting in a desolated doorway staring at us with her rheumy, puckered eyes. Or else there would be a hunchback— crooked spines being almost as common in parts of Belgium as goiters are in parts of Switzerland. But Battice had become an empty tomb, and was as lonely and as silent as a tomb. Its people—those who survived—had fled from it as from an abomination.

Beyond Battice stood another village, called Herve; and Herve was Battice all over again, with variations. At this place, during the first few hours of actual hostilities between the little country and the big one, the Belgians had tried to stem the inpouring German flood, as was proved by wrecks of barricades in the high street. One barricade had been built of wagon bodies and the big iron hods of road-scrapers; the wrecks of these were still piled at the road's edge. Yet there remained tangible proof of the German claim that they did not harry and burn indiscriminately, except in cases where the attack on them was by general concert.

Here and there, on the principal street, in a row of ruins, stood a single house that was intact and undamaged. It was plain enough to be seen that pains had been taken to spare it from the common fate of its neighbors. Also, I glimpsed one short side street that had come out of the fiery visitation whole and unscathed, proving, if it proved anything, that even in their red heat the Germans had picked and chosen the fruit for the wine press of their vengeance.

After Herve we encountered no more destruction by wholesale, but only destruction by piecemeal, until, nearing Liege, we passed what remained of the most northerly of the ring of fortresses that formed the city's defenses. The conquerors had dismantled it and thrown down the guns, so that of the fort proper there was nothing except a low earthen wall, almost like a natural ridge in the earth.

All about it was an entanglement of barbed wire; the strands were woven and interwoven, tangled and twined together, until they suggested nothing so much as a great patch of blackberry briers after the leaves have dropped from the vines in the fall of the year. To take the works the Germans had to cut through these trochas. It seemed impossible to believe human beings could penetrate them, especially when one was told that the Belgians charged some of the wires with high electricity, so that those of the advancing party who touched them were frightfully burned and fell, with their garments blazing, into the jagged wire brambles, and were held there until they died.

Before the charge and the final hand-to-hand fight, however, there was shelling. There was much shelling. Shells from the German guns that fell short or overshot the mark descended in the fields, and for a mile round these fields were plowed as though hundreds of plowshares had sheared the sod this way and that, until hardly a blade of grass was left to grow in its ordained place. Where shells had burst after they struck were holes in the earth five or six feet across and five or six feet deep. Shells from the German guns and from the Belgian guns had made a most hideous hash of a cluster of small cottages flanking a small smelting plant which stood directly in the line of fire. Some of these houses—workmen's homes, I suppose they had been—were of frame, sheathed over with squares of tin put on in a diamond pattern; and you could see places where a shell, striking such a wall a glancing blow, had scaled it as a fish is scaled with a knife, leaving the bare wooden ribs showing below. The next house, and the next, had been hit squarely and plumply amidships, and they were gutted as fishes are gutted. One house in twenty, perhaps, would be quite whole, except for broken windows and fissures in the roof—as though the whizzing shells had spared it deliberately.

I recall that of one house there was left standing only a breadth of front wall between the places where windows had been. It rose in a ragged column to the line of the roof-rafters—only, of course, there was neither roof nor rafter now. On the face of the column, as though done in a spirit of bitter irony, was posted a proclamation, signed by the burgomaster and the military commandant, calling on the vanished dwellers of this place to preserve their tranquillity.

On the side of the fort away from the city, and in the direction whence we had come, a corporal's guard had established itself in a rent-asunder house in order to be out of the wet. On the front of the house they had hung a captured Belgian bugler's uniform and a French dragoon's overcoat, which latter garment was probably a trophy brought back from the lower lines of fighting; it made you think of an old-clothes-man's shop. The corporal came forth to look at our passes before permitting us to go on. He was a dumpy, good-natured-looking Hanoverian with patchy saffron whiskers sprouting out on him.

"Ach! yes, " he said in answer to my conductor's question. "Things are quiet enough here now; but on Monday"—that would be three days before— "we shot sixteen men here—rioters and civilians who fired on our troops, and one grave-robber—a dirty hound! They are yonder. "

He swung his arm; and following its swing we saw a mound of fresh-turned clay, perhaps twenty feet in length, which made a yellow streak against the green of a small inclosed pasture about a hundred yards away. We saw many such mounds that day; and this one where the ignoble sixteen lay was the shortest of the lot. Some mounds were fifty or sixty feet in length. I presume there were distinguishing marks on the filled-up trenches where the German dead lay, but from the automobile we could make out none.

As we started on again, after giving the little Hanoverian the last treasured copy of a paper we had managed to keep that long against continual importunity, a big Belgian dog, with a dragging tail and a sharp jackal nose, loped round from behind an undamaged cow barn which stood back of the riven shell of a house where the soldiers were quartered. He had the air about him of looking for somebody or something.

He stopped short, sniffing and whining, at sight of the gray coats bunched in the doorway; and then, running back a few yards, with his head all the time turned to watch the strangers, he sat on his haunches, stuck his pointed muzzle upward toward the sky and fetched a long, homesick howl from the bottom of his disconsolate canine soul. When we turned a bend in the road, to enter the first

Paths of Glory

recognizable street of Liege, he was still hunkered down there in the rain. He finished the picture; he keynoted it. The composition of it—for me—was perfect now.

I mean no levity when I say that Liege was well shaken before taken; but merely that the phrase is the apt one for use, because it better expresses the truth than any other I can think of. Yet, considering what it went through, last month, Liege seemed to have emerged in better shape than one would have expected.

Driving into the town I saw more houses with white flags—the emblem of complete surrender—fluttering from sill and coping, than houses bearing marks of the siege. In the bombardment the shells mostly appeared to have passed above the town—which was natural enough, seeing that the principal Belgian forts stood on the hilltops westward of and overlooking the city; and the principal German batteries—at least, until the last day of fighting—were posted behind temporary defenses, hastily thrown up, well to the east and north.

Liege, squatted in the natural amphitheater below, practically escaped the fire of the big guns. The main concern of the noncombatants, they tell me, was to shelter themselves from the street fighting, which, by all accounts, was both stubborn and sanguinary. The doughty Walloons who live in this corner of Belgium have had the name of being sincere and willing workers with bare steel since the days when Charles the Bold, of Burgundy, sought to curb their rebellious spirits by razing their city walls and massacring some ten thousand of them. And quite a spell before that, I believe, Julius Caesar found them tough to bend and hard to break.

As for the Germans, checked as they had been in their rush on France by a foe whom they had regarded as too puny to count as a factor in the war, they sacrificed themselves by hundreds and thousands to win breathing space behind standing walls until their great seventeen-inch siege guns could be brought from Essen and mounted by the force of engineers who came for that purpose direct from the Krupp works.

In that portion of the town lying west of the Meuse we counted perhaps ten houses that were leveled flat and perhaps twenty that were now but burnt-out, riddled hulls of houses, as empty and useless as so many shucked pea-pods. Of the bridges spanning the river, the principal one, a handsome four-span structure of stone ornamented with stone figures of river gods, lay now in shattered fragments, choking the current, where the Belgians themselves had blown it apart. One more bridge, or perhaps two—I cannot be sure—were closed to traffic because dynamite had made them unsafe; but the remaining bridges, of which I think there were three, showed no signs of rough treatment. Opposite the great University there was a big, black, ragged scar to show where a block of dwellings had stood.

Liege, to judge from its surface aspect, could not well have been quieter. Business went on; buyers and sellers filled the side streets and dotted the long stone quays. Old Flemish men fished industriously below the wrecked stone bridge, where the debris made new eddies in the swift, narrow stream; and blue pigeons swarmed in the plaza before the Palais de Justice, giving to the scene a suggestion of St. Mark's Square at Venice.

The German Landwehr, who were everywhere about, treated the inhabitants civilly enough, and the inhabitants showed no outward resentment against the Germans. But beneath the lid a whole potful of potential trouble was brewing, if one might believe what the Germans told us. We talked with a young lieutenant of infantry who in more peaceful times had been a staff cartoonist for a Berlin comic paper. He received us beneath the portico of the Theatre Royale, built after the model of the Odeon in Paris. Two waspish rapid-fire guns stood just within the shelter of the columns, with their black snouts pointing this way and that to command the sweep of the three-cornered Place du Theatre. A company of soldiers was quartered in the theater itself. At night, so the lieutenant said, those men who were off duty rummaged the costumes out of the dressing rooms, put them on, and gave mock plays, with music. An officer's horse occupied what I think must have been the box office. It put its head out of a little window just over our heads and nickered when other horses passed. Against the side of the building were posters advertising a French company to play the Gallicized version of an American farce—"Baby Mine"—by Margaret Mayo. The borders of the posters were ornamented with prints of American flags done in the proper colors.

"Yes, Liege seems quiet enough, " said the lieutenant; "but we expect a revolt to break out at any time. We expected it last night, and the guard in the streets was tripled and doubled; and these little dears"— patting the muzzle of one of the machine guns—"were put here; and more like them were mounted on the porticoes of the Hotel de Ville and the Palais de Justice. So nothing happened in the city proper, though in the outskirts three soldiers disappeared and are supposed to have been murdered, and a high officer"—he did not give the name or the rank— "was waylaid and killed just beyond the environs.

"Now we fear that the uprising may come to-night. For the last three days the residents, in great numbers, have been asking for permits to leave Liege and go into neutral territory in Holland, or to other parts of their own country. To us this sudden exodus—there seems to be no reason for it—looks significant.

"These people are naturally turbulent. Always they have been so. Most of them are makers of parts for firearms—gunmaking, you know, was the principal industry here—and they are familiar with weapons; and many of the men are excellent shots. This increases the danger. At first they were content to ambush single soldiers who strayed into obscure quarters after dark. Now it is forbidden for less than three soldiers in a party to go anywhere at night; and they think from this that we are afraid, and are growing more daring.

"By day they smile at us and bow, and are as polite as dancing masters; but at night the same men who smile at us will cheerfully cut the throat of any German who is foolish enough to venture abroad alone.

"Besides, this town and all the towns between here and Brussels are being secretly flooded with papers printed in French telling the people that we have been beaten everywhere to the south, and that the Allies are but a few miles away; and that if they will rise in numbers and destroy the garrisons re-enforcements will arrive the next morning to hold the district against us.

"If they do rise it will be Louvain all over again. We shall burn Liege and kill all who are suspected of being in league against our troops. Assuredly many innocent ones will suffer then with the guilty; but what else can we do? We are living above a seething volcano. "

Certainly, though, never did volcano seethe more quietly.

Paths of Glory

The garrison commander would not hear of our visiting any of the wrecked Belgian fortresses on the wooded heights behind the city. As a reason for his refusal he said that explosives in the buried magazines were beginning to go off, making it highly dangerous for spectators to venture near them. However, he had no objection to our going to a certain specified point within the zone of supposed safety. With a noncommissioned officer to guide us we climbed up a miry footpath to the crest of a low hill; and from a distance of perhaps a hundred yards we looked across at what was left of Fort Loncin, one of the principal defenses.

I am wrong there. We did not look at what was left of Fort Loncin. Literally nothing was left of it. As a fort it was gone, obliterated, wiped out, vanished. It had been of a triangular shape. It was of no shape now. We found it difficult to believe that the work of human hands had wrought destruction so utter and overwhelming. Where masonry walls had been was a vast junk heap; where stout magazines had been bedded down in hard concrete was a crater; where strong barracks had stood was a jumbled, shuffled nothingness.

Standing there on the shell-torn hilltop, looking across to where the Krupp surprise wrote its own testimonials at its first time of using, in characters so deadly and devastating, I found myself somehow thinking of that foolish nursery tale wherein it is recited that a pig built himself a house of straw, and the wolf came; and he huffed and he puffed and he blew the house down. The noncommissioned officer told us an unknown number of the defenders, running probably into the hundreds, had been buried so deeply beneath the ruins of the fort in the last hours of the fighting that the Germans had been unable to recover the bodies. Even as he spoke a puff of wind brought to our nostrils a smell which, once a man gets it into his nose, he will never get the memory of it out again so long as he has a nose. Being sufficiently sick, we departed thence.

As we rode back, and had got as far as the two ruined villages, it began to rain very hard. The rain, as it splashed into the puddles, stippled the farther reaches of the road thickly with dots, and its slanting lines turned everything into one gray etching which you might have labeled Desolation! And you would make no mistake in your labeling. Then—with one of those tricks of deliberate drama by which Nature sometimes shames stage managers—the late afternoon sun came out just after we crossed the frontier, and shone on us; and on the dapper young officers driving out in carriages; and on the peaceful German country places with their formal gardens; and on a crate of fat white German pigs riding to market to be made up into sausages for the placid burghers of Aix-la-Chapelle.

Chapter 8

Three Generals and a Cook

To get to the civic midriff of the ancient and honorable French city of Laon you must ascend a road that winds in spirals about a high, steep hill, like threads cut in a screw. Doing this you come at length to the flat top of the screw—a most curiously flat top—and find on this side of you the Cathedral and the market-place, and on that side of you the Hotel de Ville, where a German flag hangs among the iron lilies in the grille-worked arms of the Republic above the front doors. Dead ahead of you is the Prefecture, which is a noble stone building, facing southward toward the River Aisne; and it has decorations of the twentieth century, a gateway of the thirteenth century and plumbing of the third century, when there was no plumbing to speak of.

We had made this journey and now the hour was seven in the evening, and we were dining in the big hall of the Prefecture as the guests of His Excellency, Field Marshal von Heeringen, commanding the Seventh Army of the German Kaiser—dining, I might add, from fine French plates, with smart German orderlies for waiters.

Except us five, and one other, the twenty-odd who sat about the great oblong table were members of the Over-General's staff. We five were Robert J. Thompson, American consul at Aix-la-Chapelle; McCutcheon and Bennett, of the Chicago Tribune; Captain Alfred Mannesmann, of the great German manufacturing firm of Mannesmann Mulag; and myself. The one other was a Berlin artist, by name Follbehr, who having the run of the army, was going out daily to do quick studies in water colors in the trenches and among the batteries. He did them remarkably well, too, seeing that any minute a shell might come and spatter him all over his own drawing board. All the rest, though, were generals and colonels and majors, and such—youngish men mostly. Excluding our host I do not believe there was a man present who had passed fifty years of age; but the General was nearer eighty than fifty, being one of the veterans of the Franco-Prussian War, whom their Emperor had ordered out of desk jobs in the first days of August to shepherd his forces in the field. At his call they came—Von Heeringen and Von Hindenberg and Von Zwehl, to mention three names that speedily became catchwords round the world— with their gray heads full of Prussian war tactics;

and very soon their works had justified the act of their imperial master in choosing them for leadership, and now they had new medals at their throats and on their breasts to overlay the old medals they won back in 1870-71.

Like many of the older officers of the German Army I met, Von Heeringen spoke no English, in which regard he was excessively unlike ninety per cent of the younger officers. Among them it was an uncommon thing in my experience to find one who did not know at least a smattering of English and considerably more than a smattering of understandable French. Even that marvelous organism, the German private soldier, was apt to astonish you at unexpected moments by answering in fair-enough English the questions you put to him in fractured and dislocated German.

Not once or twice, but a hundred times during my cruising about in Belgium and Germany and France, I laboriously unloaded a string of crippled German nouns and broken-legged adjectives and unsocketed verbs on a hickory-looking sentry, only to have him reply to me in my own tongue. It would come out then that he had been a waiter at a British seaside resort or a steward on a Hamburg-American liner; or, oftener still, that he had studied English at the public schools in his native town of Kiel, or Coblenz, or Dresden, or somewhere.

The officers' English, as I said before, was nearly always ready and lubricant. To one who spoke no French and not enough German to hurt him, this proficiency in language on the part of the German standing army was a precious boon. The ordinary double-barreled dictionary of phrases had already disclosed itself as a most unsatisfying volume in which to put one's trust. It was wearing on the disposition to turn the leaves trying to find out how to ask somebody to pass the butter and find instead whole pages of parallel columns of translated sentences given over to such questions as "Where is the aunt of my stepfather's second cousin? "

As a rule a man does not go to Europe in time of war to look up his relatives by marriage. He may even have gone there to avoid them. War is terrible enough without lugging in all the remote kinsfolk a fellow has. How much easier, then, to throw oneself on the superior educational qualifications of the German military machine. Somebody was sure to have a linguistic life net there, rigged and ready for you to drop into.

Paths of Glory

It was so in this instance, as it has been so in many instances before and since. The courteous gentlemen who sat at my right side and at my left spoke in German or French or English as the occasion suited, while old Von Heeringen boomed away in rumbling German phrases. As I ate I studied him.

Three weeks later, less a day, I met by appointment Lord Kitchener and spent forty minutes, or thereabouts, in his company at the War Office in London. In the midst of the interview, as I sat facing Kitchener I began wondering, in the back part of my head, who it was Lord Kitchener reminded me of. Suddenly the answer came to me, and it jolted me. The answer was Von Heeringen.

Physically the two men—Kitchener of Khartoum and Von Heeringen, the Gray Ghost of Metz—had nothing in common; mentally I conceived them to be unlike. Except that both of them held the rank of field marshal, I could put my finger on no point of similarity, either in personality or in record, which these men shared between them. It is true they both served in the war of 1870-71; but at the outset this parallel fell flat, too, because one had been a junior officer on the German side and the other a volunteer on the French side. One was a Prussian in every outward aspect; the other was as British as it is possible for a Briton to be. One had been at the head of the general staff of his country, and was now in the field in active service with a sword at his side. The other, having served his country in the field for many years, now sat intrenched behind a roll-top desk, directing the machinery of the War Office, with a pencil for a baton. Kitchener was in his robust sixties, with a breast like a barrel; Von Heeringen was in his shrinking, drying-up seventies, and his broad shoulders had already begun to fold in on his ribs and his big black eyes to retreat deeper into his skull. One was beaky-nosed, hatchet-headed, bearded; the other was broad-faced and shaggily mustached. One had been famed for his accessibility; the other for his inaccessibility.

So, because of these acutely dissimilar things, I marveled to myself that day in London why, when I looked at Kitchener, I should think of Von Heeringen. In another minute, though, I knew why: Both men radiated the same quality of masterfulness; both of them physically typified competency; both of them looked on the world with the eyes of men who are born to have power and to hold dominion over lesser men. Put either of these two in the rags of a beggar or the motley of a Pantaloon, and at a glance you would know him for a leader. Considering that we were supposed to be at the front on this evening at Laon, the food was good, there being a soup, and the invariable veal on which a German buttresses the solid foundations of his dinner, a salad and fruit, red wine and white wine and brandy. Also, there were flies amounting in numbers to a great multitude. The talk, like the flies, went to and fro about the table; and always it was worth hearing, since it dealt largely with first-hand experiences in the very heart of the fighting.

Yet I must add that not all the talk was talk of war. In peaceful Aix-la-Chapelle, whence we had come, the people knew but one topic. Here, on the forward frayed edge of the battle line, the men who had that day played their part in battle occasionally spoke of other things. I recall there was a discussion between Captain von Theobald, of the Artillery, and Major Humplmayer, of the Automobile Corps, on the merits of a painting that filled one of the panels in the big, handsome, overdecorated hall. The major won, which was natural enough, since, in time of peace, he was by way of being a collector of and dealer in art objects at Munich. Somebody else mentioned big-game shooting. For five minutes, then, or such a matter, the ways of big game and the ways of shooting it held the interest of half a dozen men at our curve of the table.

In such an interlude as this the listener might almost have lulled himself into the fancy that, after all, there was no war; that these courteous, gray-coated, shoulder-strapped gentlemen were not at present engaged in the business of killing their fellowmen; that this building wherein we sat, with its florid velvet carpets underfoot and its too-heavy chandeliers overhead, was not the captured chateau of the governor of a French province; and that the deep-eyed, white-fleeced, bull-voiced old man who sat just opposite was not the commander of sundry hundreds of thousands of fighting men with guns in their hands, but surely was no more and no less than the elderly lord of the manor, who, having a fancy for regimentals, had put on his and had pinned some glittering baubles on his coat and then had invited a few of his friends and neighbors in for a simple dinner on this fine evening of the young autumn.

Yet we knew that already the war had taken toll of nearly every man in uniform who was present about this board. General von Heeringen's two sons, both desperately wounded, were lying in field hospitals—one in East Prussia, the other in northern France not many miles from where we were. His second in command had two sons—his only two sons—killed in the same battle three weeks before. When, a few minutes earlier, I had heard this I stared at him, curious to see what marks so hard a stroke would leave on a man. I saw only a grave middle-aged gentleman, very attentive to the consul who sat beside him, and very polite to us all.

Prince Scharmberg-Lippe, whom we had passed driving away from the Prefecture in his automobile as we drove to it in ours, was the last of four brothers. The other three were killed in the first six weeks of fighting. Our own companion, Captain Mannesmann, heard only the day before, when we stopped at Hirson—just over the border from Belgium— that his cousin had won the Iron Cross for conspicuous courage, and within three days more was to hear that this same cousin had been sniped from ambush during a night raid down the left wing.

Nor had death been overly stingy to the members of the Staff itself. We gathered as much from chance remarks. And so, as it came to be eight o'clock, I caught myself watching certain vacant chairs at our table and at the two smaller tables in the next room with a strained curiosity.

One by one the vacant chairs filled up. At intervals the door behind me would open and an officer would clank in, dusted over with the sift of the French roads. He would bow ceremoniously to his chief and then to the company generally, slip into an unoccupied chair, give an order over his shoulder to a soldier-waiter, and at once begin to eat his dinner with the air of a man who has earned it. After a while there was but one place vacant at our table; it was next to me. I could not keep my eyes away from it. It got on my nerves—that little gap in the circle; that little space of white linen, bare of anything but two unfilled glasses. To me it became as portentous as an unscrewed coffin lid. No one else seemed to notice it. Cigars had been passed round and the talk eddied casually back and forth with the twisty smoke wreaths.

An orderly drew the empty chair back with a thump. I think I jumped. A slender man, whose uniform fitted him as though it had been his skin, was sitting down beside me. Unlike those who came before him, he had entered so quietly that I had not sensed his coming. I heard the soldier call him Excellency; and I heard him tell the soldier not to give him any soup. We swapped commonplaces, I telling him what my business there was; and for a little while he plied his knife and fork busily, making the heavy gold curb chain on his left wrist tinkle musically.

"I'm rather glad they did not get me this afternoon, " he said as though to make conversation with a stranger. "This is first-rate veal—better than we usually have here. "

"Get you? " I said. "Who wanted to get you? "

"Our friends, the enemy, " he answered. "I was in one of our trenches rather well toward the front, and a shell or two struck just behind me. I think, from their sound, they were French shells. "

This debonair gentleman, as presently transpired, was Colonel von Scheller, for four years consul to the German Embassy at Washington, more lately minister for foreign affairs of the kingdom of Saxony, and now doing staff duty in the ordnance department here at the German center. He had the sharp brown eyes of a courageous fox terrier, a mustache that turned up at the ends, and a most beautiful command of the English language and its American idioms. He hurried along with his dinner and soon he had caught up with us.

"I suggest, " he said, "that we go out on the terrace to drink our coffee. It is about time for the French to start their evening benediction, as we call it. They usually quit firing their heavy guns just before dark, and usually begin again at eight and keep it up for an hour or two. "

So we two took our coffee cups and our cigars in our hands and went out through a side passage to the terrace, and sat on a little iron bench, where a shaft of light, from a window of the room we had just quit, showed a narrow streak of flowering plants beyond the bricked wall and a clump of red and yellow woodbine on a low wall.

The rest lay in blackness; but I knew, from what I had seen before dusk came, that we must be somewhere near the middle of a broad terrace—a hanging garden rather—full of sundials and statues and flower beds, which overhung the southern face of the Hill of Laon, and from which, in daylight, a splendid view might be had of wooded slopes falling away into wide, flat valleys, and wide, flat valleys rising again to form more wooded slopes. I knew, too, from what I remembered, that the plateau immediately beneath us was flyspecked with the roofs of small abandoned villages; and that the road which ran straight from the base of the heights toward the remote river was a-crawl with supply wagons and ammunition wagons going forward to the German batteries, seven miles away, and with scouts and messengers in automobiles and on motor cycles, and the day's toll of wounded in ambulances coming back from the front.

We could not see them when we went to the parapet and looked downward into the black gulf below, but the rumbling of the wheels and the panting of the motors came up to us. With these came, also, the remote music of those queer little trumpets carried by the soldiers who ride beside the drivers of German military automobiles; and this sounded as thinly and plaintively to our ears as the cries of sandpipers heard a long way off across a windy beach.

We could hear something else too: the evening benediction had started. Now fast, now slow, like the beating of a feverish pulse, the guns sounded in faint throbs; and all along the horizon from southeast to southwest, and back again, ran flares and waves of a sullen red radiance. The light flamed high at one instant—like fireworks—and at the next it died almost to a glow, as though a great bed of peat coals or a vast limekiln lay on the farthermost crest of the next chain of hills. It was the first time I had ever seen artillery fire at night, though I had heard it often enough by then in France and in Belgium, and even in Germany; for when the wind blew out of the west we could hear in Aix-la-Chapelle the faint booming of the great cannons before Antwerp, days and nights on end.

I do not know how long I stood and looked and listened. Eventually I was aware that the courteous Von Scheller, standing at my elbow, was repeating something he had already stated at least once.

"Those brighter flashes you see, apparently coming from below the other lights, are our guns, " he was saying. "They seem to be below the others because they are nearer to us. Personally I don't think these evening volleys do very much damage, " he went on as though vaguely regretful that the dole of death by night should be so scanty, "because it is impossible for the men in the outermost observation pits to see the effect of the shots; but we answer, as you notice, just to show the French and English we are not asleep. "

Those iron vespers lasted, I should say, for the better part of an hour. When they were ended we went indoors. Everybody was assembled in the long hall of the Prefecture, and a young officer was smashing out marching songs on the piano. The Berlin artist made an art gallery of the billiard table and was exhibiting the water-color sketches he had done that day—all very dashing and spirited in their treatment, though a bit splashy and scrambled-eggish as to the use of the pigments.

A very young man, with the markings of a captain on shoulder and collar, came in and went up to General von Heeringen and showed him something— something that looked like a very large and rather ornamental steel coal scuttle which had suffered from a serious personal misunderstanding with an ax. The elongated top of it, which had a fluted, rudder-like adornment, made you think of Siegfried's helmet in the opera; but the bottom, which was squashed out of shape, made you think of a total loss.

When the general had finished looking at this object we all had a chance to finger it. The young captain seemed quite proud of it and bore it off with him to the dining room. It was what remained of a bomb, and had been loaded with slugs of lead and those iron cherries that are called shrapnel. A French flyer had dropped it that afternoon with intent to destroy one of the German captive balloons and its operator. The young officer was the operator of the balloon in question. It was his daily duty to go aloft, at the end of a steel tether, and bob about for seven hours at a stretch, studying the effects of the shell fire and telephoning down directions for the proper aiming of the guns. He had been up seven hundred feet in the air that afternoon, with no place to go in case of accident, when the Frenchman came over and tried to hit him. "It struck within a hundred meters of me, " called back the young captain as he disappeared through the dining-room doorway. "Made quite a noise and tore up the earth considerably. "

"He was lucky—the young Herr Captain, " said Von Scheller— "luckier than his predecessor. A fortnight ago one of the enemy's flyers struck one of our balloons with a bomb and the gas envelope exploded. When the wreckage reached the earth there was nothing much left of the operator— poor fellow! —except the melted buttons on his coat. There are very few safe jobs in this army, but being a captive-balloon observer is one of the least safe of them all. "

I had noted that the young captain wore in the second buttonhole of his tunic the black-and-white-striped ribbon and the black-and-white Maltese Cross; and now when I looked about me I saw that at least every third man of the present company likewise bore such a decoration. I knew the Iron Cross was given to a man only for gallant conduct in time of war at the peril of his life.

A desire to know a few details beset me. Humplmayer, the scholarly art dealer, was at my side. He had it too—the Iron Cross of the first class.

"You won that lately? " I began, touching the ribbon.

"Yes, " he said; "only the other day I received it. "

"And for what, might I ask? " said I, pressing my advantage.

"Oh, " he said, "I've been out quite a bit in the night air lately. You know we Germans are desperately afraid of night air. "

Later I learned—though not from Humplmayer—that he had for a period of weeks done scout work in an automobile in hostile territory; which meant that he rode in the darkness over the strange roads of an alien country, exposed every minute to the chances of ambuscade and barbed-wire mantraps and the like. I judge he earned his bauble.

I tried Von Theobald next—a lynx-faced, square-shouldered young man of the field guns. To him I put the question: "What have you done, now, to merit the bestowal of the Cross? "

"Well, " he said—and his smile was born of embarrassment, I thought— "there was shooting once or twice, and I—well, I did not go away. I remained. "

So after that I quit asking. But it was borne in upon me that if these gold-braceletted, monocled, wasp-waisted exquisites could go jauntily forth for flirtations with death as afore-time I had seen them going, then also they could be marvelously modest touching on their own performances in the event of their surviving those most fatal blandishments.

Pretty soon we told the Staff good night, according to the ritualistic Teutonic fashion, and took ourselves off to bed; for the next day was expected to be a full day, which it was indeed and verily. In the hotels of the town, such as they were, officers were billeted, four to the room and two to the bed; but the commandant enthroned at the Hotel de Ville looked after our comfort. He sent a soldier to nail a notice on the gate of one of the handsomest houses in Laon—a house whence the tenants had fled at the coming of the Germans—which notice gave warning to all whom it might concern that Captain Mannesmann, who carried the Kaiser's own pass, and four American Herren were, until further orders, domiciled there. And the soldier tarried to clean our boots while we slept and bring us warm shaving water in the morning.

Being thus provided for we tramped away through the empty winding streets to Number Five, Rue St. Cyr, which was a big, fine three-story mansion with its own garden and courtyard. Arriving there we drew lots for bedrooms. It fell to me to occupy one that evidently belonged to the master of the house. He must have run away in a hurry. His bathrobe still hung on a peg; his other pair of suspenders dangled over the footboard; and his shaving brush, with dried lather on it, was on the floor. I stepped on it as I got into bed and hurt my foot.

Goodness knows I was tired enough, but I lay awake a while thinking what changes in our journalistic fortunes thirty days had brought us. Five weeks before, bearing dangerously dubious credentials, we had trailed afoot—a suspicious squad—at the tail of the German columns, liable to be halted and locked up any minute by any fingerling of a sublieutenant who might be so minded to so serve us. In that stressful time a war correspondent was almost as popular, with the officialdom of the German army, as the Asiatic cholera would have been. The privates were our best friends then. Just one month, to the hour and the night, after we slept on straw as quasi-prisoners and under an armed guard in a schoolhouse belonging to the Prince de Caraman-Chimay, at Beaumont, we dined with the commandant of a German garrison in the castle of another prince of the same name—the Prince de Chimay—at the town of Chimay, set among the timbered preserves of the ancient house of Chimay. In Belgium, at the end of August, we fended and foraged for ourselves aboard a train of wounded and prisoners.

Paths of Glory

In northern France, at the end of September, Prince Reuss, German minister to Persia, but serving temporarily in the Red Cross Corps, had bestirred himself to find lodgings for us. And now, thanks to a newborn desire on the part of the Berlin War Office to let the press of America know something of the effects of their operations on the people of the invaded states, here we were, making free with a strange French gentleman's chateau and messing with an Over-General's Staff. Lying there, in another man's bed, I felt like a burglar and I slept like an oyster—the oyster being, as naturalists know, a most sound sleeper.

In the morning there was breakfast at the great table—the flies of the night before being still present—with General von Heeringen inquiring most earnestly as to how we had rested, and then going out to see to the day's killing. Before doing so, however, he detailed the competent Captain von Theobald and the efficient Lieutenant Giebel to serve for the day as our guides while we studied briefly the workings of the German war machine in the actual theater of war.

It was under their conductorship that about noon we aimed our automobiles for the spot where, in accordance with provisions worked out in advance, but until that moment unknown to us, we were to lunch with another general—Von Zwehl, of the reserves. We left the hill, where the town was, some four miles behind us, and when we had passed through two wrecked and silent villages and through three of those strips of park timber which Continentals call forests, we presently drew up and halted and dismounted where a thick fringe of undergrowth, following the line of an old and straggly thorn hedge, met the road at right angles on the comb of a small ridge commanding a view of the tablelands to the southward.

As we climbed up the banks we were aware of certain shelters which were like overgrown rabbit hutches cunningly contrived of wattled faggots and straw sheaves plaited together. They had tarpaulin interlinings and dug-out earthen floors covered over thickly with straw. These cozy small shacks hid themselves behind a screen of haws among the scattered trees which flanked an ancient fortification, abandoned many years before, I judged, by the grass-grown looks of it. Out in front, upon the open crest of the rise, staff officers were grouped about two telescopes mounted on tripods. An old man—you could tell by the hunch of his shoulders he was old—sat on a camp chair with his back to us and his face against the barrels of one of the telescopes. With his long dust-colored coat and the lacings of violent scarlet upon his cap and his upturned collar he made you think of one of those big gray African parrots that talk so fluently and bite so viciously. But when, getting nimbly up, he turned to greet us and be introduced the resemblance vanished.

There was nothing of the parrot about him now, Here was a man part watch dog and part hawk. His cheeks and the flanges of his nostrils were thickly hair-lined with those little red-and-blue veins that are to be found in the texture of good American paper currency and in the faces of elderly men who have lived much out-of-doors during their lives. His jowls were heavy and pendulous like a mastiff's. His frontal bone came down low and straight so that under the flat arch of the brow his small, very bright agate-blue eyes looked out as from beneath half-closed shutters. His hair was clipped close to his scalp and the shape of his skull showed, rounded and bulgy; not the skull of a thinker, nor yet the skull of a creator, just the skull of a natural-born fighting man. The big, ridgy veins in the back of his neck stood out like window-cords from a close smocking of fine wrinkles. The neck itself was tanned to a brickdust red. A gnawed white mustache bristled on his upper lip. He was tall without seeming to be tall and broad without appearing broad, and he was old enough for a grandfather and spry enough for his own grandchild. You know the type. Our Civil War produced it in number.

At his throat was the blue star of the Order of Merit, the very highest honor a German soldier can win, and below it on his breast the inevitable black-and-white striped ribbon. The one meant leadership and the other testified to individual valor in the teeth of danger. It was Excellency von Zwehl, commander of the Seventh Reserve Corps of the Western Army, the man who took Maubeuge from the French and English, and the man who in the same week held the imperiled German center against the French and English.

We lunched with the General and his staff on soup and sausages, with a rare and precious Belgian melon cut in thin, salmon-tinted crescents to follow for dessert. But before the lunch he took us and showed us, pointing this way and that with his little riding whip, the theater wherein he had done a thing which he valued more than the taking of a walled city. Indeed there was a certain elemental boy-like bearing of pride in him as he told us the story. If I am right in my dates the defenses of Maubeuge caved in under the batterings of the German Jack Johnsons on September sixth and the citadel surrendered September seventh. On the following day, the eighth, Von Zwehl got word that a sudden forward thrust of the Allies threatened the German center at Laon. Without waiting for orders he started to the relief. He had available only nine thousand troops, all reserves. As many more shortly re-enforced him. He marched this small army—small, that is, as armies go these Titan times—for four days and three nights. In the last twenty-four hours of marching the eighteen thousand covered more than forty English miles—in the rain. They came on this same plateau, the one which we now faced, at six o'clock of the morning of September thirteenth, and within an hour were engaged against double or triple their number. Von Zwehl held off the enemy until a strengthening force reached him, and then for three days, with his face to the river and his back to the hill, he fought.

Out of a total force of forty thousand men he lost eight thousand and more in killed and wounded, but he saved the German Army from being split asunder between its shoulder-blades. The enemy in proportion lost even more than he did, he thought. The General had no English; he told us all this in German, Von Theobald standing handily by to translate for him when our own scanty acquaintance with the language left us puzzled.

"We punished them well and they punished us well, " he added. "We captured a group of thirty-one Scotchmen—all who were left out of a battalion of six hundred and fifty, and there was no commissioned officer left of that battalion. A sergeant surrendered them to my men. They fight very well against us—the Scotch."

Since then the groundswell of battle had swept forward, then backward, until now, as chance would have it, General von Zwehl once more had his headquarters on the identical spot where he had them four weeks before during his struggle to keep the German center from being pierced. Then it had been mainly infantry fighting at close range; now it was the labored pounding of heavy guns, the pushing ahead of trench-work preparatory to another pitched battle.

Considering what had taken place here less than a month before the plain immediately before us seemed peaceful enough.

Nature certainly works mighty fast to cover up what man at war does. True, the yellow-green meadowlands ahead of us were scuffed and scored minutely as though a myriad swine had rooted there for mast. The gouges of wheels and feet were at the roadside. Under the broken hedge-rows you saw a littering of weather-beaten French knapsacks and mired uniform coats, but that was all. New grass was springing up in the hoof tracks, and in a pecking, puny sort of way an effort was being made by certain French peasants within sight to get back to work in their wasted truck patches. Near at hand I counted three men and an old woman in the fields, bent over like worms. On the crest above them stood this gray veteran of two invasions of their land, aiming with his riding whip. The whip, I believe, signifies dominion, and sometimes brute force.

Beyond the tableland, and along the succession of gentle elevations which ringed it in to the south, the pounding of the field pieces went steadily on, while Von Zwehl lectured to us upon the congenial subject of what he here had done. Out yonder a matter of three or four English miles from us the big ones were busy for a fact. We could see the smoke clouds of each descending shell and the dust clouds of the explosion, and of course we could hear it. It never stopped for an instant, never abated for so much as a minute. It had been going on this way for weeks; it would surely go on this way for weeks yet to come. But so far as we could discern the General paid it no heed—he nor any of his staff. It was his business, but seemingly the business went well.

It was late that afternoon when we met our third general, and this meeting was quite by chance. Coming back from a spin down the lines we stopped in a small village called Amifontaine, to let our chauffeur, known affectionately as The Human Rabbit, tinker with a leaky tire valve or something. A young officer came up through the dusk to find out who we were, and, having found out, he invited us into the chief house of the place, and there in a stuffy little French parlor we were introduced in due form to General d'Elsa, the head of the Twelfth Reserve Corps, it turned out. Standing in a ceremonious ring, with filled glasses in our hands, about a table which bore a flary lamp and a bottle of bad native wine, we toasted him and he toasted us.

He was younger by ten years, I should say, than either Von Heeringen or Von Zwehl; too young, I judged, to have got his training in the blood- and-iron school of Bismarck and Von Moltke of which the other two must have been brag-scholars. Both of them, I think, were Prussians, but this general was a Saxon from the South. Indeed, as I now recall, he said his home in peace times was in

Dresden. He seemed less simple of manner than they; they in turn lacked a certain flexibility and grace of bearing which were his. But two things in common they all three had and radiated from them—a superb efficiency in the trade at which they worked and a superb confidence in the tools with which they did the work. This was rather a small man, quick and supple in his movements. He had a limited command of English, and he appeared deeply desirous that we Americans should have a good opinion of the behavior of his troops and that we should say as much in what we wrote for our fellow Americans to read.

Coming out of the house to reenter our automobile I saw, across the small square of the town, which by now was quite in darkness, the flare of a camp kitchen. I wanted very much to examine one of these wheeled cook wagons at close range. An officer—the same who had first approached us to examine our papers—accompanied me to explain its workings and to point out the various compartments where the coal was kept and the fuel, and the two big sunken pots where the stew was cooked and the coffee was brewed. The thing proved to be cumbersome, which was German, but it was most complete in detail, and that, take it, was German too. While the officer rattled the steel lids the cook himself stood rigidly alongside, with his fingers touching the seams of his trousers. Seen by the glare of his own fire he seemed a clod, fit only to make soups and feed a fire box. But by that same flickery light I saw something. On the breast of his grease-spattered blouse dangled a black-and-white ribbon with a black-and-white Maltese cross fastened to it. I marveled that a company cook should wear the Iron Cross of the second class and I asked the captain about it. He laughed at the wonder that was evident in my tones.

"If you will look more closely, " he said, "you will see that a good many of our cooks already have won the Iron Cross since this war began, and a good many others will yet win it—if they live. We have no braver men in our army than these fellows. They go into the trenches at least twice a day, under the hottest fire sometimes, to carry hot coffee and hot food to the soldiers who fight. A good many of them have already been killed.

"Only the other day—at La Fere I think it was—two of our cooks at daybreak went so far forward with their wagon that they were almost inside the enemy's lines. Sixteen bewildered Frenchmen who had got separated from their company came straggling through a little forest and walked right into them. The Frenchmen thought the cook wagon with its short smoke funnel and its steel fire box was a new kind of machine gun, and they threw down their guns and surrendered. The two cooks brought their sixteen prisoners back to our lines too, but first one of them stood guard over the Frenchmen while the other carried the breakfast coffee to the men who had been all night in the trenches. They are good men, those cooks!"

So at last I found out at second hand what one German soldier had done to merit the bestowal of the Iron Cross. But as we came away, I was in doubt on a certain point and, for that matter, am still in doubt on it: I am in doubt as to which of two men most fitly typified the spirit of the German Army in this war—the general feeding his men by thousands into the maw of destruction because it was an order, or the pot-wrestling private soldier, the camp cook, going to death with a coffee boiler in his hands—because it was an order.

Chapter 9

Viewing A Battle from a Balloon

She was anchored to earth in a good-sized field. Woods horizoned the field on three of its edges and a sunken road bounded it on the fourth. She measured, I should say at an offhand guess, seventy-five feet from tip to tip lengthwise, and she was perhaps twenty feet in diameter through her middle. She was a bright yellow in color—a varnished, oily-looking yellow—and in shape suggestive of a frankfurter.

At the end of her near the ground and on the side that was underneath —for she swung, you understand, at an angle—a swollen protuberance showed, as though an air bubble had got under the skin of the sausage during the packing and made a big blister. She drooped weakly amidships, bending and swaying this way and that; and, as we came under her and looked up, we saw that the skin of the belly kept shrinking in and wrinkling up, in the unmistakable pangs of acute cramp colic.

She had a sickly, depleted aspect elsewhere, and altogether was most flabby and unreliable looking; yet this, as I learned subsequently, was her normal appearance. Being in the business of spying she practiced deceit, with the deliberate intent of seeming to be what, emphatically, she was not. She counterfeited chronic invalidism and she performed competently.

She was an observation balloon of the pattern privily chosen by the German General Staff, before the beginning of the war, for the use of the German Signal Corps. On this particular date and occasion she operated at a point of the highest strategic importance, that point being the center of the German battle lines along the River Aisne.

She had been stationed here now for more than a week—that is to say, ever since her predecessor was destroyed in a ball of flaming fumes as a result of having a bomb flung through the flimsy cloth envelope by a coursing and accurate aviator of the enemy. No doubt she would continue to be stationed here until some such mischance befell her too.

Paths of Glory

On observation balloons, in time of war, no casualty insurance is available at any rate of premium. I believe those who ride in them are also regarded as unsuitable risks. This was highly interesting to hear and, for our journalistic purposes, very valuable to know; but, speaking personally, I may say that the thing which most nearly concerned me for the moment was this: I had just been invited to take a trip aloft in this wabbly great wienerwurst, with its painted silk cuticle and its gaseous vitals—and had, on impulse, accepted.

I was informed at the time, and have since been reinformed more than once, that I am probably the only civilian spectator who has enjoyed such a privilege during the present European war. Assuredly, to date and to the best of my knowledge and belief, I am the only civilian who has been so favored by the Germans. Well, I trust I am not hoggish. Possessing, as it does, this air of uniqueness, the distinction is worth much to me personally. I would not take anything for the experience; but I do not think I shall take it again, even if the chance should come my way, which very probably it will not.

It was mid-afternoon; and all day, since early breakfast, we had been working our way in automobiles toward this destination. Already my brain chambered more impressions, all jumbled together in a mass, than I could possibly hope to get sorted out and graded up and classified in a month of trying. Yet, in a way, the day had been disappointing; for, as I may have set forth before, the nearer we came to the actual fighting, the closer in touch we got with the battle itself, the less we seemed to see of it.

I take it this is true of nearly all battles fought under modern military principles. Ten miles in the rear, or even twenty miles, is really a better place to be if you are seeking to fix in your mind a reasonably full picture of the scope and effect and consequences of the hideous thing called war. Back there you see the new troops going in, girding themselves for the grapple as they go; you see the re-enforcements coming up; you see the supplies hurrying forward, and the spare guns and the extra equipment, and all the rest of it; you see, and can, after a dim fashion, grasp mentally, the thrusting, onward movement of this highly scientific and most unromantic industry which half the world began practicing in the fall of 1914.

Finally, you see the finished fabrics of the trade coming back; and by that I mean the dribbling streams of the wounded and, in the fields and woods through which you pass, the dead, lying in windrows where they fell. At the front you see only, for the main part, men engaged in the most tedious, the most exacting, and seemingly the most futile form of day labor—toiling in filth and foulness and a desperate driven haste, on a job that many of them will never live to see finished—if it is ever finished; working under taskmasters who spare them not—neither do they spare themselves; putting through a dreary contract, whereof the chief reward is weariness and the common coinage of payment is death outright or death lingering. That is a battle in these days; that is war.

So twistiwise was our route, and so rapidly did we pursue it after we left the place where we took lunch, that I confess I lost all sense of direction. It seemed to me our general course was eastward; I discovered afterward it was southwesterly. At any rate we eventually found ourselves in a road that wound between high grassy banks along a great natural terrace just below the level of the plateau in front of Laon. We saw a few farmhouses, all desolated by shellfire and all deserted, and a succession of empty fields and patches of woodland. None of the natives were in sight. Through fear of prying hostile eyes, the Germans had seen fit to clear them out of this immediate vicinity. Anyhow, a majority of them doubtlessly ran away when fighting first started here, three weeks earlier; the Germans had got rid of those who remained. Likewise of troops there were very few to be seen. We did meet one squad of Red Cross men, marching afoot through the dust. They were all fully armed, as is the way with the German field-hospital helpers; and, for all I know to the contrary, that may be the way with the field-hospital helpers of the Allies too.

Though I have often seen it, the Cross on the sleeve-band of a man who bears a revolver in his belt, or a rifle on his arm, has always struck me as a most incongruous thing. The noncommissioned officer in charge of the squad—chief orderly I suppose you might call him—held by leashes four Red Cross dogs.

In Belgium, back in August, I had seen so-called dog batteries. Going into Louvain on the day the Belgian Army, or what was left of it, fell back into Brussels, I passed a valley where many dogs were hitched to small machine guns; and I could not help wondering what would happen to the artillery formation, and what to the discipline of the pack, if a rabbit should choose that moment for darting across the battle front.

Paths of Glory

These, however, were the first dogs I had found engaged in hospital-corps employment. They were big, wolfish-looking hounds, shaggy and sharp-nosed; and each of the four wore a collar of bells on his neck, and a cloth harness on his shoulders, with the red Maltese cross displayed on its top and sides. Their business was to go to the place where fighting had taken place and search out the fallen.

At this business they were reputed to be highly efficient. The Germans had found them especially useful; for the German field uniform, which has the merit of merging into the natural background at a short distance, becomes, through that very protective coloration, a disadvantage when its wearer drops wounded and unconscious on the open field. In a poor light the litter bearers might search within a few rods of him and never see him; but where the faulty eyesight fails the nose of the dog sniffs the human taint in the air, and the dog makes the work of rescue thorough and complete. At least we were told so.

Presently our automobile rounded a bend in the road, and the observation balloon, which until that moment we had been unable to glimpse, by reason of an intervening formation of ridges, revealed itself before us. The suddenness of its appearance was startling. We did not see it until we were within a hundred yards of it. At once we realized how perfect an abiding place this was for a thing which offered so fine and looming a target.

Moreover, the balloon was most effectively guarded against attack at close range. We became aware of that fact when we dismounted from the automobile and were clambering up the steep bank alongside. Soldiers materialized from everywhere, like dusty specters, but fell back, saluting, when they saw that officers accompanied us. On advice we had already thrown away our lighted cigars; but two noncommissioned officers felt it to be their bounden duty to warn us against striking matches in that neighborhood. You dare not take chances with a woven bag that is packed with many hundred cubic feet of gas.

At the moment of our arrival the balloon was drawn down so near the earth that its distorted bottommost extremity dipped and twisted slackly within fifty or sixty feet of the grass.

The upper end, reaching much farther into the air, underwent convulsive writhings and contortions as an intermittent breeze came over the sheltering treetops and buffeted it in puffs. Almost beneath the balloon six big draft horses stood, hitched in pairs to a stout wagon frame on which a huge wooden drum was mounted.

Round this drum a wire cable was coiled, and a length of the cable stretched like a snake across the field to where it ended in a swivel, made fast to the bottom of the riding car. It was not, strictly speaking, a riding car. It was a straight-up-and-down basket of tough, light wicker, no larger and very little deeper than an ordinarily fair- sized hamper for soiled linen. Indeed, that was what it reminded one of—a clothesbasket.

Grouped about the team and the wagon were soldiers to the number of perhaps a third of a company. Half a dozen of them stood about the basket holding it steady—or trying to. Heavy sandbags hung pendent- wise about the upper rim of the basket, looking very much like so many canvased hams; but, even with these drags on it and in spite of the grips of the men on the guy ropes of its rigging, it bumped and bounded uneasily to the continual rocking of the gas bag above it. Every moment or two it would lift itself a foot or so and tilt and jerk, and then come back again with a thump that made it shiver.

Of furnishings the interior of the car contained nothing except a telephone, fixed against one side of it; a pair of field glasses, swung in a sort of harness; and a strip of tough canvas, looped across halfway down in it. The operator, when wearied by standing, might sit astride this canvas saddle, with his legs cramped under him, while he spied out the land with his eyes, which would then be just above the top of his wicker nest, and while he spoke over the telephone.

The wires of the telephone escaped through a hole under his feet and ran to a concealed station at the far side of the field which in turn communicated with the main exchange at headquarters three miles away; which in its turn radiated other wires to all quarters of the battle front. Now the wires were neatly coiled on the ground beside the basket. A sergeant stood over them to prevent any careless foot from stepping on the precious strands. He guarded them as jealously as a hen guards her brood.

The magazine containing retorts of specially prepared gas, for recharging the envelope when evaporation and leakage had reduced the volume below the lifting and floating point, was nowhere in sight. It must have been somewhere near by, but we saw no signs of it. Nor did our guides for the day offer to show us its whereabouts. However, knowing what I do of the German system of doing things, I will venture the assertion that it was snugly hidden and stoutly protected.

These details I had time to take in, when there came across the field to join us a tall young officer with a three weeks' growth of stubby black beard on his face. A genial and captivating gentleman was Lieutenant Brinkner und Meiningen, and I enjoyed my meeting with him; and often since that day in my thoughts I have wished him well. However, I doubt whether he will be living by the time these lines see publication.

It is an exciting life a balloon operator in the German Army lives, but it is not, as a rule, a long one. Lieutenant Meiningen was successor to a man who was burned to death in mid-air a week before; and on the day before a French airman had dropped a bomb from the clouds that missed this same balloon by a margin of less than a hundred yards—close marksmanship, considering that the airman in question was seven or eight thousand feet aloft, and moving at the rate of a mile or so a minute when he made his cast.

It was the Lieutenant who said he had authority to take one of our number up with him, and it was I who chanced to be nearest to the balloon when he extended the invitation. Some one—a friend— removed from between my teeth the unlighted cigar I held there, for fear I might forget and try to light it; and somebody else—a stranger to me— suggested that perhaps I was too heavy for a passenger.

By that time, however, a kindly corporal had boosted me up over the rim of the basket and helped me to squeeze through the thick netting of guy lines; and there I was, standing inside that overgrown clotheshamper, which came up breast high on me—and Brinkner und Meiningen was swinging himself nimbly in beside me. That basket was meant to hold but one man. It made a wondrously snug fit for two; the both of us being full-sized adults at that. We stood back to back; and to address the other each must needs speak over his shoulder. The canvas saddle was between us, dangling against the calves of our legs; and the telephone was in front of the lieutenant, where he could reach the transmitter with his lips by stooping a little.

The soldiers began unhooking the sandbags; the sergeant who guarded the telephone wire took up a strand of it and held it loosely in his hands, ready to pay it out. Under me I felt the basket heave gently. Looking up I saw that the balloon was no longer a crooked sausage. She had become a big, soft, yellow summer squash, with an attenuated neck. The flaccid abdomen flinched in and puffed out, and the snout wabbled to and fro.

The lieutenant began telling me things in badly broken but painstaking English—such things, for example, as that the baglike protuberance just above our heads, at the bottom end of the envelope, contained air, which, being heavier than gas, served as a balance to hold her head up in the wind and keep her from folding in on herself; also, that it was his duty to remain aloft, at the end of his tether, as long as he could, meantime studying the effect of the German shell-fire on the enemy's position and telephoning down instructions for the better aiming of the guns—a job wherein the aeroplane scouts ably reenforced him, since they could range at will, whereas his position was comparatively fixed and stationary.

Also I remember his saying, with a tinge of polite regret in his tone, that he was sorry I had not put on a uniform overcoat with shoulder straps on it, before boarding the car; because, as he took pains to explain, in the event of our cable parting and of our drifting over the Allies' lines and then descending, he might possibly escape, but I should most likely be shot on the spot as a spy before I had a chance to explain. "However, " he added consolingly, "those are possibilities most remote. The rope is not likely to break; and if it did we both should probably be dead before we ever reached the earth. "

That last statement sank deep into my consciousness; but I fear I did not hearken so attentively as I ought to the continuation of the lieutenant's conversation, because, right in the middle of his remarks, something had begun to happen.

An officer had stepped up alongside to tell me that very shortly I should undoubtedly be quite seasick—or, rather, skysick—because of the pitching about of the basket when the balloon reached the end of the cable; and I was trying to listen to him with one ear and to my prospective traveling companion with the other when I suddenly realized that the officer's face was no longer on a level with mine. It was several feet below mine. No; it was not—it was several yards below mine. Now he was looking up toward us, shouting out his words, with his hands funneled about his mouth for a speaking trumpet. And at every word he uttered he shrank into himself, growing shorter and shorter.

It was not that we seemed to be moving. We seemed to be standing perfectly still, without any motion of any sort except a tiny teetering motion of the hamper-basket, while the earth and what was on it fell rapidly away from beneath us. At once all sense of perspective became distorted.

When on the roof of a tall building this distortion had never seemed to me so great. I imagine this is because the building remains stationary and a balloon moves. Almost directly below us was one of our party, wearing a soft hat with a flattish brim. It appeared to me that almost instantly his shoulders and body and legs vanished. Nothing remained of him but his hat, which looked exactly like a thumb tack driven into a slightly tilted drawing board, the tilted drawing board being the field. The field seemed sloped now, instead of flat.

Across the sunken road was another field. Its owner, I presume, had started to turn it up for fall planting, when the armies came along and chased him away; so there remained a wide plowed strip, and on each side of it a narrower strip of unplowed earth. Even as I peered downward at it, this field was transformed into a width of brown corduroy trimmed with green velvet.

For a rudder we carried a long, flapping clothesline arrangement, like the tail of a kite, to the lower end of which were threaded seven yellow-silk devices suggesting inverted sunshades without handles. These things must have been spaced on the tail at equal distances apart, but as they rose from the earth and followed after us, whipping in the wind, the uppermost one became a big umbrella turned inside out; the second was half of a pumpkin; the third was a yellow soup plate; the fourth was a poppy bloom; and the remaining three were just amber beads of diminishing sizes.

Probably it took longer, but if you asked me I should say that not more than two or three minutes had passed before the earth stopped slipping away and we fetched up with a profound and disconcerting jerk. The balloon had reached the tip of her hitch line.

Paths of Glory

She rocked and twisted and bent half double in the pangs of a fearful tummy-ache, and at every paroxysm the car lurched in sympathy, only to be brought up short by the pull of the taut cable; so that we two, wedged in together as we were, nevertheless jostled each other violently. I am a poor sailor, both by instinct and training. By rights and by precedents I should have been violently ill on the instant; but I did not have time to be ill.

My fellow traveler all this while was pointing out this thing and that to me—showing how the telephone operated; how his field glasses poised just before his eyes, being swung and balanced on a delicately adjusted suspended pivot; telling me how on a perfectly clear day—this October day was slightly hazy—we could see the Eiffel Tower in Paris, and the Cathedral at Rheims; gyrating his hands to explain the manner in which the horses, trotting away from us as we climbed upward, had given to the drum on the wagon a reverse motion, so that the cable was payed out evenly and regularly. But I am afraid I did not listen closely. My eyes were so busy that my ears loafed on the job.

For once in my life—and doubtlessly only once—I saw now understandingly a battle front.

It was spread before me—lines and dots and dashes on a big green and brown and yellow map. Why, the whole thing was as plain as a chart. I had a reserved seat for the biggest show on earth.

To be sure it was a gallery seat, for the terrace from which we started stood fully five hundred feet above the bottom of the valley, and we had ascended approximately seven hundred feet above that, giving us an altitude of, say, twelve hundred feet in all above the level of the river; but a gallery seat suited me. It suited me perfectly. The great plateau, stretching from the high hill behind us, to the river in front of us, portrayed itself, when viewed from aloft, as a shallow bowl, alternately grooved by small depressions and corrugated by small ridges. Here and there were thin woodlands, looking exactly like scrubby clothesbrushes. The fields were checkered squares and oblongs, and a ruined village in the distance seemed a jumbled handful of children's gray and red blocks.

The German batteries appeared now to be directly beneath us—some of them, though in reality I imagine the nearest one must have been nearly a mile away on a bee line. They formed an irregular horseshoe, with the open end of it toward us. There was a gap in the horseshoe where the calk should have been. The German trenches, for the most part, lay inside the encircling lines of batteries. In shape they rather suggested a U turned upside down; yet it was hard to ascribe to them any real shape, since they zigzagged so crazily. I could tell, though, there was sanity in this seeming madness, for nearly every trench was joined at an acute angle with its neighbor; so that a man, or a body of men, starting at the rear, out of danger, might move to the very front of the fighting zone and all the time be well sheltered. So far as I could make out there were but few breaks in the sequence of communications. One of these breaks was almost directly in front of me as I stood facing the south.

The batteries of the Allies and their infantry trenches, being so much farther away, were less plainly visible. I could discern their location without being able to grasp their general arrangement. Between the nearer infantry trenches of the two opposing forces were tiny dots in the ground, each defined by an infinitesimal hillock of yellow earth heaped before it—observation pits these, where certain picked men, who do not expect to live very long anyway, hide themselves away to keep tally on the effect of the shells, which go singing past just over their heads to fall among the enemy, who may be only a few hundred feet or a few hundred yards away from the observers.

It was an excessively busy afternoon among the guns. They spoke continually—now this battery going, now that; now two or three or a dozen together—and the sound of them came up to us in claps and roars like summer thunder. Sometimes, when a battery close by let go, I could watch the thin, shreddy trail of fine smoke that marked the arched flight of a shrapnel bomb, almost from the very mouth of the gun clear to where it burst out into a fluffy white powder puff inside the enemy's position.

Contrariwise, I could see how shells from the enemy crossed those shells in the air and curved downward to scatter their iron sprays among the Germans. In the midst of all this would come a sharp, spattering sound, as though hail in the height of the thunder shower had fallen on a tin roof; and that, I learned, meant infantry firing in a trench somewhere.

For a while I watched some German soldiers moving forward through a criss-cross of trenches; I took them to be fresh men going in to relieve other men who had seen a period of service under fire.

At first they suggested moles crawling through plow furrows; then, as they progressed onward, they shrank to the smallness of gray grub-worms, advancing one behind another. My eye strayed beyond them a fair distance and fell on a row of tiny scarlet dots, like cochineal bugs, showing minutely but clearly against the green-yellow face of a ridgy field well inside the forward batteries of the French and English. At that same instant the lieutenant must have seen the crawling red line too. He pointed to it.

"Frenchmen," he said; "French infantrymen's trousers. One cannot make out their coats, but their red trousers show as they wriggle forward on their faces."

Better than ever before I realized the idiocy of sending men to fight in garments that make vivid targets of them.

My companion may have come up for pleasure, but if business obtruded itself on him he did not neglect it. He bent to his telephone and spoke briskly into it. He used German, but, after a fashion, I made out what he said. He was directing the attention of somebody to the activities of those red trousers.

I intended to see what would follow on this, but at this precise moment a sufficiently interesting occurrence came to pass at a place within much clearer eye range. The gray grub-worms had shoved ahead until they were gray ants; and now all the ants concentrated into a swarm and, leaving the trenches, began to move in a slanting direction toward a patch of woods far over to our left. Some of them, I think, got there, some of them did not. Certain puff-balls of white smoke, and one big smudge of black smoke, which last signified a bomb of high explosives, broke over them and among them, hiding all from sight for a space of seconds. Dust clouds succeeded the smoke; then the dust lifted slowly. Those ants were not to be seen. They had altogether vanished. It was as though an anteater had come forth invisibly and eaten them all up.

Marveling at this phenomenon and unable to convince myself that I had seen men destroyed, and not insects, I turned my head south again to watch the red ladybugs in the field. Lo! They were gone too! Either they had reached shelter or a painful thing had befallen them.

The telephone spoke a brisk warning. I think it made a clicking sound. I am sure it did not ring; but in any event it called attention to itself. The other man clapped his ear to the receiver and took heed to the word that came up the dangling wire, and snapped back an answer.

"I think we should return at once, " he said to me over his shoulder. "Are you sufficiently wearied? "

I was not sufficiently wearied—I wasn't wearied at all—but he was the captain of the ship and I was not even paying for my passage.

The car jerked beneath our unsteady feet and heeled over, and I had the sensation of being in an elevator that has started downward suddenly, and at an angle to boot. The balloon resisted the pressure from below. It curled up its tail like a fat bumblebee trying to sting itself, and the guy ropes, to which I held with both hands, snapped in imitation of the rigging of a sailboat in a fair breeze. Plainly the balloon wished to remain where it was or go farther; but the pull of the cable was steady and hard, and the world began to rise up to meet us. Nearing the earth it struck me that we were making a remarkably speedy return. I craned my neck to get a view of what was directly beneath.

The six-horse team was advancing toward us at a brisk canter and the drum turned fast, taking up the slack of the tether; but, as though not satisfied with this rate of progress, several soldiers were running back and jumping up to haul in the rope. The sergeant who took care of the telephone was hard put to it to coil down the twin wires. He skittered about over the grass with the liveliness of a cricket.

Many soiled hands grasped the floor of our hamper and eased the jar of its contact with the earth. Those same hands had redraped the rim with sandbags, and had helped us to clamber out from between the stay ropes, when up came the young captain who spelled the lieutenant as an aerial spy. He came at a run. Between the two of them ensued a sharp interchange of short German sentences. I gathered the sense of what passed.

"I don't see it now, " said, in effect, my late traveling mate, staring skyward and turning his head.

"Nor do I, " answered the captain. "I thought it was yonder. " He flirted a thumb backward and upward over his shoulder.

Paths of Glory

"Are you sure you saw it?"

"No, not sure," said the captain. "I called you down at the first alarm, and right after that it disappeared, I think; but I shall make sure."

He snapped an order to the soldiers and vaulted nimbly into the basket. The horses turned about and moved off and the balloon rose. As for the lieutenant, he spun round and ran toward the edge of the field, fumbling at his belt for his private field glasses as he ran. Wondering what all this bother was about—though I had a vague idea regarding its meaning— I watched the ascent.

I should say the bag had reached a height of five hundred feet when, behind me, a hundred yards or so away, a soldier shrieked out excitedly. Farther along another voice took up the outcry. From every side of the field came shouts. The field was ringed with clamor. It dawned on me that this spot was even more efficiently guarded than I had conceived it to be.

The driver of the wagon swung his lumbering team about with all the strength of his arms, and back again came the six horses, galloping now. So thickly massed were the men who snatched at the cable, and so eagerly did they grab for it, that the simile of a hot handball scrimmage flashed into my thoughts. I will venture that balloon never did a faster homing job than it did then.

Fifty men were pointing aloft now, all of them crying out as they pointed:

"Flyer! French flyer!"

I saw it. It was a monoplane. It had, I judged, just emerged from a cloudbank to the southward. It was heading directly toward our field. It was high up—so high up that I felt momentarily amazed that all those Germans could distinguish it as a French flyer rather than as an English flyer at that distance.

As I looked, and as all of us looked, the balloon basket hit the earth and was made fast; and in that same instant a cannon boomed somewhere well over to the right. Even as someone who knew sang out to us that this was the balloon cannon in the German aviation field back of the town opening up, a tiny ball of smoke appeared against the sky, seemingly quite close to the darting flyer, and blossomed out with downy, dainty white petals, like a flower.

The monoplane veered, wheeled and began to drive in a wriggling, twisting course. The balloon cannon spoke again. Four miles away, to the eastward, its fellow in another aviation camp let go, and the sound of its discharge came to us faintly but distinctly. Another smoke flower unfolded in the heavens, somewhat below the darting airship.

Both guns were in action now. Each fired at six-second intervals. All about the flitting target the smokeballs burst—above it, below it, to this side of it and to that. They polka-dotted the heavens in the area through which the Frenchman scudded. They looked like a bed of white water lilies and he like a black dragonfly skimming among the lilies. It was a pretty sight and as thrilling a one as I have ever seen.

I cannot analyze my emotions as I viewed the spectacle, let alone try to set them down on paper. Alongside of this, big-game hunting was a commonplace thing, for this was big-game hunting of a magnificent kind, new to the world—revolving cannon, with a range of from seven to eight thousand feet, trying to bring down a human being out of the very clouds.

He ran for his life. Once I thought they had him. A shell burst seemingly quite close to him, and his machine dipped far to one side and dropped through space at that angle for some hundreds of feet apparently.

A yell of exultation rose from the watching Germans, who knew that an explosion close to an aeroplane is often sufficient, through the force of air concussion alone, to crumple the flimsy wings and bring it down, even though none of the flying shrapnel from the bursting bomb actually touch the operator or the machine.

However, they whooped their joy too soon. The flyer righted, rose, darted confusingly to the right, then to the left, and then bored straight into a woolly white cloudrack and was gone. The moment it disappeared the two balloon cannon ceased firing; and I, taking stock of my own sensations, found myself quivering all over and quite hoarse.

Paths of Glory

I must have done some yelling myself; but whether I rooted for the flyer to get away safely or for the cannon to hit him, I cannot for the life of me say. I can only trust that I preserved my neutrality and rooted for both.

Subsequently I decided in my own mind that from within the Allies' lines the Frenchman saw us—meaning the lieutenant and myself—in the air, and came forth with intent to bombard us from on high; that, seeing us descend, he hid in a cloud ambush, venturing out once more, with his purpose renewed, when the balloon reascended, bearing the captain. I liked to entertain that idea, because it gave me a feeling of having shared to some degree in a big adventure.

As for the captain and the lieutenant, they advanced no theories whatever. The thing was all in the day's work to them. It had happened before. I have no doubt it has happened many times since.

Chapter 10

In the Trenches Before Rheims

After my balloon-riding experience what followed was in the nature of an anticlimax—was bound to be anti-climactic. Yet the remainder of the afternoon was not without action. Not an hour later, as we stood in a battery of small field guns—guns I had watched in operation from my lofty gallery seat—another flyer, or possibly the same one we had already seen, appeared in the sky, coming now in a long swinging sweep from the southwest, and making apparently for the very spot where our party had stationed itself to watch the trim little battery perform.

It had already dropped some form of deadly souvenir we judged, for we saw a jet of black smoke go geysering up from a woodland where a German corps commander had his field headquarters, just after the airship passed over that particular patch of timber. As it swirled down the wind in our direction the vigilant balloon guns again got its range, and, to the throbbing tune of their twin boomings, it ducked and dodged away, executing irregular and hurried upward spirals until the cloud-fleece swallowed it up.

The driver of that monoplane was a persistent chap. I am inclined to believe he was the selfsame aviator who ventured well inside the German lines the following morning. While at breakfast in the prefecture at Laon we heard the cannoneer-sharpshooters when they opened on him; and as we ran to the windows—we Americans, I mean, the German officers breakfasting with us remaining to finish their coffee—we saw a colonel, whom we had met the night before, sitting on a bench in the old prefecture flower garden and looking up into the skies through the glasses that every German officer, of whatsoever degree, carries with him at all times.

He looked and looked; then he lowered his glasses and put them back into their case, and took up the book he had been reading.

"He got away again," said the colonel regretfully, seeing us at the window. "Plucky fellow, that! I hope we kill him soon. The airmen say he is a Frenchman, but my guess is that he is English." And then he went on reading.

Paths of Glory

Getting back to the afternoon before, I must add that it was not a bomb which the flying man threw into the edge of the woods. He had a surprise for his German adversaries that day. Soon after we left the stand of the field guns a civilian Red Cross man halted our machines to show us a new device for killing men. It was a steel dart, of the length and thickness of a fountain pen, and of much the same aspect. It was pointed like a needle at one end, and at the other was fashioned into a tiny rudder arrangement, the purpose of this being to hold it upright—-point downward—as it descended. It was an innocent-looking device—that dart; but it was deadlier than it seemed.

"That flyer at whom our guns were firing a while ago dropped this, " explained the civilian. "He pitched out a bomb that must have contained hundreds of these darts; and the bomb was timed to explode a thousand or more feet above the earth and scatter the darts. Some of them fell into a cavalry troop on the road leading to La Fere.

"Hurt anyone? Ach, but yes! Hurt many and killed several—both men and horses. One dart hit a trooper on top of his head. It went through his helmet, through his skull, his brain, his neck, his body, his leg—all the way through him lengthwise it went. It came out of his leg, split open his horse's flank, and stuck in the hard road.

"I myself saw the man afterward. He died so quickly that his hand still held his bridle rein after he fell from the saddle; and the horse dragged him—his corpse, rather—many feet before the fingers relaxed. "

The officers who were with us were tremendously interested—not interested, mind you, in the death of that trooper, spitted from the heavens by a steel pencil, but interested in the thing that had done the work. It was the first dart they had seen. Indeed, I think until then this weapon had not been used against the Germans in this particular area of the western theater of war. These officers passed it about, fingering it in turn, and commenting on the design of it and the possibilities of its use.

"Typically French, " the senior of them said at length, handing it back to its owner, the Red Cross man—"a very clever idea too; but it might be bettered, I think. " He pondered a moment, then added, with the racial complacence that belongs to a German military man

Paths of Glory

when he considers military matters: "No doubt we shall adopt the notion; but we'll improve on the pattern and the method of discharging it. The French usually lead the way in aerial inventions, but the Germans invariably perfect them."

The day wound up and rounded out most fittingly with a trip eastward along the lines to the German siege investments in front of Rheims. We ran for a while through damaged French hamlets, each with its soldier garrison to make up for the inhabitants who had fled; and then, a little later, through a less well-populated district. In the fields, for long stretches, nothing stirred except pheasants, feeding on the neglected grain, and big, noisy magpies. The roads were empty, too, except that there were wrecked shells of automobiles and bloated carcasses of dead troop horses. When the Germans, in their campaigning, smash up an automobile—and traveling at the rate they do there must be many smashed—they capsize it at the roadside, strip it of its tires, draw off the precious gasoline, pour oil over it and touch a match to it. What remains offers no salvage to friend, or enemy either.

The horses rot where they drop unless the country people choose to put the bodies underground. We counted the charred cadavers of fifteen automobiles and twice as many dead horses during that ride. The smell of horseflesh spoiled the good air. When passing through a wood the smell was always heavier. We hoped it was only dead horses we smelled there.

When there has been fighting in France or Belgium, almost any thicket will give up hideous grisly secrets to the man who goes searching there. Men sorely wounded in the open share one trait at least with the lower animals. The dying creature—whether man or beast—dreads to lie and die in the naked field. It drags itself in among the trees if it has the strength.

I believe every woodland in northern France was a poison place, and remained so until the freezing of winter sealed up its abominations under ice and frost.

Nearing Rheims we turned into a splendid straight highway bordered by trees, where the late afternoon sunlight filtered through the dead leaves, which still hung from the boughs and dappled the yellow road with black splotches, until it made you think of jaguar pelts. Midway of our course here we met troops moving toward us in force. First, as usual, came scouts on bicycles and motorcycles. One young chap had woven sheaves of dahlias and red peonies into the frame of his wheel, and through the clump of quivering blossoms the barrel of his rifle showed, like a black snake in a bouquet. He told us that troops were coming behind, going to the extreme right wing—a good many thousands of troops, he thought. Ordinarily Uhlans would have followed behind the bicycle men, but this time a regiment of Brunswick Hussars formed the advance guard, riding four abreast and making a fine show, what with their laced gray jackets and their lanes of nodding lances, and their tall woolly busbies, each with its grinning brass death's-head set into the front of it.

There was a blithe young officer who insisted on wheeling out of the line and halting us, and passing the time of day with us. I imagine he wanted to exercise his small stock of English words. Well, it needed the exercise. The skull-and-bones poison label on his cap made a wondrous contrast with the smiling eyes and the long, humorous, wrinkled-up nose below it.

"A miserable country, " he said, with a sweep of his arm which comprehended all Northwestern Europe, from the German border to the sea —"so little there is to eat! My belly—she is mostly empty always. But on the yesterday I have the much great fortune. I buy me a swine—what you call him? —a pork? Ah, yes; a pig. I buy me a pig. He is a living pig; very noisy, as you say—very loud. I bring him twenty kilometers in an automobile, and all the time he struggle to be free; and he cry out all the time. It is very droll—not? —me and the living pig, which ride, both together, twenty kilometers! "

We took some letters from him to his mother and sweetheart, to be mailed when we got back on German soil; and he spurred on, beaming back at us and waving his free hand over his head.

For half an hour or so, we, traveling rapidly, passed the column, which was made up of cavalry, artillery and baggage trains. I suppose the infantry was going by another road. The dragoons sang German marching songs as they rode by, but the artillerymen were dour and silent lot for the most part. Repeatedly I noticed that the men who worked the big German guns were rarely so cheerful as the men who belonged to the other wings of the service; certainly it was true in this instance.

Paths of Glory

We halted two miles north of Rheims in the front line of the German works. Here was a little shattered village; its name, I believe, was Brimont. And here, also, commanding the road, stood a ruined fortress of an obsolete last-century pattern. Shellfire had battered it into a gruel of shattered red masonry; but German officers were camped within its more habitable parts, and light guns were mounted in the moat.

The trees thereabout had been mowed down by the French artillery from within the city, so that the highway was littered with their tops. Also, the explosives had dug big gouges in the earth. Wherever you looked you saw that the soil was full of small, raggedy craters. Shrapnel was dropping intermittently in the vicinity; therefore we left our cars behind the shelter of the ancient fort and proceeded cautiously afoot until we reached the frontmost trenches.

Evidently the Germans counted on staying there a good while. The men had dug out caves in the walls of the trenches, bedding them with straw and fitting them with doors taken from the wreckage of the houses of the village. We inspected one of these shelters. It had earthen walls and a sod roof, fairly water-tight, and a green window shutter to rest against the entrance for a windbreak. Six men slept here, and the wag of the squad had taken chalk and lettered the words "Kaiserhof Cafe" on the shutter.

The trenches were from seven to eight feet deep; but by climbing up into the little scarps of the sharpshooters and resting our elbows in niches in the earth, meantime keeping our heads down to escape the attentions of certain Frenchmen who were reported to be in a wood half a mile away, we could, with the aid of our glasses, make out the buildings in Rheims, some of which were then on fire—particularly the great Cathedral.

Viewed from that distance it did not appear to be badly damaged. One of the towers had apparently been shorn away and the roof of the nave was burned—we could tell that. We were too far away of course to judge of the injury to the carvings and to the great rose window.

Already during that week, from many sources, we had heard the Germans' version of the shelling of Rheims Cathedral, their claim being that they purposely spared the pile from the bombardment until they found the defenders had signal men in the towers; that

Paths of Glory

twice they sent officers, under flags of truce, to urge the French to withdraw their signalers; and only fired on the building when both these warnings had been disregarded, ceasing to fire as soon as they had driven the enemy from the towers.

I do not vouch for this story; but we heard it very frequently. Now, from one of the young officers who had escorted us into the trench, we were hearing it all over again, with elaborations, when a shrapnel shell from the town dropped and burst not far behind us, and rifle bullets began to plump into the earthen bank a little to the right of us; so we promptly went away from there.

We were noncombatants and nowise concerned in the existing controversy; but we remembered the plaintive words of the Chinese Minister at Brussels when he called on our Minister—Brand Whitlock—to ascertain what Whitlock would advise doing in case the advancing Germans fired on the city. Whitlock suggested to his Oriental brother that he retire to his official residence and hoist the flag of his country over it, thereby making it neutral and protected territory.

"But, Mister Whitlock, " murmured the puzzled Chinaman, "the cannon—he has no eyes! "

We rode back to Laon through the falling dusk. The western sky was all a deep saffron pink—the color of a salmon's belly—and we could hear the constant blaspheming of the big siege guns, taking up the evening cannonade along the center. Pretty soon we caught up with the column that was headed for the right wing. At that hour it was still in motion, which probably meant forced marching for an indefinite time. Viewed against the sunset yellow, the figures of the dragoons stood up black and clean, as conventionalized and regular as though they had all been stenciled on that background. Seeing next the round, spiked helmets of the cannoneers outlined in that weird half-light, I knew of what those bobbing heads reminded me. They were like pictures of Roman centurions.

Within a few minutes the afterglow lost its yellowish tone and burned as a deep red flare. As we swung off into a side road the columns were headed right into that redness, and turning to black cinder-shapes as they rode. It was as though they marched into a fiery furnace, treading the crimson paths of glory—which are not glorious and probably never were, but which lead most unerringly to the grave.

A week later, when we learned what had happened on the right wing, and of how the Germans had fared there under the battering of the Allies, the thought of that open furnace door came back to me. I think of it yet-often.

Chapter 11

War de Luxe

"I think, " said a colonel of the ordnance department as we came out into the open after a good but a hurried and fly-ridden breakfast—"I think, " he said in his excellent Saxonized English, "that it would be as well to look at our telephone exchange first of all. It perhaps might prove of some small interest to you. " With that he led the way through a jumble of corridors to a far corner of the Prefecture of Laon, perching high on the Hill of Laon and forming for the moment the keystone of the arch of the German center. So that was how the most crowded day in a reasonably well-crowded newspaperman's life began for me—with a visit to a room which had in other days been somebody's reception parlor. We came upon twelve soldier-operators sitting before portable switchboards with metal transmitters clamped upon their heads, giving and taking messages to and from all the corners and crannies of the mid-battle-front. This little room was the solar plexus of the army. To it all the tingling nerves of the mighty organism ran and in it all the ganglia centered. At two sides of the room the walls were laced with silk-covered wires appliqued as thickly and as closely and as intricately as the threads in old point lace, and over these wires the gray-coated operators could talk—and did talk pretty constantly—with all the trenches and all the batteries and all the supply camps and with the generals of brigades and of divisions and of corps.

One wire ran upstairs to the Over-General's sleeping quarters and ended, so we were told, in a receiver that hung upon the headboard of his bed. Another stretched, by relay points, to Berlin, and still another ran to the headquarters of the General Staff where the Kaiser was, somewhere down the right wing; and so on and so forth. If war is a business these times instead of a chivalric calling, then surely this was the main office and clearing house of the business.

To our novice eyes the wires seemed snarled—snarled inextricably, hopelessly, eternally—and we said as much, but the ordnance colonel said behind this apparent disorder a most careful and particular orderliness was hidden away. Given an hour's notice, these busy men who wore those steel vises clamped upon their ears could disconnect the lines, pull down and reel in the wires, pack the batteries and the exchanges, and have the entire outfit loaded upon automobiles for speedy transmission elsewhere. Having seen what I had seen of the German military system, I could not find it in my heart to doubt this. Miracles had already become commonplaces; what might have been epic once was incidental now. I hearkened and believed.

At his command a sergeant plugged in certain stops upon a keyboard and then when the Colonel, taking a hand telephone up from a table, had talked into it in German he passed it into my hands.

"The captain at the other end of the line knows English," he said. "I've just told him you wish to speak with him for a minute." I pressed the rubber disk to my ear. "Hello!" I said.

"Hello!" came back the thin-strained answer. "This is such and such a trench"—giving the number—"in front of Cerny. What do you want to know?"

"What's the news there?" I stammered fatuously.

A pleasant little laugh tinkled through the strainer.

"Oh, it's fairly quiet now," said the voice. "Yesterday afternoon shrapnel fire rather mussed us up, but to-day nothing has happened. We're just lying quiet and enjoying the fine weather. We've had much rain lately and my men are enjoying the change."

So that was all the talk I had with a man who had for weeks been living in a hole in the ground with a ditch for an exercise ground and the brilliant prospects of a violent death for his hourly and daily entertainment. Afterward when it was too late I thought of a number of leading questions which I should have put to that captain. Undoubtedly there was a good story in him could you get it out.

We came through a courtyard at the north side of the building, and the courtyard was crowded with automobiles of all the known European sizes and patterns and shapes—automobiles for scout duty, with saw-edged steel prows curving up over the drivers' seats to catch and cut dangling wires; automobiles fitted as traveling pharmacies and needing only red- and-green lights to be regular prescription drug stores; automobile- ambulances rigged with stretchers and first-aid kits; automobiles for carrying ammunition

Paths of Glory

and capable of moving at tremendous speed for tremendous distances; automobile machine guns or machine-gun automobiles, just as suits you; automobile cannon; and an automobile mail wagon, all holed inside, like honeycomb, with two field-postmen standing up in it, back to back, sorting out the contents of snugly packed pouches; and every third letter was not a letter, strictly speaking, at all, but a small flat parcel containing chocolate or cigars or handkerchiefs or socks or even light sweaters—such gifts as might be sent to the soldiers, stamp-free, from any part of the German Empire. I wonder how men managed to wage war in the days before the automobile.

Two waiting cars received our party and our guides and our drivers, and we went corkscrewing down the hill, traversing crooked ways that were astonishingly full of German soldiers and astonishingly free of French townspeople. Either the citizens kept to their closed-up houses or, having run away at the coming of the enemy, they had not yet dared to return, although so far as I might tell there was no danger of their being mistreated by the gray-backs. Reaching the plain which is below the city we streaked westward, our destination being the field wireless station.

Nothing happened on the way except that we overtook a file of slightly wounded prisoners who, having been treated at the front, were now bound for a prison in a convent yard, where they would stay until a train carried them off to Munster or Dusseldorf for confinement until the end of the war. I counted them. —two English Tommies, two French officers, one lone Belgian—how he got that far down into France nobody could guess—and twenty-eight French cannoneers and infantrymen, including some North Africans. Every man Jack of them was bandaged either about the head or about the arms, or else he favored an injured leg as he hobbled slowly on. Eight guards were nursing them along; their bayonets were socketed in their carbine barrels. No doubt the magazines of the carbines were packed with those neat brass capsules which carry doses of potential death; but the guards, except for the moral effect of the thing, might just as well have been bare-handed. None of the prisoners could have run away even had he been so minded. The poor devils were almost past walking, let alone running. They wouldn't even look up as we went by them.

The day is done of the courier who rode horseback with orders in his belt and was winged in mid-flight; and the day of the secret

Paths of Glory

messenger who tried to creep through the hostile picket lines with cipher dispatches in his shoe, and was captured and ordered shot at sunrise, is gone, too, except in Civil War melodramas. Modern military science has wiped them out along with most of the other picturesque fol-de-rols of the old game of war. Bands no longer play the forces into the fight— indeed I have seen no more bands afield with the dun-colored files of the Germans than I might count on the fingers of my two hands; and flags, except on rare show-off occasions, do not float above the heads of the columns; and officers dress as nearly as possible like common soldiers; and the courier's work is done with much less glamour but with in-, finitely greater dispatch and certainty by the telephone, and by the aeroplane man, and most of all by the air currents of the wireless equipment. We missed the gallant courier, but then the wireless was worth seeing too.

It stood in a trampled turnip field not very far beyond the ruined Porte St. Martin at the end of the Rue St. Martin, and before we came to it we passed the Monument des Instituteurs, erected in 1899—as the inscription upon it told us—by a grateful populace to the memory of three school teachers of Laon who, for having raised a revolt of students and civilians against the invader in the Franco-Prussian War, were taken and bound and shot against a wall, in accordance with the system of dealing with ununiformed enemies which the Germans developed hereabouts in 1870 and perfected hereabouts in 1914. A faded wreath, which evidently was weeks old, lay at the bronze feet of the three figures. But the institute behind the monument was an institute no longer. It had become, over night as it were, a lazaret for the wounded. Above its doors the Red Cross flag and the German flag were crossed—emblems of present uses and present proprietorship. Also many convalescent German soldiers sunned themselves upon the railing about the statue. They seemed entirely at home. When the Germans take a town they mark it with their own mark, as cattlemen in Texas used to mark a captured maverick; after which to all intents it becomes German. We halted a moment here.

"That's French enough for you, " said the young officer who was riding with us, turning in his seat to speak—"putting up a monument to glorify three francs-tireurs. In Germany the people would not be allowed to do such a thing. But it is not humanly conceivable that they would have such a wish. We revere soldiers

Paths of Glory

who die for the Fatherland, not men who refuse to enlist when the call comes and yet take up arms to make a guerrilla warfare."

Which remark, considering the circumstances and other things, was sufficiently typical for all purposes, as I thought at the time and still think. You see I had come to the place where I could understand a German soldier's national and racial point of view, though I doubt his ability ever of understanding mine. To him, now, old John Burns of Gettysburg, going out in his high, high hat and his long, long coat to fight with the boys would never, could never be the heroic figure which he is in the American imagination; he would have been a meddlesome malefactor deserving of immediate death. For 1778 write it 1914, and Molly Pitcher serving at the guns would have been in no better case before a German court-martial. I doubt whether a Prussian Stonewall Jackson would give orders to kill a French Barbara Frietchie, but assuredly he would lock that venturesome old person up in a fortress where she could not hoist her country's flag nor invite anybody to shoot her gray head. For you must know that the German who ordinarily brims over with that emotion which, lacking a better name for it, we call sentiment, drains all the sentiment out of his soul when he takes his gun in his hand and goes to war.

Among the frowzy turnip tops two big dull gray automobiles were stranded, like large hulks in a small green sea. Alongside them a devil's darning-needle of a wireless mast stuck up, one hundred and odd feet, toward the sky. It was stayed with many steel guy ropes, like the center pole of a circus top. It was of the collapsible model and might therefore be telescoped into itself and taken down in twenty minutes, so we were informed pride-fully by the captain in charge; and from its needle-pointed tip the messages caught out of the ether came down by wire conductors to the interior of one of the stalled automobiles and there were noted down and, whenever possible, translated by two soldier- operators, who perched on wooden stools among batteries and things, for which I know not the technical names. The spitty snarl of the apparatus filled the air for rods roundabout. It made you think of a million gritty slate pencils squeaking over a million slates all together. We were permitted to take up the receivers and listen to a faint scratching sound which must have come from a long way off.

Indeed the officer told us that it was a message from the enemy that we heard.

Paths of Glory

"Our men just picked it up, " he explained; "we think it must come from a French wireless station across the river. Naturally we cannot understand it, any more than they can understand our messages—they're all in code, you know. Every day or two we change our code, and I presume they do too. "

Two of our party had unshipped their cameras by now, for the pass which we carried entitled us, among other important things, to commandeer that precious fluid, gasoline, whenever needed, and to take photographs; but we were asked to make no shapshots here. We gathered that there were certain reasons not unconnected with secret military usage why we might not take away with us plates bearing pictures of the field wireless. In the main, though, remarkably few restrictions were laid upon us that day. Once or twice, very casually, somebody asked us to refrain from writing about this thing or that thing which we had seen; but that was all.

In a corner of the turnip field close up to the road were mounds of fresh-turned clay, and so many of them were there and so closely were they spaced and for so considerable a distance did they stretch along, they made two long yellow ribs above the herbage. At close intervals small wooden crosses were stuck up in the rounded combs of earth so that the crosses formed a sort of irregular fence. A squad of soldiers were digging more holes in the tough earth. Their shovel blades flashed in the sunlight and the clods flew up in showers.

"We have many buried over there, " said an artillery captain, seeing that I watched the grave diggers, "a general among them and other officers. It is there we bury those who die in the Institute hospital. Every day more die, and so each morning trenches are made ready for those who will die during that day. A good friend of mine is over there; he was buried day before yesterday. I sat up late last night writing to his wife—or perhaps I should say his widow. They had been married only a few weeks when the call came. It will be very hard on her. "

He did not name the general who lay over yonder, nor did we ask him the name. To ask would not have been etiquette, and for him to answer would have been worse. Rarely in our wanderings did we find a German soldier of whatsoever rank who referred to his superior officer by name. He merely said "My captain" or "Our colonel. " And this was of a piece with the plan—not entirely

Paths of Glory

confined to the Germans—of making a secret of losses of commanders and movements of commands.

We went thence then, the distance being perhaps three miles by road and not above eight minutes by automobile at the rate we traveled to an aviation camp at the back side of the town. Here was very much to see, including many aeroplanes of sorts domiciled under canvas hangars and a cheerful, chatty, hospitable group of the most famous aviators in the German army—lean, keen young men all of them—and a sample specimen of the radish-shaped bomb which these gentlemen carry aloft with the intent of dropping it upon their enemies when occasion shall offer. Each of us in turn solemnly hefted the bomb to feel its weight. I should guess it weighed thirty pounds—say, ten pounds for the case and twenty pounds for its load of fearsome ingredients. Finally, yet foremost, we were invited to inspect that thing which is the pride and the brag of this particular arm of the German Army—a balloon-cannon, so called.

The balloon-gun of this size is—or was at the date when I saw it—an exclusively German institution. I believe the Allies have balloon-guns too, but theirs are smaller, according to what the Germans say. This one was mounted on a squatty half-turret at the tail end of an armored- steel truck. It had a mechanism as daintily adjusted as a lady's watch and much more accurate, and when being towed by its attendant automobile, which has harnessed within it the power of a hundred and odd draft horses, it has been known to cover sixty English miles in an hour, for all that its weight is that of very many loaded vans.

The person in authority here was a youthful and blithe lieutenant—an Iron Cross man—with pale, shallow blue eyes and a head of bright blond hair. He spun one small wheel to show how his pet's steel nose might be elevated almost straight upward; then turned another to show how the gun might be swung, as on a pivot, this way and that to command the range of the entire horizon, and he concluded the performance, with the aid of several husky lads in begrimed gray, by going through the pantomime of loading with a long yellow five-inch shell from the magazine behind him, and pretending to fire, meanwhile explaining that he could send one shot aloft every six seconds and with each shot reach a maximum altitude of between seven and eight thousand feet. Altogether it was a very pretty sight to see and most edifying. Likewise it took on an added interest when we learned that the blue-eyed youth and his brother of

Paths of Glory

a twin balloon-cannon at the front of Laon had during the preceding three weeks brought down four of the enemy's airmen, and were exceedingly hopeful of fattening their joint average before the present week had ended.

After that we took photographs ad lib and McCutcheon had a trip with Ingold, a great aviator, in a biplane, which the Germans call a double- decker, as distinguished from the Taube or monoplane, with its birdlike wings and curved tail rudder-piece. Just as they came down, after a circular spin over the lines, a strange machine, presumably hostile, appeared far up and far away, but circled off to the south out of target reach before the balloon gunman could get the range of her and the aim. On the heels of this a biplane from another aviation field somewhere down the left wing dropped in quite informally bearing two grease- stained men to pass the time of day and borrow some gasoline. The occasion appeared to demand a drink. We all repaired, therefore, to one of the great canvas houses where the air birds nest night-times and where the airmen sleep. There we had noggins of white wine all round, and a pointer dog, which was chained to an officer's trunk, begged me in plain pointer language to cast off his leash so he might go and stalk the covey of pheasants that were taking a dust-bath in the open road not fifty yards away.

The temptation was strong, but our guides said if we meant to get to the battlefront before lunch it was time, and past time, we got started. Being thus warned we did get started.

Of a battle there is this to be said—that the closer you get to it the less do you see of it. Always in my experiences in Belgium and my more recent experiences in France I found this to be true. Take, for example, the present instance. I knew that we were approximately in the middle sworl of the twisting scroll formed by the German center, and that we were at this moment entering the very tip of the enormous inverted V made by the frontmost German defenses. I knew that stretching away to the southeast of us and to the northwest was a line some two hundred miles long, measuring it from tip to tip, where sundry millions of men in English khaki and French fustian and German shoddy- wools were fighting the biggest fight and the most prolonged fight and the most stubborn fight that historians probably will write down as having been fought in this war or any lesser war. I knew this fight had been going on for weeks now back and forth upon the River Aisne and would certainly go on for weeks and perhaps months more to come. I knew these things because I had been told them; but I shouldn't have known if I hadn't been told. I shouldn't even have guessed it.

I recall that we traveled at a cup-racing clip along a road that first wound like a coiling snake and then straightened like a striking snake, and that always we traveled through dust so thick it made a fog. In this chalky land of northern France the brittle soil dries out after a rain very quickly, and turns into a white powder where there are wheels to churn it up and grit it fine. Here surely there was an abundance of wheels. We passed many marching men and many lumbering supply trains which were going our way, and we met many motor ambulances and many ammunition trucks which were coming back. Always the ambulances were full and the ammunition wagons were empty. I judge an expert in these things might by the fullness of the one and the emptiness of the other gauge the emphasis with which the fight ahead went on. The drivers of the trucks nearly all wore captured French caps and French uniform coats, which adornment the marching men invariably regarded as a quaint jest to be laughed at and cheered for.

We stopped at our appointed place, which was on the top of a ridge where a general of a corps had his headquarters. From here one had a view—a fair view and, roughly, a fan-shaped view—of certain highly important artillery operations. Likewise, the eminence, gentle and gradual as it was, commanded a mile-long stretch of the road, which formed the main line of communication between the front and the base; and these two facts in part explained why the general had made this his abiding place. Even my layman's mind could sense the reasons for establishing headquarters at such a spot.

As for the general, he and his staff, at the moment of our arrival in their midst, were stationed at the edge of a scanty woodland where telescopes stood and a table with maps and charts on it. Quite with the manner of men who had nothing to do except to enjoy the sunshine and breathe the fresh air, they strolled back and forth in pairs and trios. I think it must have been through force of habit that, when they halted to turn about and retrace the route, they stopped always for a moment or two and faced southward. It was from the southward that there came rolling up to us the sounds of a bellowing chorus of gunfire—a Wagnerian chorus, truly. That perhaps was as it should be. Wagner's countrymen were helping to make it. Now the separate reports strung out until you could count perhaps three between reports; now they came so close together that the music they made was a constant roaring which would endure for a minute on a stretch, or half a minute anyhow. But for all the noticeable heed which any uniformed men in my vicinity paid to this it might as well have been blasting in a distant stone quarry. This attitude which they maintained, coupled with the fact that seemingly all the firing did no damage whatsoever, only served to strengthen the illusion that after all it was not the actual business of warfare which spread itself beneath our eyes.

Apparently most of the shells from the Allies' side—which of course was the far side from us—rose out of a dip in the contour of the land. Rising so, they mainly fell among or near the shattered remnants of two hamlets upon the nearer front of a little hill perhaps three miles from our location. A favorite object of their attack appeared to be a wrecked beet-sugar factory of which one side was blown away.

There would appear just above the horizon line a ball of smoke as black as your hat and the size of your hat, which meant a grenade of high explosives. Then right behind it would blossom a dainty, plumy little blob of innocent white, fit to make a pompon for the hat, and that, they told us, would be shrapnel. The German reply to the enemy's guns issued from the timbered verges of slopes at our right hand and our left; and these German shells, so far as we might judge, passed entirely over and beyond the smashed hamlets and the ruined sugar-beet factory and, curving downward, exploded out of our sight.

"The French persist in a belief that we have men in those villages, " said one of the general's aides to me. "They are wasting their powder. There are many men there and some among them are Germans, but they are all dead men. "

He offered to show me some live men, and took me to one of the telescopes and aimed the barrel of it in the proper direction while I focused for distance. Suddenly out of the blur of the lens there sprang up in front of me, seemingly quite close, a zigzagging toy trench cut in the face of a little hillock. This trench was full of gray figures of the size of very small dolls. They were moving aimlessly back and forth, it seemed to me, doing nothing at all.

Then I saw another trench that ran slantwise up the hillock and it contained more of the pygmies. A number of these pygmies came

Paths of Glory

out of their trench—I could see them quite plainly, clambering up the steep wall of it—and they moved, very slowly it would seem, toward the crosswise trench on ahead a bit. To reach it they had to cross a sloping green patch of cleared land. So far as I might tell no explosive or shrapnel shower fell into them or near them, but when they had gone perhaps a third of the distance across the green patch there was a quick scatteration of their inch-high figures. Quite distinctly I counted three manikins who instantly fell down flat and two others who went ahead a little way deliberately, and then lay down. The rest darted back to the cover which they had just quit and jumped in briskly. The five figures remained where they had dropped and became quiet. Anyway, I could detect no motion in them. They were just little gray strips. Into my mind on the moment came incongruously a memory of what I had seen a thousand times in the composing room of a country newspaper where the type was set by hand. I thought of five pica plugs lying on the printshop floor.

It was hard for me to make myself believe that I had seen human beings killed and wounded. I can hardly believe it yet—that those insignificant toy-figures were really and truly men. I watched through the glass after that for possibly twenty minutes, until the summons came for lunch, but no more of the German dolls ventured out of their make- believe defenses to be blown flat by an invisible blast.

It was a picnic lunch served on board trestles under a tree behind the cover of a straw-roofed shelter tent, and we ate it in quite a peaceful and cozy picnic fashion. Twice during the meal an orderly came with a message which he had taken off a field telephone in a little pigsty of logs and straw fifty feet away from us; but the general each time merely canted his head to hear what the whispered word might be and went on eating. There was no clattering in of couriers, no hurried dispatching of orders this way and that. Only, just before we finished with the meal, he got up and walked away a few paces, and there two of his aides joined him and the three of them confabbed together earnestly for a couple of minutes or so. While so engaged they had the air about them of surgeons preparing to undertake an operation and first consulting over the preliminary details. Or perhaps it would be truer to say they looked like civil engineers discussing the working-out of an undertaking regarding which there was interest but no uneasiness. Assuredly they behaved not in the least as a general and aides would behave in a story book or on the

Paths of Glory

stage, and when they were through they came back for their coffee and their cigars to the table where the rest of us sat.

"We are going now to a battery of the twenty-one-centimeter guns and from there to the ten-centimeters, " called out Lieutenant Geibel as we climbed aboard our cars; "and when we pass that first group of houses yonder we shall be under fire. So if you have wills to make, you American gentlemen, you should be making them now before we start. " A gay young officer was Lieutenant Geibel, and he just naturally would have his little joke whether or no.

Immediately then and twice again that day we were technically presumed to be under fire—I use the word technically advisedly—and again the next day and once again two days thereafter before Antwerp, but I was never able to convince myself that it was so. Certainly there was no sense of actual danger as we sped through the empty single street of a despoiled and tenantless village. All about us were the marks of what the shellfire had done, some fresh and still smoking, some old and dry- charred, but no shells dropped near us as we circled in a long swing up to within half a mile of the first line of German trenches and perhaps a mile to the left of them.

Thereby we arrived safely and very speedily and without mishap at a battery of twenty-one-centimeter guns, standing in a gnawed sheep pasture behind an abandoned farmhouse, what was left of a farmhouse, which was to say very little of it indeed. The guns stood in a row, and each one of them—there were five in all—stared with its single round eye at the blue sky where the sky showed above a thick screen of tall slim poplars growing on the far side of the farmyard. We barely had time to note that the men who served the guns were denned in holes in the earth like wolves, with earthen roofs above them and straw beds to lie on, and that they had screened each gun in green saplings cut from the woods and stuck upright in the ground, to hide its position from the sight of prying aeroplane scouts, and that the wheels of the guns were tired with huge, broad steel plates called caterpillars, to keep them from bogging down in miry places—I say we barely had time to note these details mentally when things began to happen. There was a large and much be-mired soldier who spraddled face downward upon his belly in one of the straw-lined dugouts with his ear hitched to a telephone. Without lifting his head or turning it he sang out. At that all the other men sprang up very promptly. Before, they had been sprawled about in sunny places, smoking and sleeping, and

Paths of Glory

writing on postcards. Postcards, butter and beer—these are the German private's luxuries, but most of all postcards. The men bestirred themselves.

"You are in luck, gentlemen, " said the lieutenant. "This battery has been idle all day, but now it is to begin firing. The order to fire just came. The balloon operator, who is in communication with the observation pits beyond the foremost infantry trenches, will give the range and the distance. Listen, please. " He held up his hand for silence, intent on hearing what the man at the telephone was repeating back over the line. "Ah, that's it—5400 meters straight over the tree tops. "

He waved us together into a more compact group. "That's the idea. Stand here, please, behind Number One gun, and watch straight ahead of you for the shot—you must watch very closely or you will miss it—and remember to keep your mouth open to save your eardrums from being injured by the concussion. "

So far as I personally was concerned this last bit of advice was unnecessary—my mouth was open already. Four men trotted to a magazine that was in an earthen kennel and came back bearing a wheelless sheet- metal barrow on which rested a three-foot-long brass shell, very trim and slim and handsome and shiny like gold. It was an expensive-looking shell and quite ornate. At the tail of Number One the bearers heaved the barrow up shoulder-high, at the same time tilting it forward. Then a round vent opened magically and the cyclops sucked the morsel forward into its gullet, thus reversing the natural swallowing process, and smacked its steel lip behind it with a loud and greasy snuck! A glutton of a gun—you could tell that from the sound it made.

A lieutenant snapped out something, a sergeant snapped it back to him, the gun crew jumped aside, balancing themselves on tiptoe with their mouths all agape, and the gun-firer either pulled a lever out or else pushed one home, I couldn't tell which. Then everything—sky and woods and field and all—fused and ran together in a great spatter of red flame and white smoke, and the earth beneath our feet shivered and shook as the twenty-one-centimeter spat out its twenty-one-centimeter mouthful. A vast obscenity of sound beat upon us, making us reel backward, and for just the one-thousandth part of a second I saw a round white spot, like a new baseball, against a cloud background. The poplars, which had bent forward as if before a quick wind-squall, stood up, trembling in their tops, and we dared to breathe again. Then each in its turn the other four guns spoke, profaning the welkin, and we rocked on our heels like drunken men, and I remember there was a queer taste, as of something burned, in my mouth. All of which was very fine, no doubt, and very inspiring, too, if one cared deeply for that sort of thing; but to myself, when the hemisphere had ceased from its quiverings, I said:

"It isn't true—this isn't war; it's just a costly, useless game of playing at war. Behold, now, these guns did not fire at anybody visible or anything tangible. They merely elevated their muzzles into the sky and fired into the sky to make a great tumult and spoil the good air with a bad-tasting smoke. No enemy is in sight and no enemy will answer back; therefore no enemy exists. It is all a useless and a fussy business, signifying nothing."

Nor did any enemy answer back. The guns having been fired with due pomp and circumstance, the gunners went back to those pipe-smoking and postcard-writing pursuits of theirs and everything was as before— peaceful and entirely serene. Only the telephone man remained in his bed in the straw with his ear at his telephone. He was still couched there, spraddling ridiculously on his stomach, with his legs outstretched in a sawbuck pattern, as we came away.

"It isn't always quite so quiet hereabouts," said the lieutenant. "The commander of this battery tells me that yesterday the French dropped some shrapnel among his guns and killed a man or two. Perhaps things will be brisker at the ten-centimeter-gun battery." He spoke as one who regretted that the show which he offered was not more exciting.

The twenty-one-centimeters, as I have told you, were in the edge of the woods, with leafy ambushes about them, but the little ten-centimeter guns ranged themselves quite boldly in a meadow of rank long grass just under the weather-rim of a small hill. They were buried to their haunches—if a field gun may be said to have haunches—in depressions gouged out by their own frequent recoils; otherwise they were without concealment of any sort. To reach them we rode a mile or two and then walked a quarter of a mile through a series of chalky bare gullies, and our escorts made us stoop low and hurry fast wherever the path wound up to the crest of the bank, lest our figures, being outlined against the sky, should betray our whereabouts and, what was more important, the whereabouts of the battery to the sharpshooters in the French rifle pits forward of the French infantry trenches and not exceeding a mile from us.

We stopped first at an observation station cunningly hidden in a haw thicket on the brow of a steep and heavily wooded defile overlooking the right side of the river valley—-the river, however, being entirely out of sight. Standing here we heard the guns speak apparently from almost beneath our feet, and three or four seconds thereafter we saw five little puffballs of white smoke uncurling above a line of trees across the valley. Somebody said this was our battery shelling the French and English in those woods yonder, but you could hardly be expected to believe that, since no reply came back and no French or English whatsoever showed themselves. Altogether it seemed a most impotent and impersonal proceeding; and when the novelty of waiting for the blast of sound and then watching for the smoke plumes to appear had worn off, as it very soon did, we visited the guns themselves. They were not under our feet at all. They were some two hundred yards away, across a field where the telephone wires stretched over the old plow furrows and through the rank meadow grass, like springs to catch woodcock.

Here again the trick of taking a message off the telephone and shouting it forth from the mouth of a fox burrow was repeated. Whenever this procedure came to pass a sergeant who had strained his vocal cords from much giving of orders would swell out his chest and throw back his head and shriek hoarsely with what was left of his voice, which wasn't much. This meant a fury of noise resulting instantly and much white smoke to follow. For a while the guns were fired singly and then they were fired in salvos; and you might mark how the grass for fifty yards in front of the muzzles would lie on the earth quite flat and then stand erect, and how the guns, like shying bronchos, would leap backward upon their carriages and then slide forward again as the air in the air cushions took up the kick. Also we took note that the crews of the ten- centimeters had built for themselves dugouts to sleep in and to live in, and had covered the sod roofs over with straw and broken tree limbs. We judged they would be very glad indeed to crawl into those same shelters when night came, for they had been serving the guns all day and plainly were about as weary as men could be. To burn powder hour after hour and day after day and week after week at a foe who never sees you and whom you never see; to go at this dreary, heavy trade of war with the sober, uninspired earnestness of convicts

Paths of Glory

building a prison wall about themselves—the ghastly unreality of the proposition left me mentally numbed.

Howsoever, we arrived not long after that at a field hospital— namely, Field Hospital Number 36, and here was realism enough to satisfy the lexicographer who first coined the word. This field hospital was established in eight abandoned houses of the abandoned small French village of Colligis, and all eight houses were crowded with wounded men lying as closely as they could lie upon mattresses placed side by side on the floors, with just room to step between the mattresses. Be it remembered also that these were all men too seriously wounded to be moved even to a point as close as Laon; those more lightly injured than these were already carried back to the main hospitals.

We went into one room containing only men suffering from chest wounds, who coughed and wheezed and constantly fought off the swarming flies that assailed them, and into another room given over entirely to brutally abbreviated human fragments—fractional parts of men who had lost their arms or legs. On the far mattress against the wall lay a little pale German with his legs gone below the knees, who smiled upward at the ceiling and was quite chipper.

"A wonderful man, that little chap, " said one of the surgeons to me. "When they first brought him here two weeks ago I said to him: 'It's hard on you that you should lose both your feet, ' and he looked up at me and grinned and said: 'Herr Doctor, it might have been worse. It might have been my hands—and me a tailor by trade!'"

This surgeon told us he had an American wife, and he asked me to bear a message for him to his wife's people in the States. So if these lines should come to the notice of Mrs. Rosamond Harris, who lives at Hinesburg, Vermont, she may know that her son-in-law, Doctor Schilling, was at last accounts very busy and very well, although coated with white dust—face, head and eyebrows—so that he reminded me of a clown in a pantomime, and dyed as to his hands with iodine to an extent that made his fingers look like pieces of well-cured meerschaum.

They were bringing in more men, newly wounded that day, as we came out of Doctor Schilling's improvised operating room in the little village schoolhouse, and one of the litter bearers was a smart-faced little London Cockney, a captured English ambulance-hand,

Paths of Glory

who wore a German soldier's cap to save him from possible annoyance as he went about his work. Not very many wounded had arrived since the morning—it was a dull day for them, the surgeons said—but I took note that, when the Red Cross men put down a canvas stretcher upon the courtyard flags and shortly thereafter took it up again, it left a broad red smear where it rested against the flat stones. Also this stretcher and all the other stretchers had been so sagged by the weight of bodies that they threatened to rip from the frames, and so stained by that which had stained them that the canvas was as stiff as though it had been varnished and revarnished with many coats of brown shellac. But it wasn't shellac. There is just one fluid which leaves that brown, hard coating when it dries upon woven cloth.

As I recall now we had come through the gate of the schoolhouse to where the automobiles stood when a puff of wind, blowing to us from the left, which meant from across the battlefront, brought to our noses a certain smell which we already knew full well.

"You get it, I see," said the German officer who stood alongside me. "It comes from three miles off, but you can get it five miles distant when the wind is strong. That"—and he waved his left arm toward it as though the stench had been a visible thing—"that explains why tobacco is so scarce with us among the staff back yonder in Laon. All the tobacco which can be spared is sent to the men in the front trenches. As long as they smoke and keep on smoking they can stand—that!

"You see," he went on painstakingly, "the situation out there at Cerny is like this: The French and English, but mainly the English, held the ground firSt. We drove them back and they lost very heavily. In places their trenches were actually full of dead and dying men when we took those trenches.

"You could have buried them merely by filling up the trenches with earth. And that old beet-sugar factory which you saw this noon when we were at field headquarters—it was crowded with badly wounded Englishmen.

"At once they rallied and forced us back, and now it was our turn to lose heavily. That was nearly three weeks ago, and since then the ground over which we fought has been debatable ground, lying

Paths of Glory

between our lines and the enemy's lines—a stretch four miles long and half a mile wide that is literally carpeted with bodies of dead men. They weren't all dead at first. For two days and nights our men in the earthworks heard the cries of those who still lived, and the sound of them almost drove them mad. There was no reaching the wounded, though, either from our lines or from the Allies' lines. Those who tried to reach them were themselves killed. Now there are only dead out there—thousands of dead, I think. And they have been there twenty days. Once in a while a shell strikes that old sugar mill or falls into one of those trenches. Then—well, then, it is worse for those who serve in the front lines. "

"But in the name of God, man, " I said, "why don't they call a truce— both sides—and put that horror underground? "

He shrugged his shoulders.

"War is different now, " he said. "Truces are out of fashion. "

I stood there and I smelled that smell. And I thought of all those flies, and those blood-stiffened stretchers, and those little inch-long figures which I myself, looking through that telescope, had seen lying on the green hill, and those automobiles loaded with mangled men, and War de Luxe betrayed itself to me. Beneath its bogus glamour I saw war for what it is—the next morning of drunken glory.

Chapter 12

The Rut of Big Guns in France

Let me say at the outset of this chapter that I do not set up as one professing to have any knowledge whatsoever of so-called military science. The more I have seen of the carrying-on of the actual business of war, the less able do I seem to be to understand the meanings of the business. For me strategy remains a closed book. Even the simplest primary lessons of it, the A B C's of it, continue to impress me as being stupid, but none the less unplumbable mysteries.

The physical aspects of campaigning I can in a way grasp. At least I flatter myself that I can. A man would have to be deaf and dumb and blind not to grasp them, did they reveal themselves before him as they have revealed themselves before me. Indeed, if he preserved only the faculty of scent unimpaired he might still be able to comprehend the thing, since, as I have said before, war in its commoner phases is not so much a sight as a great bad smell. As for the rudiments of the system which dictates the movements of troops in large masses or in small, which sacrifices thousands of men to take a town or hold a river when that town and that river, physically considered, appear to be of no consequence whatsoever, those elements I have not been able to sense, even though I studied the matter most diligently. So after sundry months of first-hand observation in one of the theaters of hostilities, I tell myself that the trade of fighting is a trade to be learned by slow and laborious degrees, and even then may be learned with thoroughness only by one who has a natural aptitude for it. Either that, or else I am most extraordinarily thick-headed, for I own that I am still as complete a greenhorn now as I was at the beginning.

Having made the confession which is said to be good for the soul, and which in any event has the merit of blunting in advance the critical judgments of the expert, since he must pity my ignorance and my innocence even though he quarrel with my conclusions, I now assume the role of prophet long enough to venture to say that the day of the modern walled fort is over and done with. I do not presume to speak regarding coast defenses maintained for the purposes of repelling attacks or invasions from the sea. I am speaking with regard to land defenses which are assailable by land

Paths of Glory

forces. I believe in the future great wars—if indeed there are to be any more great wars following after this one—that the nations involved, instead of buttoning their frontiers down with great fortresses and ringing their principal cities about with circles of protecting works, will put their trust more and more in transportable cannon of a caliber and a projecting force greater than any yet built or planned. I make this assertion after viewing the visible results of the operations of the German 42-centimeter guns in Belgium and France, notably at Liege in the former country and at Maubeuge in the latter.

Except for purposes of frightening non-combatants the Zeppelins apparently have proved of most dubious value; nor, barring its value as a scout—a field in which it is of marvelous efficiency—does the aeroplane appear to have been of much consequence in inflicting loss upon the enemy. Of the comparatively new devices for waging war, the submarine and the great gun alone seem to have justified in any great degree the hopes of their sponsors.

Since I came back out of the war zone I have met persons who questioned the existence of a 42-centimeter gun, they holding it to be a nightmare created out of the German imagination with intent to break the confidence of the enemies of Germany. I did not see a 42-centimeter gun with my own eyes, and personally I doubt whether the Germans had as many of them as they claimed to have; but I talked with one entirely reliable witness, an American consular officer, who saw a 42-centimeter gun as it was being transported to the front in the opening week of the war, and with another American, a diplomat of high rank, who interviewed a man who saw one of these guns, and who in detailing the conversation to me said the spectator had been literally stunned by the size and length and the whole terrific contour of the monster.

Finally, I know from personal experience that these guns have been employed, and employed with a result that goes past adequate description; but if I hadn't seen the effect of their fire I wouldn't have believed it were true. I wouldn't have believed anything evolved out of the brains of men and put together by the fingers of men could operate with such devilish accuracy to compass such utter destruction. I would have said it was some planetic force, some convulsion of natural forces, and not an agency of human devisement, that turned Fort Loncin inside out, and transformed it within a space of hours from a supposedly impregnable stronghold into a hodgepodge of complete and hideous ruination. And what befell Fort Loncin on the hills behind Liege befell Fort Des Sarts outside of Maubeuge, as I have reason to know. When the first of the 42-centimeters emerged from Essen it took a team of thirty horses to haul it; and with it out of that nest of the Prussian war eagle came also a force of mechanics and engineers to set it up and aim it and fire it.

Here, too, is an interesting fact that I have not seen printed anywhere, though I heard it often enough in Germany: by reason of its bulk the 42- centimeter must be mounted upon a concrete base before it can be used. Heretofore the concrete which was available for this purpose required at least a fortnight of exposure before it was sufficiently firm and hardened; but when Fraulein Bertha Krupp's engineers escorted the Fraulein's newest and most impressive steel masterpiece to the war, they brought along with them the ingredients for a new kind of concrete; and those who claim to have been present on the occasion declare that within forty-eight hours after they had mixed and molded it, it was ready to bear the weight of the guns and withstand the shock of their recoil.

This having been done, I conceive of the operators as hoisting their guns into position, and posting up a set of rules—even in time of war it is impossible to imagine the Germans doing anything of importance without a set of rules to go by—and working out the distance by mathematics, and then turning loose their potential cataclysms upon the stubborn forts which opposed their further progress. From the viewpoint of the Germans the consequences to the foe must amply have justified the trouble and the cost. For where a 42-centimeter shell falls it does more than merely alter landscape; almost you might say it alters geography.

In the open field, where he must aim his gun with his own eye and discharge it with his own finger, I take it the Kaiser's private soldier is no great shakes as a marksman. The Germans themselves begrudgingly admitted the French excelled them in the use of light artillery. There was wonderment as well as reluctance in this concession. To them it seemed well-nigh incredible that any nation should be their superiors in any department pertaining to the practice of war. They could not bring themselves fully to understand it. It remained as much a puzzle to them as the unaccountable obstinacy of the English in refusing to be budged out of their position by displays of cold steel, or to be shaken by the volleying,

Paths of Glory

bull-like roar of the German charging cry, which at first the Germans counted upon as being almost as efficacious as the bayonet for instilling a wholesome fear of the German war god into the souls of their foes.

While giving the Frenchmen credit for knowing how to handle and serve small field-pieces, the Germans nevertheless insisted that their infantry fire or their skirmish fire was as deadly as that of the Allies, or even deadlier. This I was not prepared to believe. I do not think the German is a good rifle shot by instinct, as the American often is, and in a lesser degree, perhaps, the Englishman is, too. But where he can work the range out on paper, where he has to do with mechanics instead of a shifting mark, where he can apply to the details of gun firing the exact principles of arithmetic, I am pretty sure the German is as good a gunner as may be found on the Continent of Europe today. This may not apply to him at sea, for he has neither the sailor traditions nor the inherited naval craftsmanship of the English; but judging by what I have seen I am quite certain that with the solid earth beneath him and a set of figures before him and an enemy out of sight of him to be damaged he is in a class all by himself.

A German staff officer, who professed to have been present, told me that at Manonvilla—so he spelled the name—a 42-centimeter gun was fired one hundred and forty-seven times from a distance of 14,000 meters at a fort measuring 600 meters in length by 400 meters in breadth—a very small target, indeed, considering the range—and that investigation after the capture of the fort showed not a single one of the one hundred and forty-seven shots had been an outright miss. Some few, he said, hit the walls or at the bases of the walls, but all the others, he claimed, had bull's-eyed into the fort itself.

Subsequently, on subjecting this tale to the acid test of second thought I was compelled to doubt what the staff officer had said. To begin with, I didn't understand how a 42-centimeter gun could be fired one hundred and forty-seven times without its wearing out, for I have often heard that the larger the bore of your gun and the heavier the charge of explosives which it carries, the shorter is its period of efficiency.. In the second place, it didn't seem possible after being hit one hundred and forty-seven times with 42-centimeter bombs that enough of any fort of whatsoever size would be left to permit of a tallying-up of separate shots. Ten shots properly placed should have razed it; twenty more should have blown its leveled remainder to powder and scattered the powder.

Paths of Glory

Be the facts what they may with regard to this case of the fort of Manonvilla—if that be its proper name—I am prepared to speak with the assurance of an eyewitness concerning the effect of the German fire upon the defenses of Maubeuge. What I saw at Liege I have described in a previous chapter of this volume. What I saw at Maubeuge was even more convincing testimony, had I needed it, that the Germans had a 42- centimeter gun, and that, given certain favored conditions, they knew how to handle it effectively.

We spent the better part of a day in two of the forts which were fondly presumed to guard Maubeuge toward the north—Fort Des Sarts and Fort Boussois; but Fort Des Sarts was the one where the 42-centimeter gun gave the first exhibition of its powers upon French soil in this war, so we went there first. To reach it we ran a matter of seven kilometers through a succession of villages, each with its mutely eloquent tale of devastation and general smash to tell; each with its group of contemptuously tolerant German soldiers on guard and its handful of natives, striving feebly to piece together the broken and bankrupt fragments of their worldly affairs.

Approaching Des Sarts more nearly we came to a longish stretch of highway, which the French had cleared of visual obstructions in anticipation of resistance by infantry in the event that the outer ring of defenses gave way before the German bombardment. It had all been labor in vain, for the town capitulated after the outposts fell; but it must have been very great labor. Any number of fine elm trees had been felled and their boughs, stripped now of leaves, stuck up like bare bones. There were holes in the metaled road where misaimed shells had descended, and in any one of these holes you might have buried a horse. A little gray church stood off by itself upon the plain. It had been homely enough to start with. Now with its steeple shorn away and one of its two belfry windows obliterated by a straying shot it had a rakish, cock-eyed look to it.

Just beyond where the church was our chauffeur halted the car in obedience to an order from the staff officer who had been detailed by Major von Abercron, commandant of Maubeuge, to accompany us on this particular excursion. Our guide pointed off to the right. "There, " he said, "is where we dropped the first of our big ones when we were trying to get the range of the fort. You see our guns were posted at a point between eight and nine kilometers away and at the start we overshot a trifle. Still to the garrison yonder it must have been an unhappy foretaste of what they might shortly expect, when they saw the forty- twos striking here in this field and saw what execution they did among the cabbage and the beet patches. "

We left the car and, following our guide, went to look. Spaced very neatly at intervals apart of perhaps a hundred and fifty yards a series of craters broke the surface of the earth. Considering the tools which dug them they were rather symmetrical craters, not jagged and gouged, but with smooth walls and each in shape a perfect funnel. We measured roughly a typical specimen. Across the top it was between fifty and sixty feet in diameter, and it sloped down evenly for a depth of eighteen feet in the chalky soil to a pointed bottom, where two men would have difficulty standing together without treading upon each other's toes. Its sides were lined with loose pellets of earth of the average size of a tennis ball, and when we slid down into the hole these rounded clods accompanied us in small avalanches.

We were filled with astonishment, first, that an explosive grenade, weighing upward of a ton, could be so constructed that it would penetrate thus far into firm and solid earth before it exploded; and, second, that it could make such a neat saucer of a hole when it did explode. But there was a still more amazing thing to be pondered. Of the earth which had been dispossessed from the crevasse, amounting to a great many wagonloads, no sign remained. It was not heaped up about the lips of the funnel; it was not visibly scattered over the nearermost furrows of that truck field. So far as we might tell it was utterly gone; and from that we deduced that the force of the explosion had been sufficient to pulverize the clay so finely and cast it so far and so wide that it fell upon the surface in a fine shower, leaving no traces unless one made a minute search for it. Noting the wonder upon our faces, the officer was moved to speak further in a tone of sincere admiration, touching on the capabilities of the crowning achievement of the Krupp works:

"Pretty strong medicine, eh? Well, wait until I have shown you American gentlemen what remains of the fort; then you will better understand. Even here, out in the open, for a radius of a hundred and fifty meters, any man, conceding he wasn't killed outright, would be knocked senseless and after that for hours, even for days, perhaps, he would be entirely unnerved. The force of the concussion appears to have that effect upon persons who are at a considerable distance—it rips their nerves to tatters. Some seem numbed and dazed; others develop an acute hysteria.

Paths of Glory

"Highly interesting, is it not? Listen then; here is something even more interesting: Within an inclosed space, where there is a roof to hold in the gas generated by the explosion or where there are reasonably high walls, the man who escapes being torn apart in the instant of impact, or who escapes being crushed to death by collapsing masonry, or killed by flying fragments, is exceedingly likely to choke to death as he lies temporarily paralyzed and helpless from the shock. I was at Liege and again here, and I know from my own observations that this is true. At Liege particularly many of the garrison were caught and penned up in underground casements, and there we found them afterward dead, but with no marks of wounds upon them—they had been asphyxiated."

I suppose in times of peace the speaker was a reasonably kind man and reasonably regardful of the rights of his fellowmen. Certainly he was most courteous to us and most considerate; but he described this slaughter-pit scene with the enthusiasm of one who was a partner in a most creditable and worthy enterprise.

Immediately about Des Sarts stood many telegraph poles in a row, for here the road, which was the main road from Paris to Brussels, curved close up under the grass-covered bastions. All the telegraph wires had been cut, and they dangled about the bases of the poles in snarled tangles like love vines. The ditches paralleling the road were choked with felled trees, and, what with the naked limbs, were as spiky as shad spines. Of the small cottages which once had stood in the vicinity of the fort not one remained standing. Their sites were marked by flattened heaps of brick and plaster from which charred ends of rafters protruded. It was as though a giant had sat himself down upon each little house in turn and squashed it to the foundation stones.

As a fort Des Sarts dated back to 1883. I speak of it in the past tense, because the Germans had put it in that tense. As a fort, or as anything resembling a fort, it had ceased to be, absolutely. The inner works of it—the redan and the underground barracks, and the magazines, and all—were built after the style. followed by military engineers back in 1883, having revetments faced up with brick and stone; but only a little while ago—in the summer of 1913, to be exact—the job of inclosing the original works with a glacis of a newer type had been completed. So when the Germans came along in the first week of September it was in most respects made over into a modern fort. No doubt the re-enforcements of reserves that hurried into it to strengthen the regular garrison counted themselves lucky men to have so massive and stout a shelter from which to fight an enemy who must work in the open against them. Poor devils, their hopes crumbled along with their walls when the Germans brought up the forty-twos.

We entered in through a breach in the first parapet and crossed, one at a time, on a tottery wooden bridge which was propped across a fossé half full of rubble, and so came to what had been the heart of the fort of Des Sarts. Had I not already gathered some notion of the powers for destruction of those one-ton, four-foot-long shells, I should have said that the spot where we halted had been battered and crashed at for hours; that scores and perhaps hundreds of bombs had been plumped into it. Now, though, I was prepared to believe the German captain when he said probably not more than five or six of the devil devices had struck this target. Make it six for good measure. Conceive each of the six as having been dammed by a hurricane and sired by an earthquake, and as being related to an active volcano on one side of the family and to a flaming meteor on the other. Conceive it as falling upon a man-made, masonry-walled burrow in the earth and being followed in rapid succession by five of its blood brethren; then you will begin to get some fashion of mental photograph of the result. I confess myself as unable to supply any better suggestion for a comparison. Nor shall I attempt to describe the picture in any considerable detail. I only know that for the first time in my life I realized the full and adequate meaning of the word chaos. The proper definition of it was spread broadcast before my eyes.

Appreciating the impossibility of comprehending the full scope of the disaster which here had befallen, or of putting it concretely into words if I did comprehend it, I sought to pick out small individual details, which was hard to do, too, seeing that all things were jumbled together so. This had been a series of cunningly buried tunnels and arcades, with cozy subterranean dormitories opening off of side passages, and still farther down there had been magazines and storage spaces. Now it was all a hole in the ground, and the force which blasted it out had then pulled the hole in behind itself. We stood on the verge, looking downward into a chasm which seemed to split its way to infinite depths, although in fact it was probably not nearly so deep as it appeared. If we looked upward there, forty feet above our heads, was a wide riven gap in the earth crust.

Near me I discerned a litter of metal fragments. From such of the scraps as retained any shape at all, I figured that they had been part of the protective casing of a gun mounted somewhere above. The missile which wrecked the gun flung its armor down here. I searched my brain for a simile which might serve to give a notion of the present state of that steel jacket. I didn't find the one I wanted, but if you will think of an earthenware pot which has been thrown from a very high building upon a brick sidewalk you may have some idea of what I saw.

At that, it was no completer a ruin than any of the surrounding debris. Indeed, in the whole vista of annihilation but two objects remained recognizably intact, and these, strange to say, were two iron bed frames bolted to the back wall of what I think must have been a barrack room for officers. The room itself was no longer there. Brick, mortar, stone, concrete, steel reinforcements, iron props, the hard-packed earth, had been ripped out and churned into indistinguishable bits, but those two iron beds hung fast to a discolored patch of plastering, though the floor was gone from beneath them. Seemingly they were hardly damaged. One gathered that a 42-centimeter shell possessed in some degree the freakishness which we associate with the behavior of cyclones.

We were told that at the last, when the guns had been silenced and dismounted and the walls had been pierced and the embrasures blown bodily away, the garrison, or what was left of it, fled to these lowermost shelters. But the burrowing bombs found the refugees out and killed them, nearly all, and those of them who died were still buried beneath our feet in as hideous a sepulcher as ever was digged. There was no getting them out from that tomb. The Crack of Doom will find them still there, I guess.

To reach a portion of Des Sarts, as yet un-visited, we skirted the gape of the crater, climbing over craggy accumulations of wreckage, and traversed a tunnel with an arched roof and mildewed brick walls, like a wine vault. The floor of it was littered with the knapsacks and water bottles of dead or captured men, with useless rifles broken at the stocks and bent in the barrels, and with suchlike riffle. At the far end of the passage we came out into the open at the back side of the fort.

"Right here," said the officer who was piloting us, "I witnessed a sight which made a deeper impression upon me than anything I have seen in this campaign. After the white flag had been hoisted by the survivors and we had marched in, I halted my men just here at the entrance to this arcade. We didn't dare venture into the redan, for sporadic explosions were still occurring in the ammunition stores. Also there were fires raging. Smoke was pouring thickly out of the mouth of the tunnel. It didn't seem possible that there could be anyone alive back yonder.

"All of a sudden, men began to come out of the tunnel. They came and came until there were nearly two hundred of them—French reservists mostly. They were crazy men—crazy for the time being, and still crazy, I expect, some of them. They came out staggering, choking, falling down and getting up again. You see, their nerves were gone. The fumes, the gases, the shock, the fire, what they had endured and what they had escaped—all these had distracted them. They danced, sang, wept, laughed, shouted in a sort of maudlin frenzy, spun about deliriously until they dropped. They were deafened, and some of them could not see but had to grope their way. I remember one man who sat down and pulled off his boots and socks and threw them away and then hobbled on in his bare feet until he cut the bottoms of them to pieces. I don't care to see anything like that again—even if it is my enemies that suffer it."

He told it so vividly, that standing alongside of him before the tunnel opening I could see the procession myself—those two hundred men who had drained horror to its lees and were drunk on it.

We went to Fort Boussois, some four miles away. It was another of the keys to the town. It was taken on September sixth; on the next day, September seventh, the citadel surrendered. Here, in lieu of the 42-centimeter, which was otherwise engaged for the moment, the attacking forces brought into play an Austrian battery of 30-centimeter guns. So far as I have been able to ascertain this was the only Austrian command which had any part in the western campaigns. The Austrian gunners shelled the fort until the German infantry had been massed in a forest to the northward. Late in the afternoon the infantry charged across a succession of cleared fields and captured the outer slopes. With these in their possession it didn't take them very long to compel the surrender of Fort Boussois, especially as the defenders had already been terribly cut up by the artillery fire.

The Austrians must have been first-rate marksmen. One of their shells fell squarely upon the rounded dome of a big armored turret which was sunk in the earth and chipped off the top of it as you would chip your breakfast egg. The men who manned the guns in that revolving turret must all have died in a flash of time. The impact of the blow was such that the leaden solder which filled the interstices of the segments of the turret was squeezed out from between the plates in curly strips, like icing from between the layers of a misused birthday cake.

Back within the main works we saw where a shell had bored a smooth, round orifice through eight meters of earth and a meter and a half of concrete and steel plates. Peering into the shaft we could make out the floor of a tunnel some thirty feet down. To judge by its effects, this shell had been of a different type from any others whose work we had witnessed. Apparently it had been devised to excavate holes rather than to explode, and when we asked questions about it we speedily ascertained that our guide did not care to discuss the gun which had inflicted this particular bit of damage.

"It is not permitted to speak of this matter, " he said in explanation of his attitude. "It is a military secret, this invention. We call it a mine gun. "

Every man to his taste. I should have called it a well-digger.

Erect upon the highest stretch of riddled walls, with his legs spraddled far apart and his arms jerking in expressive gestures, he told us how the German infantry had advanced across the open ground. It had been hard, he said, to hold the men back until the order for the charge was given, and then they burst from their cover and came on at a dead run, cheering.

"It was very fine, " he added. "Very glorious. "

"Did you have any losses in the charge? " asked one of our party.

Paths of Glory

"Oh, yes, " he answered, as though that part of the proceeding was purely an incidental detail and of no great consequence. "We lost many men here—very many—several thousands, I think. Most of them are buried where you see those long ridges in the second field beyond."

In a sheltered corner of a redoubt, close up under a parapet and sheathed on its inner side with masonry, was a single grave. The pounding feet of many fighting men had beaten the mound flat, but a small wooden cross still stood in the soil, and on it in French were penciled the words:

"Here lies Lieutenant Verner, killed in the charge of battle."

His men must have thought well of the lieutenant to take the time, in the midst of the defense, to bury him in the place where he fell, for there were no other graves to be seen within the fort.

Paths of Glory

Chapter 13

Those Yellow Pine Boxes

It was late in the short afternoon, and getting close on to twilight, when we got back into the town. Except for the soldiers there was little life stirring in the twisting streets. There was a funeral or so in progress. It seemed to us that always, no matter where we stopped, in whatsoever town or at whatsoever hour, some dead soldier was being put away. Still, I suppose we shouldn't have felt any surprise at that. By now half of Europe was one great funeral. Part of it was on crutches and part of it was in the graveyard and the rest of it was in the field.

Daily in these towns back behind the firing lines a certain percentage of the invalided and the injured, who had been brought thus far before their condition became actually serious, would die; and twice daily, or oftener, the dead would be buried with military honors.

So naturally we were eyewitnesses to a great many of these funerals. Somehow they impressed me more than the sight of dead men being hurriedly shoveled under ground on the battle front where they had fallen. Perhaps it was the consciousness that those who had these formal, separate burials were men who came alive out of the fighting, and who, even after being stricken, had a chance for life and then lost it. Perhaps it was the small show of ceremony and ritual which marked each one—the firing squad, the clergyman in his robes, the tramping escort—that left so enduring an impress upon my mind. I did not try to analyze the reasons; but I know my companions felt as I did.

I remember quite distinctly the very first of these funerals that I witnessed. Possibly I remember it with such distinctness because it was the firSt. On our way to the advance positions of the Germans we had come as far as Chimay, which is an old Belgian town just over the frontier from France. I was sitting on a bench just outside the doorway of a parochial school conducted by nuns, which had been taken over by the conquerors and converted into a temporary receiving hospital for men who were too seriously wounded to stand the journey up into Germany. All the surgeons on duty here were Germans, but the nursing force was about equally divided between nuns and Lutheran deaconesses who had been brought overland for

Paths of Glory

this duty. Also there were several volunteer nurses—the wife of an officer, a wealthy widow from Dusseldorf and a school-teacher from Coblenz among them. Catholic and Protestant, Belgian and French and German, they all labored together, cheerfully and earnestly doing drudgery of the most exacting, the most unpleasant sorts.

One of the patronesses of the hospital, who was also its manager ex officio, had just left with a soldier chauffeur for a guard and a slightly wounded major for an escort. She was starting on a three-hundred-mile automobile run through a half subdued and dangerous country, meaning to visit base hospitals along the German frontier until she found a supply of anti-tetanus serum. Lockjaw, developing from seemingly trivial wounds in foot or hand, had already killed six men at Chimay within a week. Four more were dying of the same disease. So, since no able-bodied men could be spared from the overworked staffs of the lazarets, she was going for a stock of the serum which might save still other victims. She meant to travel day and night, and if a bullet didn't stop her and if the automobile didn't go through a temporary bridge she would be back, she thought, within forty-eight hours. She had already made several trips of the sort upon similar missions. Once her car had been fired at and once it had been wrecked, but she was going again. She was from near Cologne, the wife of a rich manufacturer now serving as a captain of reserves. She hadn't heard from him in four weeks. She didn't know whether he still lived. She hoped he lived, she told us with simple fortitude, but of course these times one never knew.

It was just before sundown. The nuns had gone upstairs to their little chapel for evening services. Through an open window of the chapel just above my head their voices, as they chanted the responses between the sonorous Latin phrases of the priest who had come to lead them in their devotions, floated out in clear sweet snatches, like the songs of vesper sparrows. Behind me, in a paved courtyard, were perhaps twenty wounded men lying on cots. They had been brought out of the building and put in the sunshine. They were on the way to recovery; at least most of them were. I sat facing a triangular-shaped square, which was flanked on one of its faces by a row of shuttered private houses and on another by the principal church of the town, a fifteenth-century structure with outdoor shrines snuggled up under its eaves. Except for the chanting of the nuns and the braggadocio booming of a big cock-pigeon, which had flown down from the church tower to forage for spilt grain almost under my feet, the place was quiet. It was so quiet that when a little column of men turned into the head of the street which wound past the front of the church and off to the left, I heard the measured tramping of their feet upon the stony roadway fully a minute before they came in sight. I was wondering what that rhythmic thumping meant, when one of the nursing sisters came and closed the high wooden door at my back, shutting off the view of the wounded men.

There appeared a little procession, headed by a priest in his robes and two altar-boys. At the heels of these three were six soldiers bearing upon their shoulders a wooden box painted a glaring yellow; and so narrow was the box and so shallow-looking, that on the instant the thought came to me that the poor clay inclosed therein must feel cramped in such scant quarters. Upon the top of the box, at its widest, highest point, rested a wreath of red flowers, a clumsy, spraddly wreath from which the red blossoms threatened to shake loose. Even at a distance of some rods I could tell that a man's inexpert fingers must have fashioned it.

Upon the shoulders of the bearers the box swayed and jolted.

Following it came, first, three uniformed officers, two German nurses and two surgeons from another hospital, as I subsequently learned; and following them half a company of soldiers bearing their rifles and wearing side arms. As the small cortege reached a point opposite us an officer snapped an order and everybody halted, and the gun-butts of the company came down with a smashing abruptness upon the cobbles. At that moment two or three roughly clad civilians issued from a doorway near by. Being Belgians they had small cause to love the Germans, but they stopped in their tracks and pulled off their caps. To pay the tribute of a bared head to the dead, even to the unknown dead, is in these Catholic countries of Europe as much a part of a man's rule of conduct as his religion is.

The priest who led the line turned my way inquiringly. He did not have to wait long for what was to come, nor did I. Another gate farther along in the nunnery wall opened and out came six more soldiers, bearing another of these narrow-shouldered coffins, and accompanied by a couple of nurses, an officer and an assistant surgeon. At sight of them the soldiers brought their pieces up to a salute, and held the posture rigidly until the second dead man in his yellow box had joined the company of the first dead man in his.

Paths of Glory

Just before this happened, though, one of the nurses of the nunnery hospital did a thing which I shall never forget. She must have seen that the first coffin had flowers upon it, and in the same instant realized that the coffin in whose occupant she had a more direct interest was bare. So she left the straggling line and came running back. The wall streamed with woodbine, very glorious in its autumnal flamings. She snatched a trailer of the red and yellow leaves down from where it clung, and as she hurried back her hands worked with magic haste, making it into a wreath. She reached the second squad of bearers and put her wreath upon the lid of the box, and then sought her place with the other nurses. The guns went up with a snap upon the shoulders of the company. The soldiers' feet thudded down all together upon the stones, and with the priest reciting his office the procession passed out of sight, going toward the burial ground at the back of the town. Presently, when the shadows were thickening into gloom and the angelus bells were ringing in the church, I heard, a long way off, the rattle of the rifles as the soldiers fired goodnight volleys over the graves of their dead comrades.

On the next day, at Hirson, which was another of our stopping points on the journey to the front, we saw the joint funeral of seven men leaving the hospital where they had died during the preceding twelve hours, and I shan't forget that picture either. There was a vista bounded by a stretch of one of those unutterably bleak backways of a small and shabby French town. The rutted street twisted along between small gray plaster houses, with ugly, unnecessary gable-ends, which faced the road at wrong angles. Small groups of towns-people stood against the walls to watch.

There was also a handful of idling soldiers who watched from the gateway of the house where they were billeted.

Seven times the bearers entered the hospital door, and each time as they reappeared, bringing one of the narrow, gaudy, yellow boxes, the officers lined up at the door would salute and the soldiers in double lines at the opposite side of the road would present arms, and then, as the box was lifted upon the wagon waiting to receive it, would smash their guns down on the bouldered road with a crash. When the job of bringing forth the dead was done the wagon stood loaded pretty nearly to capacity. Four of the boxes rested crosswise upon the flat wagon-bed and the other three were racked lengthwise on top of them. Here, too, was a priest in his robes, and here were

Paths of Glory

two altar boys who straggled, so that as the procession started the priest was moved to break off his chanting long enough to chide his small attendants and wave them back into proper alignment. With the officers, the nurses and the surgeons all marching afoot marched also three bearded civilians in frock coats, having the air about them of village dignitaries. From their presence in such company we deduced that one of the seven silent travelers on the wagon must be a French soldier, or else that the Germans had seen fit to require the attendance of local functionaries at the burial of dead Germans.

As the cortege—I suppose you might call it that—went by where I stood with my friends, I saw that upon the sides of the coffins names were lettered in big, straggly black letters. I read two of the names—Werner was one, Vogel was the other. Somehow I felt an acuter personal interest in Vogel and Werner than in the other five whose names I could not read.

Wherever we stopped in Belgium or in France or in Germany these soldiers' funerals were things of daily, almost of hourly occurrence. And in Maubeuge on this evening, even though dusk had fallen, two of the inevitable yellow boxes, mounted upon a two-wheeled cart, were going to the burying ground. We figured the cemetery men would fill the graves by lantern light; and knowing something of their hours of employment we imagined that with this job disposed of they would probably turn to and dig graves by night, making them ready against the needs of the following morning. The new graves always were ready. They were made in advance, and still there were rarely enough of them, no matter how long or how hard the diggers kept at their work. At Aix-la-Chapelle, for example, in the principal cemetery the sexton's men dug twenty new graves every morning. By evening there would be twenty shaped mounds of clay where the twenty holes had been. The crop of the dead was the one sure crop upon which embattled Europe might count. That harvest could not fail the warring nations, however scanty other yields might be.

In the towns in occupied territory the cemeteries were the only actively and constantly busy spots to be found, except the hospitals. Every schoolhouse was a hospital; indeed I think there can be no schoolhouse in the zone of actual hostilities that has not served such a purpose. In their altered aspects we came to know these schoolhouses mighty well. We would see the wounded going in on stretchers and the dead coming out in boxes. We would see how the blackboards, still scrawled over perhaps with the chalked sums of lessons which never were finished, now bore pasted-on charts dealing in nurses' and surgeons' cipher-manual, with the bodily plights of the men in the cots and on the mattresses beneath. We would see classrooms where plaster casts and globe maps and dusty textbooks had been cast aside in heaps to make room on desktops and shelves for drugs and bandages and surgical appliances. We would see the rows of hooks intended originally for the caps and umbrellas of little people; but now from each hook dangled the ripped, bloodied garments of a soldier—gray for a German, brown-tan for an Englishman, blue-and-red for a Frenchman or a Belgian. By the German rule a wounded man's uniform must be brought back with him from the place where he fell and kept handily near him, with tags on it, to prove its proper identity, and there it must stay until its owner needs it again—if ever he needs it again.

We would see these things, and we would wonder if these schoolhouses could ever shake off the scents and the stains and the memories of these present grim visitations—wonder if children would ever frolic any more in the courtyards where the ambulances stood now with red drops trickling down from their beds upon the gravel. But that, on our part, was mere morbidness born of the sights we saw. Children forget even more quickly than their elders forget, and we knew, from our own experience, how quickly the populace of a French or Flemish community could rally back to a colorable counterfeit of their old sprightliness, once the immediate burdens of affliction and captivity had been lifted from off them.

From a jumbled confusion of recollection of these schoolhouse-hospitals sundry incidental pictures stick out in my mind as I write this article. I can shut my eyes and visualize the German I saw in the little parish school building in the abandoned hamlet of Colligis near by the River Aisne. He was in a room with a dozen others, all suffering from chest wounds. He had been pierced through both lungs with a bullet, and to keep him from choking to death the attendants had tied him in a half erect posture. A sort of hammock-like sling passed under his arms, and a rope ran from it to a hook in a wall and was knotted fast to the hook. He swung there, neither sitting nor lying, fighting for the breath of life, with an unspeakable misery looking out from his eyes; and he was too far spent to lift a hand to brush away the flies that swarmed upon his face and his lips and upon his bare, throbbing throat. The flies dappled the faces of his fellow sufferers with loathsome black dots; they literally masked his. I preserve a memory which is just as vivid of certain things I saw in a big institution in Laon. Although in German hands, and nominally under German control, the building was given over entirely to crippled and ailing French prisoners. These patients were minded and fed by their own people and attended by captured French surgeons. In our tour of the place I saw only two men wearing the German gray. One was the armed sentry who stood at the gate to see that no recovering inmate slipped out, and the other was a German surgeon- general who was making his daily round of inspection of the hospitals and had brought us along with him. Of the native contingent the person who appeared to be in direct charge was a handsome, elderly lady, tenderly solicitous of the frowziest Turco in the wards and exquisitely polite, with a frozen politeness, to the German officer. When he saluted her she bowed to him deeply and ceremoniously and silently. I never thought until then that a bow could be so profoundly executed and yet so icily cold. It was a lesson in congealed manners.

As we were leaving the room a nun serving as a nurse hailed the German and told him one of her charges was threatening to die, not because of his wound, but because he had lost heart and believed himself to be dying.

"Where is he? " asked the German.

"Yonder, " she said, indicating a bundled-up figure on a pallet near the door. A drawn, hopeless face of a half-grown boy showed from the huddle of blankets. The surgeon-general cast a quick look at the swathed form and then spoke in an undertone to a French regimental surgeon on duty in the room. Together the two approached the lad.

"My son, " said the German to him in French, "I am told you do not feel so well to-day. "

The boy-soldier whispered an answer and waggled his head despondently. The German put his hand on the youth's forehead.

"My son, " he said, "listen to me. You are not going to die—I promise you that you shall not die. My colleague here"—he indicated the French doctor—"stands ready to make you the same promise. If you won't believe a German, surely you will take your own countryman's professional word for it, " and he smiled a little

Paths of Glory

smile under his gray mustache. "Between us we are going to make you well and send you, when this war is over, back to your mother. But you must help us; you must help us by being brave and confident. Is it not so, doctor? " he added, again addressing the French physician, and the Frenchman nodded to show it was so and sat down alongside the youngster to comfort him further.

As we left the room the German surgeon turned, and looking round I saw that once again he saluted the patrician French lady, and this time as she bowed the ice was all melted from her bearing. She must have witnessed the little byplay; perhaps she had a son of her own in service. There were mighty few mothers in France last fall who did not have sons in service.

Yet one of the few really humorous recollections of this war that I preserve had to do with a hospital too; but this hospital was in England and we visited it on our way home to America. We went—two of us—in the company of Lord Northcliffe, down into Surrey, to spend a day with old Lord Roberts. Within three weeks thereafter Lord Roberts was dead where no doubt he would have willed to die—at the front in France, with the sound of the guns in his ears, guarded in his last moments by the Ghurkas and the Sikhs of his beloved Indian contingent. But on this day of our visit to him we found him a hale, kindly gentleman of eighty-two who showed us his marvelous collection of firearms and Oriental relics and the field guns, all historic guns by the way, which he kept upon the terraces of his mansion house, and who told us, among other things, that in his opinion our own Stonewall Jackson was perhaps the greatest natural military genius the world had ever produced. Leaving his house we stopped, on our return to London, at a hospital for soldiers in the grounds of Ascot Race Course scarcely two miles from Lord Roberts' place. The refreshment booths and the other rooms at the back and underside of the five-shilling stand had been thrown together, except the barber's shop, which was being converted into an operating chamber; and, what with its tiled walls and high sloped ceiling and glass front, the place made a first-rate hospital.

It contained beds for fifty men; but on this day there were less than twenty sick and crippled Tommies convalescing here. They had been brought out of France, out of wet and cold and filth, with hurried dressings on their hurts; and now they were in this bright, sweet, wholesome place, with soft beds under them and clean linen on their bodies, and flowers and dainties on the tables that stood alongside them, and the gentlefolk of the neighborhood to mind them as volunteer nurses.

There were professional nurses, of course; but, under them, the younger women of the wealthy families of this corner of Surrey were serving; and mighty pretty they all looked, too, in their crisp blue-and-white uniforms, with their arm badges and their caps, and their big aprons buttoned round their slim, athletic young bodies. I judge there were about three amateur nurses to each patient. Yet you could not rightly call them amateurs either; each of them had taken a short course in nursing, it seemed, and was amply competent to perform many of the duties a regular nurse must know. Lady Aileen Roberts was with us during our tour of the hospital. As a daily visitor and patroness she spent much of her time here and she knew most of the inmates by name. She halted alongside one bed to ask its occupant how he felt. He had been returned from the front suffering from pneumonia.

He was an Irishman. Before he answered her he cast a quick look about the long hall. Afternoon tea was just being served, consisting, besides tea, of homemade strawberry jam and lettuce sandwiches made of crisp fresh bread, with plenty of butter; and certain elderly ladies had just arrived, bringing with them, among other contributions, sheaves of flowers and a dogcart loaded with hothouse fruit and a dozen loaves of plumcake, which last were still hot from the oven and which radiated a mouth-watering aroma as a footman bore them in behind his mistress. The patient looked at all these and he sniffed; and a grin split his face and an Irish twinkle came into his eyes.

"Thank you, me lady, for askin', " he said; "but I'm very much afeared I'm gettin' better. "

We might safely assume that the hospitals and the graveyard of Maubeuge would be busy places that evening, thereby offering strong contrasts to the rest of the town. But I should add that we found two other busy spots, too: the railroad station—where the trains bringing wounded men continually shuttled past—and the house where the commandant of the garrison had his headquarters. In the latter place, as guests of Major von Abercron, we met at dinner that night and again after dinner a strangely mixed company. We met many officers and the pretty American wife of an officer, Frau Elsie von, Heinrich, late of Jersey City, who had made an

Paths of Glory

adventurous trip in a motor ambulance from Germany to see her husband before he went to the front, and who sent regards by us to scores of people in her old home whose names I have forgotten. We met also a civilian guest of the commandant, who introduced himself as August Blankhertz and who turned out to be a distinguished biggame hunter and gentleman aeronaut. With Major von Abercron for a mate he sailed from St. Louis in the great balloon race for the James Gordon Bennett Cup. They came down in the Canadian woods and nearly died of hunger and exposure before they found a lumber camp. Their balloon was called the Germania. There was another civilian, a member of the German secret-service staff, wearing the Norfolk jacket and the green Alpine hat and on a cord about his neck the big gold token of authority which invariably mark a representative of this branch of the German espionage bureau; and he was wearing likewise that transparent air of mystery which seemed always to go with the followers of his ingenious profession.

During the evening the mayor of Maubeuge came, a bearded, melancholy gentleman, to confer with the commandant regarding a clash between a German under-officer and a household of his constituents. Orderlies and attendants bustled in and out, and somebody played Viennese waltz songs on a piano, and altogether there was quite a gay little party in the parlor of this handsome house which the Germans had commandeered for the use of their garrison staff.

At early bedtime, when we stepped out of the door of the lit-up mansion into the street, it was as though we had stepped into a far-off country. Except for the tramp of a sentry's hobbed boots over the sidewalks and the challenging call of another sentry round the corner the town was as silent as a town of tombs. All the people who remained in this place had closed their forlorn shops where barren shelves and emptied showcases testified to the state of trade; and they had shut themselves up in their houses away from sight of the invaders. We could guess what their thoughts must be. Their industries were paralyzed, and their liberties were curtailed, and every other house was a breached and worthless shell. Among ourselves we debated as we walked along to the squalid tavern where we had been quartered, which of the spectacles we had that day seen most fitly typified the fruitage of war—the shattered, haunted forts lying now in the moonlight beyond the town, or the brooding conquered, half-destroyed town itself. I guess, if it comes to that, they both typified it.

Chapter 14

The Red Glutton

As we went along next day through the town of Maubeuge we heard singing; and singing was a most rare thing to be hearing in this town. In a country where no one smiles any more who belongs in that country, singing is not a thing which you would naturally expect to hear. So we turned off of our appointed route.

There was a small wine shop at the prow of a triangle of narrow streets. It had been a wine shop. It was now a beer shop. There had been a French proprietor; he had a German partner now. It had been only a few weeks—you could not as yet measure the interval of time in terms of months—since the Germans came and sat themselves down before Maubeuge and blew its defenses flat with their 42-centimeter earthquakes and marched in and took it. It had been only these few weeks; but already the Germanizing brand of the conqueror was seared deep in the galled flanks of this typically French community. The town-hall clock was made to tick German time, which varied by an even hour from French time. Tacked upon the door of the little cafe where we ate our meals was a card setting forth, with painful German particularity, the tariff which might properly be charged for food and for lodging and drink and what not; and it was done in German-Gothic script, all very angular and precise; and it was signed by His Excellency, the German commandant; and its prices were predicated on German logic and the estimated depth of a German wallet. You might read a newspaper printed in German characters, if so minded; but none printed in French, whether so minded or not.

So when we entered in at the door of the little French wine shop where the three streets met, to find out who within had heart of grace to sing 'O Strassburg, O Strassburg', so lustily, lo and behold, it had been magically transformed into a German beer shop. It was, as we presently learned, the only beer shop in all of Maubeuge, and the reason for that was this: No sooner had the Germans cleared and opened the roads back across Belgium to their own frontiers than an enterprising tradesman of the Rhein country, who somehow had escaped military service, loaded many kegs of good German beer upon trucks and brought his precious cargoes overland a hundred miles and more southward. Certainly he could not have moved the lager caravan without the consent and aid of the Berlin war office. For all I know to the contrary he may have been financed in that competent quarter. That same morning I had seen a field weather station, mounted on an automobile, standing in front of our lodging place just off the square. It was going to the front to make and compile meteorological reports. A general staff who provided weather offices on wheels and printing offices on wheels—this last for the setting up and striking off of small proclamations and orders—might very well have bethought themselves that the soldier in the field would be all the fitter for the job before him if stayed with the familiar malts of the Vaterland. Believe me, I wouldn't put it past them.

Anyway, having safely reached Maubeuge, the far-seeing Rheinishman effected a working understanding with a native publican, which was probably a good thing for both, seeing that one had a stock of goods and a ready-made trade but no place to set up business, and that the other owned a shop, but had lost his trade and his stock-in-trade likewise. These two, the little, affable German and the tall, grave Frenchman, stood now behind their counter drawing off mugs of Pilsener as fast as their four hands could move. Their patrons, their most vocal and boisterous patrons, were a company of musketeers who had marched in from the north that afternoon. As a rule the new levies went down into France on troop trains, but this company was part of a draft which for some reason came afoot.

Without exception they were young men, husky and hearty and inspired with a beefish joviality at having found a place where they could ease their feet, and rest their legs, and slake their week-old thirst upon their own soothing brews. Being German they expressed their gratefulness in song. We had difficulty getting into the place, so completely was it filled. Men sat in the window ledges, and in the few chairs that were available, and even in the fireplace, and on the ends of the bar, clunking their heels against the wooden baseboards. The others stood in such close order they could hardly clear their elbows to lift their glasses. The air was choky with a blended smell derived from dust and worn boot leather and spilt essences of hops and healthy, unwashed, sweaty bodies. On a chair in a corner stood a tall, tired and happy youth who beat time for the singing with an empty mug and between beats nourished himself on drafts from a filled mug which he held in his other hand. With us was a German officer. He was a captain of reserves and a person of considerable wealth. He shoved his way to the bar and laid down upon its sloppy surface two gold coins and said something to a petty officer who was directing the distribution of the refreshments.

The noncom. hammered for silence and, when he got it, announced that the Herr Hauptmann had donated twenty marks' worth of beer, all present being invited to cooperate in drinking it up, which they did, but first gave three cheers for the captain and three more for his American friends and afterward, while the replenished mugs radiated in crockery waves from the bar to the back walls, sang for us a song which, so far as the air was concerned, sounded amazingly like unto Every Little Movement Has a Meaning All Its Own. Their weariness was quite fallen away from them; they were like schoolboys on a frolic. Indeed, I think a good many of them were schoolboys.

As we came out a private who stood in the doorway spoke to us in fair English. He had never been in America, but he had a brother living in East St. Louis and he wanted to know if any of us knew his brother. This was a common experience with us. Every third German soldier we met had a brother or a sister or somebody in America. This soldier could not have been more than eighteen years; the down on his cheeks was like corn silk. He told us he and his comrades were very glad to be going forward where there would be fighting. They had had no luck yet. There had been no fighting where they had been. I remembered afterward that luck was the word he used.

We went back to the main street and for a distance the roar of their volleying chorus followed us. Men and women stood at the doors of the houses along the way. They were silent and idle. Idleness and silence seemed always to have fallen as grim legacies upon the civilian populace of these captured towns; but the look upon their faces as they listened to the soldiers' voices was not hard to read. Their town was pierced by cannonballs where it was not scarified with fire; there was sorrow and the abundant cause for sorrow in every house; commerce was dead and credit was killed; and round the next turning their enemy sang his drinking song. I judge that the thrifty Frenchman who went partner with the German stranger in the beer traffic lost popularity that day among his fellow townsmen.

We were bound for the railway station, which the Germans already had rechristened Bahnhof. Word had been brought to us that trains of wounded men and prisoners were due in the course of the afternoon from the front, and more especially from the right wing;

Paths of Glory

and in this prospect we scented a story to be written. To reach the station we crossed the river Sambre, over a damaged bridge, and passed beneath the arched passageway of the citadel which the great Vauban built for the still greater Louis XIV, thinking, no doubt, when he built it, that it would always be potent to keep out any foe, however strong. Next to its stupid massiveness what most impressed us this day was its utter uselessness as a protection. The station stood just beyond the walls, with a park at one side of it, but the park had become a timber deadfall. At the approach of the enemy hundreds of splendid trees had been felled to clear the way for gunfire from the inner defenses in the event that the Germans got by the outer circle of fortresses. After the Germans took the forts, though, the town surrendered, so all this destruction had been futile. There were acres of ragged stumps and, between the stumps, jungles of overlapping trunks and interlacing boughs from which the dead and dying leaves shook off in showers. One of our party, who knew something of forestry, estimated that these trees were about forty years old.

"I suppose, " he added speculatively, "that when this war ends these people will replant their trees. Then in another forty years or so another war will come and they will chop them all down again. On the whole I'm rather glad I don't live on this continent. "

The trains which were expected had not begun to arrive yet, so with two companions I sat on a bench at the back of the station, waiting. Facing us was a line of houses. One, the corner house, was a big black char. It had caught fire during the shelling and burned quite down. Its neighbors were intact, except for shattered chimneys and smashed doors and riddled windows. The concussion of a big gunfire had shivered every window in this quarter of town. There being no sufficient stock of glass with which to replace the broken panes, and no way of bringing in fresh supplies, the owners of the damaged buildings had patched the holes with bits of planking filched from more complete ruins near by. Of course there were other reasons, too, if one stopped to sum them up: Few would have the money to buy fresh glass, even if there was any fresh glass to buy, and the local glaziers—such of them as survived—would be serving the colors. All France had gone to war and at this time of writing had not come back, except in dribbling streams of wounded and prisoners.

These ragged boards, sparingly nailed across the window sockets, gave the houses the air of wearing masks and of squinting at us through narrow eye slits. The railroad station was windowless, too, like all the buildings round about, but nobody had closed the openings here, and it gaped emptily in fifty places, and the raw, gusty winds of a North European fall searched through it.

In this immediate neighborhood few of the citizens were to be seen. Even those houses which still were humanly habitable appeared to be untenanted; only soldiers were about, and not so very many of them. A hundred yards up the tracks, on a siding, a squad of men with a derrick and crane were hoisting captured French field guns upon flat cars to be taken to Berlin and exhibited as spoils of conquest for the benefit of the stay-at-homes. A row of these cannons, perhaps fifty in all, were ranked alongside awaiting loading and transportation. Except for the agonized whine of the tackle-blocks and the buzzing of the flies the place where we sat was pretty quiet. There were a million flies, and there seemed to be a billion. You wouldn't have thought, unless you had been there to see for yourself, that there were so many flies in the world. By the time this was printed the cold weather had cured Europe of its fly plague, but during the first three months I know that the track of war was absolutely sown with these vermin. Even after a night of hard frost they would be as thick as ever at midday—as thick and as clinging and as nasty. Go into any close, ill-aired place and no matter what else you might smell, you smelled flies too.

As I sit and look back on what I myself have seen of it, this war seems to me to have been not so much a sight as a stench. Everything which makes for human happiness and human usefulness it has destroyed. What it has bred, along with misery and pain and fatted burying grounds, is a vast and loathsome stench and a universe of flies.

The smells and the flies; they were here in this railroad station in sickening profusion.

I call it a railroad station, although it had lost its functions as such weeks before. The only trains which ran now were run by the Germans for strictly German purposes, and so the station had become a victualing point for troops going south to the fighting and a way hospital for sick and wounded coming back from the fighting. What, in better days than these, had been the lunch room was a place for the redressing of hurts. Its high counters, which once held sandwiches and tarts and wine bottles, were piled with snowdrifts of

Paths of Glory

medicated cotton and rolls of lint and buckets of antiseptic washes and drug vials. The ticket booth was an improvised pharmacy. Spare medical supplies filled the room where formerly fussy customs officers examined the luggage of travelers coming out of Belgium into France. Just beyond the platform a wooden booth, with no front to it, had been knocked together out of rough planking, and relays of cooks, with greasy aprons over their soiled gray uniforms, made vast caldrons of stews—always stews—and brewed so-called coffee by the gallon against the coming of those who would need it. The stuff was sure to be needed, all of it and more too. So they cooked and cooked unceasingly and never stopped to wipe a pan or clean a spoon.

At our backs was the waiting room for first-class passengers, but no passengers of any class came to it any more, and so by common consent it was a sort of rest room for the Red Cross men, who mostly were Germans, but with a few captured Frenchmen among them, still wearing their French uniforms. There were three or four French military surgeons—prisoners, to be sure, but going and coming pretty much as they pleased. The tacit arrangement was that the Germans should succor Germans and that the Frenchmen should minister to their own disabled countrymen among the prisoners going north, but in a time of stress—and that meant every time a train came in from the south or west—both nationalities mingled together and served, without regard for the color of the coat worn by those whom they served.

Probably from the day it was put up this station had never been really and entirely clean. Judged by American standards Continental railway stations are rarely ever clean, even when conditions are normal. Now that conditions were anything but normal, this Maubeuge station was incredibly and incurably filthy. No doubt the German nursing sisters who were brought here tried at first, with their German love for orderliness, to keep the interior reasonably tidy; but they had been swamped by more important tasks. For two weeks now the wounded had been passing through by the thousands and the tens of thousands daily. So between trains the women dropped into chairs or down upon cots and took their rest in snatches. But their fingers didn't reSt. Always their hands were busy with the making of bandages and the fluffing of lint.

By bits I learned something about three of the women who served on the so-called day shift, which meant that they worked from early morning until long after midnight. One was a titled woman who had volunteered for this duty. She was beyond middle age, plainly in poor health herself and everlastingly on the verge of collapse from weakness and exhaustion. Her will kept her on her feet. The second was a professional nurse from one of the university towns—from Bonn, I think. She called herself Sister Bartholomew, for the German nurses who go to war take other names than their own, just as nuns do. She was a beautiful woman, tall and strong and round-faced, with big, fine gray eyes. Her energy had no limits. She ran rather than walked. She had a smile for every maimed man who was brought to her, but when the man had been treated, and had limped away or had been carried away, I saw her often wringing her hands and sobbing over the utter horror of it all. Then another sufferer would appear and she would wipe the tears off her cheeks and get to work again. The third—so an assistant surgeon confided to us—was the mistress of an officer at the front, a prostitute of the Berlin sidewalks, who enrolled for hospital work when her lover went to the front. She Was a tall, dark, handsome girl, who looked to be more Spaniard than German, and she was graceful and lithe even in the exceedingly shapeless costume of blue print that she wore. She was less deft than either of her associates but very willing and eager. As between the three—the noblewoman, the working woman and the woman of the street—the medical officials in charge made no distinction whatsoever. Why should they? In this sisterhood of mercy they all three stood upon the same common ground. I never knew that slop jars were noble things until I saw women in these military lazarets bearing them in their arms; then to me they became as altar vessels.

Lacking women to do it, the head surgeon had intrusted the task of clearing away the dirt to certain men. A sorry job they made of it. For accumulated nastiness that waiting room was an Augean stable and the two soldiers who dawdled about in it with brooms lacked woefully in the qualities of Hercules. Putting a broom in a man's hands is the best argument in favor of woman's suffrage that I know of, anyhow. A third man who helped at chores in the transformed lunch room had gathered up and piled together in a heap upon the ground near us a bushel or so of used bandages—grim reminders left behind after the last train went by— and he had touched a match to the heap in an effort to get rid of it by fire. By reason of what was upon them the clothes burned slowly, sending up a smudge of acrid smoke to mingle with smells of carbolic acid and iodoform, and the scent of boiling food, and of things infinitely less pleasant than these.

Paths of Glory

Presently a train rolled in and we crossed through the building to the trackside to watch what would follow. Already we had seen a sufficiency of such trains; we knew before it came what it would be like: In front the dumpy locomotive, with a soldier engineer in the cab; then two or three box cars of prisoners, with the doors locked and armed guards riding upon the roofs; then two or three shabby, misused passenger coaches, containing injured officers and sometimes injured common soldiers, too; and then, stretching off down the rails, a long string of box cars, each of which would be bedded with straw and would contain for furniture a few rough wooden benches ranging from side to side. And each car would contain ten or fifteen or twenty, or even a greater number, of sick and crippled men.

Those who could sit were upon the hard benches, elbow to elbow, packed snugly in. Those who were too weak to sit sprawled upon the straw and often had barely room in which to turn over, so closely were they bestowed. It had been days since they had started back from the field hospitals where they had had their first-aid treatment. They had moved by sluggish stages with long halts in between. Always the wounded must wait upon the sidings while the troop trains from home sped down the cleared main line to the smoking front; that was the merciless but necessary rule. The man who got himself crippled became an obstacle to further progress, a drag upon the wheels of the machine; whereas the man who was yet whole and fit was the man whom the generals wanted. So the fresh grist for the mill, the raw material, if you will, was expedited upon its way to the hoppers; that which already had been ground up was relatively of the smallest consequence.

Because of this law, which might not be broken or amended, these wounded men would, perforce, spend several days aboard train before they could expect to reach the base hospitals upon German soil, Maubeuge being at considerably less than midway of the distance between starting point and probable destination. Altogether the trip might last a week or even two weeks—a trip that ordinarily would have lasted less than twelve hours. Through it these men, who were messed and mangled in every imaginable fashion, would wallow in the dirty matted straw, with nothing except that thin layer of covering between them and the car floors that jolted and jerked beneath them. We knew it and they knew it, and there was nothing to be done. Their wounds would fester and be hot with fever. Their clotted bandages would clot still more and grow stiffer and harder with each dragging hour. Those who lacked overcoats and blankets—and some there were who lacked both—would half freeze at night. For food they would have slops dished up for them at such stopping places as this present one, and they would slake their thirst on water drawn from contaminated wayside wells and be glad of the chance. Gangrene would come, and blood poison, and all manner of corruption. Tetanus would assuredly claim its toll. Indeed, these horrors were already at work among them. I do not tell it to sicken my reader, but because I think I should tell it that he may have a fuller conception of what this fashionable institution of war means— we could smell this train as we could smell all the trains which followed after it, when it was yet fifty yards away from us.

Be it remembered, furthermore, that no surgeon accompanied this afflicted living freightage, that not even a qualified nurse traveled with it. According to the classifying processes of those in authority on the battle lines these men were lightly wounded men, and it was presumed that while en route they would be competent to minister to themselves and to one another. Under the grading system employed by the chief surgeons a man, who was still all in one piece and who probably would not break apart in transit, was designated as being lightly wounded. This statement is no attempt upon my part to indulge in levity concerning the most frightful situation I have encountered in nearly twenty years of active newspaper work; it is the sober, unexaggerated truth.

And so these lightly wounded men—men with their jaws shot away, men with holes in their breasts and their abdomens, men with their spine tips splintered, men with their arms and legs broken, men with their hands and feet shredded by shrapnel, men with their scalps ripped open, men with their noses and their ears and their fingers and toes gone, men jarred to the very marrow of their bones by explosives—these men, for whom ordinarily soft beds would have been provided and expert care and special food, came trundling up alongside that noisome station; and, through the door openings from where they were housed like dumb beasts, they looked out at us with the glazed eyes of dumb suffering beasts.

As the little toy-like European cars halted, bumping together hard, orderlies went running down the train bearing buckets of soup, and of coffee and of drinking water, and loaves of the heavy, dark German bread. Behind them went other men—bull-necked strong men picked for this job because of their strength. Their task was to bring back in their arms or upon their shoulders such men as were past walking. There were no stretchers. There was no time for stretchers. Behind this train would be another one just like it and behind that one, another, and so on down an eighty-mile stretch of dolorous way. And this, mind you, was but one of three lines carrying out of France and Belgium into Germany victims of the war to be made well again in order that they might return and once more be fed as tidbits into the maw of that war; it was but one of a dozen or more such streams, threading back from as many battle zones to the countries engaged in this wide and ardent scheme of mutual extermination.

Half a minute after the train stopped a procession was moving toward us, made up of men who had wriggled down or who had been eased down out of the cars, and who were coming to the converted buffet room for help. Mostly they came afoot, sometimes holding on to one another for mutual support. Perhaps one in five was borne bodily by an orderly. He might be hunched in the orderly's arms like a weary child, or he might be traveling upon the orderly's back, pack-fashion, with his arms gripped about the bearer's neck; and then, in such a case, the pair of them, with the white hollow face of the wounded man nodding above the sweated red face of the other, became a monstrosity with two heads and one pair of legs.

Here, advancing toward us with the gait of a doddering grandsire, would be a boy in his teens, bent double and clutching his middle with both hands. Here would be a man whose hand had been smashed, and from beyond the rude swathings of cotton his fingers protruded stiffly and were so congested and swollen they looked like fat red plantains. Here was a man whose feet were damaged. He had a crutch made of a spade handle. Next would be a man with a hole in his neck, and the bandages had pulled away from about his throat, showing the raw inflamed hole. In this parade I saw a French infantryman aided along by a captured Zouave on one side and on the other by a German sentry who swung his loaded carbine in his free hand. Behind them I saw an awful nightmare of a man—a man whose face and bare cropped head and hands and shoes were all of a livid, poisonous, green cast. A shell of some new and particularly devilish variety had burst near him and the fumes which it generated in bursting had dyed him green. Every man would have, tied about his neck or to one of his buttonholes, the German field-doctor's card telling of the nature of his hurt and the place where he had sustained it; and the uniform of nearly every one would be discolored with dried blood, and where the coat gaped open you marked that the harsh, white cambric lining was made harsher still by stiff, brownish- red streakings.

In at the door of the improvised hospital filed the parade, and the wounded men dropped on the floor or else were lowered upon chairs and tables and cots—anywhere that there was space for them to huddle up or stretch out. And then the overworked surgeons, French and German, and the German nursing sisters and certain of the orderlies would fall to. There was no time for the finer, daintier proceedings that might have spared the sufferers some measure of their agony. It was cut away the old bandage, pull off the filthy cotton, dab with antiseptics what was beneath, pour iodine or diluted acid upon the bare and shrinking tissues, perhaps do that with the knife or probe which must be done where incipient mortification had set in, clap on fresh cotton, wind a strip of cloth over it, pin it in place and send this man away to be fed—providing he could eat; then turn to the next poor wretch. The first man was out of that place almost before the last man was in; that was how fast the work went forward.

One special horror was spared: The patients made no outcry. They gritted their teeth and writhed where they lay, but none shrieked out. Indeed, neither here nor at any of the other places where I saw wounded men did we hear that chorus of moans and shrieks with which fiction always has invested such scenes. Those newly struck seemed stunned into silence; those who had had time to recover from the first shock of being struck appeared buoyed and sustained by a stoic quality which lifted them, mute and calm, above the call of tortured nerves and torn flesh. Those who were delirious might call out; those who were conscious locked their lips and were steadfast. In all our experience I came upon just two men in their senses who gave way at all. One was a boy of nineteen or twenty, in a field hospital near Rheims, whose kneecap had been smashed. He sat up on his bed, rocking his body and whimpering fretfully like an infant. He had been doing that for days, a nurse told us, but whether he whimpered because of his suffering or at the thought of going through life with a stiffened leg she did not know. The other was here at Maubeuge. I helped hold his right arm steady while a surgeon took the bandages off his hand. When the wrapping came away a shattered finger came with it—it had rotted off, if you care to know that detail—and at the sight the victim uttered growling, rasping, animal-like sounds. Even so, I think it was the thing he saw more than the pain of it that overcame him; the pain he could have borne. He had been bearing it for days.

I particularly remember one other man who was brought in off this first train. He was a young giant. For certain the old father of Frederick the Great would have had him in his regiment of Grenadier Guards. Well, for that matter, he was a grenadier in the employ of the same family now. He hobbled in under his own motive power and leaned against the wall until the first flurry was over. Then, at a nod from one of the shirt-sleeved surgeons, he stretched himself upon a bare wooden table which had just been vacated and indicated that he wanted relief for his leg—which leg, I recall, was incased in a rude, splintlike arrangement of plaited straw. The surgeon took off the straw and the packing beneath it. The giant had a hole right through his knee, from side to side, and the flesh all about it was horribly swollen and purplish- black. So the surgeon soused the joint, wound and all, with iodine; the youth meanwhile staring blandly up at the ceiling with his arms crossed on his wide breast. I stood right by him, looking into his face, and he didn't so much as bat an eyelid. But he didn't offer to get up when the surgeon was done with treating him. He turned laboriously over on his face, pulling his shirt free from his body as he did so, and then we saw that he had a long, infected gash from a glancing bullet across the small of his back. He had been lying on one angry wound while the other was redressed. You marveled, not that he had endured it without blenching, but that he had endured it at all.

The train stayed with us perhaps half an hour, and in that half hour at least a hundred men must have had treatment of sorts. A signal sounded and the orderlies lifted up the few wasted specters who still remained and toted them out. Almost the last man to be borne away was injured in both legs; an orderly carried him in his arms. Seeing the need of haste the orderly sought to heave his burden aboard the nearest car. The men in that car protested; already their space was overcrowded. So the patient orderly staggered down the train until he found the crippled soldier's rightful place and thrust him into the straw just as the wheels began to turn. As the cars, gathering speed, rolled by us we could see that nearly all the travelers were feeding themselves from pannikins of the bull-meat stew. Wrappings on their hands and sometimes about their faces made them doubly awkward, and the hot tallowy mess spilt in spattering streams upon them and upon the straw under them.

Paths of Glory

They were on their way. At the end of another twenty-four hour stretch they might have traveled fifty or sixty or even seventy miles. The place they left behind them was in worse case than before. Grease spattered the earth; the floor of the buffet room was ankle deep, literally, in discarded bandages and blood-stiffened cotton; and the nurses and the doctors and the helpers dropped down in the midst of it all to snatch a few precious minutes of rest before the next creaking caravan of misery arrived. There was no need to tell them of its coming; they knew. All through that afternoon and night, and through the next day and night, and through the half of the third day that we stayed on in Maubeuge, the trains came back. They came ten minutes apart, twenty minutes apart, an hour apart, but rarely more than an hour would elapse between trains. And this traffic in marred and mutilated humanity had been going on for four weeks and would go on for nobody knew how many weeks more.

When the train had gone out of sight beyond the first turn to the eastward I spoke to the head surgeon of the German contingent—a broad, bearded, middle-aged man who sat on a baggage truck while an orderly poured a mixture of water and antiseptics over his soiled hands.

"A lot of those poor devils will die?" I suggested.

"Less than three per cent of those who get back to the base hospitals will die," he said with a snap of his jaw, as though challenging me to doubt the statement. "That is the wonder of this war—that so many are killed in the fighting and that so few die who get back out of it alive. These modern scientific bullets, these civilized bullets"—he laughed in self-derision at the use of the word—"they are cruel and yet they are merciful too. If they do not kill you outright they have a little way, somehow, of not killing you at all."

"But the bayonet wounds and the saber wounds?" I said. "How about them?"

"I have been here since the very first," he said; "since the day after our troops took this town, and God knows how many thousands of wounded men—Germans, Englishmen, Frenchmen, Turcos, some Belgians—have passed through my hands; but as yet I have to see a man who has been wounded by a saber or a lance. I saw one bayonet wound yesterday or the day before. The man had fallen on his own bayonet and driven it into his side. Shrapnel wounds? Yes. Wounds

Paths of Glory

from fragments of bombs? Again, yes. Bullet wounds? I can't tell you how many of those I have seen, but surely many thousands. But no bayonet wounds. This is a war of hot lead, not of cold steel. I read of these bayonet charges, but I do not believe that many such stories are true."

I didn't believe it either.

The train which followed after the first, coming up out of France, furnished for us much the same sights the first one had furnished, and so, with some slight variations, did the third train and the fourth and all the rest of them. The station became a sty where before it had been a kennel; the flies multiplied; the stenches increased in volume and strength, if such were possible; the windows of the littered waiting room, with their cracked half panes, were like ribald eyes winking at the living afflictions which continually trailed past them; the floors looked as though there had been a snowstorm.

A train came, whose occupants were nearly all wounded by shrapnel. Wounds of the head, the face and the neck abounded among these men—for the shells, exploding in the air above where they crouched in their trenches, had bespattered them with iron pebbles. Each individual picture of! suffering recurred with such monotonous and regular frequency that after an hour or so it took something out of the common run—an especially vivid splash of daubed and crimson horror—to quicken our imaginations and make us fetch out our note books. I recall a young lieutenant of Uhlans who had been wounded in the breast by fragments of a grenade, which likewise had smashed in several of his ribs. He proudly fingered his newly acquired Iron Cross while the surgeon relaced his battered torso with strips of gauze. Afterward he asked me for a cigar, providing I had one to spare, saying he had not tasted tobacco for a week and was perishing for a smoke. We began to take note then how the wounded men watched us as we puffed at our cigars, and we realized they were dumbly envying us each mouthful of smoke. So we sent our chauffeur to the public market with orders to buy all the cigars he could find on sale there. He presently returned with the front and rear seats of the automobile piled high with bundled sheaves of the brown weed—you can get an astonishingly vast number of those domestic French cigars for the equivalent of thirty dollars in American money—and we turned the whole cargo over to the head nurse on condition that, until the supply was exhausted, she give a cigar to every hurt soldier who might crave one, regardless of his nationality. She cried as she thanked us for the small charity.

"We can feed them—yes, " she said, "but we have nothing to give them to smoke, and it is very hard on them. "

A little later a train arrived which brought three carloads of French prisoners and one carload of English. Among the Frenchmen were many Alpine Rangers, so called—the first men we had seen of this wing of the service—and by reason of their dark blue uniforms and their flat blue caps they looked more like sailors than soldiers. At first we took them for sailors. There were thirty-four of the Englishmen, being all that were left of a company of the West Yorkshire Regiment of infantry. Confinement for days in a bare box car, with not even water to wash their faces and hands in, had not altogether robbed them of a certain trim alertness which seems to belong to the British fighting man. Their puttees were snugly reefed about their shanks and their khaki tunics buttoned up to their throats.

We talked with them. They wanted to know if they had reached Germany yet, and when we told them that they were not out of France and had all of Belgium still to traverse, they groaned their dismay in chorus.

"We've 'ad a very 'ard time of it, sir, " said a spokesman, who wore sergeant's stripes on his sleeves and who told us he came from Sheffield. "Seventeen 'ours we were in the trench, under fire all the time, with water up to our middles and nothing to eat. We were 'olding the center and when the Frenchies fell back they didn't give our chaps no warning, and pretty soon the Dutchmen they 'ad us flanked both sides and we 'ad to quit. But we didn't quit until we'd lost all but one of our officers and a good 'alf of our men. "

"Where was this? " one of us asked.

"Don't know, sir, " he said. "It's a blooming funny war. You never knows the name of the place where you're fighting at, unless you 'ears it by chance. "

Then he added:

Paths of Glory

"Could you tell us, sir, 'ow's the war going? Are we giving the Germans a proper 'iding all along the line?"

We inquired regarding their treatment. They didn't particularly fancy the food—narsty slop, the sergeant called it—although it was reasonably plentiful; and, being true Englishmen, they sorely missed their tea. Then, too, on the night before their overcoats had been taken from them and no explanations vouchsafed.

"We could 'ave done with them," said the speaker bitterly; "pretty cold it was in this 'ere car. And what with winter coming on and everything I call it a bit thick to be taking our overcoats off of us."

We went and asked a German officer who had the convoy in charge the reason for this, and he said the overcoats of all the uninjured men, soldiers as well as prisoners, had been confiscated to furnish coverings for such of the wounded as lacked blankets. Still, I observed that the guards for the train had their overcoats. So I do not vouch for the accuracy of his explanation.

It was getting late in the afternoon and the fifth train to pull in from the south since our advent on the spot—or possibly it was the sixth— had just halted when, from the opposite direction, a troop-train, long and heavy, panted into sight and stopped on the far track while the men aboard it got an early supper of hot victuals. We crossed over to have a look at the new arrivals.

It was a long train, drawn by one locomotive and shoved by another, and it included in its length a string of flat cars upon which were lashed many field pieces, and commandeered automobiles, and even some family carriages, not to mention baggage wagons and cook wagons and supply wagons. For a wonder, the coaches in which the troops rode were new, smart coaches, seemingly just out of the builders' hands. They were mainly first and second class coaches, varnished outside and equipped with upholstered compartments where the troopers took their luxurious ease. Following the German fashion, the soldiers had decorated each car with field flowers and sheaves of wheat and boughs of trees, and even with long paper streamers of red and white and black. Also, the artists and wags of the detachment had been busy with colored chalks. There was displayed on one car a lively crayon picture of a very fierce, two-tailed Bavarian lion eating up his enemies—a nation at a bite. Another car bore a menu:

Paths of Glory

Russian caviar

Servian rice meat English roast beef

Belgian ragout French pastry

Upon this same car was lettered a bit of crude verse, which, as we had come to know, was a favorite with the German private. By my poor translation it ran somewhat as follows:

> For the Slav, a kick we have,
> And for the Jap a slap;
> The Briton too—we'll beat him blue,
> And knock the Frenchman flat.

Altogether the train had quite the holidaying air about it and the men who traveled on it had the same spirit too. They were Bavarians—all new troops, and nearly all young fellows. Their accouterments were bright and their uniforms almost unsoiled, and I saw that each man carried in his right boot top the long, ugly-looking dirk-knife that the Bavarian foot-soldier fancies. The Germans always showed heat when they found a big service clasp-knife hung about a captured Englishman's neck on a lanyard, calling it a barbarous weapon because of the length of the blade and long sharp brad-awl which folded into a slot at the back of the handle; but an equally grim bit of cutlery in a Bavarian's bootleg seemed to them an entirely proper tool for a soldier to be carrying.

The troops—there must have been a full battalion of them—piled off the coaches to exercise their legs. They skylarked about on the earth, and sang and danced, and were too full of coltish spirits to eat the rations that had been brought from the kitchen for their consumption. Seeing our cameras, a lieutenant who spoke English came up to invite us to make a photograph of him and his men, with their bedecked car for a background. He had been ill, he said, since the outbreak of hostilities, which explained why he was just now getting his first taste of active campaigning service.

"Wait, " he said vaingloriously, "just wait until we get at the damned British. Some one else may have the Frenchmen—we want to get our hands on the Englishmen. Do you know what my men say? They say they are glad for once in their lives to enjoy a fight where the policemen won't interfere and spoil the sport. That's the

Paths of Glory

Bavarian for you—the Prussian is best at drill, but the Bavarian is the best fighter in the whole world. Only let us see the enemy—that is all we ask!

"I say, what news have you from the front? All goes well, eh? As for me I only hope there will be some of the enemy left for us to kill. It is a glorious thing—this going to war! I think we shall get there very soon, where the fighting is. I can hardly wait for it. " And with that he hopped up on the steps of the nearest car and posed for his picture.

Having just come from the place whither he was so eagerly repairing I might have told him a few things. I might for example have told him what the captain of a German battery in front of La Fere had said, and that was this:

"I have been on this one spot for nearly three weeks now, serving my guns by day and by night. I have lost nearly half of my original force of men and two of my lieutenants. We shoot over those tree tops yonder in accordance with directions for range and distance which come from somewhere else over field telephone, but we never see the men at whom we are firing. They fire back without seeing us, and sometimes their shells fall short or go beyond us, and sometimes they fall among us and kill and wound a few of us. Thus it goes on day after day. I have not with my own eyes seen a Frenchman or an Englishman unless he was a prisoner. It is not so much pleasure—fighting like this. "

I might have told the young Bavarian lieutenant of other places where I had been—places where the dead lay for days unburied. I might have told him there was nothing particularly pretty or particularly edifying about the process of being killed. Death, I take it, is never a very tidy proceeding; but in battle it acquires an added unkemptness. Men suddenly and sorely stricken have a way of shrinking up inside their clothes; unless they die on the instant they have a way of tearing their coats open and gripping with their hands at their vitals, as though to hold the life in; they have a way of sprawling their legs in grotesque postures; they have a way of putting their arms up before their faces as though at the very last they would shut out a dreadful vision. Those contorted, twisted arms with the elbows up, those spraddled stark legs, and, most of all, those white dots of shirts—those I had learned to associate in my own mind with the accomplished fact of mortality upon the field.

Paths of Glory

I might have told him of sundry field hospitals which I had lately visited. I could recreate in my memory, as I shall be able to recreate it as long as I live and have my senses, a certain room in a certain schoolhouse in a French town where seven men wriggled and fought in the unspeakable torments of lockjaw; and another room filled to capacity with men who had been borne there because there was nothing humanly to be done for them, and who now lay very quietly, their suetty-gray faces laced with tiny red stripes of fever, and their paling eyes staring up at nothing at all; and still another room given over entirely to stumps of men, who lacked each a leg or an arm, or a leg and an arm, or both legs or both arms; and still a fourth room wherein were men—and boys too—all blinded, all learning to grope about in the everlasting black night which would be their portion through all their days. Indeed for an immediate illustration of the products of the business toward which he was hastening I might have taken him by the arm and led him across two sets of tracks and shown him men in the prime of life who were hatcheled like flax, and mauled like blocks, and riddled like sieves, and macerated out of the living image of their Maker.

But I did none of these things. He had a picture of something uplifting and splendid before his eyes. He wanted to fight, or he thought he did, which came to the same thing.

So what I did was to take down his name and promise to send him a completed copy of his picture in the care of his regiment and brigade; and the last I saw of him he was half out of a car window waving good-by to us and wishing us auf wiedersehen as he was borne away to his ordained place.

As we rode back through the town of Maubeuge in the dusk, the company which had sung O Strassburg in the Franco-German beer shop at the prow of the corner where the three streets met were just marching away. I thought I caught, in the weaving gray line that flowed along like quicksilver, a glimpse of the boy who was so glad because he was about to have some luck.

In two days fourteen thousand wounded men came back through Maubeuge, and possibly ten times that many new troops, belonging to the first October draft of a million, passed down the line. In that week fifty thousand wounded men returned from the German right wing alone.

Paths of Glory

He's a busy Red Glutton. There seems to be no satisfying his greed..

Chapter 15

Belgium—The Rag Doll of Europe

I have told you already, how on the first battlefield of any consequence that was visited by our party I picked up, from where it lay in the track of the Allies' retreat, a child's rag doll. It was a grotesque thing of print cloth, with sawdust insides. I found it at a place where two roads met. Presumably some Belgian child, fleeing with her parents before the German advance, dropped it there, and later a wagon or perhaps a cannon came along and ran over it. The heavy wheel had mashed the head of it flat.

In impressions which I wrote when the memory of the incident was vivid in my mind, I said that, to me, this shabby little rag doll typified Belgium. Since then I have seen many sights. Some were dramatic and some were pathetic, and nearly all were stirring; but I still recall quite clearly the little picture of the forks of the Belgian road, with a background of trampled fields and sacked houses, and just at my feet the doll, with its head crushed in and the sawdust spilled out in the rut the ongoing army had made. And always now, when I think of this, I find myself thinking of Belgium.

They have called her the cockpit of Europe. She is too. In wars that were neither of her making nor her choosing she has borne the hardest blows—a poor little buffer state thrust in between great and truculent neighbors. To strike at one another they must strike Belgium. By the accident of geography and the caprice of boundary lines she has always been the anvil for their hammers. Jemmapes and Waterloo, to cite two especially conspicuous examples among great Continental battles, were fought on her soil. Indeed, there is scarcely an inch of her for the possession of which men of breeds not her own—Austrians and Spaniards, Hanoverians and Hollanders, Englishmen and Prussians, Saxons and Frenchmen—have not contended. These others won the victories or lost them, kept the spoils or gave them up; she wore the scars of the grudges when the grudges were settled. So there is a reason for calling her the cockpit of the nations; but, as I said just now, I shall think of her as Europe's rag doll—a thing to be clouted and kicked about; to be crushed under the hoofs and the heels; to be bled and despoiled and ravished.

Paths of Glory

Thinking of her so, I do not mean by this comparison to reflect in any wise on the courage of her people. It will be a long time before the rest of the world forgets the resistance her soldiers made against overbrimming odds, or the fortitude with which the families of those soldiers faced a condition too lamentable for description.

Unsolicited, so competent an authority as Julius Caesar once gave the Belgians a testimonial for their courage. If I recall the commentaries aright, he said they were the most valorous of all the tribes of Gaul. Those who come afterward to set down the tale and tally of the Great War will record that through the centuries the Belgians retained their ancient valor.

First and last, I had rather exceptional opportunities for viewing the travail of Belgium. I was in Brussels before it surrendered and after it surrendered. I was in Louvain when the Germans entered it and I was there again after the Germans had wrecked it. I trailed the original army of invasion from Brussels southward to the French border, starting at the tail of the column and reaching the head of it before, with my companions, I was arrested and returned by another route across Belgium to German soil.

Within three weeks thereafter I started on a ten-day tour which carried me through Liege, Namur, Huy, Dinant and Chimay, and brought me back by Mons, Brussels, Louvain and Tirlemont, with a side trip to the trenches before Antwerp—roughly, a kite-shaped journey which comprehended practically all the scope of active operations among the contending armies prior to the time when the struggle for western Flanders began. Finally, just after Antwerp fell, I skirted the northern frontiers of Belgium and watched the refugees pouring across the borders into Holland. I was four times in Liege and three times in Brussels, and any number of times I crossed and recrossed my own earlier trails. I traveled afoot; in a railroad train, with other prisoners; in a taxi-cab, which we lost; in a butcher's cart, which we gave away; in an open carriage, which deserted us; and in an automobile, which vanished.

I saw how the populace behaved while their little army was yet intact, offering gallant resistance to the Germans; I saw how they behaved when the German wedge split that army into broken fragments and the Germans were among them, holding dominion with the bayonet and the bullet; and finally, six weeks later, I saw how they behaved when substantially all their country, excluding a

Paths of Glory

strip of seaboard, had been reduced to the state of a conquered fief held and ruled by force of arms.

By turns I saw them determined, desperate, despairing, half rebellious, half subdued; resigned with the resignation of sheer helplessness, which I take it is a different thing from the resignation of sheer hopelessness. It is no very pleasant sight to see a country flayed and quartered like a bloody carcass in a meat shop; but an even less pleasant thing than that is to see a country's heart broken. And Belgium to-day is a country with a broken heart.

These lines were written with intent to be printed early in January. By that time Christmas was over and done with. On the other side of the Atlantic Ocean, in lieu of the Christmas carols, the cannon had rung its brazen Christmas message across the trenches, making mockery of the words: "On earth peace, good will toward men. " On our side of the ocean the fine spirit of charity and graciousness which comes to most of us at Christmastime and keeps Christmas from becoming a thoroughly commercialized institution had begun to abate somewhat of its fervor.

To ourselves we were saying, many of us: "We have done enough for the poor, whom we have with us always. " But not always do we have with us a land famous for its fecundity that is now at grips with famine; a land that once was light-hearted, but where now you never hear anyone laugh aloud; a land that is half a waste and half a captive province; a land that cannot find bread to feed its hungry mouths, yet is called on to pay a tribute heavy enough to bankrupt it even in normal times; a land whose best manhood is dead on the battleground or rusting in military prisons; whose women and children by the countless thousands are either homeless wanderers thrust forth on the bounty of strangers in strange places, or else are helpless, hungry paupers sitting with idle hands in their desolated homes—and that land is Belgium.

Having been an eyewitness to the causes that begot this condition and to the condition itself, I feel it my duty to tell the story as I know it. I am trying to tell it dispassionately, without prejudice for any side and without hysteria. I concede the same to be a difficult undertaking.

Some space back I wrote that I had been able to find in Belgium no direct proof of the mutilations, the torturings and other barbarities which were charged against the Germans by the Belgians. Though fully a dozen seasoned journalists, both English and American, have agreed with me, saying that their experiences in this regard had been the same as mine; and though I said in the same breath that I could not find in Germany any direct evidence of the brutalities charged against the Belgians by the Germans, the prior statement was accepted by some persons as proof that my sympathy for the Belgians had been chilled through association with the Germans. No such thing. But what I desire now is the opportunity to say this: In the face of the present plight of this little country we need not look for individual atrocities. Belgium herself is the capsheaf atrocity of the war. No matter what our nationality, our race or our sentiments may be, none of us can get away from that.

Going south into France from the German border city of Aix-la-Chapelle, our automobile carried us down the Meuse. On the eastern bank, which mainly we followed during the first six hours of riding, there were craggy cliffs, covered with forests, which at intervals were cleft by deep ravines, where small farms clung to the sides of the steep hills. On the opposite shore cultivated lands extended from the limit of one's vision down almost to the water. There they met a continuous chain of manufacturing plants, now all idle, which stretched along the river shore from end to end of the valley. Culm and flume and stack and kiln succeeded one another unendingly, but no smoke issued from any chimney; and we noted that already weeds were springing up in the quarry yards and about the mouths of the coal pits and the doorways of the empty factories.

Considering that the Germans had to fight their way along the Meuse, driving back the French and Belgians before they trusted their columns to enter the narrow defiles, there was in the physical aspect of things no great amount of damage visible. Stagnation, though, lay like a blight on what had been one of the busiest and most productive industrial districts in all of Europe. Except that trains ran by endlessly, bearing wounded men north, and fresh troops and fresh supplies south, the river shore was empty and silent.

In twenty miles of running we passed just two groups of busy men. At one place a gang of German soldiers were strengthening the temporary supports of a railroad bridge which had been blown up by the retiring forces and immediately repaired by the invaders. In another place a company of reserves were recharging cases of artillery shells which had been sent back from the front in carload lots. There were horses here —a whole troop of draft horses which had been worn out in that relentless, heartbreaking labor into which war sooner or later resolves itself. The drove had been shipped back this far to be rested and cured up, or to be shot in the event that they were past mending.

I had seen perhaps a hundred thousand head of horses, drawing cannon and wagons, and serving as mounts for officers in the first drive of the Germans toward Paris, and had marveled at the uniformly prime condition of the teams. Presumably these sorry crow-baits, which drooped and limped about the barren railroad yards at the back of the siding where the shell loaders squatted, had been whole-skinned and sound of wind and joint in early August.

Two months of service had turned them into gaunt wrecks. Their ribs stuck through their hollow sides. Their hoofs were broken; their hocks were swelled enormously; and, worst of all, there were great raw wounds on their shoulders and backs, where the collars and saddles had worn through hide and flesh to the bones. From that time on, the numbers of mistreated, worn-out horses we encountered in transit back from the front increased steadily. Finally we ceased to notice them at all.

I should explain that the description I have given of the prevalent idleness along the Meuse applied to the towns and to the scattered workingmen's villages that flanked all or nearly all the outlying and comparatively isolated factories. In the fields and the truck patches the farming folks—women and old men usually, with here and there children—bestirred themselves to get the moldered and mildewed remnants of their summer-ripened crops under cover before the hard frost came.

Invariably we found this state of affairs to exist wherever we went in the districts of France and of Belgium that had been fought over and which were now occupied by the Germans. Woodlands and cleared places, where engagements had taken place, would, within a month or six weeks thereafter, show astonishingly few traces of the violence and death that had violated the peace of the countryside. New grass would be growing in the wheel ruts of the guns and on the sides of the trenches in which infantry had screened itself. As though they took pattern by the example of Nature, the peasants would be afield, gathering what remained of their harvests—even plowing and harrowing the ground for new sowing. On the very edge of the battle front we saw them so engaged, seemingly paying less heed to the danger of chance shell-fire than did the soldiers who passed and repassed where they toiled.

In the towns almost always the situation was different. The people who lived in those towns seemed like so many victims of a universal torpor. They had lost even their sense of inborn curiosity regarding the passing stranger. Probably from force of habit, the shopkeepers stayed behind their counters; but between them and the few customers who came there was little of the vivacious chatter one has learned to associate with dealings among the dwellers in most Continental communities. We passed through village after village and town after town, to find in each the same picture—men and women in mute clusters about the doorways and in the little squares, who barely turned their heads as the automobile flashed by. Once in a while we caught the sound of a brisker tread on the cobbled street; but when we looked, nine times in ten we saw that the walker was a soldier of the German garrison quartered there to keep the population quiet and to help hold the line of communication.

I think, though, this cankered apathy has its merciful compensations. After the first shock and panic of war there appears to descend on all who have a share in it, whether active or passive, a kind of numbed indifference as to danger; a kind of callousness as to consequences, which I find it difficult to define in words, but which, nevertheless, impresses itself on the observer's mind as a definite and tangible fact. The soldier gets it, and it enables him to endure his own discomforts and sufferings, and the discomforts and sufferings of his comrades, without visible mental strain. The civic populace get it, and, as soon as they have been readjusted to the altered conditions forced on them by the presence of war, they become merely sluggish, dulled spectators of the great and moving events going on about them. The nurses and the surgeons get it, or else they would go mad from the horrors that surround them. The wounded get it, and cease from complaint and lamenting.

It is as though all the nerve ends in every human body were burnt blunt in the first hot gush of war. Even the casual eyewitness gets it. We got it ourselves; and not until we had quit the zone of hostilities did we shake it off. Indeed, we did not try. It made for subsequent sanity to carry for the time a drugged and stupefied imagination.

Paths of Glory

Barring only Huy, where there had been some sharp street fighting, as attested by shelled buildings and sandbag barricades yet resting on housetops and in window sills, we encountered in the first stage of our journey no considerable evidences of havoc until late in the afternoon, when we reached Dinant. I do not understand why the contemporary chronicles of events did not give more space to Dinant at the time of its destruction, and why they have not given it more space subsequently.

I presume the reason lies in the fact that the same terrible week which included the burning of Louvain included also the burning of Dinant; and in the world-wide cry of protestation and distress which arose with the smoke of the greater calamity the smaller voice of grief for little ruined Dinant was almost lost. Yet, area considered, no place in Belgium that I have visited—and this does not exclude Louvain—suffered such wholesale demolition as Dinant.

Before war began, the town had something less than eight thousand inhabitants. When I got there it had less than four thousand, by the best available estimates. Of those four thousand more than twelve hundred were then without food from day to day except such as the Germans gave them. There were almost no able-bodied male adults left. Some had fled, some were behind bars as prisoners of the Germans, and a great many were dead. Estimates of the number of male inhabitants who had been killed by the graycoats for offenses against the inflexible code set up by the Germans in eastern Belgium varied. A cautious native whispered that nine hundred of his fellow townsmen were "up there"—by that meaning the trenches on the hills back of the town. A German officer, newly arrived on the spot and apparently sincere in his efforts to alleviate the misery of the survivors, told us that, judging by what data he had been able to gather, between four and six hundred men and youths of Dinant had fallen in the house-to-house conflicts between Germans and civilians, or in the wholesale executions which followed the subjugation of the place and the capture of such ununiformed belligerents as were left.

In this instance subjugation meant annihilation. The lower part of the town, where the well-to-do classes lived, was almost unscathed. Casual shell-fire in the two engagements with the French that preceded the taking of Dinant had smashed some cornices and shattered some windows, but nothing worse befell. The lower half, made up mainly of the little plaster-and-stone houses of working people, was gone, extinguished, obliterated. It lay in scorched and crumbled waste; and in it, as we rode through, I saw, excluding soldiers, just two living creatures. Two children, both little girls, were playing at housekeeping on some stone steps under a doorway where there was no door, using bits of wreckage for furniture. We stopped a moment to watch them. They had small china dolls.

The river, flowing placidly along between the artificial boundaries of its stone quays, and the strange formation of cliffs, rising at the back to the height of hundreds of feet, were as they had been. Soldiers paddled on the water in skiffs and thousands of ravens flickered about the pinnacles of the rocks, but between river and cliff there was nothing but ruination—the graveyard of the homes of three thousand people.

Yes, it was the graveyard not alone of their homes but of their prosperity and their hopes and their ambitions and their aspirations— the graveyard of everything human beings count worth having. This was worse than Hervé or Battice or Visé, or any of the leveled towns we had seen. Taken on the basis of comparative size, it was worse even than Louvain, as we discovered later. It was worse than anything I ever saw —worse than anything I ever shall see, I think.

These hollow shells about us were like the picked cadavers of houses. Ends of burnt and broken rafters stood up like ribs. Empty window openings stared at us like the eye sockets in skulls. It was not a town upon which we looked, but the dead and rotting bones of a town.

Just over the ragged line that marked the lowermost limits of the destructive fury of the conquerors, and inside the section which remained intact, we traversed a narrow street called—most appropriately, I thought—the Street of Paul the Penitent, and passed a little house on the shutters of which was written, in chalked German script, these words: "A Grossmutter"—grandmother—"ninety-six years old lives here. Don't disturb her. " Other houses along here bore the familiar line, written by German soldiers who had been billeted in them: "Good people. Leave them alone! "

The people who enjoyed the protection of these public testimonials were visible, a few of them. They were nearly all women and children. They stood in their shallow doorways as our automobile went by bearing four Americans, two German officers and the orderly of one of the officers— for we had picked up a couple of chance passengers in Huy—and a German chauffeur. As we interpreted their looks, they had no hate for the Germans. I take it the weight of their woe was so heavy on them that they had no room in their souls for anything else.

Just beyond Dinant, at Anseremme, a beautiful little village at the mouth of a tiny river, where artists used to come to paint pictures and sick folks to breathe the tonic balsam of the hills, we got rooms for the night in a smart, clean tavern. Here was quartered a captain of cavalry, who found time—so brisk was he and so high-spirited— to welcome us to the best the place afforded, to help set the table for our belated supper, and to keep on terms of jovial yet punctilious amiability with the woman proprietor and her good-looking daughters; also, to require his troopers to pay the women, in salutes and spoken thanks, for every small office performed.

The husband of the older woman and the husband of one of the daughters were then serving the Belgian colors, assuming that they had not been killed or caught; but between them and this German captain a perfect understanding had been arrived at. When the head of the house fixed the prices she meant to charge us for our accommodations, he spoke up and suggested that the rate was scarcely high enough; and also, since her regular patrons had been driven away at the beginning of the war, he advised us that sizable tips on our leaving would probably be appreciated.

Next morning we rose from a breakfast—the meat part of it having been furnished from the German commissary—to find twenty lancers exercising their horses in a lovely little natural arena, walled by hills, just below the small eminence whereon the house stood. It was like a scene from a Wild West exhibition at home, except that these German horsemen lacked the dash of our cowpunchers. Watching the show from a back garden, we stood waist deep in flowers, and the captain's orderly, when he came to tell us our automobile was ready, had a huge peony stuck in a buttonhole of his blouse. I caught a peep at another soldier, who was flirting with a personable Flemish scullery maid behind the protection of the kitchen wall. The proprietress and her daughters stood at the door to wave us good-by and to wish us, with apparent sincerity, a safe journey down into France, and a safe return.

Paths of Glory

To drop from this cozy, peaceful place into the town of Dinant again was to drop from a small earthly paradise into a small earthly hell. Somewhere near the middle of the little perdition our cavalry captain pointed to a shell of a house.

"A fortnight ago, " he told us, "we found a French soldier in that house — or under it, rather. He had been there four weeks, hiding in the basement. He took some food with him or found some there; at any rate, he managed to live four weeks. He was blind, and nearly deaf, too, when we found out where he was and dug him out — but he is still alive. "

One of us said we should like to have a look at a man who had undergone such an entombment.

"No, you wouldn't, " said the captain; "for he is no very pleasant sight. He is a slobbering idiot. "

In the Grand Place, near the shell-riddled Church of Notre Dame — built by the Bishops in the thirteenth century, restored by the Belgian Government in the nineteenth, and destroyed by the German guns in the twentieth — a long queue of women wound past the doorway of a building where German noncommissioned officers handed out to each applicant a big loaf of black soldier bread.

"Oh, yes; we feed the poor devils, " the German commandant, an elderly, scholarly looking man of the rank of major, said to us when he had come up to be introduced. "When our troops entered this town the men of the lower classes took up arms and fired at our soldiers; so the soldiers burned all their houses and shot all the men who came out of those houses.

"All this occurred before I was sent here. Had I been the commander of the troops, I should have shot them without mercy. It is our law for war times, and these Belgian civilians must be taught that they cannot fire on German soldiers and not pay for it with their lives and their homes. With the women and children, however, the case is different. On my own responsibility I am feeding the destitute. Every day I give away to these people between twelve hundred and fifteen hundred loaves of bread; and I give to some who are particularly needy rations of tea and sugar and coffee and rice. Also, I sell to the butcher shops fresh and salt meat from our military stores at cost, requiring only that they, in turn, shall sell it at no more than a fair profit. So long as I am stationed here I shall do this, for I cannot let them starve before my eyes. I myself have children."

It was like escaping from a pesthouse to cross the one bridge of Dinant that remained standing on its piers, and go winding down the lovely valley, overtaking and passing many German wagon trains, the stout, middle-aged soldier drivers of which drowsed on their seats; passing also one marching battalion of foot-reserves, who, their officers concurring, broke from the ranks to beg newspapers and cigars from us. On the mountain ash the bright red berries dangled in clumps like Christmas bells, and some of the leaves of the elm still clung to their boughs; so that the wide yellow road was dappled like a wild-cat's back with black splotches of shadow. Only when we curved through some village that had been the scene of a skirmish or a reprisal did the roofless shells and the toppled walls of the houses, standing gaunt and ugly in the sharp sunlight, make us realize that we were still in the war tracks.

As nearly as we could tell from our brief scrutiny a great change had come over the dwellers in southern Belgium. In August they had been buoyant and confident of the ultimate outcome and very proud of the behavior of their little army. Even when the Germans burst through the frontier defenses and descended on them in innumerable swarms they were, for the most part, not daunted by those evidences of the invaders' numerical superiority and of their magnificent equipment. The more there were of the Germans the fewer of them there would be to come back when the Allies, over the French border, fell on them. This we conceived to be the mental attitude of the villagers and the peasants; but now they were different. The difference showed in all their outward aspects—in their gaits; in their drooped shoulders and half-averted faces; and, most of all, in their eyes. They had felt the weight of the armed hand, and they must have heard the boast, filtering down from the officers to the men, and from the men to the native populace, that, having taken their country, the Germans meant to keep it; that Belgium, ceasing to be Belgium, would henceforth be set down on the map as a part of Greater Prussia.

Seeing them now, I began to understand how an enforced docility may reduce a whole people to the level of dazed, unresisting automatons. Yet a national spirit is harder to kill than a national boundary—so the students of these things say. A little flash of flaming hate from the dead ashes of things; a quick, darting glance of

Paths of Glory

defiance; a hissed word from a seemingly subdued man or woman; a shrill, hostile whoop from a ragged youngster behind a hedge—things such as these showed us that the courage of the Belgians was not dead. It had been crushed to the ground, but it had not been torn up by the roots. The roots went down too far. The under dog had secret dreams of the day to come, when he should not be underneath, but on top.

Even had there been no abandoned custom-houses to convince us of it, we should have known when we crossed from southern Belgium into northern France; for in France the proportion of houses that had suffered in punitive attacks was, compared with Belgium, as one to ten. Understand, I am speaking of houses that had been deliberately burned in punishment, and not of houses that stood in the way of the cannon and the rapid-fire guns, and so underwent partial or complete destruction as the result of an accidental yet inevitable and unavoidable process. Of these last France, to the square mile, could offer as lamentably large a showing as Belgium; but buildings that presented indubitable signs of having been fired with torches rather than with shells were few.

Explaining this and applauding it, Germans of high rank said it presented direct and confirmatory proof of their claim that sheer wanton reprisals were practically unknown in their system of warfare. Perhaps I can best set forth the German attitude in this regard by quoting a general whom we interviewed on the subject:

"We do not destroy for the pleasure it gives us. We destroy only when it is necessary. The French rural populace are more rational, more tractable and much less turbulent than the Belgians. To a much greater degree than the Belgians they have refrained from acts against our men that would call for severe retaliatory measures on our part. Consequently we have spared the houses and respected the property of the French noncombatants."

Personally I had a theory of my own. So far as our observations went, the people living immediately on both sides of the line were an interrelated people, using the same speech and being much alike in temperament, manners and mode of conduct. I reached the private conclusion that, because of the chorus of protest that arose from all the neutral countries, and particularly from the United States, against the severities visited on Belgium in August and September, the word went forth to the German forces in the field that the scheme of punishment for offenders who violated the field code should be somewhat softened and relaxed. However, that is merely a personal theory. I may be absolutely wrong about it. The German general who interpreted the meaning of the situation may have been absolutely right about it. Certainly the physical testimony was on his side.

Also, it seemed to me, the psychology of the people—particularly of the womenfolk—in northern France was not that of their neighboors over the frontier. In a trade way the small shopkeepers here faced ruin; the Belgians already had been ruined. The Frenchwomen, whose sons and brothers and husbands and fathers were at the front, walked in the shadow of a great fear, as you might tell by a look into the face of any one of them. They were as peppercorns between the upper millstone and the nether, and the sound of the crunching was always in their ears, even though their turn to be ground up had not yet come.

For the Belgian women, however, the worst that might befall had already happened to them; their souls could be wrung no more; they had no terror of the future, since the past had been so terrible and the present was a living desolation of all they counted worth while. You might say the Frenchwomen dreaded what the Belgians endured. The refilled cup was at the lips of France; Belgium had drained it dry.

Yet in both countries the women generally manifested the same steadfast and silent patience. They said little; but their eyes asked questions. In the French towns we saw how bravely they strove to carry on their common affairs of life, which were so sadly shaken and distorted out of all normality by the earthquake of war.

For currency they had small French coins and strange German coins, and in some places futile-looking, little green-and-white slips, issued by the municipality in denominations of one franc and two francs and five francs, and redeemable in hard specie "three months after the declaration of peace." For wares to sell they had what remained of their depleted stocks; and for customers, their friends and neighbors, who looked forward to commercial ruin, which each day brought nearer to them all. Outwardly they were placid enough, but it was not the placidity of content. It bespoke rather a dumb, disciplined acceptance by those who have had fatalism literally thrust on them as a doctrine to be practiced.

Paths of Glory

Looking back on it I can recall just one woman I saw in France who maintained an unquenchable blitheness of spirit. She was the little woman who managed the small cafe in Maubeuge where we ate our meals. Perhaps her frugal French mind rejoiced that business remained so good, for many officers dined at her table and, by Continental standards, paid her well and abundantly for what she fed them; but I think a better reason lay in the fact that she had within her an innate buoyancy which nothing—not even war—could daunt.

She was one of those women who remain trig and chic though they be slovens by instinct. Her blouse was never clean, but she wore it with an air. Her skirt testified that skillets spit grease; but in it she somehow looked as trim as a trout fly. Even the hole in her stocking gave her piquancy; and she had wonderful black hair, which probably had not been combed properly for a month, and big, crackling black eyes. They told us that one day, a week or two before we came, she had been particularly cheerful—so cheerful that one of her patrons was moved to inquire the cause of it.

"Oh, " she said, "I am quite content with life to-day. I have word that my husband is a prisoner. Now he is out of danger and you Germans will have to feed him—and he is a great eater! If you starve him then I shall starve you. "

At breakfast Captain Mannesmann, who was with us, asked her in his best French for more butter. She paused in her quick, bird-like movements— for she was waitress, cook, cashier, manager and owner, all rolled into one—and cocking a saucy, unkempt head at him asked that the question be repeated. This time, in his efforts to be understood, he stretched his words out so that unwittingly his voice took on rather a whining tone.

"Well, don't cry about it! " she snapped. "I'll see what I can do. "

Returning from the battle front our itinerary included a long stretch of the great road that runs between Paris and Brussels, a road much favored formerly by auto tourists, but now used almost altogether for military purposes. Considering that we traversed a corner of the stage of one of the greatest battles thus far waged—Mons—and that this battle had taken place but a few weeks before, there were remarkably few evidences remaining of it.

Paths of Glory

With added force we remarked a condition that had given us material for wonderment in our earlier journeyings. Though a retreating army and an advancing army, both enormous in size, had lately poured through the country, the houses, the farms and the towns were almost undamaged.

Certain contrasts which took on a heightened emphasis by reason of their brutal abruptness, abounded all over Belgium. You passed at a step, as it were, from a district of complete and irreparable destruction to one wherein all things were orderly and ordered, and much as they should be in peaceful times. Were it not for the stagnated towns and the depression that berode the people, one would hardly know these areas had lately been overrun by hostile soldiers and now groaned under enormous tithes. In isolated instances the depression had begun to lift. Certain breeds of the polyglot Flemish race have, it appears, an almost unkillable resilience of temper; but in a town a mile away all those whom we met would be like dead people who walked.

Also, there were many graves. If we passed a long ridged mound of clay in a field, unmarked except by the piled-up clods, we knew that at this spot many had fought and many had fallen; but if, as occurred constantly, one separate mound or a little row of separate mounds was at the roadside, that probably meant a small skirmish. Such a grave almost always was marked by a little wooden cross, with a name penciled on it; and often the comrades of the dead man had hung his cap on the upright of the cross. If it were a French cap or a Belgian the weather would have worn it to a faded blue-and-red wisp of worsted. The German helmets stood the exposure better. They retained their shape.

On a cross I saw one helmet with a bullet hole right through the center of it in front. Sometimes there would be flowers on the mound, faded garlands of field poppies and wreaths of withered wild vines; and by the presence of these we could tell that the dead man's mates had time and opportunity to accord him greater honor than usually is be-stowed on a soldier killed in an advance or during a retreat.

Mons was reached soon, looking much as I imagine Mons must always have looked; and then, after a few stretching and weary leagues, Brussels—to my mind the prettiest and smartest of the capital cities of Europe, not excluding Paris. I first saw Brussels when

Paths of Glory

it was as gay as carnival— that was in mid-August; and, though Liege had fallen and Namur was falling, and the German legions were eating up the miles as they hurried forward through the dust and smoke of their own making, Brussels still floated her flags, built her toy barricades, and wore a gay face to mask the panic clutching at her nerves.

Getting back four days later I found her beginning to rally from the shock of the invasion. Her people, relieved to find that the enemy did not mean to mistreat noncombatants who obeyed his code of laws, were going about their affairs in such odd hours as they could spare from watching the unending gray freshet that roared and pounded through their streets. The flags were down and the counterfeit light-heartedness was gone; but essentially she was the same Brussels.

Coming now, however, six weeks later, I found a city that had been transformed out of her own customary image by captivity and hunger and hard-curbed resentment. The pulse of her life seemed hardly to beat at all. She lay in a coma, flashing up feverishly sometimes at false rumors of German repulses to the southward.

Only the day before we arrived a wild story got abroad among the starvelings in the poorer quarters that the Russians had taken Berlin and had swept across Prussia and were now pushing forward, with an irresistible army, to relieve Brussels. So thousands of the deluded populace went to a bridge on the eastern outskirts of the town to catch the first glimpse of the victorious oncoming Russians; and there they stayed until nightfall, watching and hoping and—what was more pitiable —believing.

From what I saw of him I judged that the military governor of Brussels, Major Bayer, was not only a diplomat but a kindly and an engaging gentleman. Certainly he was wrestling most manfully, and I thought tactfully, with a difficult and a dangerous situation. For one thing, he was keeping his soldiers out of sight as much as possible without relaxing his grip on the community. He did this, he said, to reduce the chances of friction between his men and the people; for friction might mean a spark and a spark might mean a conflagration, and that would mean another and greater Louvain. We could easily understand that small things might readily grow into great and serious troubles. Even the most docile-minded man would be apt to resent in the wearer of a hated uniform what he

Paths of Glory

might excuse as over-officiousness or love of petty authority were the offender a policeman of his own nationality. Brooding over their own misfortunes had worn the nerves of these captives to the very quick.

In any event, be the outcome of this war what it may, I do not believe the Belgians can ever be molded, either by kindness or by sternness, into a tractable vassal race. German civilization I concede to be a magnificent thing—for a German; but it seems to press on an alien neck as a galling yoke. Belgium under Berlin rule would be, I am sure, Alsace and Lorraine all over again on a larger scale, and an unhappier one. She would never, in my humble opinion, be a star in the Prussian constellation, but always a raw sore in the Prussian side.

In Major Bayer's office I saw the major stamp an order that turned over to the acting burgomaster ten thousand bags of flour for distribution among the more needy citizens. We were encouraged to believe that this was by way of a free gift from the German Government. It may have been made without payment or promise of payment. In regard to that I cannot say positively; but this was the inference we drew from the statements of the German officers who took part in the proceeding. As for the acting burgomaster, he stood through the scene silent and inscrutable, saying nothing at all. Possibly he did not understand; the conversation—or that part of it which concerned us—was carried on exclusively in English. His face, as he bowed to accept the certified warrant for the flour, gave us no hint of his mental processes.

Major Bayer claimed a professional kinship with those of us who were newspaper men, as he was the head of the Boy Scout movement in Germany and edited the official organ of the Boy Scouts. He had a squad of his scouts on messenger duty at his headquarters—smart, alert-looking youngsters. They seemed to me to be much more competent in their department than were the important-appearing German Secret Service agents who infested the building. The Germans may make first-rate spies—assuredly their system of espionage was well organized before the war broke out—but I do not think they are conspicuous successes as detectives: their methods are so delightfully translucent.

Major Bayer had been one of the foremost German officers to set foot on Belgian soil after the severance of friendly relations between the two countries. "I believe, " he said, "that I heard the first shot fired in this war. It came from a clump of trees within half an hour after our advance guard crossed the boundary south of Aachen, and it wounded the leg of a captain who commanded a company of scouts at the head of the column. Our skirmishers surrounded the woods and beat the thickets, and presently they brought forth the man who had fired the shot. He was sixty years old, and he was a civilian. Under the laws of war we shot him on the spot. So you see probably the first shot fired in this war was fired at us by a franc-tireur. By his act he had forfeited his life, but personally I felt sorry for him; for I believe, like many of his fellow countrymen who afterward committed such offenses, he was ignorant of the military indefensibility of his attack on us and did not realize what the consequences would be.

"I am sure, though, that the severity with which we punished these offenses at the outset was really merciful, for only by killing the civilians who fired on us, and by burning their houses, could we bring home to thousands of others the lesson that if they wished to fight us they must enlist in their own army and come against us in uniforms, as soldiers. "

Within the same hour we were introduced to Privy Councilor Otto von Falke, an Austrian by birth, but now, after long service in Cologne and Berlin, promoted to be Director of Industrial Arts for Prussia. He had been sent, he explained, by order of his Kaiser, to superintend the removal of historic works of art from endangered churches and other buildings, and turn them over to the curator of the Royal Belgian Gallery, at Brussels, for storage in the vaults of the museum until such time as peace had been restored and they might be returned with safety to their original positions.

"So you see, gentlemen, " said Professor von Falke, "the Germans are not despoiling Belgium of its wealth of pictures and statues. We are taking pains to preserve and perpetuate them. They belong to Belgium—not to us; and we have no desire to take them away. Certainly we are not vandals who would wantonly destroy the splendid things of art, as our enemies have claimed. "

He was plainly a sincere man and he was much in love with his work; that, too, was easy to see. Afterward, though, the thought came to us that, if Belgium was to become a German state by right of seizure and conquest, he was saving these masterpieces of Vandyke

Paths of Glory

and Rubens, not for Belgium, but for the greater glory of the Greater Empire.

However, that was beside the mark. What at the moment seemed to us of more consequence even than rescuing holy pictures was that all about us were sundry hundreds of thousands of men, women and children who did not need pictures, but food. You had only to look at them in the streets to know that their bellies felt the grind of hunger. Famine knocked at half the doors in that city of Brussels, and we sat in the glittering cafe of the Palace Hotel and talked of pictures!

We called on Minister Brand Whitlock, whom we had not seen—McCutcheon and I—since the Sunday afternoon a month and a half before when we two left his official residence in a hired livery rig for a ride to Waterloo, which ride extended over a thousand miles, one way and another, and carried us into three of the warring countries. Mention of this call gives me opportunity to say in parenthesis, so to speak, that if ever a man in acutely critical circumstances kept his head, and did a big job in a big way, and reflected credit at a thousand angles on himself and the country that had the honor to be served by him, that man was Brand Whitlock. To him, a citizen of another nation, the people of forlorn Brussels probably owe more than to any man of their own race.

Grass was sprouting from between the cobbles of the streets in the populous residential districts through which we passed on the way from the American Ministry to our next stopping place. Viewed at a short distance each vista of empty street had a wavy green beard on its face; and by this one might judge to what a low ebb the commerce and the pleasure of the city had fallen since its occupation. There was one small square where goats and geese might have been pastured. It looked as though weeks might have passed since wagon wheels had rolled over those stones; and the town folks whose houses fronted on the little square lounged in their doorways, with idle hands thrust into their pockets, regarding us with lackluster, indifferent eyes. It may have been fancy, but I thought nearly all of them looked griped of frame and that their faces seemed drawn. Seeing them so, you would have said that, with them, nothing mattered any more.

We saw a good many people, though, who were taking for the moment an acute and uneasy interest in their own affairs, at the big

Paths of Glory

city prison, where we spent half an hour or so. Here, in a high-walled courtyard, we found upward of two hundred offenders against small civic regulations, serving sentences ranging in length from seven days to thirty. Perhaps one in three was a German soldier, and probably one in ten was a woman or a girl; the rest were male citizens of all ages, sizes and social grading, a few Congo negroes being mixed in. Most of the time they stayed in their cells, in solitary confinement; but on certain afternoons they might take the air and see visitors in the bleak and barren inclosure where they were now herded together.

By common rumor in Brussels the Germans were shooting all persons caught secretly peddling copies of French or English papers or unauthorized and clandestine Belgian papers; since only orthodox German papers were permitted to be sold. The Germans themselves took no steps to deny these stories, but in the prison we found a large collection of forlorn newsdealers. Having been captured with the forbidden wares in their possession, they had mysteriously vanished from the ken of their friends; but they had not been "put against the wall, " as they say in Europe. They had been given fourteen days apiece, with a promise of six months if they transgressed a second time.

One little man, with the longest and sleekest and silkiest black whiskers I have seen in many a day, recognized us as Americans and drew near to tell us his troubles in a confidential whisper. By his bleached indoor complexion and his manners anyone would have known him for a pastry cook or a hairdresser. A hairdresser he was; and in a better day than this, not far remote, had conducted a fashionable establishment on a fashionable boulevard.

"Ah, I am in one very sad state, " he said in his twisted English. "I start for Ostend to take winter garments for my two small daughters, which are there at school, and they arrest me—these Germans—and keep me two days in a cowshed, and then bring me back here and put me here in this so-terrible-a-place for two weeks; and all for nothing at all. "

"Didn't you have a pass to go through the lines? " I asked. "Perhaps that was it. "

"I have already a pass, " he said; "but when they search me they find in my pockets letters which I am taking to people in Ostend. I do not know what is in those letters. People ask me to take them to friends of theirs in Ostend and I consent, not knowing it is against the rule. They read these letters—the Germans—and say I am carrying news to their enemies; and they become very enrage at me and lock me up. Never again will I take letters for anybody anywhere.

"Oh, sirs, if you could but see the food we eat here! For dinner we have a stew—oh, such a stew! —and for breakfast only bread and coffee who is not coffee! " And with both hands he combed his whiskers in a despair that was comic and yet pitiful.

He was standing there, still combing, as we came away.

Chapter 16

Louvain the Forsaken

It was Sunday when I saw Louvain in the ashes of her desolation. We were just back then from the German trenches before Antwerp; and the hollow sounds of the big guns which were fired there at spaced intervals came to our ears as we rode over the road leading out from Brussels, like the boomings of great bells. The last time I had gone that way the country was full of refugees fleeing from burning villages on beyond. Now it was bare, except for a few baggage trains lumbering along under escort of shaggy gray troopers. Perhaps I should say they were gray- and-yellow troopers, for the plastered mud and powdered dust of three months of active campaigning had made them of true dirt color.

Oh, yes; I forgot one other thing: We overtook a string of wagons fitted up as carryalls and bearing family parties of the burghers to Louvain to spend a day among the wreckage. There is no accounting for tastes. If I had been a Belgian the last thing I should want my wife and my baby to see would be the ancient university town, the national cradle of the Church, in its present state. Nevertheless there were many excursionists in Louvain that day.

The Germans had taken down the bars and sight-seers came by autobusses from as far away as Aix-la-Chapelle and from Liege and many from Brussels. They bought postal cards and climbed about over the mountain ranges of waste, and they mined in the debris mounds for souvenirs. Altogether, I suppose some of them regarded it as a kind of picnic. Personally I should rather go to a morgue for a picnic than to Louvain as it looks to-day. I tried hard, both in Germany among the German soldiers and in Belgium among the Belgians, to get at the truth about Louvain. The Germans said the outbreak was planned, and that firing broke out at a given signal in various quarters of the town; that, from windows and basements and roofs, bullets rained on them; and that the fighting continued until they had smoked the last of the inhabitants from their houses with fire and put them to death as they fled. The Belgians proclaimed just as stoutly that, mistaking an on marching regiment for enemies, the Germans fired on their own people; and then, in rage at having committed such an error and to cover it up, they turned on the townspeople and mixed massacre with pillaging and burning for the better part of a night and a day.

I could, I think, sense something of the viewpoint of each. To the Belgian, a German in his home or in his town was no more than an armed housebreaker. What did he care for the code of war? He was not responsible for the war. He had no share in framing the code. He took his gun, and when the chance came he fired—-and fired to kill. Perhaps, at first, he did not know that by that same act he forfeited his life and sacrificed his home and jeopardized the lives and homes of all his neighbors. Perhaps in the blind fury of the moment he did not much care.

Take the German soldier: He had proved he was ready to meet his enemy in the open and to fight him there. When his comrade fell at his side, struck down by an unseen, skulking foe, who lurked behind a hedge or a chimney, he saw red and he did red deeds. That in his reprisals he went farther than some might have gone under similar conditions is rather to have been expected. In point of organization, in discipline, and in the enactment of a terribly stern, terribly deadly course of conduct for just such emergencies, his masters had gone farther than the heads of any modern army ever went before. You see, all the laboriously built-up ethics of civilized peace came into direct conflict with the bloody ethics of war, which are never civilized, and which frequently are born in the instant and molded on the instant to suit the purposes of those who create them. And Louvain is perhaps the most finished and perfect example we have in this world to-day to show the consequences of such a clash.

I am not going to try to describe Louvain. Others have done that competently. The Belgians were approximately correct when they said Louvain had been destroyed. The Germans were technically right when they said not over twenty per cent of its area had been reduced; but that twenty per cent included practically the whole business district, practically all the better class of homes, the university, the cathedral, the main thoroughfares, the principal hotels and shops and cafes. The famous town hall alone stood unscathed; it was saved by German soldiers from the common fate of all things about it. What remained, in historic value and in physical beauty, and even in tangible property value, was much less than what was gone forever.

Paths of Glory

I sought out the hotel near the station where we had stayed, as enforced guests of the German army, for three days in August. Its site was a leveled gray mass, sodden, wrecked past all redemption; ruined beyond all thought of salvage. I looked for the little inn at which we had dined. Its front wall littered the street and its interior was a jumble of worthlessness. I wondered again as I had wondered many times before what had become of its proprietor—the dainty, gentle little woman whose misshapen figure told us she was near the time for her baby.

I endeavored to fix the location of the little sidewalk cafe where we sat on the second or the third day of the German occupation—August twenty-first, I think, was the date—and watched the sun go out in eclipse like a copper disk. We did not know it then, but it was Louvain's bloody eclipse we saw presaged that day in the suddenly darkened heavens. Even the lines of the sidewalks were loSt. The road was piled high with broken, fire-smudged masonry. The building behind was a building no longer. It was a husk of a house, open to the sky, backless and front-less, and fit only to tumble down in the next high wind.

As we stood before the empty railroad station, in what I veritably believe to be the forlornest spot there is on this earth, a woman in a shawl came whining to sell us postal cards, on which were views of the desolation that was all about us.

"Please buy some pictures, " she said in French. "My husband is dead. "

"When did he die? " one of us asked.

She blinked, as though trying to remember.

"That night, " she said as though there had never been but one night. "They killed him then—that night. " "Who killed him? " "They did. "

She pointed in the direction of the square fronting the station. There were German soldiers where she pointed—both living ones and dead ones. The dead ones, eighty-odd of them, were buried in two big crosswise trenches, in a circular plot that had once been a bed of ornamental flowers surrounding the monument of some local notable. The living ones were standing sentry duty at the fence that flanked the railroad tracks beyond.

Paths of Glory

"They did," she said; "they killed him! Will you buy some postal cards, m'sieur? All the best pictures of the ruins!"

She said it flatly, without color in her voice, or feeling or emotion. She did not, I am sure, flinch mentally as she looked at the Germans. Certainly she did not flinch visibly. She was past flinching, I suppose.

The officer in command of the force holding the town came, just before we started, to warn us to beware of bicyclists who might be encountered near Tirlemont.

"They are all franc-tireurs—those Belgians on wheels," he said. "Some of them are straggling soldiers, wearing uniforms under their other clothes. They will shoot at you and trust to their bicycles to get away. We've caught and killed some of them, but there are still a few abroad. Take no chances with them. If I were in your place I should be ready to shoot first."

We asked him how the surviving populace of Louvain was behaving.

"Oh, we have them—like that!" he said with a laugh, and clenched his hand up in a knot of knuckles to show what he meant. "They know better than to shoot at a German soldier now; but if looks would kill we'd all be dead men a hundred times a day." And he laughed again.

Of course it was none of our business; but it seemed to us that if we were choosing a man to pacify and control the ruined people of ruined Louvain this square-headed, big-fisted captain would not have been our first choice.

It began to rain hard as our automobile moved through the wreckage-strewn street which, being followed, would bring us to the homeward road—home in this instance meaning Germany. The rain, soaking into the debris, sent up a sour, nasty smell, which pursued us until we had cleared the town. That exhalation might fully have been the breath of the wasted place, just as the distant, never-ending boom of the guns might have been the lamenting voice of the war-smitten land itself.

Paths of Glory

I remember Liege best at this present distance by reason of a small thing that occurred as we rode, just before dusk, through a byway near the river. In the gloomy, wet Sunday street two bands of boys were playing at being soldiers. Being soldiers is the game all the children in Northern Europe have played since the first of last August.

From doorways and window sills their lounging elders watched these Liege urchins as they waged their mimic fight with wooden guns and wooden swords; but, while we looked on, one boy of an inventive turn of mind was possessed of a great idea. He proceeded to organize an execution against a handy wall, with one small person to enact the role of the condemned culprit and half a dozen others to make up the firing squad.

As the older spectators realized what was afoot a growl of dissent rolled up and down the street; and a stout, red-faced matron, shrilly protesting, ran out into the road and cuffed the boys until they broke and scattered. There was one game in Liege the boys might not play.

The last I saw of Belgium was when I skirted her northern frontier, making for the seacoast. The guns were silent now, for Antwerp had surrendered; and over all the roads leading up into Holland refugees were pouring in winding streams. They were such refugees as I had seen a score of times before, only now there were infinitely more of them than ever before: men, women and children, all afoot; all burdened with bags and bundles; all dressed in their best clothes— they did well to save their best, since they could save so little else— all or nearly all bearing their inevitable black umbrellas.

They must have come long distances; but I marked that none of them moaned or complained, or gave up in weariness and despair. They went on and on, with their weary backs bent to their burdens and their weary legs trembling under them; and we did not know where they were going— and they did not know. They just went. What they must face before them could not equal what they left behind them; so they went on.

That poor little rag doll, with its head crushed in the wheel tracks, does not after all furnish such a good comparison for Belgium, I think, as I finish this tale; for it had sawdust insides—and Belgium's vitals are the vitals of courage and patience.

Printed in the United Kingdom
by Lightning Source UK Ltd.
125309UK00001B/257/A